STRANGERS IN THE LAND

THE ZOMBIE BIBLE – BOOK 3

STANT LITORE

Westmarch Publishing

2015

– THE SILVER EDITION –

FIRST PUBLISHED IN 2012

The characters and events portrayed in this book are fictitious. Any similarity to real persons, living or dead, is coincidental and not intended by the author.

Stant Litore is a pen name for Daniel Fusch.

Cover art © 2015 by Lauren K. Cannon.
Cover design by Roberto Calas.

A Westmarch Publishing release.

ISBN: 978-1-942458-14-2

Previous edition published by 47North, an imprint of Amazon Publishing.

You can reach Stant Litore at:
http://stantlitore.com
zombiebible@gmail.com
http://www.facebook.com/stant.litore
@thezombiebible

PRAISE FOR STANT LITORE'S
THE ZOMBIE BIBLE

"Heartbreaking and wonderful." – *Conflictium*

"I find myself riveted to Stant's prose, not only because I'm eager to find out the characters' fate but because his words are so beautiful. The story has stayed with me days after reading it. I highly recommend." – Denise Grover Swank, author of *The Curse Keepers*

"Stant Litore has been doing fascinating phantasmagorical things with zombies in biblical times." – Jeff Vandermeer, author of *Annihilation*

"Beautifully composed and frighteningly well-researched... Well worth the read... Beyond the rich historical background and the desperate fight for survival, *Strangers in the Land* is a story about otherness, what it means to be a 'stranger'... Far from being 'just another zombie book', it is a remarkably clear look at what it means to impose a system of inequality among a culture."
– *Examiner.com*

"To say I loved this book would be an understatement. I could not put it down." – *The Seattle Post-Intelligencer*

"*The Zombie Bible* is philosophy played out in bleak landscapes. It's psychology set to the harsh strains of Prokofiev. Litore's prose is lean and hungry; his characters are faceted all-round like various colored stones; his scenes pulse with blood and life, ring with metal or reek of sweat and undeath." – Marc McDermott, Amazon.com

"Like Cormac McCarthy's novels, *I Will Hold My Death Close* does not pull its punches. A beautiful, brilliant tale, it offers a pretty bleak picture of the human condition and the human struggle against the terrors of this world." – Andrew Hallam, Ph.D., Metropolitan State University of Denver

"Litore's vibrant writing . . . rips the lid off of the King James version and reveals to us a world of intense human hopes, dreams and pathos, with a liberal dose of horror seething in the shadows. You've never seen anything like this before." – Richard Ellis Preston, Jr., author of *Romulus Buckle and the City of the Founders*

"Intensely troubling and sharply beautiful. I highly anticipate the opportunity to reread it." – Timothy Widman, *Wandering Paths*

"Gruesome and human and lyrical and horrible, *The Zombie Bible* is like nothing you have ever read. Once you're in, you'll stay."
– S.G. Redling, author of *Flowertown* and *Damocles*

"Stant rebuilds the zombie mythology from the ground up."
– Rob Kroese, author of *Mercury Falls* and *Schrodinger's Gat*

"What Litore has done ... I call it the de-sanitisation of the gospel: a visceral, messy, human take on a message of a visceral and tangible hope." – Siku, creator of *The Manga Bible* and *Drink It!*

"A good novel should go for the throat; *Death Has Come up into Our Windows* goes for your heart, rips it out and eats it before your eyes." – Lucinda Rose, *Rose Reads*

CONTENTS

MAPS

BASED LOOSELY ON
THE EVENTS OF JUDGES 4

CIRCA 1160 BC

for my daughters River and Inara
may their lives be full and free

HISTORIAN'S NOTE

IN THE THIRTEENTH CENTURY BC, several wandering tribes of Hebrews were crossing the desert. They were a young and vigorous people, flushed with life. Few of them had ever seen a walking corpse.

They were freshly displaced from the fertile fields of the Nile, where the dead were carefully contained; indeed, many Hebrew workers had broken their backs in hard labor, making or hauling brick to build the high tombs in which the cities of Kemet (that land the Greeks called Egypt) housed their dead. Those of Kemet cherished the memory of their dead and did all they could to send the deceased to the judgment hall well prepared.

There, the recently deceased handed its heart to the gods, to be weighed in scales against the feather of virtue. Often, the heart, burdened by the evils of this life, proved heavier than the feather. Then, the people of Kemet believed, the soul was cast back into the body. Deprived of the fruitful fields beyond death, it rose from its sarcophagus in a mind-devouring hunger.

The bodies of the dead must be securely entombed against this possibility. Hoping that any wakeful dead might yet find peace, the people of Kemet inscribed the insides of the tombs with hieroglyphics and magnificent art—spells and prayers and histories, everything that a risen corpse might need to remember who it had been. Perhaps, if a corpse could be made to remember the life it had lived and its hope of new life beyond death's river, the spirit might return to its gray eyes and it might offer an acceptable sacrifice and atonement using the incense, fruits, and ornate vessels of fine drink that its relatives had left with it in the tomb. Then lie down in the sarcophagus and return to the hall of judgment with a lightened heart. So those of Kemet hoped as they slid closed the massive doors of the tombs.

In our own era, several unwary archaeologists have slid open those same doors to find themselves food for the cursed and hungry dead—a testament to the utter forgetfulness of death and the smallness of the human voice, which even with its strongest stories and most beautiful pictographs cannot yet reach across death's river to bring messages or remembrance to the lost.

In time, Kemet adopted other practices for securing a successful journey across death's river. The brains of the dead they scooped free of the skull, and the other organs too, placing them in canopic jars. Mummification effectively prevented resurrection; the bodies were now but hollow shells closely enshrouded in linens. In time, the plague became virtually unknown in Kemet. Yet that cultural legacy of a pronounced concern for the well-being of the newly dead persisted. Over the centuries, the brick tombs grew greater and more magnificent, and many laborers—both Hebrews and men of other ethnicities— died in the toil of making them.

In caring so meticulously for their own dead, the people of Kemet oppressed bitterly the living members of other tribes, and the tale of the revolt of the tribes is among the most dramatic of the stories that come down to us from our spiritual ancestors. The Hebrews have left us many folktales and songs that tell of the coming of their Lawgiver and his confrontation with the Pharaoh, their liberation from oppression, and their march into the wilderness to find their own land and their own deity.

The story is well known and frequently retold. Yet most modern storytellers end their tales and let their voices fall still after the celebratory departure, the exodus from Kemet; it is hard for us to gaze steadily at the dark years in the desert and the trials that turned a frightened people of former slave workers into the hardened, efficient, and even brutal tribes that a generation later invaded fertile Canaan, slaughtering many of its people and setting up their tents in the valleys near the burned and smoking towns.

What happened to these people in the desert?

***

Their exodus from a land lush with food yet dark with oppression into barren hills with few oases strikes us as both magnificent and naïve, perhaps in equal measure. The Hebrews starved in the desert, and thirsted, and even lamented the loss of a life of enslavement that at least had not required any of them to be responsible for their own provision. Better to be oxen pulling brick than be men,

3

some of them cried. It is too hard to be men. The women offered their own complaints: along the Nile, their more lovely daughters may have been prey for lusty overseers, but at least they had been fed and clothed.

This season of innocent misery came to an unanticipated and terrible end one night when the dead stumbled, groaning, out of the rocks and canyons and fell upon the tents. We do not know where these dead came from, or why they were so many. Dead have been known to travel together en masse, shambling slowly like animal herds across an empty landscape until they encounter food. It is possible some other tribe had succumbed to the illness and had slouched into the dry hills without direction or destination, there to wait for years or even centuries until drawn by the noise of the Hebrew camp.

We do know that the death toll was severe. Even if we accept the Hebrews' written memories as the most extravagant of exaggerations, the loss of life must have been catastrophic. When dawn came, the Hebrews faced the hard reality that many of their people had been eaten and many others bitten. Some of the latter were already lurching unsteadily to their feet, their hands reaching to clutch at the survivors.

**

How the Lawgiver ended the pestilence is a narrative that I will refer to elsewhere, not here; it is at any rate no story to tell after dark. More important is the way of life the survivors adopted in their fierce intent never to suffer such a crisis a second time.

That time of terror in the wilderness redefined how the Hebrews understood their world and their duties within it. They saw themselves now as alone—desperately alone in a complex and threatening world they had been taught to believe was simple; in the empty desert they had few things to rely on. In their need for certainty, they established a Covenant with the God they had encountered in the desolate wastes, and they chiseled the first words of their Pact into tablets of hard stone, which they then kept with them always in a sacred Ark. In Kemet, they had seen contracts written on scrolls of papyrus, a vegetable material that perished if exposed to moisture; the desert demanded that a covenant as important as this one be recorded on some substance less fragile. Only a contract written into stone that would last as long as the earth could assure them of its reliability.

Among other exacting rules, the Covenant demanded a sharp separation between the living and the dead. The living were to clean their hands and arms up to the elbows before and after touching any dead meat, and the meat of some animals could not be touched at all; they were not to touch with their naked hands the body of any dead man or woman; they were not to leave any dead body unburied, for any reason. The punishments for breaking the Covenant were severe, even as the promised reward for keeping it was great: an eternal inheritance in a clean and fertile land and divine protection from the hungry dead.

One consequence of that Covenant was a profound and lasting distrust of tribes not their own. The Hebrews both envied and feared the less restricted lives of their neighbors, who lived by no exacting Covenant. To cite one example of the many customs that worried and at times disgusted the Hebrews, some of their neighbors left their enemy dead unburied after a raid or buried the dead too shallow. How terrible it must have been to walk among the fallen, unclothing the slain and checking for bites that they may have concealed in their fear even from their own people. The Hebrews believed it was better to simply bury all the bodies—bury them deep if the soil was soft or pile high a cairn of stones over each corpse to crush it securely to the ground so that none might ever rise, moaning, to catch and devour the living.

The commandments by which the Hebrews lived left no room for unwary haste or compromise, whether with one's own dead or with another's: pile high the cairn, and if necessity required that in doing so you touch the bodies of the dead with ungloved hands, then wait afterward outside the camp for the required seven days until your uncleanness had passed.

To minds hardened by the crisis in the desert, compromise meant the deaths of others in your tribe. Those might be deaths you couldn't predict or prevent, but as they rose, wailing, those dead would cry out your guilt to God.

***

Studying the fragmentary but eloquent records these tribes left behind, I find myself struck with both admiration and horror. Admiration for their ability to both survive and establish a code of law that would permit them to remain human while surviving. And horror at their readiness to exterminate or enslave other peoples who were less aware and therefore less cautious of the ravenous dead.

In our own time, this globe has suffered one mass genocide at least once every decade for more than a century. Despite this, we are today a sheltered people, and we are losing our memory. Yet it is vitally important that we remember. Like the Hebrews, we are at a moment of terrible choice, where we too must decide what we will do with those who live as "strangers" among us, those who labor in our towns or starve in our streets. Those who speak a strange language and who some of us choose to believe are not of our People.

Some of us have already made the choice. Some of us appoint watchmen with authority to hold and harass and contain the strangers we fear. Some of us erect fences along the border of the land or gaze at the sky and shiver in fear of falling planes.

The ancient records hold lessons for us, hard lessons we too often ignore. Our ancestors, like the Hebrews, yearned for the durability of their covenant passionately enough to write it in stone—not in tablets within an Ark, but on the pedestal of the Statue of Liberty. We will at times regret and wish to deny the covenants and the commitments our fathers made, regardless of whether they were right or wrong, foolish or wise. And at times we will fear their consequences, real or imagined. Yet if we cannot honor the covenants we make with those who live among us, then we may prove equally unable to honor the covenants we make with God, or with our own kin, or with ourselves. Like the Hebrews, we are newly come to a land we now consider our own, and though we think of ourselves as one constituted people, a people set apart, we remain in fact many tribes intermingled, giving worship to many gods both sacred and secular.

In the lean years to come, when the dead moan outside our walls and our homesteads, nothing will matter more to our ability to survive—and to remain true and human—than our readiness to honor the covenants that our fathers and that we ourselves, the living, have made with each other. To do otherwise is to forget that we are strongest together, and that God, who does not make promises lightly, has issued us no guarantee that the ideas that save us will come from a banker in Chicago rather than an assistant electrician in Los Angeles. And to do otherwise is to be less than who we've said we will be.

***

Our narrative opens a few brief generations after the desert. A people without a standing military or any significant arsenal, the Hebrew tribes had raided when they saw land worth taking; now, having taken it, they were weary, and most of them desired only rest and the chance of a new life in a lush and fertile land. The aggressive deforestation of later centuries would let in the desert, but in 1160 BC, the land of promise was not as it is today. Israel was more humid then, and in some places richly forested, a land of milk and honey.

Many of the Hebrews were eager to keep to their own kin on their own lands, trusting in the judges of the Law to arbitrate disputes and keep the region clean of the dead.

The Canaanites who had lived in the land before them now had few leaders and fewer armed men; with those few who remained, the Hebrews had made a covenant in the valley that the priests later named Weeping because of their regret for the truce established there. Now most of the Canaanites kept to themselves in small settlements of wooden houses or hovels, or lived and worked among the Hebrews as slaves or second-class laborers. Yet their presence had already begun to change the Hebrews they lived among. Though many of the Hebrew encampments still consisted of tents amid pastures filled with herds, in places a few houses of cedar could already be seen, a few vineyards, a few olive presses.

PART 1
SHILOH

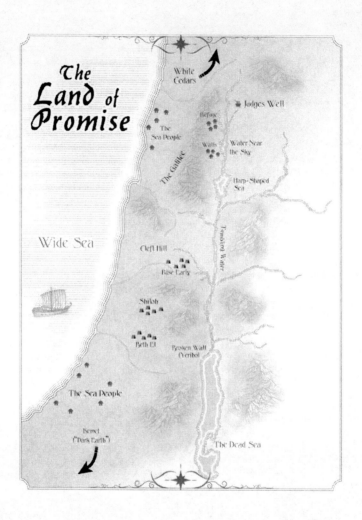

NAVI

THE PEOPLE OF THE COVENANT had many judges, but only one *navi* who told them the future and the past and found truth. She heard their pleas four times a week from a wooden seat her husband had carved for her beneath the great olive tree on its hill near Shiloh. The tree had branches that spread wider than the roof of a cedar house, and it had been standing there, tall and green, when Yeshua the war leader first led their ancestors to the land. Still rich with life, it served now as a visible reminder to all who came before the *navi*'s seat that the fertility and possession of this land of promise, this land of milk and honey and olive groves, came with a high cost: the keeping of the Law and the Covenant, that commitment to ways of living that alone kept the People clean and secure in a world where heathen tribes or the living dead might rise up in the night and devour them.

To keep the Covenant meant olive oil and abundant fields of wheat and barley, many births among the flocks, and many children.

To break it—that meant a curse: blight and barrenness and unclean death.

Let the People look to the *navi*'s seat and remember this.

Devora the *navi* sat there now with the full authority of the Law at her back, her eyes hard among early wrinkles, her graying hair glowing in that softened light that comes before sunset. A massive, broad-shouldered man stood behind her with a stout ashen spear ending in a bronze head and the long, uncut hair that was the visible sign of his vow. As a nazarite, Zadok lived a life that had no meaning but the wielding of the spear and the defense of the tribe of Levi. He had trained his body for this. Zadok was not a farmer, a tanner, a vintner, or a priest. He was one who preserved life and dealt death when needed. In all the land, only four others shared his vow.

Two supplicants had just turned from Devora's seat to make their way down the slope, one with a relieved look, the other with a scowl. Their argument over the possession of a bull had nearly drawn blood, and the details of the case were such that the seventy judges in Shiloh could not decide it and had sent the two men to the olive tree. But no vision had come to Devora to reveal where there was guilt and where there was not, and in her frustration the *navi* had resolved the matter by deciding that both men together would take the bull and give the animal to the priests, who would offer it up as an *olah*, a burnt offering before God. In this one act they would sacrifice their dispute and atone for the discord they'd brought to the camps of the People. This case, like others that day, had reminded Devora how divided the People were, how provisional their commitment to the covenants they'd made with God and with each other. In light of the evil news this morning had brought to the valley below, this division alarmed Devora. She sat very still, anxious to end the day's judgments and return to the camp. She was intensely grateful for Zadok's steadying presence behind her.

The people gathered on the slope below parted to let the two supplicants by. There were maybe thirty men and women, some standing, others seated on great slabs of rock that past supplicants had pulled free of the scree on the west side of the hill near the cairns of the dead. Beyond the supplicants lay the valley, filled with the white tents of Shiloh. That land was lush with tall grasses and stands of oak and terebinth near the water; faint from the far slopes across the river came the lowing of herds, many of them her husband's. The slow river wound eastward on its way to meet the Tumbling Water, which ran through all the land from the Galilee hills in the north to the dead sea in the south where no fish were—and where the salt in the water was so thick a man could lie on the surface without sinking. Where the salt on the shore stood in tall white pillars, shaped like tents or women or creatures the Hebrews had not met before even in nightmares. Like so many reminders that the land was strange to them and they still strangers in it, and their possession of its fields and waters a blessing that could yet be revoked, a promise that could yet be rescinded.

As Devora looked out over the supplicants, she decided she had time before sundown to sit in decision over one more case. It was her responsibility to see as

15

many as she could, yet she was weary. She yearned for a restful Sabbath meal with her husband. The cases of the day had not succeeded in distracting her from her real worry—the armed camp that had set up a few miles down-river around the tent of a chieftain called Barak ben Abinoam, bringing with it news of walking dead in the north.

Devora searched the supplicants' eyes—herdsmen, levites, craftsmen—for some sign of an easy case, though only the most difficult were sent to her. A stir among those lowest on the slope drew her attention. People were drawing together as though to form a wall as a woman approached them, climbing unsteadily up the hill with a bundle clutched in her arms. Her lank hair hung forward over her face, and she was wrapped in a blanket that looked to be coarse wool. A salmah, the poorest of garments. One shoulder was free of the wool, bare and dirtied with the stain of a long and sweaty walk. Devora did not recognize her from the nearby camp at Shiloh nor from any of the herders' camps in the surrounding valleys. She might have come a long way, wearing nothing but that salmah and her long, ragged hair, and carrying nothing but that bundle she held.

One of the supplicants, a white-robed levite, stepped directly into her way and must have said something that Devora couldn't hear from her seat; she saw the young woman—a girl, really—lift her head and spit in the levite's face. The man lifted his hand but did not strike, as though reluctant to touch with his bare skin this woman who came strange and dirtied to the *navi*'s hill.

The other supplicants formed a circle around the girl. A few who did not share the levite's hesitation began shoving her, as though to push her back down the slope. Seeing the girl stumble to her knees, Devora hissed through her teeth. She didn't want complications; the day had been tiring enough. The seat of decision was hers and there would be no stoning or reviling or barring of any supplicant from her hill unless it was at her word. She wanted to know what was going on, and quickly. She lifted her hand.

"Let the girl come!" she called, her voice sharp and clear in the late afternoon heat.

Silence fell over the hill.

The supplicants stepped away from the girl, a few of them with visible reluctance, and left an open path to the bare, trampled space before the *navi*'s seat. Now all their eyes were on Devora; she felt them, even as she kept her own on the girl who was stumbling the last fifty paces up to the olive tree. The *navi* put up her hand once the girl had come near enough, and the girl stood there with her eyes lowered, her shoulders shaking, her hands clutching the bundle as tightly as though it were her very life.

Devora knew at once something was wrong, badly wrong, and Zadok stirred almost imperceptibly behind her; he felt it too. The bundle the girl held drew the *navi*'s gaze.

"What brings you here, girl?" she said softly, without lifting her eyes from the bundle. "Who has wronged you?" Those four words were her ritual, her invitation to any who came to speak with her beneath the olive. Her promise that she would hear them before making a judgment.

The girl shook without speaking, and Devora saw the terror and wild hope in the girl's eyes. She also saw that this was not a girl of their People; her sharp cheekbones and the kohl beneath her eyes, smeared from the girl's tears, betrayed her. She was a Canaanite girl, though it was possible she was captive or wife to one of the People. Her features were those of the north, of the Galilee hills, and the state of her sandals and the half-healed scrapes on her shins beneath the ragged hem of her garment told the story of a long journey on foot, carrying her bundle down out of the hills to this olive tree.

The anguish in the girl's eyes was a loud demand, though silent; it made Devora wary. The girl was heathen, keeper of no Covenant, a threat to the sons of the People. Devora wanted suddenly to turn the girl away. She could do this easily. The girl was not of the People. And she had not been sent here by the seventy judges—she had walked right to this hill and tried to shove through the supplicants who were already waiting. Devora could just send the girl to Shiloh to wait.

Yet.

This girl had come willingly to the olive tree, in a land her strange, soft people had once possessed. She had come even as any daughter of the People might, to seek the *navi*'s knowledge and the *navi*'s justice. And the words of the Law spoke of how the People were to treat such as her:

> *Shelter the stranger you find in your land, for you also were strangers in the land of Kemet where none gave you shelter. Forget not your suffering in the land of Kemet.*

Even had there been no such words in the Law, this girl had come to her. To the *navi*. With that anguish, that demand in her eyes.

She could not be turned away.

Devora felt a chill, a premonition that was instinct and not prophecy. She made her voice stern. "Who has wronged you, girl?" But suddenly that seemed the wrong question. She could see it in the girl's eyes. Whatever this girl might tell her, it would not be a situation where justice could be meted out between her and another. Whatever judgment she would ask would not be one Devora was prepared to make.

"*Navi*—" The girl's voice broke. Her hands whitened around the bundle she held.

"You stand before the Law and the Covenant," Devora said sharply. "Why have you come, Canaanite?"

"Help me." The girl's voice was raw from crying. The plea in her tear-reddened eyes was one of panic, one woman's cry to another. "They say you approach the Hebrew God without any veil between you. Please. Beg him to help me."

Her hand shaking, the girl peeled away one corner of the bundle, and Devora wrinkled her nose at a stench of ripe decay. The bundle was a swaddled infant, less than a week old; the girl's back was to the other supplicants below, and only she and Devora and Zadok behind the *navi*'s seat could see the infant. See what was wrong. Devora's breath hissed between her teeth.

Unclean! A wild cry in her mind, a cry as ancient and forlorn as broken tombs in a desert place. A cry her people had made around fires in the wilderness long before she or anyone she knew was born. *Unclean!*

The infant opened its reddened eyes and reached its hands feebly toward the *navi*, tiny fingers clutching at the air. Its mouth opened and let out a high-pitched moan.

Devora felt terribly cold. The child's skin was gray. Much of the infant's left leg was gone, where some creature had bitten into it and torn away flesh and soft cartilage, perhaps only a moment before the child's mother had been able to rescue it.

Its eyes gazed on the *navi*, but those eyes were dull and dry like small stones.

The infant was not alive.

It would never again draw milk from the young Canaanite's breasts. It would never crawl or learn to walk. Its hair would never grow even a fingernail's width, nor would it ever void its bowels.

But it *would* hunger.

Devora listened to that high, unwavering moan for one long moment, feeling not only chilled but old: the ache in her wrists and fingers, the sharp needles that lived in her back. Swallowing against the dryness in her throat, she motioned to the man who stood behind her. After an instant's hesitation, Zadok set aside his spear and plucked from the girdle about his waist two gloves of dried goatskin. He drew them on, then moved forward quickly to seize the child.

The girl shrieked, tried to leap away with her infant, but the man caught her arm, pulled her savagely back, even as she kicked at him and screamed, her eyes dark with horror. He took up the baby by its remaining leg, wrenching it from her. He held the girl away from his body, and she clawed wildly at his arm, thrashing. Her salmah fell open, revealing a body thin and wasted, with great folds of skin slack from a childbirth that could not have happened more than a couple of weeks before.

"*Navi!*" the girl screamed. "*Navi!*"

The man hesitated, looked to Devora, even as the girl fought his grip. The infant wriggled in the air, hissing like an asp, its small arms moving. The people below on the slope could see it now, and several of them cried out.

Devora tensed. That corpse writhing in the nazarite's grip was her most terrible fear made flesh. "Zadok," she said—

Then, between one beat of Devora's heart and the next, it happened.

The air around her *heated*, as though the *navi* were standing in a desert. A dry and violent heat that overcame her and swept into her. Devora knew what it meant; it was the *shekinah*, the holy presence of God, the same heat that dwelled over the Ark in the Tent of Meeting at Shiloh. Devora braced herself, and then the vision came. The seeing of what might happen.

She saw shambling figures lurching through the valley below. Some of them were on the slope below her, others were by the river. Still more were among the tents, small at this distance. Herds of them, all swaying as they walked. Arms lifted as though yearning for an embrace. The scent of decay stank sweetly in Devora's nostrils. She coughed painfully and passed her hand over her eyes, which burned now with strain.

Her vision cleared, mercifully. There was only the girl screaming and Zadok the nazarite with the child clutched in his hand. And the supplicants below with ashen faces, the hill on which they stood, and around them the wide fields of heather and barley under a pale sky. No other dead, only that small, moaning infant.

Her lips tasted of salt; in the heat of God's presence all

the moisture had been baked from them, leaving only that taste behind.

She forced herself to breathe. Deeply, fully. It was the future she had seen, but it was not the truth. Not yet. It couldn't be. It mustn't be. In her mind, she heard the screams outside her mother's tent, screams that went on and on until they died in a gasp of breath. That was a memory, that was the past. She tried to shove it back as she turned cold eyes on the Canaanite girl. Thirty years ago, her people had brought the unclean death into the land. Now it was happening again.

"Please, *navi*," the girl cried, her face twisted in pain and fear. "Please, pray to the Hebrew God. There must be something the gods can do. He didn't die of illness or hunger or any wild animal. It's *unjust*. The gods have to give him back! Please, *navi*, please, *navi!*"

The girl's cries pulled at her, but Devora could not afford to pity her. The miracle the girl hoped for was not Devora's to provide. It was brutally clear what she had to do, to avert what she had just foreseen. Her life had been a series of acts of extreme and necessary justice. Keeping the Law, protecting the People—this mattered more than one girl's pain. She met the Canaanite's eyes and made her voice hard as the edge of a blade. "Don't be foolish, girl. Only one thing can be done. Go home; your husband will give you more children." Devora turned to Zadok. "Do what must be done," she said.

The nazarite gave her a grim nod. Unlike the others who'd taken the nazarite vow, Zadok ben Zefanyah had not made his covenant with the high priest, but with the *navi*. Devora had been there the night his father died defending the priests, had been the one person in the camp to stop and speak with the boy as he stood by his father's corpse.

His vow and the events of his life had shaped him, she knew, into a man who grieved deeply but did not flinch; when the corpses he'd seen and the acts that had been required of him returned to his heart in the dark hours of the night, he would drown the memory of them in the heaviness of barley beer (the only violation of his vow that he permitted himself) or in the sweet softness of a woman's body. The dawn would find him slumped over his cup or over his lover's breasts, weeping. But his cries would pass. He would stand, unsteadily a moment, then leave the beer-house or the woman's tent and return to his covenant and his duty. And whatever that next day required, he would not flinch.

He did not flinch now. He held the Canaanite girl at arm's length and set the bundled infant upon the ground. Then he took up his long-hafted spear from where he had set it aside.

"*No!*" The girl began to shriek. "You Hebrew bitch!" she cried. "*You Hebrew bitch!*" The scream tore its way out of her throat, raw and frantic, as she tried to struggle past Zadok.

Devora closed her eyes, said a short prayer under her breath. She could hear the murmur of the supplicants— none of whom had moved. She heard the tiny moan from the corpse that had been an infant; it ended in a hard *thock* of bronze driven into flesh. A choked, sobbing noise from the mother, as though a scream had caught in her throat and would be lodged there for every night of her remaining years. The *navi* kept her eyes closed a moment more.

When she looked on the world again, the girl was on her knees, her face ashen, still making that choked sound. Zadok stood beside her; he'd cast his spear to the grass. Down the hill, some of the other supplicants were on their knees as well, overcome by horror. The bundle at Zadok's feet didn't move or make any sound.

Grimly, Devora rose to her feet. Too old, she felt too old today. Much too old for seeing…this. She stepped forward until she stood by Zadok and the Canaanite, with the small corpse at her feet. Glanced down at it. The head had been crushed entirely; one of the little hands was still curled as if to grasp at some flesh warmer than its own. There was no blood beneath the body, nor any on the bronze head of Zadok's spear that lay beside it, for only living things bleed.

It was a small, mangled thing, without face or any color to its skin. It did not seem ever to have been human. There was a burn of moisture in Devora's eyes; she forbade it. If no one had been watching she would have sat down beside that body and remained there until the world was old.

She glanced up, noted the position of the sun. Perhaps two hours before dark. Dusk would come swiftly, and with it the Sabbath bride. They must be in the tents before then or sleep on the heather; from sunset this day to sunset the next, she must rest. Yet she could not simply hurry to the tents and leave this body unburied through the Sabbath.

She whispered the words of one of the six hundred and thirteen *mitzvot*, commandments given to their fathers in

24

the desert for keeping the camp clean of disease and the dead:

> *You shall bury the flesh of the dead, and raise above it a cairn of stones, that God will see it, and remember, and make the land clean.*

The People sheltered and hid from the dead within the mighty tent of the Law, and the poles of that tent were the living pillars of the Covenant, strong and binding promises between the tribes and God and between the tribes and each other; yet the roots of those pillars were intricate and fragile, for those roots were the acts of the People that upheld and sustained the Covenant. Devora sat in her seat of decision to pass judgment wherever the roots had been broken or eaten away by unclean choices, in order to keep the whole tent of the Law from collapsing and crushing the People beneath it. Now she could sense that mighty canvas of the Law tearing in the wind and heat of her vision. What this day had brought to her. News of herds of dead moving through the high Galilee, a migration of corpses into the land such as she had never before heard or imagined. And one of them brought even here, to her feet, at the olive tree.

Her hands were trembling; she could not still them.

"We must bury it," she whispered. "And we must hurry."

CAIRNS FOR THE DEAD

SOME HORRORS DEMAND that we have words to explain them, but Devora had none. She stepped past Zadok and the girl to gaze down the slope at the ashen-faced supplicants. Behind her, the girl's sobs became high-pitched and sharp, like the sounds of some small animal dying in pain. Devora took a steadying breath, carefully sewing her heart shut. She did what had to be done.

A wind sprang up, pulling at her hair and her dress. She raised her voice over it. "This hill is cleansed," she called to them, "and a cairn will be raised."

"*Selah*," the supplicants murmured back. *Always*. And the wind took away their voices. Their eyes were wide; they stared into a darkness that was their own fear and their own expectation and their own waking at night. They had come here to stand before the olive tree to receive justice, rather than visiting justice upon each other in blood and heat and the glinting of knives. Now they were pale. They had heard rumors of the moaning of the dead in the high Galilee and the coming of armed men to seek aid from all the tribes, but the Canaanite woman today had brought that distant terror that they could ignore here to this very hill above the tents of Shiloh and the holy Ark itself. Surely the hunger cry of the dead infant meant some savage and irremediable justice had been visited upon them, upon the land and the People. That God who sat in decision over the Hebrews and over the whole earth had taken away his hand of protection. That they were no longer supplicants but rather men marked for death and burial.

The cleansing and the silencing of this one small, restless corpse brought no comfort. They gazed at the *navi*, awaiting some judgment or vision from God. She felt the weight of their need, their demands on her.

But what could Devora tell them? That she had foreseen the dead moving across the holy valley in great herds and didn't yet know what God wished her to do to prevent it? They didn't need to hear that.

"Go back to your tents," she cried at last. "The *navi* has left her seat."

They gazed up at her listlessly.

"Go home! Observe the Sabbath. Live by the Law, and the land will be clean."

Some of those standing or sitting on the slope below her had been there before the sun rose to offer the earth its warm kiss. Some had been months in Shiloh while their cases were debated among those levites appointed to sit in decision over the People, before they'd been referred at last to the *navi* who received special insight from God. Yet now they didn't complain; they began leaving the hill, one after the other. Some of them walking slowly back to the tents, some quickly as though fleeing. As though they understood that their demands on the Law and on God were rescinded or postponed. Perhaps, in the days ahead, they would wait in silence to hear whether the valley would fill with the voices of the dead preparing to feed or with the clack of stone against stone as cairns were raised over the corpses to hold them unrising to the earth.

Devora watched for a few moments as they moved away through the heather. Delaying her next task. She lifted her eyes, gazing across this land of promise from her high place, and listened to the wind move in the olive leaves. Softly as the wind, she heard the Canaanite weeping.

She didn't turn yet to face that mother and the infant in need of burial. She couldn't. There was little time, but she needed one moment to breathe. She glanced down at the valley, at the mighty flock of white tents perched like cranes by the river. That was Shiloh. A yearning lit in her for a quiet meal and rest in her husband's tent. But she knew there would be no rest for her tonight, no real rest.

The men from the Galilee had pitched their tents a few miles downriver to the east. She could see them from here. Not a permanent camp like Shiloh, but a hasty one, mostly small tents that could be rolled up and carried on a man's back. In the high land where those men lived, the dead were feeding, groping through fields of wild barley or along creek-banks, hunting animals or men or women. Or reaching through windows for infants asleep in the cedar houses built by the Canaanites.

Years since she'd seen one of the unclean dead.

Except in her dreams.

Except whenever she lay her head down and closed her

eyes and pursued sleep through the weeds and fens of her nightmares.

Turning, Devora found Zadok standing over the infant with his back to her, and the girl still on her knees. She had drawn her salmah back around her, but Devora recalled how thin and exhausted her body had looked, as though the journey to her olive tree and the ordeal she suffered in her heart had bled the girl's body of all her strength and health. The Canaanite glanced up at the *navi* with swollen eyes.

"A cairn," the girl said. "You said a cairn. Please. My child. He needs to go into the water. He's not a Hebrew. Please. He must pass into the fish, and the fish into the people, so that he can come back."

Devora went cold with horror at the thought. What if it took only one unclean corpse to defile an entire lake, all the fish in it, all those who ate of the fish? Who could say what would happen? Thirty years ago, the heathen dead had wandered, moaning, into Shiloh camp and devoured much of what mattered to young Devora. She had known since that day what a peril the Canaanites and their customs could be.

"Enough," she cried. "I'll have none of your heathen ways, girl. They've brought this on us. Your gloves, Zadok."

When the nazarite didn't answer, Devora stepped toward him, glanced at his face, and received a shock. That face showed no expression: Zadok simply stood with his dark eyes fixed on the small body.

"Zadok?"

No answer.

Alarmed, Devora approached him, trying to catch his eyes with hers. He didn't move or show that he'd heard her. His massive body just breathed in and out, his chest moving like a great bear's, his entire attention on the corpse. Devora's heart beat faster. It had been a long time since one of these moods had overtaken Zadok. It used to happen every time he stilled one of the unclean corpses— but the last had been nearly ten years ago, and the one before that had been four years earlier.

The worst time, when he was still but a youth, Zadok had stood completely still for almost two days. When he'd come out of it at last, he'd been violent, enraged, lashing about with his spear. For a few minutes, then he'd collapsed from exhaustion. He'd slept for a day and a half and woken with no memory of his fit, nor any clear memory of the death that had prompted it. Zadok and two other nazarites had been clearing an oak grove of dead, several hours upriver from Shiloh. Some caravan merchant had died there, then risen; he'd eaten his wife and one of his slaves, and the rest had fled, leaving three bodies restless and unburied. The dead had surprised Zadok in the trees, but he'd dealt with them. Afterward, one of the other nazarites had stayed beside him while Zadok stood still as a tree, his memories gripping at his heart. The other had run to Shiloh with word, and had told Devora. After a quick word to her husband, the *navi* had hurried out to the grove, and she had been there sitting by Zadok when he woke at last.

But that had been over twenty years ago.

She had no idea how long this one would last.

The *navi* glanced at the declining sun. Felt the small, sharp teeth of panic. The Sabbath was coming; they had to get back to the tents. But they could *not* leave a corpse on the open ground, with no stones over it. Her breath hissed through her teeth.

She struck Zadok hard across the face.

He didn't even blink.

Devora's right hand stung, and she rubbed it with her left. Her heart was pounding now. She glanced about, cursing under her breath. Wishing she'd kept the supplicants at the hill rather than dispersing them. The area was quiet now but for the wind. There were only the three of them—Zadok, the Canaanite girl, and the *navi*. Alone with the tiny corpse.

"What's wrong with him?" the Canaanite whispered.

"The dead are a shock to anyone," Devora muttered. She must do without Zadok. She caught the hems of the goatskin gloves at his wrists and peeled them free of his hands, one, then the other, careful not to touch the fingers or the palm, anywhere the leather might have touched the corpse. Under her breath, she recited the words of the Law. That was a ritual of hers when she needed calm.

> *You shall not touch the flesh of the dead, for the dead body is unclean. If a man touches the flesh of the dead, you shall put him from your camp and watch him. Seven days you shall put him from your camp, until his uncleanness has passed.*

The gloves were much too large for her; her hands felt silly inside them, and she worried they would slip off her fingers, which were damp with sweat. She kept her hands curled to prevent this. She reached for the infant.

"Leave him alone!" the girl whispered, without looking up.

31

"You brought this child to me," Devora said. "Now it is my task to do what I must." The *navi* took the tiny body in her hands, lifting it carefully, not letting the gloves slip. The infant was very light, as though she held a bundle of leaves. She hooked the swaddling cloth with one gloved finger, lifting it from the ground too. She could wrap the body in it later.

For an instant she glanced at Zadok's spear where it lay in the grass. That bronze spearhead would probably make digging a grave easier. But she shook her head. The spear was Zadok's. She would leave it with him.

"Come, girl." She began walking briskly down the slope.

***

In the lee of the west slope there were cairns in great number, several hundred of them, orderly stacks of flat stones like stunted pillars set in the earth, a forest of monuments. Some of the dead beneath them had died of age or illness, a few from bloodshed, some from a judgment of death by stoning. Set a little apart from the others—because the bodies beneath them were defiled—a stretch of eight and sixty cairns marked the resting places of those who had died the unclean death on that terrible night thirty years ago, when the walking dead had come to Shiloh.

Carrying the infant's body at arm's length, Devora moved slowly among the cairns, weighted down by the crushing burden of the past, which even the Covenant could only partially lighten. Behind her the Canaanite followed numbly.

Devora lay the infant by the cairns of the defiled, and the Canaanite knelt by the body, her head lowered, her hands clutching her knees. Devora left her there and hurried to a bit of scree nearby where a rockslide some years before had exposed the guts of the earth. Beyond the scree and the curve of the hill she could see the white tents of Shiloh again, as alluring to her as a flock of white doves alighting in a dry wilderness. But the tents must wait.

The stones she gathered had to be large ones—large enough to crush the dead to the earth. The corpse's head had been shattered; it would not hunger again. Yet it was unclean and might spread the blight to anything it touched. You couldn't know what might sicken from it—living people or living crops. So you pile stone above a dead body, any dead body, no matter how dead or how still the body may look. The time in the desert, when Devora's ancestors had seen corpses rise moaning to their feet, had taught them to take no chances, none.

***

Devora felt the strain in her arms as she carried the last of six slabs of rock from the scree to the place she'd chosen beside the other cairns. Sweat began to trickle down her back, making her itch. Devora tried to move quickly, but her fatigue was catching up with her. After more than forty years of life, her body was aging; there were days when she felt no pain, and days like this one when the weariness was as present as the breath in her lungs. Devora glanced back once to see Zadok standing still as a cairn himself by the olive tree on the slope above. She chewed on bitter words for Zadok in the privacy of her heart, but those words were quickly swallowed in remorse. She'd left him up there, trapped in who knew what darkness of the heart. Spearing the dead had brought back memories for him, too. She should have expected that. She should have taken up spear or stone herself and borne the burden of that act on her own shoulders, even as she was now bearing the burden of this stone. Her face heated with shame; the nazarite's vow was to defend her life, not to suffer in her place.

The Canaanite girl still knelt by the small body. At first, Devora had feared the girl might grab the infant and flee, but she seemed to be in shock. The salmah had slipped from her shoulder, nearly baring one breast, which was so swollen with milk that her skin was red and each vein could be clearly seen. It must have hurt terribly, yet the girl did not appear to notice. Nor did she cover herself. She just stared listlessly at an empty spot of ground beside the infant and did not twitch or do anything but breathe as Devora approached.

With a groan, the *navi* let the rock fall to the earth beside that scrap of flesh and bone that had once been a child. Then rested a moment, breathing hard. She didn't spare the Canaanite another glance. Just listened to the beating of her heart and the breath coming in and out of her body. Calm. She needed calm. She glanced again at the sun, held up her hand—four fingers' width between that blaze of heat and the tops of the hills. Little time, little time. She didn't intend to spend the Sabbath on this hill among the cairns, with a weeping Canaanite girl and a nazarite lost in his own private nightmare. She needed to get back. She needed to tell the priests of her vision. Needed the solace of her husband's arms—she knew well that her own nightmares would visit her tonight, after dark.

Taking up a jagged rock to use for a shovel, Devora began digging in the soil beside the body, parting the roots of weeds and hollowing out an infant-sized resting place in the warm ground, as though shaping a small womb in the earth for the child's body to return to. She panted as she worked. A quick glance at Zadok—he had not moved.

"Don't put him in the ground," the Canaanite said, her eyes sore and red.

Devora didn't look up. "You can't take it from the hill," she said quietly. "Or to any water the People might drink."

"You've taken everything from us," the girl said. "Everything. Our men toil like slaves in your fields. Your priests burn our gods." A quiver of despair in her voice. "Can I not even care for the body of *my child*?"

Devora cast the jagged rock aside and reached for one of her stones. Each was roughly rectangular, about the length of her arm and the height of her hand. Grasping the edge of a stone with both her hands and digging in with her fingers, she lifted and tipped, rolling the stone into position. Her back itched furiously, and her arms and shoulders and neck burned with pain.

"I hate you," the girl whispered. "I hate you."

Devora glanced at the Canaanite girl, a rebuke ready. But she was caught by the girl's visible anguish and cold defiance. The Canaanite wasn't the kind of heathen Devora might have expected to meet. She carried in her hand no trivial god of wood or stone. She had no war paint. This stranger in her land was only a girl, one who had suffered and labored in the birth tent to bring one small life into the land to set against all the unclean death. The midwives had pulled that infant wet and helpless from this woman's own body and handed it to her as it cried in its horror at the strangeness of the world beyond the womb. Devora thought of those moments she'd never known but had witnessed, when the mother and the infant weep together and the midwives press warm, moist cloths to the mother's exhausted and torn body to stop the blood.

The grief in the Canaanite's eyes was so intense it was nearly feral. It took Devora aback; the rebuke died on her lips. She had felt grief before—grief that tore at her in the night. But whatever this stranger was feeling, *that* Devora had never felt. For a moment Devora pressed her own hand to her belly, and something clenched tight about her heart. She had never brought any child crying into the land. What would it have been like to bear one, from one harvest season nearly to the next, feel it growing inside her, and birth one, and then lose one?

The Canaanite's travails had not ended with the lifting of her child to her breast. It could not have been many days later when she'd risen and stumbled all the way here out of the settlements in the high Galilee, carrying that bitten infant, her own body still bleeding from its birth.

She must have needed to rest often, near fainting, only to push herself unsteadily to her feet again. Perhaps the infant had been alive and feverish when she began her long, desperate walk. Perhaps it had died along the way, then risen to the mother's horror with that low cry of hunger. Yet the girl had kept carrying it, kept on her feet, all the way here, to the *navi*'s olive tree. It might have taken her days. Perhaps Devora's words of comfort had been colder than she'd realized; perhaps there was no husband. Perhaps it was the husband who had bitten the infant and eaten its leg. She didn't know. She only knew that the Canaanite girl had come here alone, carrying her infant across a land that had once been hers and her people's.

"The cairn is a necessity," Devora said softly. "It is also a promise. A promise to the dead that the People will not forget. A promise that even God will look down and see the cairn and remember. And a promise to the living *and* the dead that the unclean death will end here, at these stones, and spread no further. We must bury the child the Hebrew way. Or more children may die."

She wished she might wipe sweat from her face, but dared not lift the gloves to touch her skin. She kept her eyes on the Canaanite, saw that her words meant little to her.

"Girl," the *navi* called softly, "what is your name?"

"Hurriya." The girl's eyes were hopeless. "I am Hurriya. The father was Malachi ben Aharon."

"That is a Hebrew name," Devora said sharply.

"He *was* Hebrew," the girl said. "A laborer at an olive press near Judges' Well. My father sold me to him when I was twelve."

Devora cast an uneasy glance at the cairn she'd raised.

The father had been Hebrew. If he were here, he might beg the *navi* to sing the Words of Going for his son.

"Did the child have a name?"

"No," Hurriya whispered. "He was only seven days old. I knew in my heart you couldn't help him. But the hope. The hope was all I had."

The horror of it made Devora's throat tighten. On the eighth day, every male Hebrew child was circumcised and given a name. This infant had perished without name and without any mark of the Covenant upon its flesh. It was not of the People. It was not of *any* People—it had no name. Yet if no Words of Going were sung over the cairn, this infant and its father would be forgotten. God might see the cairn, but how would God know who was beneath it? The thought of one of the People being unremembered—that was the grasp of a cold hand about her heart.

She let out her breath and returned her focus to the physical work of raising the cairn. She arranged three great stones in a triangle around the little pit she'd dug—that made a wall, or a frame, for the cairn. Like the foundation of a small house, a house for the dead. She reached for the infant and lowered what was left of it into the small depression she'd made in the earth.

Muscles that she probably hadn't used since she was a young girl were screaming at her. She clenched her teeth and lifted one of the other stones. With a groan that felt like her bones were coming loose from each other, she slammed the stone down across the top of the cairn's foundation, covering half of the small grave, forming half a roof. Her gloved fingers still clenched tight about the edge of the stone, she lay over it, wheezing. For a moment she just lay there.

Finish. She had to finish this.

She pushed herself up.

Only two more stones. One to complete the roof and one to sit atop the cairn, sealing it. Two more, only two. The infant was already half concealed. She could do this.

But she could still hear that moan, that unliving moan, in her mind. Worse, she could hear the moans outside her mother's tent, thirty years ago, and the screams. Her hands began shaking again. If she were to close her eyes, she'd be *there*, in that tent, as a child. She used to visit that tent in her dreams, night after night. But it had been a long time now since she had. She knew she would be there tonight. When that happened, she couldn't be alone. After so long—she feared the dreams would shatter her, that her body would convulse and clench up and she would sob in her blankets until morning. She couldn't afford that kind of weakness, that kind of terror. Israel couldn't afford it. She needed her husband tonight.

She lifted the next stone, straining. A cry ripped from her throat as she let the great rock fall into place, roofing the cairn. As she gulped in air, her palms flat against the cold stone, she felt the slightest tremor in the ground, through her knees.

She lifted her eyes.

Three horses were riding up the valley below toward her hill at a swift canter, one well ahead of the other two. They were sleek animals, good ones, probably trades from across the Water. They were riding from the northeast, from the northern camp, and with the sun behind her Devora could see them clearly. The riders were tall men, one broad-shouldered with a thick, dark beard. The other two lean and wiry.

Taking a breath, she returned her attention to the cairn. It must be finished. The earth was cool against her knees, but strands of her hair had strayed across her face, sweaty from the exertion. Not how she would have chosen to meet men of her People: on her knees, sweaty, and dirtied. She hissed through her teeth. Burying this corpse was more important than her dignity. She reached for the last of the stones. She would finish this, and then she would hear what these men wanted, these men who'd taken up the spear when the dead rose, and ridden out of the north.

MEN FROM THE GALILEE

THE FIRST OF THE RIDERS pulled well ahead of the other two; he rode at a gallop right up the slope, only slowing when he reached the cairns, so as not to break his horse's legs against some mound of stone. Horses were rare in the land, a gift of God to any who possessed one. Sacred in their own way and not to be risked heedlessly. The man riding this one checked his steed, slid from its back, and strode toward Devora among the cairns without any sign of deference or respect for the *navi*.

Ignoring his approach, Devora was fighting to lift the last stone into place, and she nearly passed out from the exertion and from the pain in her back.

Suddenly the weight was gone, and she nearly fell. Blinking sweat from her eyes, she found that Zadok had taken the stone from her and was raising it to the top of the cairn as effortlessly as though he were lifting no more weight than a full waterskin. The stone settled into place with a reassuring *clack* of rock against rock.

Zadok!

Her whole body lightened with relief.

The nazarite turned to her, his eyes grim but present. "*Navi*," he said quietly.

"About time," she gasped, then swayed on her feet. Zadok's hand caught her arm, and for a moment she leaned against him, just breathing, heedless of the impropriety. But she had no time to rest or breathe; the war-leader was approaching between the cairns. The Canaanite looked numbly on without rising from where she knelt. Devora's own limbs were shaky, but she forced herself to step away from Zadok and stand without support. Her dress was smeared with soil and sweat; there was dirt beneath her nails and scrapes on her hands. She felt filthy, and vaguely defiled, though her naked skin had not touched the corpse. She longed desperately for a cold river to dip into and dry clothes, but there wasn't time.

The stranger stopped when he was near enough to speak without shouting. A lean man, tall with the height of the northern tribes, his hair braided in the war knot. One of his eyelids drooped a little. That would have made another man look sleepy; it made this man look sinister, secretive. His lip had a bit of curl in it. As his gaze took in Devora and Zadok, then lingered on the Canaanite, that curl twisted into a sneer.

Devora braced herself, not liking the look of this man.

"A heathen," the man called out, without bothering to introduce himself. "Even in Shiloh I find the stink of them."

The Canaanite looked up from the cairn, and her eyes burned hot.

"She's a supplicant," Devora said quietly. "Let her be."

The man spat to the side, and Devora tensed. This was where the dead were buried—how *dare* he— "Who are you, stranger?" she demanded.

He showed his teeth. His hard, cold eyes glanced past her, at Zadok. "I am Nimri ben Nabaoth, of Naphtali tribe. I lead herdsmen in the hills above Judges' Well. Why does the woman speak for you?"

"She is the *navi*," Zadok said. "She speaks for God."

"Ha. Ask God to choose a man for the next *navi*."

"Perhaps he will," Devora said smoothly. "You've come from Barak's camp?"

"I've come from *my* camp. Barak happens to be camping near me."

The other two riders were approaching now. They dismounted some distance from the cairns to approach on foot, showing respect for the holy ground where the dead were buried, and for the *navi*. Nimri glanced over his shoulder at them, tensing slightly. Then he shook his head and shot Zadok a look. "Let *them* talk to this woman if they want." Then he mounted his horse. "The high priest—I can find him down there?" He jerked his head toward the white tents.

"It is nearly the Sabbath," Zadok said.

Devora didn't say anything. Her hands were clenched with rage.

"After the Sabbath, then," Nimri said, his tone dismissive. His gaze flicked across them all once, contempt for the woman who spoke for God and a violent hate in his eyes when he glanced at the Canaanite. Then he turned his horse and kicked it into a canter, nearly riding down the other two men. The men leapt to the side, and then

Nimri ben Nabaoth was past, and he and his horse tore down the slope as quickly as they'd come.

"If that is the kind of man mothers raise in the northern tribes," Devora muttered under her breath, but didn't finish the thought. The other two were near now. One of them stepped forward, his eyes glancing at the nazarite and the two women. Devora took a careful look at the war-leader approaching her. His hands were rough from working an olive press; his legs were long and lean. There were few wrinkles in his suntanned face. Some of that was youth. Devora suspected the rest was that this was not a man who worried much or deliberated much. A great, slanting scar crossed his nose and cheeks, probably a witness to the efficacy of Sea Coast iron and to the youth's ability to face it head-on, without fleeing. Or, Devora supposed, a witness to this man's inability to duck.

She nodded at the man, and he halted a few strides from her. Then the man looked the two women over, appraising them for a moment as he might appraise slaves he wished to purchase for his bedding. The Canaanite didn't appear to notice; she still knelt by that cairn, her head down, silent in her suffering. But Devora flushed, and her eyes went cold. "Do you also come to insult God's *navi*?"

The newcomer cast a glance back at Nimri, his face amused. "That is a proud man. Nimri insults everybody. Someone will gut him with a spear one day. But we are all proud men in the north." He looked back at her, grinned. "I like you. They did not tell me the *navi* was a lovely woman."

"The *navi* has been a woman for three generations."

"God's ways are strange," the northerner remarked. "They *did* say you were a woman. They didn't say you were beautiful. I am told the last *navi* was a wrinkled old thing. Not every doe ages well." He glanced at Zadok. "Is she yours?"

Devora seethed, but Zadok spoke before she could. "I serve her. I have taken the nazarite vow." Zadok's voice was calm, but every line of the man's body was tense, watchful.

"The hair. I saw." For the first time, the northerner's voice deepened with awe. "We haven't seen you in the north, but we've *heard*. They say a nazarite knows no trade but the spear. They say he fights like ten men."

"They are wrong," Zadok said grimly. "I fight like twenty."

"Ha!" The northerner slapped his thigh in appreciation and pointed at the nazarite. "I like you too."

Devora lifted her voice. "What is your name and your tribe, stranger?"

"I am Omri." He drew himself up. "Of Zebulun tribe."

"And what are the chieftains of the north doing in Shiloh valley, Omri of Zebulun tribe? There are no dead here. Does Barak ben Abinoam lie in his tent enjoying his wines while the dead feast?"

The amusement faded from Omri's face. "We've come to find what visions God has sent the *navi*," he said, the flirtation gone from his voice. "And to ask the *kohannim* for the Ark."

"God sent a vision this very day," Devora replied. "I have seen the dead lurching through fields of barley and wheat. In numbers greater than the cranes in the marshes.

I have seen the whole land defiled and blighted. It is God's warning. This is what might happen. You and the men in that camp must see that it doesn't."

Omri looked stricken by her words; he fell silent. The other man's face grew grimmer, colder. Devora considered him curiously. Dark, curling hair about a sun-roughened face. He held in his right hand a tall staff with its top swaddled in wool and its end planted firmly in the earth. That made Devora think of a herdsman, but the man's hands were stained with red and purple—the juices of grapes. A vintner, then. Perhaps he needed the staff because he was infirm. Yet he did not lean on it. He wore a heavy wool cloak, which was strange in this heat. He did not bear scars across his face as Omri did, but his dark eyes and the set of his shoulders spoke of a wrath and a strength barely restrained. There was something lethal about this man. She would not care to be alone with him. She felt sure she could remind Omri of his place, and hers, but this other man…

"When we left," Omri muttered, "there were just a few wandering herds of corpses up by White Cedars. The northernmost encampments were at risk. Nimri's, mostly. We sent word to other tribes. Set our camp down there—" He waved at the valley. "Where else would we all gather but Shiloh? Though it means leaving our barley and our vineyards undefended for a few days, we need help." His face flushed with anger. "We need *much* help, if God has shown you—that. If I am not hearing only a woman's fears."

Devora ignored the comment, focusing instead on what Omri was implying. "How many men have come, Omri?"

"Five hundred and fifty," he said.

Devora started. "So few?"

"Maybe less now. A few slipped away as we came down out of the hills. They did not want to leave their farms unwatched." He showed his teeth.

Fear gripped her heart. "How many tribes?" Her voice breathless with horror.

"Zebulun and Naphtali have come. A few from Issachar, very few—but Laban is their chieftain, and when he lifts his axe, he's an entire raid by himself." Omri's eyes glinted. "The northern tribes have gathered. But the others…the chieftains of Reuben sent this message to us in the hour before dawn today: *Let Barak defend his vineyard, and we will defend ours.*"

Three tribes. Only three. Three could not take the Ark of the Covenant with them, nor the blessing of the *kohannim* who stood before God for the People. Three tribes out of twelve could not take God with them into the north.

"Omri, not in all our years in possession of this land have the People risen with so few as five hundred and fifty men." Devora felt her control slipping. The infant, the weeping of the Canaanite girl, the vision of the dead devouring the land, the shock of Omri's news—it was too much.

"The other tribes feel no threat," he muttered.

"What threatens one tribe threatens all. Have our People forgotten the desert?" Her fear rose like a river in flood. "Where is Barak? Why hasn't he come himself? I would speak with *him*, Omri."

"He is here."

The man who'd spoken was Omri's companion, the grim, lethal one. He cast his wool cloak back over his shoulder, revealing a bronze breast-piece, polished though dented from past raids. Bronze greaves strapped to his calves. He took a step forward; as he did, he unwound the cloth about the head of his staff to reveal a lethal slice of bronze that flashed in the lowering sun. A spear, not a staff.

Zadok took his place by Devora's side, tall and menacing, and the man did not approach nearer.

"Barak is here," the man said. His voice was strange, rasping a little as though he rarely used it, as though he rarely indulged in conversation with other men or with women. Yet his voice rose from deep in his chest and was powerful. "And *I* would ask things of God's *navi*."

BARAK

BARAK WAS A MAN WHO liked to have warm earth under his hands, or the cool, healthy skin of green vines. His vineyards were not the best in Eretz Israel, but they were close. His presses gave wine that sold not only to the sons of the People but even to merchants traveling through on their way to the great cities on the coast. Over the door of his house hung a bronze spear and a shield, from the days when he'd led the men of the north in repelling a raid of young warriors from those coastal cities. Though he'd had four hundred men at his back, he'd fought in those days only to defend his own house, which to his mind was his whole tribe.

His wife, a Canaanite, had died half a year ago in pregnancy, both she and the child, and at times the pain of it hit him so hard he stood still in the middle of his vines under the hot sun, vision gone wet with tears, just waiting to be able to breathe again. He hadn't taken another wife yet, though he must do so soon or his seed would be lost. Yet his grief was bitter, and he did not forgive Hadassah for leaving him nor God for taking her.

He would never forget the fire he'd felt in her flesh as she died; she'd been burning up from the inside, and his child had burned inside her. And then, between one breath and the next, she was gone, and what was left of her retained its warmth for a time and then cooled slowly, like a charred coal. He had remained with her body until the sun rose, defiling his hand each time he touched her face to feel her warmth dying away. In the morning, he'd carried her to the slopes above his vineyard. Set her in the earth, raised a cairn above her. Pitched a tent beside the stones that marked her memory and remained there seven days until his uncleanness passed.

When the seven days ended, he had returned to his cedar house and found his slaves and his wife's mother with ashes in their hair, mourning by the hearth. Without a word to his mother-in-law, he'd gone to her alcove and dug out her gods from beneath her bedding. He had tolerated them for the sake of his Canaanite wife. Now she was gone. God had taken her. He feared what else God might take from him. He'd made it halfway to the hearth before Hadassah's mother had flown at him, screaming and snatching at the gods with her aged hands.

She had screamed and kicked at him, and in the end he'd had to tie her, binding her at the wrists, ankles, and knees. He'd left her rolling on the floor behind him as he'd burned her gods, one after the other. She had shrieked and called him vile things and spat at him, but he had not turned his head or responded, until the flames were licking at the carved face of the last of her gods. By then she was out of breath and sobbing.

"Burn," he'd murmured without turning to face her. He had kept his eyes on the flames. "When God is near, everything unclean catches fire. Nothing unclean must remain in my house. I will invite no more fire in my house."

He watched the coals long into the night, ignoring the weeping of his wife's mother. Seven days. His wife Hadassah had been dead only seven days.

***

Now, months later, Barak stood before the *navi*, taking her measure. The *navi* was aging but lovely; she was not tall, but the way she stood and the hardness in her eyes conveyed presence and command—something he had never seen before or expected to see in a woman. The man standing behind her was a giant, and his legend as giant as he, but unlike his chieftains, Barak ignored the nazarite. After an initial glance, he ignored the Canaanite girl too, though her face pulled at his heart, troubling him; she looked so much like Hadassah.

But Barak did not like to be distracted from a thing that he needed. He focused on the *navi*.

"What would you ask?" Devora's voice sounded a little hoarse. Good. She was off her guard, then.

Barak lifted his voice, intending to speak in a way that demanded her submission, but to his own surprise he found that his tone grew hard with anger.

"Each year, we in the hills send a tenth of our harvest to Shiloh. To *feed* Shiloh. So you can speak to God, protect us from the dead." Barak thought grimly of the caravans moving south through the hills—and of the screams of Hadassah's mother as the fire devoured her gods. He had done his part to keep Law and Covenant. "Now the dead have come," he said. "What happened?"

"What happened." Devora's face tightened. "Each year fewer tithes come. Each year fewer children are dedicated to the priesthood. Each year as I sit in decision here, I hear more offenses against the Law and the Covenant, more lawlessness in the land. And now, this day, I hear that the People have need of spears to protect them, and only three tribes have come. It is not Shiloh that has failed."

Barak's eyes glinted with anger. But he held his tongue. That this *woman* should take him to task…but the *navi* was set apart from all women. She was *kadosh*, she was holy. She was God's. A man could not strike her. Nor could a man ignore her words.

"I demand assurances of God." Barak planted the end of his spear haft into the earth, but he did not lean on it. "I have heard things in the hills that touch my mind with fear. Who is to say El will stride before us against the unburied dead?"

"Have the men of this land become weak, brittle? Moseh the Lawgiver but lifted his hand, and raiders from another tribe tumbled into the dust—for he knew God was near. Do you and your men know nothing but your own fright, roaring louder in your hearts than anything else you might hear?"

"I hear *you*," Barak said grimly. "And I believe you hear God. If God is with us, *navi*, I will not fear." Barak held her gaze. He did not know what he would find when he returned to the north, what he would have to face. But this woman did. This woman could see what would happen, see what God might give and what God might take away. He would not allow himself to lose his temper with her; he needed her. His men needed her. "I'll not lead men on a raid they won't survive or to a battle I can't win. If we have no sign that God is with us, if you will not go with us into the north, then I will go home to my vineyard, and likely each of the men will seek out his own door, to stand in defense of his own home, until the dead come. Let all other men fend for themselves."

DEVORA'S DECISION

"...IF YOU WILL NOT GO..."

Dread sat in Devora's breast, a clammy mass wrapped in damp, clinging cloth. If Barak did not lead the tribes into the north, surely the vision she had seen would become real. And the infant she had buried would be only the first of many. The cold presence of all the cairns on the slope seemed suddenly intense; the outlines of those farther up the hill stood sharp against the sky, a demand. Like so many silent watchers waiting to see if the judge and *navi* of Israel would keep her promise. That the unclean death would stop with the raising of these stones and devour no more of the land's children, whether Hebrew or heathen.

But there were *dead* in the north, many dead. To go with the men—it would be like returning to the night of the attack on Shiloh, or to that other, earlier night in her mother's tent. She could hear, faint and distant, the death-shrieks outside that tent. She held the memory at bay with an effort of will.

Behind her, Zadok growled low in his throat, like a wolf coming awake at a threat to his own.

Devora fought to stay calm. "Do I look like a man to you, Barak ben Abinoam? Like one who takes up the spear?"

Omri actually *leered* at her—as if thinking that, no, she didn't look like a man to him—but Devora ignored him.

"We both go, or neither, *navi*," Barak said.

"He is right," Omri said. "The men are frightened."

"When God calls a man to take up the spear," Devora cried, "he does not ask him to count the enemy."

Barak's eyes narrowed.

"*I* do not count them," Omri said. His smile didn't touch his eyes. "I am here. I am ready for a fight. That jackal Nimri is too. But other men shake in their tents or their houses. Maybe they have grown old and weak in their hearts. Or maybe they are just sleepy—who knows? Those with a bit of loot, a few fine garments, a girl or two, are ready to rest. I have brought home no slaves and have little to put in my house. So I'm not done with the spear. But there has been a lot of fighting: the raids of the Sea People, strife with the Horse People east of the river, threats from the chieftains of White Cedars to our north. But now no spearmen come out of White Cedars to raid us, only the unclean dead."

"Will you come?" Barak asked, his voice cold and quiet.

Devora swallowed. "You would force the hand of God's *navi*."

"I would."

For a moment Devora glimpsed grief in the man's eyes, a grief deep as a scream but silent.

"I have heard the dead near my vineyard," Barak said, "and I have done what I could to gather men to silence them. But I am not Moseh. I am not Yeshua, or Othniel, or Ehud. And God has taken much from me." His eyes were dark and intense. "Like a woman, God promises out of one corner of the mouth and curses out of the other. Let God send a sign that she favors us. Let God send the Ark—or send you."

The wind had picked up again, and strands of Devora's hair flicked across her vision. Her throat felt very dry.

The men's eyes were on her. They were so strange, these men of the north. Hardly better than heathen. Perhaps they *were* half-heathen. More than any other tribes in Israel, they'd mingled with other peoples who burned *olah* before gods of the sea or gods of the rain or gods of the forested hills. With people who did not cleanse their bodies or wash to the elbows before they ate. People who ate foods that defiled them. People who touched the dead bodies of their kin, who raised no cairns over their dead or who fed them to fish. People who defiled the land.

Devora exhaled slowly. She thought of the chieftains losing their courage and returning each to his own territory, and each man to his own crop. The thought horrified her. Those dead she'd seen in her vision—they would devour each homestead, each tent, as easily as a child might pluck berries.

Yet to go *with* these men, to seek out the dead herself—it would be like riding right into her memories.

Her mother's screams were louder, nearer. The green leaves above her tossed in a sudden gust. There was sharp pain in her palms. Slowly she forced her hands to open, saw where her nails had cut her skin.

She sat in decision over the People, with the Law at her

back like an old woman with a hand on her shoulder to guide her. But what would guide her in *this* decision?

As if in answer, a wave of heat and a wave of vision. Again she saw the slouching dead moving through barley fields, and recoiled from the sight. For an instant she glimpsed a young woman wielding a bronze peg, a tent peg. A young woman with eyes that hurt to look at.

Then the vision passed, and there were only Barak and Omri before her, and Zadok behind her, and the Canaanite girl weeping silently by her child's cairn.

But it was enough. For the vision had shown her what she needed to know—that the dead could be dealt with, and that Barak ben Abinoam could not deal with them alone. Once, long years ago, Devora had hid shaking in her mother's tent, helpless in her terror, while everyone she knew died. She would not let that kind of fear determine her choices now.

She motioned Barak closer.

When the northern chieftain stood before her, Devora spoke softly, for his ears alone. "There will be screaming in the Galilee. But the God who gives me these—visions— he is the same God who parted the sea for Moseh. He gave our fathers bread in the desert. He has shattered walls and broken the spears of chieftains whom men feared. He makes the barley grow and gives heat and light to the earth. And with this God, with *this* God you have made your covenant, Barak." Her voice had dropped, and he leaned in to hear. "Learn not to demand assurances," she whispered.

"Nevertheless," he murmured, "you will go?"

"I will go," she said.

Seeing the relief in his face, she realized that for all his bravado, Barak hadn't been sure she would come—or what he would do if she refused.

"I would like to meet the woman who mothered you," Devora said. "She must have torn out her hair in exasperation."

"She is ten years beneath a cairn," Barak said.

Devora made a small noise in her throat. Barak did indeed have all the traits of a man who had little to do with women and had neither wife nor mother to counsel him or soften his edges. But enough. She had made her decision, it was done. Though she felt so cold. She must turn now to practical matters.

"Provide a white tent," she said. "One befitting God's *navi* to whom the priests at Shiloh listen. My husband has a horse that I will ask for, so you need provide no more than the tent."

"It will be done." Barak nodded. "I will send one of the chieftains for you after the Sabbath, *navi.*" The man began walking back to his horse. Omri gave the *navi* another look and grinned at her, then followed Barak.

"Barak!" Devora called out suddenly.

He turned.

"Something else God has shown to me. You have approached God with doubt and demands and not as your fathers' fathers did. The renown for this victory will not go to you or to your kin or to your tribe. God has shown me that he will deliver the dead into the hands of women."

For a moment there was silence on the hillside.

"Then let us hope those women know what to do with them," Barak said, and turned from her.

THE ANGEL OF DEATH

As BARAK AND OMRI mounted and rode away from the cairns, Devora looked after them, troubled. It occurred to her suddenly that she might be vulnerable among these men of the north, who only granted a grudging acknowledgment of her holy position. Clearly, Nimri and Omri looked at her and saw only a woman, rather than a levite anointed by God. Yet Shiloh's women were set apart from all the women of their People. Many of them had been dedicated as children to the service of the Most Holy God. They wove the clothing that the high priest wore when he entered the *shekinah*, the holy presence within the Tent of Meeting. Their hands carried incense to the door of that Tent, preparing a sweet scent for God. They were not as other women.

Now the behavior of these three men of the Galilee reminded her that women elsewhere in the land had *not* been dedicated to such holy service. Women elsewhere might anoint their bodies or their bedding with sweet scents for men, but none of those other women carried sweet scents before God. And their lives were more slave-like. They might be beaten, for instance, if they failed to please their father or their brother or their husband, whatever man was their keeper. They might be deprived of food or bartered away if their man tired of them. That bartering was against the Covenant, but she knew such things occurred. Devora sensed that the women of the north lived different lives than those she had known.

She felt Zadok beside her, a tall, firm presence. "Ride north with me after the Sabbath, Zadok," she said. "God's *navi* needs a nazarite beside her."

"Your will, *navi*," he murmured.

She lowered her head. "I am glad you—woke—so quickly," she said.

He didn't answer. Devora could feel his shame. Like a drumbeat in the air.

"I should have remembered," she said. "I shouldn't have placed that burden on you."

"I have taken the nazarite vow—"

"Yes," Devora said. "You have taken the vow. And I was wrong to abuse it."

Before Zadok could answer, the *navi* turned and approached the Canaanite where she knelt by the cairn, holding her salmah closed with one hand. If there had been scant time before, the arrival of the riders had only made her urgency greater. The sun was nearly touching the far ridge; the Sabbath bride was already walking across the eastern hills toward them. And she must yet decide what to do with the heathen girl.

Devora stopped when she stood near the Canaanite.

"You are unclean," the *navi* said to her, for the girl had carried a corpse for several days. "I cannot bring you to the tents at Shiloh. But I can find you some place to sleep at the edge of the camp."

The girl didn't look at her. Her face was pale and exhausted, as though she herself were one of the dead, whose cairn had been inadequate to hold her to the earth. "Leave me here," she whispered. "Let me die near my child." She lowered her head, leaned it against the cairn. Began singing softly, Canaanite words that Devora didn't know. It sounded like a go-to-sleep song, one of the simple, slow melodies mothers sing to infants. Despite her need for haste, Devora watched her a moment, caught. Her own mother had sung to her once like that, other melodies, but just as soft.

Then Devora sighed. "Zadok, carry her."

The Canaanite's voice fell still. The nazarite's mouth twisted in distaste, but he didn't hesitate. As he stepped toward her, Hurriya looked up at last, her eyes hot. "Don't you touch me!"

"He won't hurt you, girl. Nor will he touch your skin. Come, now." Devora gripped the girl's left arm near the shoulder through the thin wool she wore, careful not to touch her bare skin, for she was unclean. She lifted Hurriya to her feet. Hurriya looked wildly from her to the nazarite.

"We are not going to hurt you," Devora said again.

The girl acquiesced as Zadok lifted her into his arms, her body rigid with tension. Devora shook her head. She could not leave the girl on the hill; she was a supplicant. The *navi* had an obligation to her. But neither did she know what to do with her.

Devora led the way, and she and Zadok circled the hill. The nazarite was watchful. They could see, below in the valley, the two horsemen racing the dusk, hurrying back to their own camp. As Devora and her nazarite reached the slope beneath the olive tree, the *navi* glanced up toward her seat.

And gasped.

No. No, this couldn't be. Her body went rigid with attention; she stopped breathing. Was it only a trick of the light, of the setting sun? It *must* be. Yet even as she gazed, she saw—she was *certain* she saw—

She broke into a run, ignoring Zadok's shout behind her. Climbing the hill was an exertion, and her sides burned, but she forced herself on and came quickly to the olive tree. Even as she approached, she knew that it had been no trick of the light. The tree was changing. The edges of its long leaves crinkling, drying. As though the tree were dying one of the long deaths of trees, accelerated into the brevity of a handful of days, quickened so that she could *see* the death, even as one might see a fever taking a child's body, relentlessly, from one brief hour to the next. She reached up, touched her fingers to one of the yellowing leaves. The edge of the leaf crumbled even as she touched it; it was dry, brittle. She let out a low cry and leapt back from the tree, taking in all of it. The leaves along one entire half of the tree were drying away, dying— the half of the tree that faced the north.

"Are you hurt, *navi?*" Zadok called, hurrying to her side, leaving the Canaanite standing below.

"The tree," she gasped.

Zadok approached quickly, his gaze darting to the branches. She heard him suck in his breath. For a long moment they stood quite still. The tree appeared to wither even as they watched; whatever part this olive tree, like all others in the land, had shared in the Covenant of God, it was now dissolving away, like papyrus exposed to water. The sight of it drew all the warmth out of Devora's body, left her shivering. She thought of the unclean flesh she had laid in the earth on this very hill, so near the tree's roots, and a low moan rose in her throat. She closed her lips tightly to hold it in.

"What does it mean, *navi*?" Zadok breathed.

Devora let her hand fall from the branch. "It means— the promise is revoked. That the unclean dead will overwhelm the land because we have broken Covenant with God. That blight and plague will no longer pass over us without touching our soil." She stared helplessly at the tree. "It's the *malakh ha-mavet*, Zadok. The *malakh ha-mavet*. The angel of death."

CRIES IN THE OLIVES

"IT IS ONLY ONE TREE," Zadok said as they hurried
down the long slope toward the tents. He carried the
Canaanite girl in his arms as if she weighed no more than a
linen cloth. Their voices were hushed, breathless as they
rushed through the heather at nearly a run, the slope
already cast into shadow. Less than an hour now before
dark, when the Sabbath would come like a bride to the
People, her face veiled by the night sky, to free the People
from work, give them rest, remind them they were free
and possessors of a land of their own, with no overseer's
whip and no foreign gods to take from them their labor
and their harvests.

But though it was customary to greet the bride with
song or with a slapping of hands against thighs and
exuberant shouts, tonight the delight of Sabbath barely
touched Devora's heart as she struggled to keep pace with
Zadok's mighty strides. Her heart was clutched in the
withering roots of that olive tree. Her face very pale.

"It is *not* only one tree," Devora protested. "What
sickens one plant can kill an entire crop. What sickens

within one woman's heart can poison an entire People. You know this, Zadok. Why else did you take the nazarite vow?"

"It is *one* tree," Zadok said, "and all about me I see a land fertile and lush, a land of olives and great herds."

"This day I have seen the land filled with herds of the ravenous dead." Devora's voice shook. "Zadok ben Zefanyah, the Law will defend the People from the dead," Devora breathed, "but only if the People live by it. How many times have I sat in judgment over acts that tear at the very roots of the Covenant? Brothers killing brothers or robbing them. Bodies left unburied. And always, I hear of—of *her* people, mingling with ours. Of Hebrew men who permit deities of wood and clay to reside in their homes, or who dance at Canaanite festivals in the hill country. Zadok! What *if*—"

Zadok made no answer, and Devora did not voice her fears. Her side burned; though she was aging, she was the *navi* and she climbed and descended this hill often. And her need and her anxiety drove her. Yet their haste was taking its toll on her, and her growing dread seemed to choke away her breath.

Glancing at the silent girl Zadok carried, Devora wanted badly to hate her, to loathe her for the withering that was coming on the land, a blight in which her strange people and their small, useless gods had surely played some part. And hate would be easier on her than this cold, clinging dread. But the little flame of hate flickered out; she could not sustain it. The girl was too weak to hate.

Hurriya was a ruin, barely alive; she'd likely been held together only by her need to seek out the *navi*, to bring her that tiny corpse and beg for the impossible. Now the Canaanite stared out at the valley and at the white tents they were approaching. Unblinking, apparently unaware of the day or the hour or of anything but what lay within her own heart, in her own grief.

The *malakh ha-mavet!*

Every Hebrew child knew the story. How the night before their fathers' exodus from a foreign land, the *malakh ha-mavet* had visited the homes of the men and women of Kemet, from the lowest farm worker to the home of Pharaoh himself. And in each home, the firstborn had been struck with the uncleanness, the fever, the drying out and convulsing of the body, then the quick tossing of the spirit into the empty dark and the stillness of a corpse cooling slowly on its bed. And then, in the hours before dawn, when the Nile was calm and quiet as a lake, the firstborn rose hungering, and the grieving of their parents turned to shrieks of terror as son devoured father and daughter devoured mother, as parents turned on the bodies of their children with spades or shovels or sharpened styluses. That night of the risen dead had left every house in Kemet spattered with blood.

Every dwelling place but the Hebrews'.

For God's hand had covered them.

The Hebrews commemorated that night each spring at the festival of Pesach, the Passing Over, even as they commemorated the time of wandering in the desert each harvest at Sukkot, the Feast of Tents. Each year, the *kohannim* reminded the gathered celebrants in the fields about Shiloh that so long as they kept the Covenant and lived by the Law, God's hand would cover Israel. Their sons and their daughters would be as many as the stars in the night sky; their tribes would grow as fruitful as the branches of the olive tree.

But now the olive tree above Shiloh had withered.

The three in the heather were approaching the camp swiftly; Devora could see men and women among the white tents ahead. She found that she was reciting one of the *mitzvot* softly, though she barely had breath for it; for once, the words of the Law brought her little calm. The burn in her side was fierce.

***

When they had approached within shouting distance of the camp, they halted where a dip in the land would conceal the girl's uncleanness from the sight of the tents. While Devora leaned forward with her hands on her legs above the knees, gasping for breath, Zadok took his cloak and, with only a moment's hesitation, laid it out across the weeds and blossoms. Then he placed the girl gently on it. He would need to find a new cloak; he would not get this one back.

The girl lifted her hand and caught at Devora's sleeve. The *navi* tensed.

"I heard you talking with the men," she whispered. "There are more dead. Many more dead."

"Yes," Devora said.

"We're all going to die. Like my child."

"We most certainly are not," Devora snapped.

"They came out of the olive grove. There were eight of them, and their bodies had been torn open and eaten on, as though a lion or a wolf had been at them. But they were walking, they were *walking*." The girl's eyes showed their whites.

"I know," Devora said.

"Malachi was at the olive press, and they *ate* him. They snarled like animals. They dragged him down and tore at him and *ate* him."

Devora shivered.

"I was in the shack, and I tried to hold the door. I tried to keep them out—I tried—I tried—" She began weeping, without tears. "They were too strong. They wanted the baby—they wanted my baby—"

In her mind Devora could hear the shrieks of her mother again, dying outside the tent. "I know," she said again, her voice hoarse. The girl's misery seemed terribly familiar, a dark mirror of Devora's own. The girl had come to her seat for judgment, but there was never any forgiveness for the deaths of your kin. Whether you could have prevented their deaths or not, they were gone. Devora knew this too well.

Some days a woman can only save one life, the old *navi* Naomi had tried to tell her when she was a girl. Yet surely if that one life were always your own, that was an abomination in the eyes of the God who sits in decision over the living and the dead. Unable to look away from Hurriya's quiet misery, Devora realized that the Canaanite, like she herself, stood alone and still breathing among the corpses of her kin. And even if Hurriya survived her heart's grief and her body's anguish, she would still stand there, every night of her life, every morning. Though she had sacrificed everything she had and everything she was as she struggled out of the hills, wasting her body away as she bore her dying infant in her arms, still her child and its father were dead. She, she only, was alive. There would never be forgiveness for that. Devora knew this; she had fled alone out of the death of her parents' camp when she was twelve, had listened and waited for mercy, and had received only barrenness in her womb and night terrors when her memories came back to her in the dark, and hard burdens to carry.

Devora felt that she must say something. She could not just leave this girl grieving here in that woolen cloth that could only be called a garment by an act of the imagination, with her body thin and exhausted and torn from childbirth, her breasts swollen with milk that had become futile, a curse to her.

"You did what you could," Devora told her after a moment. "Try to sleep, and forget."

"Forget," Hurriya whispered. She began to laugh softly, helplessly. Letting go of Devora's sleeve, she curled up, bringing her knees to her chest as though to protect an unborn child, though she had only her own ravaged heart to protect, only her own body to shield.

Devora exchanged a look with Zadok, then stood.

"I can get bedding for her," Zadok said. "But if we leave her here weeping, a wolf will come for her."

"Guard her tonight, for me."

"Your will, *navi*."

Devora's shoulders sagged beneath the weight of her unseen burdens. What if the girl *did* die out here? She glanced at Zadok, saw the weariness in his eyes.

Shelter the stranger you find in your land.

Yet like Hurriya fleeing her hills, Devora had done what she could. It was not enough, but only a small crescent of the sun was visible now above the hills. She'd lingered too long already.

"When your uncleanness has passed," she said without looking at the girl, "you can wash linens in the camp, be given meals, a place to sleep. Until we know if any kin live who can claim you. Forget, girl. That is all you can do. There will be other children."

The girl just sobbed. The sound wrenched at the *navi's* heart.

Devora turned and hurried toward the white tents, walking fast.

SHILOH

SHILOH CAMP was both a monument and a defense against the past. It lay on the land like a great map beneath the gaze of God that charted the People's history and their orientation toward their deity. The *kohannim* boasted that no matter where a Hebrew found himself in the land, he always knew which direction he was facing. For a People whose fathers had lost a generation wandering in the desert and hiding from the restless dead, knowing where things were was vitally important. Where there was water, where there was sand, where there were quail to eat or deer to hunt. Where there were enemies and where there were kin. Where you were and where God was in relation to you.

The camp was a great square, tilted so that its points faced north, west, east, and south. The eastern quadrant held the tents of the *kohannim*, the priests who'd gone through seven-day rites of purification and cleansing and could now approach God's presence without fear, bringing burnt offerings to atone for the uncleanness of the tribes. The doors of their tents faced east, toward the Tumbling

71

Water, the great river the People had crossed when they took the land. Their tents faced the past.

The western tents held those levites who were not of the priesthood. Scribes and craftsmen and the young dedicates who were brought to Shiloh as children, to be raised as levites if they were boys or to be raised as wives for them if they were girls.

The southern quadrant held the tents of the seventy judges appointed to resolve disputes. These faced the vast settlements of Benyamin and Yudah tribes, the most populous in the land.

And across the camp, facing north and away from the People, as though keeping watch toward those hills where there were still many heathen, stood the tents of the nazarites, those who'd taken the harshest of vows to defend the Ark, the holy tribe of Levi, the priests, and the *navi*. In the midst of their tents lay a great cleared space of dirt and sand where the nazarites danced the spears each morning, training for battles with either the living or the dead. The nazarites were few. There were in fact only five in Shiloh this year. Though in the north there were raids from the fortified towns on the coast or from the heathen settlements in White Cedars where the hilltops were high enough for snow, those were the concern of the northern tribes. The rest of the land had lain quiet for a generation. Few now took the nazarite vow or kept it. Many of the older nazarites had even gone through the rites to be released of their vows. Of the generation who remembered the night the dead had come to Shiloh, only Zadok was left.

And finally, broad and mighty at the utmost east of the camp, standing between the People and their terrible past, stood the Tent of Meeting, many-colored and stretched over a frame of wooden poles. It was the reason for Shiloh's existence. Within it, behind a heavy veil, was the *kodesh kodashim*, the Holy of Holies, which held the Ark of the Covenant. Inside that great chest of wood and gold were tablets of stone on which were inscribed the Ten, the words spoken by God to the People at Har Sinai, the words that had initiated the Covenant, the first words of the Law. And above that Ark, in an empty space between the outspread wings of carved golden angels, dwelled the *shekinah*, the heat and presence of their ancient desert God.

Even in their ancestors' time when Shiloh had moved often, this Tent had never been raised *within* the camp. It always stood just outside, in hope that the uncleanness of the People would not offend God to wrath. In the outer part of the Tent, in a tiny censer prepared by levite women and placed before the veil, incense was burned at all hours, to sweeten the scent of the camp, so it would be easier for God to live near them. The *kohannim* taught that this God they'd found in the desert was not like the handcrafted gods of wood and stone that the heathen revered, gods who might be housed within your own tent without fear, small gods who were powerless to protect those who honored them from either the spears of the living or the teeth of the dead.

No, the Hebrews' God was *el kadosh*. He was a mighty and holy God, and the unclean dead and the unclean living alike would wither if they approached him. At all times he was set apart from the camp, so that if his anger burst into flame, perhaps only a small part of the camp would burn, those tents nearest him. He must be approached with care.

73

His heat could kindle not only against the enemies of the People, living or dead, but against the People themselves. For though the *kohannim* believed this strange God had consented and chosen to dwell among the Hebrews alone out of all the peoples in all the lands beneath the sun, the *kohannim* also remembered that before this God, all peoples, even theirs, were small. If God's slightest fingertip touched the land, that touch might dry a river or scorch crops. What then would happen if, looking about and seeing the evil the People too often did to each other, how the People too often failed to care for the living or confine the dead, what if God in wrath should strike the land with his fist? Would not the very hills smoke?

***

Devora passed the Tent of Meeting as she hurried into Shiloh, and she passed the charred earth beside it, that silent memorial to the night of wrath thirty years past. Her heart hardened at the sight of it. That night it had been Canaanites who had brought the unclean death to the camp. The heathen who could not be trusted to place their dead beneath cairns or to keep their camps clean of dead meat or even to wash their own arms up to the elbows before lifting their fingers to their mouths. The heathen who all but *invited* the coming of the unclean dead.

At the doors of the white tents, the *kohannim* and their wives stood singing, in robes and gowns of white with embroidered hems. The men sang first, deep voices lifted in ululation to greet the Sabbath bride, who came over the hills clothed in the *shekinah*. Even before the men's voices fell silent, their wives lifted their own, lovely voices calling out their worship of the God who gives and takes away, the God who stirs new life in the womb and closes us each in the womb of the earth when our brief lives have ended.

The men and women of Shiloh camp inclined their heads respectfully as the *navi* passed, and despite her haste Devora slowed her walk enough that she could pass them with dignity—though her white gown was stained and torn in places from her work in raising the cairn, and her feet were sore within her sandals. The song she heard all about her was a comfort; it eased the anxiety that had choked her after the withering of her olive tree. With so many men and women singing a greeting to God, it was unthinkable that God was not here among them. Perhaps the withering had only been a warning, nothing more.

As she approached the high priest's tent—her husband's was still many tents beyond it, in the western part of the camp—Devora halted and looked at the high priest and his wife as they sang outside the door of their tent. She had to tell him, she realized. She had to tell the *kohannim* of her vision.

Eleazar ben Phinehas ben Eleazar ben Aharon was the head of Levi tribe and the one man who might pass within the last veil to speak face-to-face with the *shekinah*, the hot presence that dwelled over the Ark. He alone could give offerings there, sending up a sweet smoke to renew the Covenant between God and People. Among all the People, only he was permitted by Law to speak without the veil between him and the divine ears.

Only he.

Except that God, too, could draw aside the veil. Without consulting priest or levites, the *shekinah* might sometimes fall upon a *navi*, showing the prophet things that otherwise only God's eyes would see. It was an uneasy relationship, that of the high priest and the *navi*.

Eleazar's robe was white like the other priests', but over it he wore the *ephod*, a loose garment gold like the sun. And over that he wore an ornamented bronze breast-piece. It was the sign of his office, the *hoshen mishpat*, the breast-piece of decision. Embedded in the *hoshen* were twelve smooth river stones from the Tumbling Water, on which had been inscribed the names of the Hebrew tribes, and also two stones with no letters on them, one dark as a cow's eye, the other pale as dead flesh. The *urim* and *thummim*, a last resort, a device for divining God's will in uncertain matters.

Beside Eleazar stood Hannah, his wife, in a white levite's gown with the blue sash of the midwives about her hips. Her head tilted back in song. She was a tall woman, nearly as tall as the priest; she had always towered over Devora.

"Eleazar!" Devora called out.

The priest stopped his song, and his wife beside him fell silent. They looked at Devora curiously. Disheveled as she was, the *navi* likely was a strange sight to them.

Devora found herself out of breath, trying to gasp out what was in her heart. "*Kohen*, there are dead—the olive tree—it withered—and there are dead. So many." She swallowed, gathered herself. "God sent a vision."

"What did he show you?" Eleazar murmured. There was respect in his tone, but wariness too.

Briefly, Devora told of her vision, of the lurching herds.

"This is horrible!" Hannah gasped. And Devora saw in the other woman's eyes that she too remembered the night of wrath thirty years before. No one who had been there would ever forget it.

Eleazar's eyes had become windows into a desolate place. "What you have seen is like cold water on my heart," he said after a moment. "The men of the Galilee sent a messenger here today."

Devora stiffened. "What did he say?"

"He said the other tribes were refusing to come at Barak's call. He asked for the Ark." Eleazar looked grim.

It was said that in the days of Yeshua when the People took possession of lands east of the Tumbling Water, the levites had carried the Ark on stout poles in advance of the host. The few dead walking in those valleys had stumbled out of the fields with their lifted arms and their moaning voices, only to wither before the Ark like dry wheat before a desert wind. So it was said.

"But they have come with only three tribes, *navi*. They cannot take the Ark. They think God does not care if his People are divided or together."

"Maybe we should talk, all of us, after the Sabbath," Devora said quickly. "What I've seen—if there are so many dead—"

"We are one People, *navi*."

"I *know* that. But perhaps it's time to cast the *urim and thummim*, to find out if God *wishes* to go north with the men. Why else would he have sent me such visions?"

"Perhaps. But right now it is time to greet the bride,"

Eleazar said, cutting her off. And he turned toward the door of his tent.

"Eleazar, please—"

"We will talk after the Sabbath, *navi*." He spoke without turning and disappeared into his tent.

Devora stood a moment, afflicted again by a terrible sense of not having done enough. Hannah gave her an understanding look but said nothing. Devora turned to leave, then stopped. Fresh to her mind had come the sight of the Canaanite curled up like a wounded animal in her travel-stained *salmah*, nothing but a woolen blanket to shelter her body and her grief.

"Hannah," Devora called.

The priest's wife had her hand at the door of the tent. She glanced back at the *navi*.

"Hannah, please. After the Sabbath. There is a girl at the edge of the camp. Zadok is tending her. She is weak from childbirth and likely ill. She'll need ointment, and herbs, and warm water and cloths. You'll know what else she needs better than I. Will you go to her, Hannah?"

Hannah gave her a curious look. "Who is she?"

The *navi* paused. She could hear the sides of the tent flapping slightly as a wind moved through the camp. It seemed to her that the wind carried to her the sound of a faint moan, as if from the hill. Then a quiet, gasping sob, the grief of a bereaved woman. Perhaps visions came to her ears this day and not only to her eyes. Or perhaps she only imagined it. "A supplicant," she said. She could not say *a heathen*, nor explain why it suddenly seemed so important to her that someone see to the girl. She had no time to argue with Hannah.

Hannah gave a small nod. "I will see to her. Good Sabbath, *navi*." She paused. "The other wives are dining with us. Will you join us?"

"Not tonight," Devora said.

Then she walked swiftly, almost at a run, toward her husband Lappidoth's tent. All through the camp, the priests' songs were falling silent; the Sabbath had arrived.

And then Devora *did* run, forgetful of dignity.

THE MAN WHO DEFENDED HIS CATTLE

DEVORA HAD BEEN twelve the first time she had seen him; he had been twenty. She was traveling alone on her way to Shiloh after the dead had devoured her mother's camp and all her kin. By night she lay in the weeds, shivering. By day she moved with caution, listening for any moaning dead and keeping away from any cart paths or any living men she saw, who might be tempted by a girl alone and without the protection of her tribe. It was easy to tell at a distance whether a figure striding through barley or tall grass was living or dead, for the dead staggered and lurched, but either the living or the dead could be dangerous to her. She was the only one left of all the men and women and children she knew; the fourteen others in her camp were dead. She was weak from hunger, and she hurried from one small pond or mud hole to the next, anxious for water.

The day she first saw Lappidoth was the second day of her flight.

She heard the moaning first, faint but unmistakable over the music of nearby water, and for a long time she stood still, terribly still, in grass higher than her chin. When she moved a little, as silently as she could, she came to a stream and saw the dead—and *him*—on the other bank. He was defending his herd from them. One of the cows had been torn apart; the others huddled in the middle of the stream. There were four corpses attacking. One was naked with a great gash in its side, its ribs white in the sun. Another of the dead had only one arm, yet it clawed at the air with the other as it came at the herdsman.

The young man had cast aside his cloak so that they could not grasp at it to pull him toward their biting teeth; he wore only his loincloth and a cattleherder's gloves, his body covered in a sheen of sweat. He held a flint hatchet, and he ducked and darted among the dead like a desert fox among serpents. Devora watched, breathless. The herdsman was so careful not to touch them with his hands, not to defile himself. He brought his hatchet down at one of the corpses' heads, shearing away the ear, then neatly flipped the hatchet about in his hand and swung his right arm back, driving the flint blade into the corpse's head. Then he leapt back out of the others' reach; they staggered after him. Devora held her breath, her heart in her throat. The dead hissed, and she could hear again her mother's shrieks and the shambling feet of the dead in her camp. Devora shrank back, though it meant the tall grass obscured her sight a little.

Even as she watched, eyes wide, one of the dead closed with the herder while his hatchet clove another's head; leaving the hatchet stuck in the first corpse's skull, the man ducked beneath the second's grasp and got his gloved hands on its hips. In a moment he lifted the rotting corpse high above his head and hurled it bodily into the stream.

The corpse in the stream splashed on its back like a turtle trying to right itself in the water. There was no time for the herder to try retrieving his hatchet; the corpse that was still on its feet was reaching for him. He leapt to the side, grasped a fistful of its hair in his gloved hand, and tried to pull it from its feet, but the corpse's scalp peeled free with the hair and the thing was still grasping for him, moaning, a bared patch of its skull shining in the sun. Devora bit her hand to smother a scream. She wanted to flee, to get far, far away from the dead, but something in her held her there, hiding in the tall grass, watching. Her own camp had been helpless against the dead, but this man wasn't. Her eyes shone with admiration.

The man stumbled; he fell to the dirt and then rolled fast to his left as the corpse turned and staggered after him. He got up into a crouch and then sprinted across the sand, putting distance between himself and the corpse. The other unclean corpse had risen from the water and was coming at him too. The man ran to the water's edge and bent and took up two large stones in his hands, one a blunt river stone the size of a clay bowl, the other a jagged rock that had been broken in two sometime before and would serve for a hatchet. With his eyes hard, one rock in either hand, he turned to face the oncoming dead.

***

In the end, they lay at his feet, unmoving. The herdsman stood panting, the rocks still clutched in his hands, dripping brown, viscous fluid, his head lowered. He might have been praying, or mourning, or simply spending all his energy just breathing, just staying on his feet.

She had watched him for so long. A warmth lit in her heart.

But he was a man, a strange man, and she was still a girl. She slipped away through the grass; glancing once over her shoulder, she saw through the tall blades his face lifted, peering after her. He must have heard her rustling retreat. He must have looked up. Her heart pounded, and she fled. She didn't stop running until her sides burned and her legs gave out under her.

The man gave her something to think about on the long walk to Shiloh. Something other than her mother's face. By day as she walked—drinking from small streams and chewing on grass to dull the bite of hunger, her ears attentive for any sound of the dead—she thought about the man and the way he had stood between the moaning dead and the riverbank. The way the sun had blazed on his bare shoulders and arms. She had not known what a man was, not really. There had been men in the encampment where she and her mother lived, and there had been her father, though they were gone now. They had been merely adults, taller and mysterious beings. Now she had seen a man. It seemed to her she had never truly seen one before. Her heart thrilled at it. The memory and wonder of it gave her the strength to keep placing one foot before the other.

But at night there was no escape from her terrors.

At night she lay awake, shivering, as the breeze tossed the blades of grass overhead. She could only lie still, listening, imagining terrible noises in the dark. Remembering how she'd wakened to see her mother's torso disappearing through the flap of the tent; something had her feet, was dragging her out. Her mother clutching frantically at the rug. The whites of her eyes.

Then she was gone; the rug slid out behind her. Devora had trembled, staring at the tent flap as her mother's screams broke the night, terrible screams. The sound of teeth tearing flesh. Screams that went on and on. Devora had covered her ears and just rocked back and forth, too scared even to cry.

Sometime in the hours that followed, Devora had taken up a clay pestle her mother had used to grind meal, the pestle cool in her hand, and had waited, shaking. At sunrise, a gray hand with strips of its flesh hanging loose had peeled aside the door of the tent, and her mother's face had peered in. What was *left* of her mother's face. Much of the flesh about her jaw had been chewed away, the bone showing under one gashed cheek. The corpse's dull eyes had looked directly at Devora, its mouth opening in a hiss.

Afterward, she had fled her mother's tent and the remains within it. The encampment had been full of the dead, shuffling back and forth. One of them was her father—who had been eaten as he slept in another tent. He had been weak. He had not saved her mother, or her— had done *nothing* to help them. Seeing her come out of the tent, he moaned, and then they were all moaning at her, all of her dead kin, and she ran. Ran fast and far across the low slopes, until she couldn't hear them anymore.

When the world was dark, there was no escape from the memories of her mother's camp. But by day, as Devora stumbled and half ran at times through the long grass, uphill and down, she forced the night shivers from her mind and dreamed instead of the man she'd seen fighting for his cattle, the man who, unlike her father, slew the dead and defended his own. His strong hands and the way the sunlight glistened on his back. She thought of him holding her, taking her in his arms, pressing his mouth to her throat as she had sometimes seen her father do with her mother. The warmth of that dream sustained her on the long walk. Whispering to God as she moved through the weeds, she vowed that she would find that man again one day.

***

Yet it was four and a half years before she saw the herdsman again, and in that time the entire shape of her life had changed. She had become the *navi*, had faced the dead again, had seen the fire in the tents. She'd even been kissed, but the man who'd kissed her was now beneath a cairn.

The year she turned sixteen, there was a rich harvest in the land, and more people than usual came to the Feast of Tents, that gathering where the men and women of the land leave their permanent camps or their towns and come to pitch tents in the fields near Shiloh for seven nights, in memory of their time of wandering in the desert. Many of the young women danced hill dances they'd learned from the Canaanites or the wilder desert dances of their own

People. For the first time, Devora danced too—for she found her herdsman by accident as she spoke with a few chieftains among the tents pitched by Ephraim tribe. Their eyes met, and she excused herself from that moment of council, because some things are more important than talk or planning or Shiloh itself.

She danced that night for Lappidoth, whose eyes shone as he watched her. She knew he did not remember her; probably he had not seen her face that other time. Probably he had seen only a movement of the tall grass as she ran. But now he gazed upon her, and she burned as he looked at her, burned as though he'd touched her. How she danced! She let her hips sing of her desire as she moved in the moonlight; she had thought of him so many times as she lay waiting for sleep.

After the fires at the Feast of Tents were coals and the people had gone to sleep, she rose from her place and sought out his tent. There was no woman there; he was alone. She slipped onto the wool carpet he lay on and woke him with a whisper in his ear, a whisper she herself could not hear, for her heart and the blood in her ears were louder. It was the boldest moment in her life. She had no family, no tent of her own, only the visions that came to her sometimes from the God of the Covenant and the memory of her first sight of this man, a memory she'd held close for years. Those two were the only things she had, the only things that meant anything to her then. She whispered to him about her longing, how strong and like a man he'd looked to her when she had first seen him. Then his hands grasped her arms and he pulled her beneath him; she gasped as she felt his weight on her. His face above hers was struck with wonder, like a man who has been told that though he had never known it, he is the son of a chieftain. Or like a desert man on a long journey who crests a hill to find an unexpected, clear lake at his feet. "Who are you, girl?" he asked hoarsely.

"Devora," she whispered. "Your wife."

***

Before the Feast of Tents was finished, Devora and Lappidoth stood beneath a canopy together, and it seemed to the young *navi* that all Israel celebrated with them. They had reason to. The nazarites, though now few in number, had fulfilled their vows well, cleansing the low valleys of the restless dead. It was becoming rare to hear of a corpse walking. And though the Feast of Tents was a reminder of deprivation and hunger in the desert, it was also a reminder that beneath the sheltering roof of the Law, the People had *survived* the desert.

When Devora and Eleazar and the *kohannim* met and talked in the afternoons, they spoke of the need to push all the tribes to make sure that none of the Canaanites sent their dead to the water or left bodies unburied. And that none of their own people did either.

During the short, warm summer nights, Devora's mind was on other matters.

***

For thirty years, Devora had hidden away the memory of her mother's camp, and Lappidoth had found less reason to fear for his herd. Now the dead were back.

As the reverent hush of Sabbath fell over Shiloh camp, Devora drew aside the heavy canvas door of her husband's tent and found Lappidoth already within, seated cross-legged on his red cushions, and she found with warmth in her heart that he was the same man she had seen fighting for his cattle, the same man she'd danced for. He was still strong, and sturdy as an oak. Life in this lush land had been good to him. The fine threads and fringes on the rugs and cushions within the tent he shared with her were a sign of his wealth. He had many cattle in the fields and ten hired herdsmen and was an astute trader. In his lap he held a great clay bowl of grains, and before him was a round wafer of unleavened bread, about the size of his two hands.

"You're not eating the Sabbath meal with Hannah and the priests' wives?" His voice was a low rumble in the dimness.

Her throat felt tight. "I'd rather eat here with you, my husband."

He nodded and held out his hand to the cushions at his side. She went to him and knelt gracefully there by him. He pressed a clay bowl into her hands; it was filled with water. Devora set it before her and washed her hands and arms up to the elbows as the *mitzvot* required, then her face. The water felt cool against her skin, and she sighed softly as some of the sweat and dirt of the day flowed away into the bowl. Lappidoth took up a piece of the unleavened bread, breaking it in two.

After a moment Devora set the bowl behind her and leaned against his side, her head on his shoulder, as she had often done long ago, as a young woman. She pressed her face to his garment, which smelled of cattle, and cried without tears, her body shaking as though coming apart. Lappidoth's calloused hands were warm and comforting on her back.

She just let him hold her. He waited, neither eating the bread nor pressing her to eat, and not asking her any question. He just held her.

After a while she whispered, "There is a windstorm in my heart."

Lappidoth put his arm about her, held her tightly to him. With his other hand, he took a small stone and set it beside the bread. "This is my wife's heart," he rumbled. Then covered the stone with his cupped hand. "This is my love for my wife, covering her heart. That the winds may pass over without tearing through her."

She smiled despite the tightness in her breast. "I love you," she whispered.

Yet as she gazed at his hand cupped protectively about that small stone, she shivered. His words reminded her of what she'd seen at the olive tree, and her worry howled louder inside her. What if God had removed *his* hand?

SCREAMS IN THE NIGHT

THE *NAVI* BOLTED AWAKE with a cry, clutching at her breast. She sat up, heaving for air. The pain and terror of her dream so violent, she felt she'd black out. A roaring in her ears.

Then her husband's strong arms were about her, his voice low in her ear, murmuring to her, calming her. He caressed her hair as he spoke, almost as he might caress the neck of one of his horses, calming it after a rearing and a cry of panic. Horses, nightmares, the ravaging dead— nothing ever really fazed Lappidoth. Devora clutched him, her heart pounding, grateful that in the spinning dark there was one thing to cling to.

She gulped in great breaths of cold night air, her wool covers tangled about her legs, her body nude but for a sheen of sweat. She hated this. *Hated* waking like this. It was always a few moments before she even really knew who she was. She reached for the wool, drew it up about her. Lappidoth laid her gently back and helped her cover herself; his body was pressed to hers, warm and firm. He kissed her cheek and neck. "Shhh," he murmured. "Shhh, Devora."

Devora realized he was kissing away tears. Her face was moist. "Don't let me go back to sleep," she whispered.

Lappidoth's arm squeezed her, a promise. He shifted so that his hip rested on hers, so that his body partly covered her beneath the wool. It comforted her. He was large and warm, and his weight held her to the present, to this specific moment in his tent, in his bedding.

After a moment she put her arms around him, though her hands still trembled behind his back. He didn't try to make love to her, just held her, occasionally kissing her face, the line of her jaw, her lips. Devora listened to her husband's breathing, like that of some huge animal in the dark. She could feel his heart beating where his chest pressed to her. She began to breathe more slowly. Full, deep breaths, filling her body with air and life. Her heart stopped racing.

She pressed her face into the soft place between her husband's neck and his shoulder and breathed in his scent. He had always been a distraction to her, a distraction from everything.

She felt him stir against her hip, and her senses came alert. She moved her fingers slowly over his back, thinking. She held her breath a moment, then decided that if he wanted her again, she would voice no protest, though she also wouldn't invite it—she wanted only to be held. But lovemaking too would distract her from the past and the future. And she knew with an ache between her ribs that each time he touched her might be the last.

His large, thick hands began to caress her arms slowly, though he made no other movement. His breathing was a little faster. After a moment he murmured her name in that soft growl of his, and she caught her breath, remembering the night he first said her name that way—repeating it a moment after she made a gift of it.

***

Some time later, she found herself warmed and content and safe as she lay under him and felt his strong body on her and inside her. She loved the way his breathing felt after he finished. She drank in the smell of him.

"I'll ride with you," he murmured.

She gasped, her content fading. "No, you won't," she whispered, worry sharp within her.

He lifted himself up on his elbows, and she looked into his eyes in the dark. "I'd be ashamed to stay," he said. He had faced the dead before.

She lifted her hand to cup his face, felt the roughness of his beard against her palm. He covered her hand with his own. A large hand, a herdsman's hand. Once strong, so strong. Now so wrinkled, the veins thick like cords, but— so beautiful. Her husband was a man who sat with others in the evening and discussed the Law. He was a quiet man, though furious when roused. For an instant, heat rushed into her, scorching her, not a passion-heat but a God-heat, and she saw her strong, gentle husband in the grip of the dead, many of them, *so many*, the unclean dead tearing him off his horse and bearing him to the ground, their nails and teeth digging into his flesh. She gasped, and the vision left her, leaving dizziness in its wake. The tent spun around her a moment, and to keep herself from spinning with it she clutched Lappidoth's arms as tightly as she had during their love. She forced herself to breathe, and the world stilled.

Kisses soft and moist on her brow, on her eyelids. His rumbling voice. "Are you all right?"

She kept her eyes closed, fearing the tent would spin again. "Please, husband," she whispered. "I beg you. Stay, defend your cattle. You have no herds in the north." She felt the tension in him, but he didn't speak. "I will be with armed men, I will be safe. I will serve our God better knowing you are here." She opened her eyes at last, saw the pain in his. It made her ache. Making him promise to stay, when she left and put herself at risk, was cruel. But he was not a young man now. And what she had *seen*!

She spoke softly, hoping to save his pride. Her wonderful, strong, aging husband. The sharpness of worry in her heart. "Please. Stay, and take your best yearling bull to Eleazar. A sacrifice to the Most High, so he'll give us victory and bring me safe home."

He looked at her for a long moment, then nodded. She let out the breath she'd been holding, and Lappidoth kissed her slowly, warmly. Then he moved within her, making her cry out, startled. It had been long since they'd made love more than once.

This time, it was more effort than passion, but she did not care. She clung to him, felt the warmth of him, kissed his shoulders and neck, and thought, This is my husband, my husband. He was the one thing in the world that was truly hers and that she need sacrifice to no other and to no duty. She drove the visions from her mind, wishing she did not have to leave this tent. For a while—for a little while—she let herself forget everything, everything, and clung fiercely to him, willing this night and the Sabbath day that would follow and the night after to be without ending.

WIND IN THE CAMP

A FEW MILES AWAY, Barak also endured a restless night. The wind had picked up, and he lay in his pavilion with his eyes open, grateful for the roar of the wind against the canvas. The noise prevented him from imagining that he could hear the moans of the dead.

Hadassah's mother had known the dead were in the hills before he did, and his vines had realized it even before her. They had even tried to tell him; how many mornings had he stood, his brow furrowed, holding a blighted leaf or a withered stalk in his hand? The grapes had begun to dry up like raisins, right there on the vines that should have fed and fattened them. Even the ground began to look gray rather than that deep, rich earth color he'd always seen before.

Then the moaning began. At first very distant—on the extreme edge of hearing, in the faint hours before dawn when sleep changes how everything in the world feels, even the air on your skin. He had bolted up in bed and strained to hear, only to have the sound fade like the cry of a heathen god on the high air. He shivered once, but lay back down to sleep. He had imagined it. He must have.

But Hadassah's mother was certain. He found her each night standing at the door of their cedar house, gazing toward the hills. He had to put his hands firmly on her shoulders and, speaking softly, half-coax, half-force her to her bed.

The blight on the vines grew worse. Such a sickening of the plants was a terrifying thing. If a man's wife sickened, he could drape a shawl over her shoulders and order her to bed. When a crop sickened…that was an unnatural thing, and he could only stand helplessly by, seeing neither cause nor cure. Praying to God with a dry mouth and a heart clamorous with horror. On crops they all depended, and on God who, fickle as a woman, brought rain or withheld it as she pleased.

One night he heard the moans and was no longer able to ignore them. The dead were nearer now, wandering aimlessly about, perhaps on the slopes of the nearer hills. Shaking, he stumbled out the door to stand at the edge of the vineyard, gazing straight up at the sharp and brittle stars so that he wouldn't need to look at the dark, brooding silhouettes of the hills to the east.

"God!" he cried in a hoarse, loud whisper. "Is it not enough you took Hadassah? And the child she would have given me?"

There was no answer. He almost felt he could hear the vines withering as he stood there, a dry rustling sound, like brush on a desert wind, very loud in the silence between distant moans. A rage burned low in his belly, though he didn't know if it was directed at the land that was betraying him or at the dead whose distant moans were now too loud to ignore, or at God, who, like a woman, could not be trusted to keep her promises. Both women and God might abandon a man one day. Leave him crying amid his vines.

He turned and went inside and slammed shut the cedar bar across the door for the first time in years, the first since the last, worst raids from the Sea People. But he could not shut out the moans of the dead.

***

Rolling onto his side in the tent, Barak gazed at where his bronze shield and spear and breast-piece were propped against one of the poles that framed his tent—gear he had taken from a Sea Coast raider he'd killed. With a sigh, he got to his feet and began arming himself, strapping bronze greaves to his shins, settling a leather jerkin over his shoulders and then the breast-piece over that, lifting his spear and testing its heft. He didn't know how near dawn it was, but it was surely near enough.

By the time he stepped outside, the wind had settled again and the camp was quiet, most of the men asleep except for sentries and a few of the chieftains arguing in low voices around a nearby fire. Laban was there, as broad-shouldered as a nazarite, and Omri too. Barak walked toward them, his bronze clinking slightly.

"Get the men ready," he said. "It's time to leave."

Laban gave him an uneasy glance, and Omri looked startled, but they both stood without comment and began moving through the camp, calling out for their men. After a moment, those men began to emerge from their tents, their weary faces drawn with fear.

Barak stood amid the shouts of men gathering their gear without taking much notice of it. He looked to the north, at the silhouettes of hills against the sky. Up there, north of the settlements at Walls and Refuge, was a narrow valley of vineyards and barley fields and his own homestead, his own house of cedar and thatch. A few days, and he could be standing again at his own door, stepping inside to a warm welcome, Hadassah's soft body pressed to his, her kisses moist on his throat.

No.

Hadassah was gone.

A fresh pang of grief in his breast, surprisingly sharp. He drew in a shuddering breath and banished both grief and memory. Began moving through the camp. There was much to see to.

A shout made him turn; Nimri was walking toward him in haste, his eyes bright with that fanatical fury Barak knew too well. Barak kept walking, forcing Nimri to fall in alongside him.

"What is it, Nimri?"

"It's the Sabbath, that's what." A snarl in the man's voice.

Barak's eyes hardened. "The Law says: if your cattle fall in a ditch, it is no violation of the Covenant to haul them out. I have no cows in a ditch, but I may have dead in my vineyard. No other tribes are coming, Nimri. We've wasted enough time here."

Nimri's face twisted. "What I'd expect," he muttered, "from a man who took a heathen girl to wife."

Barak stopped short, and his voice went cold. "My father was a Hebrew, Nimri. My mother too."

"I do not deny it." Nimri smirked, then cast a glance down toward Barak's groin, and sneered when he lifted his eyes. "Yet you stink of them."

Barak fought his anger. He had no time for this. His fingers twitched, but he did not reach for the knife at his hip. "Before you insult me again, think carefully about whether you want a battle with *me*." If his voice had been cold a moment before, it was ice now. "Stay here and wait if you will. I will leave horses, such as I have; you can catch up when you've done as we agreed."

Nimri tried to speak, but Barak held up his hand. "Enough," he growled, and turned away, walking on through the camp. His back was tense, but he did not expect a knife in it; Nimri was trouble, but he was no coward. Barak did not look over his shoulder to see if Nimri still stood there or whether he had gone back to his tents. He just proceeded through his own camp, stopping a man every once in a while to give a command or ask a question. Already men were folding the tents. The wind was back, and all about Barak loose canvas flapped in the wind, with a sound like a hundred giant birds all taking flight at once. Strangely, the sound calmed him a little. Surely a camp that could make that much noise would prove large enough to cleanse their land of the dead.

If Nimri had spoken as he had in the hearing of other men, Barak could not have ignored it. But he ignored what he could afford to, for he was used to it. Since the day he had seen Hadassah by the well in Walls and looked into her dark eyes, the day he'd met with her father and taken her to his house, he had heard the jeering of other Hebrews. That he, who had been known as a man raiders from the sea might fear—that he should take a heathen girl as a wife rather than a slave.

Still struggling with his anger, Barak reflected that at least Nimri would be out of his camp for a while. And perhaps Nimri was the kind of man he should leave behind to push at the priests of Shiloh, in any case. A man with a passionate faith in the power of God and his Ark and his Law, but who would not be awed by any other man, even a levite, even a priest. Nimri would not be likely to back down at a refusal.

MISHPAT

DAWN'S COLD LIGHT. The Sabbath bride had visited the People for a night and a day. This was now the morning that followed. Lappidoth had already left to see about a horse for his wife. In his tent, Devora dressed swiftly but with purpose; she was acutely aware that what she wore this day, and what she carried with her, might be as important as any words she spoke. Even as she cinched tight the girdle about her white dress—white, the color of the Levi tribe—her fingers faltered an instant. She glanced at the bundles and parcels at the back of the tent, her eyes drawn to one long, slender bundle in a corner, half-concealed beneath the rest, a bundle bound with a red cord. Two things there must go with her as well, two things she had not taken in her hands in a long time. If she was to ride into the north and see fields that were occupied by the hungry dead, she could not leave it to others to carry out her judgments. To do so would be to invite a kind of blindness. The kind that kept her from seeing the weight that the burden of executing her judgments placed on Zadok's shoulders.

It should have been her hand that silenced the infant, not only her hand that buried it. It must be her hand that attended to the dead.

God had given her visions of things to come. That meant the burden was hers. It was right that it should be. She had never borne a child, but she was a woman of the People and she understood how to bear burdens, she understood how to shoulder those hard necessities required to preserve life. She had once carried a corpse in her arms like a beloved child a mile through dank reeds because it was unthinkable that another should have to.

Devora moved to the goatskin bundle and unwrapped it. Took up the scarlet cord first and held it in her hand a moment. Then she gently drew aside the goatskin, revealing the item it had concealed: a blade longer than her arm, polished to a sheen, slender and feminine in its delicacy. A hilt of white bone. She gazed at it grimly. Both the blade and the cord she held were heathen in origin, yet they were items that had proven useful to the People and had been consecrated for their uses, even as the fields and hills that had once been possessed only by the Canaanites were now places set apart and chosen out of all lands for the Hebrews, places holy in their own way.

"We must have a truce, you and I." Devora spoke to the sword and to the memories it recalled for her. "I will lift you and carry you with me, because the dead are in the land again and there will be butchery to do before the land is clean. But you mustn't expect me to use you. Only when I must. You were once unclean with the blood of a woman who was the best woman in Israel, the wisest. I will not like you or the necessity of carrying you. I unbind you and will need you ready to my hand, but don't think that I carry you as a man would, with any joy in your beauty."

The blade lay there mute yet eloquent in the shimmer of dawn light on its cold metal. Iron, the only iron blade she'd ever seen. Sea People had smithied it, in their walled towns on the coast to the west. The blade had come to Devora as a gift in the darkest of circumstances. After she'd done what she must, she'd wrapped it tightly in that goat hide and bound it and bound with it the pain of that day. Released now, that pain leapt at her and clawed at her heart as she gazed on the sharp metal.

"I will name you Mishpat," she whispered to the blade, "the Judgment. That will help us both remember what you are and what you are not."

A judgment on the dead. A judgment on her. The swift cut of decision, severing what limbs must be severed from the body of the People so that the rest of the body might thrive and not decay.

She considered the blade a few moments, as if watching for some sign of its consent to the name. Idly she wrapped the scarlet cord about her hand, feeling its coarse, aged fiber against her skin. Then bound it about her waist like a girdle. A dark mood fell over her, and she pressed her hand to her belly with a gentleness that would have surprised any who saw her.

She listened for a long moment, but heard nothing there. An ache opened within her, deep as the ravines of the Tumbling Water. There was no life stirring within her after the lovemaking of the past two nights. As *navi*, she would have known if there were; she felt certain of it. Tears stung her eyes; she blinked them away.

She knew her barrenness to be a judgment on her for the choices she'd had to make as a younger woman. As with any shattering of Covenant, barrenness had been visited on her, even as barrenness and blight now threatened the People and the land itself.

"Devora?"

She turned, saw Lappidoth at the door of the tent, peering in. She drew in her breath. She could be vulnerable, here in his tent. Once she stepped outside, she could not be. Out there, where she was going, weakness would be lethal—for her, and for her People.

Lappidoth came to her, sat beside her, and put his arms about her. "I'd nearly forgotten you had that," he murmured into her hair, and she knew he meant Mishpat. "You are taking it?"

"I am. It has only ever been used for one thing. Where God is sending me, I may need it." Devora closed her eyes, just feeling his warmth. "Why have you never been angry?" she whispered. "I deceived you when I came to you."

She had not told him she was barren, or why. Yet he had sheltered her in his tent all these years, not because she was the *navi* but because she was a woman, a woman he loved. Nor had he ever taken a second wife—though this meant his seed would not be passed on. He had once told her there was only one woman he wished to see bearing his child within her.

This morning might be the last she would ever see him.

"You didn't know." His voice a rumble at her ear, his presence heavy and strong in the dim light.

"I feared it," she murmured. Then she shook her head, breathed out slowly, straightening her back, refusing to lean any longer into his arms. She wanted to, so badly, but she could ill afford to begin this morning weak. Tears were a luxury reserved for women who did not have a People in their care. Her eyes hardened again, with purpose and with denial of all weariness.

"Sarah was barren," she said suddenly. "Our father Abraham's wife. Her body aged and she bore no child, and bitterness ate at her heart. Then two men came to her husband's tents beneath the oak trees. Only they weren't men, they were *malakhim*, angels of *El adonai* our God."

Lappidoth pressed his face to her neck with a soft sound in his throat, to comfort her.

"They said to Abraham, we bring you *niv sefatayim*, fruitful words from the God in high places. A year from now your wife will give birth to a boy." Devora lifted a hand as she spoke, moving her fingers gently through her husband's hair. "Sarah was within the tent, concealed from the sight of men who were strange to her. When she heard the words, she laughed. A cold laugh, for she did not think God could bring anything green and alive out of the desert she felt her body had become." Devora's voice fell, became soft. "But a year later, she had the boy. Then she laughed a second time, with tears. Isaak I name you, she said to the boy as he suckled at her breast, Isaak, my laughter.

"I have tried to live a life as holy and set apart, as *kadosh*, as Sarah's," she whispered, "but when I was a girl I broke the Covenant twice, and God remembers it."

Lappidoth's arms were around her.

"There will be no laughter for me in my old age." She gave him a small, bitter smile. "And perhaps I will not come back from the hills."

"You *will* come back," her husband growled. She could hear in his voice that her words had upset him. He gripped her chin suddenly, turned her face toward his. His eyes were fierce in the dim light. "You have a covenant with me, not only with God. And how can you keep it from beneath a cairn? You will come back." And rather than wait for an answer, he kissed her.

At that moment there were shouts outside, sharp cries of fear. Devora stiffened, and Lappidoth's eyes went dark with alarm. Swiftly he rose from beside her. He strode toward the tent door, cast it to the side. Devora got to her feet, had time to cry, "Wait!" but then Lappidoth was already through the door, and gone.

Devora's heart pounded. She started toward the door, stopped. Glanced back at the blade that lay unsheathed on the rug. It looked lethal. A moment ago she had been mourning her inability to bear new life. That blade was meant to sever life.

Another cry outside, a scream. This time one of pain.

With a moan of dread, Devora bent and took up the blade, then hurried out the door.

THE SOUNDING
OF THE SHOFAR

DEVORA BURST from her husband's tent and was nearly trampled down by a man on horseback; she let out a cry and sprang back, tripping. Then the man was past with a glance at her over his shoulder as he rode, and Devora had a shock. For his eyes and his cheekbones were those of the northern tribes. And in one hand he carried a long knife, nearly the length of a man's arm between elbow and wrist. The knife was red with blood.

Then man and horse were gone amid the tents. Lappidoth was nowhere to be seen. Devora broke into a run, moving as quickly as her long woolen skirt would permit, Mishpat's hilt cold in her hand. She didn't understand, couldn't understand! But she sensed the camp, *God*'s camp, was under some kind of raid. As she dashed through the tents, others began to bolt past her running the other way. There were screams and, somewhere ahead, the clang of bronze striking against bronze. Panic choked her.

The commotion was coming from near the Tent of Meeting. Holding Mishpat out to her side, she darted past the tents, dodging to the side as another horse galloped past her. Caught a glimpse of the rider's face. Hebrew. Another northern face. Her heart burned hot within her. That Barak—that Barak!—*what had he done?*

There were levites on the ground among the tents now—their white robes gashed open and reddened with blood. She ran faster, leaping over the bodies, breathing hard, a stitch in her side. Then she was around the last of the priests' tents, and she could see the Tent of Meeting and the scorched earth around it and high on its pole near the Tent, the ram's horn, the *shofar*, untouched, no alarm blown. Had there been no time?

Several northern men were dismounted by the pole, and one was bent over the body of a fallen priest. Zadok and another nazarite were fighting to get into the Tent, the door barred by a lean man whose face was turned away from her; the man held a bronze blade and a round shield. Zadok lunged in with his spear, but the man caught the spear on the edge of his shield and spun the shield in one quick, smooth motion, ripping the spear out of Zadok's grasp and sending it clattering away. The other nazarite had only a knife in his hand, and he danced in place, awaiting an opening.

Devora had only a moment to take in the scene—the battle at the door, great gashes in the side of the tent, the body in the dirt, and the men moving away from the pole now to flank Zadok—when there was a bellow like a bull's voice to her left, and her husband leapt around one of the tents with a tent pole uplifted in his hands. Lappidoth ran at the men and drove the end of the pole into one's face, sending the man sprawling limp some distance away. He spun the pole at another man's head, but the man ducked. Then Devora was at her husband's side, screaming loud enough to drown out her fear, and they were facing three from the northern tribes, tall, lean men wielding staves of cedar. They carried no shields; those staves served them for both attack and defense. The blade wavered in her grip; these were living men, men of the People, and she had only once before in her life raised Mishpat against another's life. But these men meant to kill *her husband*. They meant to defile the Tent of Meeting, *had* defiled it. And they meant to kill Lappidoth.

Everything in her went cold.

She swung the blade.

The eyes of the men facing her widened in horror at the sight of this white-robed levite woman bearing down on them with a blade of iron that seemed not of this land or any other, slender metal, a white slice of death such as they had only seen perhaps in the hands of men of the Sea Coast during raids from the walled towns in the west. The strangeness of the sight and the hesitation it provoked was lethal; Devora's blade slashed across the face of the man in the middle. A spray of blood, some of it spattered warm across Devora's neck and her cheek. The *navi*'s heart was pounding. She screamed again and swept the blade down at the legs of the man to the right, even as Lappidoth blocked the man's club from striking her; the iron blade slid through sinew and bone as though they were milk, and the man crumpled with a shrill cry.

As her husband faced the last of the three, Devora caught a glimpse of the Tent of the Meeting past the enemy's shoulder. The second nazarite lay still on the ground, a pool of blood beneath his head. Zadok had taken up the fallen man's knife and was dancing to the left, then the right, with the kind of grace one sees in desert asps or in the lethal mamba of Kemet, the serpent that strikes unseen from the trees. But Zadok could not get within the northern man's reach; the man's war braid and the colored stones he'd woven into his belt declared him a chieftain of men, one who had survived many harsh raids in the north. In less time than the beat of a heart, Devora's eyes took in the nazarite's peril and the great cuts in the side of the holy Tent.

The Tent had been violated; there was at least one man within who had not been consecrated or prepared to enter the *shekinah* and who dared to bear sharp bronze before Holy God. Yet no fire blazed from the Tent to wither the northern man where he stood, which Devora couldn't understand. But then, these were not strangers in the land who raided the Tent but men who partook of the Covenant and the promise. Perhaps God, whose ways were not the ways of men and women who walk on the earth, was waiting for his Hebrews to clean up the evil of their own. She didn't have time to think of it—it was only a silent cry of astonished horror in her mind.

Other northern men had emerged from among the tents to the right, one with a bloodied spear. Devora sprang away from her husband and his opponent, bolted the few steps to the pole by the Tent. She reached up for the peg from which hung the shofar, the curved ram's horn, the voice of the People's need or the People's might. Snatched it from its peg and lifted it to her lips. Blew on it the *t'qiah*, the notes of challenge and alarm.

The call was deep and clear; after a moment the call seemed to return, doubled, from the slopes of the hills.

There were shouts in the camp. And footsteps, white-robed men rallying to the Tent at the call of the horn. Somewhere, a woman's scream. Hannah, the midwife. That was Hannah's voice.

There was no time for thought or judgment, only action. Devora ran toward the other northern men who were closing on Zadok and her husband, looping the shofar about her neck by its leather cord as she ran. She brought Mishpat up, and the blade was slender and violent like a scream out of God's mind in the desert. She knew no art of its use, but she was furious and desperate, and one of the men fell back before the rage in her eyes, and the other took the blade across his right shoulder and spun to his left and dropped to his knees, where Devora's sandalled foot took him in the face.

Then a third man was before her with a club in either hand, and the *navi* was slashing the blade in great strokes through the air that made her arms ache and left her open and vulnerable had she known it. But the other man simply avoided her strokes and did not strike, his eyes round with astonishment. Perhaps he guessed she was the *navi*; perhaps it was only that he found himself met in the dance of spears by a woman and didn't know what to do. But then other men of the camp were behind Devora and at her side, and the northern man fell back. Powerful arms wrapped around Devora from behind, pinning her own upper arms so that she could hardly swing the blade. She screamed and kicked back at her assailant. Heard a rough, low voice in her ear. "Easy, Devora, easy. It's over, it's over."

111

Lappidoth.

She collapsed back in his arms, panting for air, and Mishpat hung limp at her side. She was shaking. She just let his arms hold her for a moment, then the reality of what had happened seized her. "The Ark!" she cried.

Lappidoth released her, and she turned to the Tent. Zadok stood there with a shallow cut along his cheek, his hand gripped fierce about the invader's throat. Somehow he had gotten past the enemy's blade and taken the man's throat in his hand and wrenched him from his feet. Now the man had been forced to his knees, and the nazarite loomed over him, squeezing his throat, his other hand holding the man's right wrist at a cruel angle, though the northerner stubbornly clung to his sword's hilt and would not drop it.

With a start, Devora realized she knew the man.

Nimri. This was Nimri, that chieftain of Naphtali who had spoken so scornfully by the cairns, before the Sabbath. Her heart went hard and cold.

Zadok's eyes were those of a killer, but in a moment, two of the camp's other three surviving nazarites were beside him, and they pulled Zadok loose, muttering low words in his ears. One of them then kicked the invader onto his back, then held him down with a foot over his throat while his companion disarmed him. Zadok stood silently by, his eyes still hot with rage, his hands flexing as though it were taking all his will to keep from leaping upon Nimri and choking away his life.

But Devora spared the men little attention, for now she could see through the wide door of the Tent of Meeting.

And what she saw winded her.

Within, the altar had been toppled to the side, and two northern men lay slain beside it. A white-robed priest knelt by them, clutching his belly from which a darkness flowed that could only be his life leaving him. A spear lay discarded to the side, its bronze head wet with the priest's blood. In his hand, the dying priest still held the flint knife that was used in preparing sacrifices for the altar; this morning, it had sacrificed only the two northern men who lay dead within. Beyond the priest was the veil that concealed the *kodesh kodashim*, the Holy of Holies, from the eyes of those who hadn't been consecrated to meet God face-to-face like a lover. But the veil had been ripped aside, like a rape. Through the tear, Devora could see the Ark of the Covenant tipped on its side and its lid fallen away, revealing the scrolls of the Law and the two stone tablets on which were chiseled, durable as the land itself, the words of the Ten.

The bleeding man turned toward the door, but even before she could see his face, Devora could tell who he was from the *hoshen mishpat* he wore.

"Eleazar!"

The priest's eyes showed recognition; then he swayed and fell.

In another moment Devora was within the Tent, despite the sacrilege of it; she knelt and lifted Eleazar's head to her lap and cupped his face in her hands, her heart stricken with ice. This was the high priest of her People, struck down by a spear within the very walls of the Tent of God. Those walls stirred loudly in the wind, and the veil fluttered, a fragile thing.

"No," Devora said, her voice thick. "Oh no."

Eleazar's gaze lifted, focused on her though dull with pain. "Ark," he gasped. "They wanted the Ark. Told them. Law forbade. Ark can only go—where *all* the tribes go. Not just two or three."

"Shh," Devora whispered, and brushed strands of lank, sweaty hair away from his face. "Don't talk. Just rest, *kohen*. Just rest. Until Hannah is here."

His mouth worked a moment without words. Then: "No time. Your vision. The dead. You must go. Where God needs you to be."

"Please don't talk," Devora said, desperate. She took cloth and pressed it to his wound, but the dark blood kept pulsing out. He was dying. Devora felt a firm hand on her shoulder and didn't need to glance up to know Lappidoth was there with her, silent and strong behind her. As he had always been.

"My sons," Eleazar rasped. "In Beth El camp. Send for them."

"We will," Devora said, gripping his hand tightly.

Gazing past Devora's shoulder as if at the sky, Eleazar gasped, "Don't let the People be—eaten—or—or burned—"

Devora didn't understand, but she nodded. Everything in her felt wrung tight.

"*Sh'ma*," Eleazar forced the words out. "*Sh'ma Yisrael adonai eloheinu, adonai echad.*" Hear O Israel, Adonai our God, Adonai is One. A Hebrew's death prayer, since the time in the desert. Speaking it, Eleazar was saying, *I may die, but I die in service to Holy God, as my fathers did before me. You who live, see that you do likewise.*

The breath left his body in a long sigh that stopped abruptly. A sound more terrible in its way than the moans of the dead. Devora stared down at him. He was gone. The high priest of Israel. Gone. She'd been too late. Once again, as on that other night three decades before, when there'd been fire in the tents and many who'd mattered to her had perished, she'd come too late.

Gently Devora laid the priest back on the bloodstained rugs that floored the Tent. She took his left hand and placed it on his chest, then brought his right up to join it. Even as she did, another woman entered on silent feet and knelt across the body from her, then took the priest's face in her hands. This other woman was weeping breathlessly. It was Hannah. She too had arrived too late.

"He is dead, Hannah," Devora said gently. "You mustn't touch the body. When it cools, he'll be unclean."

Hannah shook her head, her eyes wet with her tears.

Devora lowered her head, her own grief rising within her like a wind. She and Eleazar had never been close, though they had shared a bond, as had all the survivors of that terrible night so many years ago. The bond that all the old shared, that none of the young could truly understand. Devora had seen the others who had lived through that night die in recent years, of old age or disease or weariness. Maybe a day would come when only she would be left. She alone.

As she looked down, her gaze caught on Eleazar's breast-piece and the stones placed within it. The stones on which were carved the names of the tribes, and the *other* two stones. The *urim*, dark as a horse's eyes, and the *thummim*, pale like dead flesh. Gently, reverently, Devora lifted those two from the breast-piece; Hannah, lost in her weeping, didn't appear to notice. For a moment she held them in her hand. The stones were very small. They were rarely used.

"Does your hand still cover Israel?" the *navi* whispered.

She cast the stones. Letting them roll across the rugs within the Tent. Held her breath as she waited to see which would stop rolling first.

The two stones rolled.

The *urim* settled, dark on the earth-colored threads. The *thummim*, the "no" stone, rolled a little farther.

Devora let her breath out slowly.

The *urim* had stopped first.

The "yes" stone.

The answer was yes.

She rose and picked up the stones. One, then the next. Held them in her hand, pressed them to her lips. She needed a moment, just a moment. She was shaking.

The answer had been yes.

Her fist tightened until her nails dug into her palm and she felt she could feel the *urim* and *thummim* pressing right against her bones, through her skin. She drew in a fresh breath with a hiss. God still covered his People. Provisionally, perhaps, but God was still here. *Still* here.

Hannah's weeping behind her was quiet.

Devora could act again with the authority of God's *navi*. And action and judgment would be needed. For a great violation of the Covenant had been committed.

Devora rose stiffly to her feet and left the tent, emerging into the morning sun. The shofar still hung about her throat, Mishpat in her right hand. She gazed numbly at the blood on the iron. She'd meant to wield Mishpat against the unclean dead, not the living. Wind tugged at the slashed sides of the Tent before her, though within the recesses of the Tent the veil hung limp, gashed and still, as though that veil were God's hymen, torn and then held to be of little value. A flicker of heat lit somewhere on the cold plain of her grief and grew until the flames consumed her heart. Lappidoth spoke to her, but she did not hear him. She saw Zadok standing near and she said quietly, "Take me to him."

The nazarite nodded, his face still hard with violence. He turned and led the way, and heeding neither Hannah's weeping nor the cries of the wounded, Devora moved through the camp. Rage burning in her heart. She did not even feel her husband's gaze on her.

She found Nimri held out in the heather beyond the Tent, between two nazarites who had pulled him away from the camp as though he were unclean. Now he stood among the purple blossoms, and the wind tugged at his hair. He hardly seemed to notice Devora approaching, but when he saw Zadok, he spat like a cat. The other two nazarites gazed at the *navi* with something in their eyes that she had never seen there before. Awe, perhaps. Devora's long, silvered hair bannered in the wind; her white gown, though dirtied and splashed with blood, billowed about her legs in a way that suggested a mighty bird swooping through the heather. The shofar about her neck, Mishpat held out bloodied at her side.

Devora stopped when she stood before Nimri, her eyes hot with fury.

"Whose command?" she demanded. "Who sent you here?"

Nimri lifted his chin. He'd been bruised about the face, and the marks of Zadok's fingers were dark on his throat. "Go home to your tent, woman."

117

"I am the *navi* of Israel, Nimri! *Why are you here?*" Her voice cracked sharp as a lash in the air.

He watched her a moment, a brooding look in his eyes. "Asking for the Ark."

For an instant there was only the wind in the heather.

"You might try leaving your spears behind when you ask," Devora said. "Where is Barak?"

"He's left for the north, woman." Nimri sneered at her. "I'm to meet him there at Walls, with you and the Ark."

"Left? This morning?" It made no sense. His camp was only a few miles away. Surely he would have waited an hour or two for Nimri to return.

"Yesterday."

Devora cried out, enraged. "On the *Sabbath*! Has he forgotten the *whole* Covenant?"

"What does a woman know of the Covenant?" Nimri's voice went quiet with menace. "Judgment, of either Barak or the dead, is for men to decide. You have no place here. Get back to your husband's tent."

Devora struck him.

His head whipped back, and then he looked at her with rage-darkened eyes and blood on his lip. His face reddening. Devora held his gaze, her eyes hard. "I speak a *navi*'s judgment and a *navi*'s curse," she said, and at the words, a little color left the man's face.

Devora's words welled from some hot pool of fury within her, and heat washed through her body, the heat that had always presaged for her the nearness of God and the nearness of the future. Her voice hard as the tablets in the Ark on which were chiseled the Covenant of their People. "You will come once at each planting and once at each harvest to Shiloh. You will come on foot, without sandals or waterskin, relying on the mercy of the levites to give you water to drink and oils for your feet. You will bring to them a white bull, without blemish, and beg the priest to sacrifice it for you, to atone for this day's evil. You will do this year after year, until the priests release you."

She drew in a hissing breath. "That is my judgment." Her voice rose, shrill and cold. "*This* is my curse. Nimri ben Nabaoth, until the priests release you, you will take up no spear nor blade nor any implement of metal, nor any bludgeon, nor so much as lift your hand to strike another man. The instant you do, your hand will wither and your whole body will be struck with the white sickness—for with your own hand you struck down a priest of our God. And my friend." For he had been. She knew in this moment that he had been. However uneasy they had at times been with each other.

Devora was almost shrieking the words now, the heat of the future, of prophecy and curse, crackling along her skin, making her hairs rise. Nimri's face had gone white. "You will be a leper, unclean, begging at the roadside with stumps where your hands were. Your manhood will decay and fall off. You will be spat upon by all who are true to their Covenant. I, Devora, the *navi*, who sees what God sees, I speak this curse. Whatever covenants you made with Barak ben Abinoam, you must abide the consequences of their breaking, for you will never again march with other armed men."

WORDS OF GOING

DEVORA HAD SEEN too many burials; this one was harder than most, for it seemed to promise other burials to come. An hour after banishing Nimri from the camp, Devora led a procession through the heather and up the slope of her hill to the forest of stone cairns. As she climbed, she glanced to the east and saw that Barak's camp had indeed slipped away. The tents there were gone, leaving only spaces of trampled dirt amid the weeds. Like guilty men leaving a corpse. Her face tightened. Nimri had spoken mockingly of Barak ben Abinoam, yet Barak had left him behind to bring the Ark and the *navi* north. What commands had Barak given him? Had Barak meant to seize the Ark by force? In either case, for loosing this wolf on the tents of Levi, Barak had much to answer for.

Behind the *navi*, twenty priests climbed the hill, and Shiloh's last few nazarites climbed with them, each bearing a body safely wrapped in a linen shroud. Behind the bearers walked women from the camp, veiled in their grief like northern girls, climbing in silence. The morning's terror had left them too exhausted even to weep. Hannah was with them. Zadok walked just behind the *navi*, carrying Eleazar in his shroud.

Devora led them among the cairns without word or cry, but her mind was loud within her, and she could not calm it. She struggled to understand how this thing could have happened, that *Hebrew* men—Hebrew, not heathen— should try to seize the Ark from the priests by force. She knew the People had been spreading out through the land, further and further from the Ark and from God and from the Law at Shiloh. What if they were ceasing to be a People—becoming mere scattered encampments, no longer tribes but homesteads, isolated among the homes of heathen? She repressed a shudder. Was that why the dead had come, surging out of the cedar forests in the far north? To drive the People together again, like scattered deer fleeing a storm, rushing together down long slopes to gather in one valley, before one Law?

Or were the People altogether forsaken, and the dead here merely because God's hand had been removed from covering Shiloh and the land? The *urim* and *thummim* had suggested otherwise. Yet. She remembered the *malakh ha-mavet* and the way the Tent of Meeting had been cut open and no fire from God had withered those who toppled altar and Ark. Devora did not know, *could* not know, if the herds of dead moving in the north were a chastisement meant to drive the People together, or a revocation entire of the Covenant and the promise.

Here among the cairns, the men from Shiloh set out the bodies in a great line, as they had once before, thirty years ago, after another attack on the camp. Devora stood by the bodies, her head bowed, feeling the memory settle heavy on her shoulders. All about her, the men gathered up stones, mighty stones to bury the dead. Zadok stopped a moment beside the *navi* without speaking, just giving her the comfort and solidity of his presence. She glanced up at his face, saw it drawn with pain. The memories were heavy on *his* shoulders too.

Devora looked out over the cairns. Many of the corpses beneath them, especially the oldest ones, had become anonymous now, hidden in a field of dead whose names she didn't know. One of the cairns was even crumbled in upon itself, as much a ruin as the body it buried. For the human memory is short, and even when we write it in stone we quickly forget and the stones crumble and even those stones then forget.

The men laid Eleazar in a shallow grave and then piled the stones above him, a house humbler than the pyramids of Kemet but alike in purpose and no less effective. Devora wished for a moment that she could see his face, but he was shrouded, and then there were stones over him and she couldn't see even his shape, and his laughter and his love for his wife and his exuberance for the Law were buried forever.

When the cairns were finished, Devora stood facing Eleazar's with her arms folded, preternaturally straight and still, her gaze fixed on the pile of rock. She lifted her voice, clear on the crisp air, chanting the Words of Going. There were words in that lament that were Hebrew, and there were words of Kemet, for many generations of their mothers and grandmothers had sung those words over the bodies of their sons, beaten to death in the labor of raising the great tombs and cities of the dead in that land of river and dark earth. In those words could be heard the tears of all the women of the People and all the tears the men had feared to shed. The song was older than the *Shirat ha'Yam*, older than the praisesongs of the *kohannim*, older than any *navi* or any vision given to man or woman by the God of their Covenant. The People had known death and loss and despair, and the screaming in the desert, before they had known God.

Devora sang for Eleazar and for the other dead priests, and for the nazarite Nimri had slain. And, after the briefest hesitation in her heart, she sang even for a small child, a nameless child with a Hebrew father and a heathen mother, who had died somewhere in the north and then been buried here. She sang for the child because the infant's mother had no way to say farewell herself, here, so far from the water. She sang for the child because of her dreams and her terrors of the night before. Because when the unclean death separates child and mother, some atonement must be made, some words of parting. There were no words in the Law that demanded she sing over a child who was not of the People. But there was a Law written on her heart that did demand it.

***

The young Canaanite didn't stand as Devora approached her on the outskirts of the camp, her blade still held in one hand, her throat a little hoarse from singing over the cairns. Hurriya was lying in thick pelts that Zadok must have thrown there on the earth, and nearby there was another hide rumpled, where Zadok had probably slept. The *navi* considered her a moment. This wouldn't be easy. Bracing herself, she stepped toward the girl.

"I need a guide in the Galilee," Devora said.

Hurriya lifted herself up on her elbows with an effort, and the pelt that covered her fell away from her. Devora recoiled half a step, appalled at her condition. The girl smelled of sweat and blood and dirt; her face was very pale, and her salmah looked stiffened. Devora wondered how long it had been since either that woolen cloth or the girl within it had been washed. There were hollows under Hurriya's eyes as she looked up at the *navi*.

Perhaps the Canaanite girl had kin in the north. Someone who could care for her there.

"I thought I was *unclean*," the girl said, and the bitterness in her voice was like a slap.

Devora glanced about quickly, noting a discarded waterskin and a cloth that had probably been brought here in the morning with bread in it. She let out her breath slowly. The girl had been fed at least and given water to drink. But she had given birth to a child not long ago, and her body had not healed well from it. The walk down from the Galilee, in exhaustion and terror, must have been brutal. It was a wonder the girl was even conscious.

"You've lived all your life in those hills," Devora said. "Neither I nor Zadok have ever been in the Galilee. And you know more about what's happening there than anyone in this camp." She didn't add that she would trust a heathen before she'd trust that dog Barak and his chieftains. "If Zadok rigs a sidesaddle for you, can you ride a horse?" she asked aloud.

Hurriya just sank back and closed her eyes. "I've never ridden a horse."

"You'll ride before me on my husband's horse, then."

She shook her head, pale with misery. "Let me die, *navi*," she whispered.

"I am *not* going to do that," Devora said sharply. "You came to me. I have an obligation to you, girl; I mean to keep it. I am taking you north. You can show me when to turn to the left, when to the right, until we get there." She thought for a moment. "We will have to get you your own waterskin, and keep your skin covered at all times, to prevent contact. You *are* unclean." Her heart sank; she couldn't bear to lose the hours it would take to gather up a spare waterskin and food and supplies for the girl and to beg clothing for her from one of Shiloh's women, clothing that could not be returned. She had to leave, now. She meant to catch Barak.

"I am unclean," Hurriya repeated. "This whole *land* is unclean." Hurriya began laughing, a cold, bitter laughter that shook her until she coughed and clenched up in pain. Devora gazed down at her in dismay.

"I don't care what you do," Hurriya whispered after a few moments. "Tie me to your horse if you like. I don't care."

Before she could reply, Devora heard hooves behind her and turned toward the tents. There were two horses approaching, one dark as beer from Kemet, and massive, the other smaller and white, with a dark patch near its nose. On the dark horse rode Zadok, who seemed even more massive in the saddle. He wore a breast-piece of bronze, and his spear was strapped to the side of his saddle, counterbalanced on the other side by several waterskins—bless him, that solved one problem—and a small pack. The man's face was grim. He sat that dark horse like danger and threat incarnate.

Lappidoth rode the white horse, his face drawn and pale. Devora cried out when she saw him, fearing for a moment that he meant to ride with her, whether she willed or no. But he saw her face and shook his head.

"The horse is only for you, Devora," he said. "I am staying."

Devora blushed. Of course. When Lappidoth her husband made a promise, he kept it.

"His name was Arvad, the wanderer," Lappidoth told her gravely as he halted near her, "for he was wild on the steppes before a caravan from Midian brought him to Shiloh. Now he is Shomar, because he guards his rider." He slid from the horse's back. Zadok drew his horse up beside but stayed in the saddle.

"I need speed more than safety," Devora said. She noted the bedroll and other supplies attached to Shomar's saddle. Her heart was warm with love for the man. Here was one man in Israel who kept his covenants, all of them, every one.

"Oh, he is fast, wife." Lappidoth shook his head and patted Shomar's neck. Devora stroked the other side of the horse's neck, marveling at the animal's beauty. She felt powerful muscles move beneath her hand when the horse turned its head to nuzzle her ear. Devora's eyes shone. Horses were rare in the land.

"He is fast enough," Lappidoth said, "but then, Barak's men have few horses. They will be on foot. So safety *will* matter more than speed. I will not have my wife falling from a fast, nervous horse who startles at an asp on some hillside far from my tent." The horse whickered, and Lappidoth caressed the animal's chin. "He is a good horse," he said slowly.

"There are three other nazarites still alive in Shiloh," Lappidoth added in a lower voice. "Will you take them with you, wife?"

Devora shook her head. "They'll be needed here. And Zadok rides with me. I am *kadosh*. Why should I fear to journey in the land of our People?"

Lappidoth looked troubled. "You are *kadosh*. Yet men lifted arms against you this morning. The Ark is *kadosh*. Yet men turned it on its side, trying to drag it from the Tent where we meet God. Eleazar was *kadosh*. Yet he lies dead."

Devora swallowed against a tightness in her throat at these grim reminders of the day's evil.

The men of the north had much to answer for.

"I do not trust the northern tribes," Lappidoth said.

"Nor do I. But they will have what they want. They will have the *navi*, to remind them God is with them as they cleanse the land."

"Wife," Lappidoth said, and the hard, urgent way he said the word made her focus on him.

"Take the men," he said. "Please. You are *kadosh*, and it has not been my way to command you or to govern you too firmly. But please take the men."

She hesitated a long moment, then shook her head.

"Shiloh is my home," she said softly. "Husband. Shiloh is my home. I can't leave it without its spears. Thank you—for worrying for me. No one will harm me while Zadok is with me. Even if they should wish to."

But Zadok's own brow was furrowed, as though he himself was uncertain of the merit of either accepting or refusing Lappidoth's plea. His eyes were pools of grief and guilt—a guilt Devora knew too well. The burden that settled, hot and tight, in your breast when you could not save those lives that were your responsibility.

Quietly Zadok dismounted and helped Devora bind Mishpat to her saddle.

After a long, searching stare at Zadok, Lappidoth gave his wife a brisk nod. Seeing this, Devora's heart went warm with gratitude—for a husband who could remain behind without it breaking his pride and his strength, and who could watch a younger man guard his wife without jealousy, and who could trust her when she said she would be all right.

"I know Zadok will keep you safe," Lappidoth said gruffly. "He is an able man."

"And you are a good man, my husband," she whispered. "You have my heart."

"Just bring Shomar back." He forced a smile. "I traded ten head of my cattle for him. I have never seen a finer horse."

He stepped back, and Devora tried to think of some further word of farewell, but words failed her. She just held his gaze, her eyes full of her heart. Zadok bent and lifted the Canaanite from the ground, careful not to touch her bare flesh, his face grim at the small cry of pain she made. He settled her into the saddle before Devora, then gave Shomar a pat on the gelding's rump and muttered, "Keep these women safe, horse."

Devora put her arm about the Canaanite's waist and held her tight, fearful the girl would panic and spook the horse. Hurriya's eyes were wide. "Shomar is my husband's," Devora whispered near her ear. "He will not let you fall."

The Canaanite gave a terse nod. "Don't leave me alone with him," she whispered.

"What? The horse?"

"That man." The girl was gazing at Zadok, wide-eyed.

"Peace, girl. Zadok won't harm you."

Though affronted for Zadok's sake, Devora was grateful to see the girl's fear. Fear was better than numbness, better than despair. It meant her heart was still beating, her blood still loud in her ears. That was perhaps the best Devora could hope for; she didn't want the girl to die on her along the way. And making sure she didn't would give the *navi* something to distract her from the vast lake of grief that lay dark beneath her feet, ready to swallow her.

"*Navi*," Zadok murmured. "Hannah sends a message."

She glanced down at his hard face. She was certain she could guess what the wife of Eleazar had in her heart.

"She says, *I call for judgment on Barak ben Abinoam, who killed my husband and the high priest of Israel.* She asks you to do this for her in memory of the day in the reeds. She says you have always protected her and those bound to her."

"That is true." She gazed to the north, thought of the shambling dead, and wondered if God had already prepared a bitter judgment over the men of the north, Barak and others. "Barak will atone for what his men have done," she said.

As Zadok remounted his own steed, Devora glanced back at Lappidoth, and the man looked wearier than she had ever seen him. "God be with you, Devora," he called to her.

"And with you, Lappidoth," she said.

She dug in her heels. *"Hai!"*

Shomar carried her over the uneven ground at something near a gallop, and the tents sprang away behind; then they were in the heather, Devora and her horse, riding around the edge of the camp. She glanced back once, her hair streaming across her face in the wind. Saw Lappidoth still standing by Hurriya's discarded bedding, one hand lifted. Gazing after her.

STRANGERS IN THE LAND

DEVORA, THE *NAVI* and judge of Israel, rode from
Shiloh with Hurriya before her and Zadok beside her.
They rode as though their horses had caught the scent of
God and were rushing to find him. Yet God was behind
them, not before, and the blasphemy of that torn veil had
perhaps ensured that God would not follow them into the
north. Devora spurred Shomar on, almost cruelly, her
insides so hot with rage that she saw nothing to the left or
to the right. She rode blind. Her only thought was to find
Barak ben Abinoam and demand of him a dire atonement
for the evil of this day. That he could have treated their
God—*el kadosh*, the weighty, the mighty, who could rise
over the land in fire and storm and scorch it to a desert
that would not bear seed for a thousand years, or who
could fall gentle as rain and urge wheat from the soil that
would grow at his touch taller than the height of a man—
that Barak could have approached this God, *this* God, and
treated him as a mere object to be acquired and moved
about. Did he think he was dealing with one of the

wooden not-gods of the Canaanites, a mute thing that you might carry in the palm of your hand? She hissed Barak's name as she rode, and the midmorning sun lifting over the land found her horse streaking through the fields, and Zadok on his own steed a spear's cast behind her, laboring to catch up.

***

Yet she could not keep that pace; it left Hurriya shaking and faint. Devora didn't know how much of that was her anguish and how much of it fear of being on horseback, but the sight of her pain cooled the *navi's* fury, and she slowed, consoling herself with the thought that Barak and his men were on foot.

So they trotted their horses northward through fields white for harvest. From time to time, Devora leaned to the side and let her fingers trail through the high wheat or plucked up some to chew as they went. This was the *land*, beloved of their mothers and fathers, and its beauty pulled at Devora's heart and abated her anger, almost brought her tears. The day was long and her wrath burned out, though no doubt it would flicker into fresh fire when she caught up with Barak at last. With the land of promise rich and fruitful about her, a kind of quiet awe settled over her. Each field and each hill about her was shaped delicately by the hands of God, each one with a name and a story. Here, the dead seemed only a tale told to frighten. An impossibility. Yet there in the north, where the hills were taller—they were there, somewhere. Hurriya's pale face was testimony to it.

Riding with Hurriya before her in the saddle and her arm about the girl's waist was a strange experience. With the exception of Lappidoth, Devora had never spent so many hours so near another person. This Canaanite girl in her arms neither spoke nor cried as Shomar carried them through the wheat; she simply rested limp against Devora's shoulder, taking shallow breaths. Sometimes she slept. Devora began to feel a strange protectiveness, riding with her like this. She could feel the warmth of Hurriya's body through her salmah.

***

They passed Cleft Hill on their left in the early afternoon and saw the tiny wooden houses of Rise Early clustered beneath the slope, with olive presses just outside the town and barley fields behind it. That had once been a walled town, one of the strongest of the Canaanite towns, but it had never really been rebuilt after the Hebrews had taken violent possession of it. Devora spared the cookfires one uneasy glance as they passed. Strangers in their land, so many in their land.

An hour or two later, Devora lifted her hand for a halt and brought Shomar to a stop by a wide pond north of Rise Early and let him drink. Zadok lifted the Canaanite from Shomar's back and laid her gently by the edge of the water beneath one of the leafy terebinth trees growing there. In their branches cicadas sang loud as thunder, recalling moments from Devora's girlhood in Shiloh, where a hundred such insects had roared in a line of terebinths outside the girls' tent.

Zadok walked a little way from where Hurriya rested. Then stopped and gazed, brooding, at the pool. Devora tended to her horse, patting down his flanks with her own shawl. Then she stroked Shomar's neck for a few moments and whispered soft words.

Devora glanced at Hurriya, who had her eyes closed. The *navi* smiled slightly, still warm from holding her. She supposed the girl was asleep. After a moment, Devora joined Zadok at the water's edge, and they walked along the bank for a while in silence. A kingfisher darted in and out of the water. She glanced to the north. From here the land rose steadily, climbing toward the Galilee and toward the snow-capped mountains of White Cedars in the north beyond. In the near distance, Devora could see the Hills of Teaching and of Cleansing towering over the land. There was smoke rising from the slope of Cleansing, but not enough for it to be a camp of armed men. Probably herdsmen. If they were nearer, they'd probably hear the bleating of goats.

The earth at the bank was soft here, nearly mud. "But no hoofprints," the *navi* murmured. "Nor feet. Barak and his men didn't stop here."

"I will finish looking," Zadok said quietly. "Go back and rest, *navi*."

She glanced at him—his face was tight with grief.

"You fought well," Devora said softly. "It is not your fault the high priest is dead."

Pain flashed across his eyes.

"My father died that night," he said.

Devora had no need to ask what *that night* meant. For her too it would always be *that night*.

"He died defending the Ark, and the levites, and the *navi*. I was seven. He threw me within his tent, commanded my mother to hold me there. I have never forgotten his face. I will not give to the fulfilling of my covenant less than my father gave to it."

Another silence. She did not break it; she knew the importance of silence when the heart is sore.

"I fought well," he said at last. "But the high priest is still dead."

He just looked out over the water. Devora felt stiff, as though she'd slept badly. She could not yet cry for Eleazar or the other dead in Shiloh.

She thought of pressing him, but it would do little good until he was ready to speak. After a moment she left him standing there in the reeds.

Returning to where the Canaanite lay in the damp grass beside the water, Devora saw with a sinking of her heart that Hurriya was weeping. The young woman was gazing up at the branches above her, her tears leaving pale streaks through the dirt and sweat on her face. Devora approached and knelt by her, very near but not touching, folding her hands in her lap. The girl looked only half-alive, lying there pale in her anguish amid the lush vegetation.

"Do you have any kin in the Galilee?" the *navi* asked softly.

"Leave me alone," Hurriya whispered. She was looking at the pond. "I want to die here. Here, where it is so beautiful. Where there's water. Please just leave me here."

The vulnerability in her voice tugged at Devora, and angered her. "I lost all my kin, girl," she said sharply. "Everyone I knew of as my tribe. All of them. Mother, father, the elders, the other children I'd known. In a single night, they were gone. You can't let yourself speak of dying. There are always other people who need you. Right now I do; you're my guide. There must be others in the north, kin who need you. Someone we can take you to."

Hurriya shook her head. Then whispered something Devora couldn't hear. The *navi* leaned closer, and Hurriya repeated: "Sister."

"A sister, yes. At Judges' Well?" Devora asked.

Hurriya was silent for a few heartbeats. "There was this olive tree," she said, her voice hoarse. She sounded not as though she were speaking to Devora but as though she were speaking to herself, aloud, because she needed to. "The tallest one. Anath would climb to the very top. I'd call up to her. Could never get her to come down. She said up there she could see the whole sky and the goddess's face." Hurriya stared at the water. "I want to tell her—I saw the whole sky too, and the goddess's face. In my little—" Her voice broke. "For only a few days. A few days." She sobbed.

Devora felt a flicker of unease at the mention of a deity not her own, a deity she couldn't trust, but the girl's sobs quashed her unease and took her whole attention, for though nearly silent, Hurriya's sobs seemed to shake her whole body and risk breaking her. It was clear the girl would never make it into the north like this, and Devora *did* have an obligation to her. The girl had come to her, and she was suffering.

With a sigh Devora took the Canaanite into her arms, wrapping the salmah tighter about her and then holding her. Hurriya was shaking; Devora held her pressed close with one arm, and with her other she tore off a bit of her dress and dipped the linen in the water beside them. The water was very cool.

Gently, and taking care not to brush Hurriya's face with her fingertips, Devora washed her face with the cloth, clearing away the grime of travel and grief. "There," she said softly when the left side of Hurriya's face was clean, "a woman can at least mourn in dignity."

Hurriya made no answer, and Devora finished, then rolled up the cloth and laid it gently in Hurriya's palm, in case she wanted it.

"Are you bleeding?" she asked, keeping her voice low so that the nazarite wouldn't hear. She could see Zadok out of the corner of her eye; he'd finished his circuit of the pool and was tending the horses.

"What do you care, Hebrew?"

"By the Covenant, girl, be civil. I am trying to help you."

"I don't want your help."

"Another ride and you may." Devora tried to dampen her frustration. "Let me tend you." There was no other woman here to do so, Hebrew or Canaanite, so Devora would have to care for the girl herself. Stranger or no.

Hurriya made no sign of assent or denial. Devora cast a quick glance about her, then called out, "Zadok, look away and do not approach, please."

The nazarite didn't turn toward them. "Your will, *navi*," he said. His voice cold with his own grief.

With great care, Devora unwrapped Hurriya's salmah. Keeping the cloth over her arms, Devora gripped her above the elbows and lowered her gently onto her salmah like a blanket. Seeing her body unclothed, Devora gasped. Her breasts were still swollen in a way that must have been torture. Dried blood on the girl's left thigh and leg, though not enough to endanger her. Gently Devora took the scrap of linen from the girl's hand where she'd clutched it loosely, wet it again in the pool, and slowly washed her thighs and her womanhood. Then she rose and walked grimly to Shomar, to her saddlebag, retrieving the spare waterskin.

Zadok was currying his own horse. "Is she well?"

"No woman's well who's just had a child," Devora said curtly, and walked back.

She knelt again beside the young woman, who was no longer crying but only gazing up at the branches. Devora recalled what she'd said about the olive tree and her sister. The protectiveness she'd felt for the girl earlier was fiercer now, and she wondered at it but had no time to think too much about it, for the girl's need was so great. She had forgotten for the moment that she was Hebrew and Hurriya was heathen. Or rather, it wasn't that she'd forgotten it—it was that the fact that Hurriya was a young woman grieving and in pain seemed so visible and immediate that the other fact paled before it like a torch in bright sunlight. Devora submersed the waterskin in the pool until it was full. Lifted the skin to the girl's lips. "Drink," she said. "Small swallows."

She watched as Hurriya drank slowly, and tilted the waterskin up for her until the young woman lifted her hands and grasped it. Devora let her have it.

"I forgot how far you'd walked," she murmured. "My mind was on—other things. I'm sorry."

Hurriya took a few last swallows, then lowered the skin to her side. Her eyes were a little more alert. "Why are you doing this? When you despise me."

A twinge of guilt. "I don't despise you, girl."

"You despise my people."

Devora paused. "You came before my olive tree. You are my responsibility, my care." Her tone was fierce and it surprised her.

Hurriya lay back. "I'm grateful for the water."

Devora nodded.

"My people—there are only remnants of us in the land." Hurriya closed her eyes. "And most Hebrews see us as labor, either in the fields or in their beds. You're different. You see us as a threat."

Devora hesitated a moment, a turmoil within her. She was trying to sort through her feelings for this strange girl.

"You Canaanites invite the rising of the dead," she said at last. "When the People came to the land and there were raids between our tribes and yours, you tossed your own dead into the water and left ours unburied." Her voice went low and intense. "The unburied dead cry out to God. They moan. Ceaselessly. They even rise from the earth and walk, seeking burial, feeding to sustain their walking until that burial is given to them."

"I have seen that," Hurriya whispered.

***

When they left the pond, the slow pace of their riding made Devora hiss in exasperation, but her own body was grateful for it. Already her thighs burned from chafing against the saddle, and the rolling gait of her husband's gelding promised her livid bruises later. The girl actually moaned for the first few minutes of their ride, then mercifully fell asleep, though the look of misery did not leave her face even in slumber. Devora yearned to pronounce some curse against Barak as dire as the one she'd given Nimri. She should not have had to chase after his army on horseback. She should not have had to take this girl with her as a guide—she could have left the girl dying at the edge of Shiloh camp and been done with her. Yet she knew she could never have done that.

As they rode, Devora began watching the rising hillsides, alert for moving figures. Already, she feared to catch some glimpse of an unsteady, lurching corpse. But there were none. Which only made her more anxious. They'd left the barley fields of Manasseh tribe behind and were climbing toward the high lakes of the north.

Hurriya snored softly as she slept against Devora's shoulder. She was still so pale, and her body so thin within her salmah, as though God had formed her not out of a man's rib but out of leaves and dry twigs.

She was so small, so vulnerable. At one point, the *navi*'s hand twitched with a powerful urge to stroke Hurriya's hair in comfort, and Devora reminded herself angrily that the girl was unclean.

Devora had never caressed another woman's hair, and it was some time before the memory came to her of her own mother caressing hers, and singing softly to her, when she was eleven. Before she'd bled and before the walking corpses had come to her mother's camp. Though it surprised her to realize it, this memory of her mother brought Devora no pain or fear, only warmth and well-being. It felt good, riding in the late summer heat with Hurriya in her arms and with the warm strength of Shomar beneath them, bearing them both. It felt good. Though her thighs and rear were sore, Devora found herself nearly dozing, lulled by the warmth of the girl she held and the smooth, rolling rhythm of the horse, and would startle awake after a few minutes of drowsy stupor. For a time, she forgot what they were riding to and what they were riding from.

Until she glanced back at Zadok and felt the darkness touch her heart again. The nazarite hadn't forgotten. His face was grim as a man's who'd just stood by while his brother died.

***

After a while, Hurriya woke. She seemed more alert. With each mile she looked about her more, her face drawn with pain but the worst of her anguish fading from her eyes as though each step Shomar took was erasing an earlier step. Erasing the long nightmare of her walk to the *navi*'s seat. As though her child and her pain had never been. As though all of that had happened in the dark dream country, not in her waking life. Yet she remained terribly pale. Devora made her drink often.

They came to the high country, and Zadok emerged from his brooding and began watching the tall grasses and the scree on the slopes. There were a few hours of light yet, as the days this time of year were long. Devora began asking Hurriya softly for advice on the way they should take, and to her pleased surprise the weary girl offered an occasional gesture or word of direction. They picked their way among well-traveled paths into the broken hills that hid from their eyes the Kinnor, the Harp-Shaped Sea. They passed the two peaks of the Hittim, skirting them on the east. Devora considered Hurriya's wan face and then glanced at the smoke that hung over the tiny settlement on one of the hills. They could stop, perhaps, and ask for herbs for the girl. Yet she was in haste, and there would be women with herbs following Barak's camp, she was certain. Uneasy, Devora pressed on.

Hurriya cast a glance at the settlement too, but without any expression of longing. Perhaps she simply didn't care.

The Kinnor Sea called to Devora's heart as they moved carefully along the cliffs that confined it on the west. Near the shore, the water was that shade of blue that water only gets when it is viciously cold, for the shadow of the hills lay over it. Innumerable white birds dipped and glided over the water, far below the women and the nazarite. Their voices came up to them in faint, shrill cries, like the voices of God's own host diving out of the sky to give battle. Even from this height, Devora could make out little houses clustered near the water and small boats on the surface.

"*Kinnor*, the harp," Devora whispered. "I have never seen this sea. It is beautiful."

"*Kenar*," Hurriya said.

Devora glanced at her. "What?"

"*Kenar*. The sea is *Kenar*. Not *Kinnor*."

She frowned. "Is that a Canaanite word?"

"It's Canaanite. Look." She gestured at the water. "My mother told me there are more fish in that water than there are men and women on the earth, and a god sleeps at the bottom of the sea, and his name is Kenar. The fish swim out of his dreams into the water, and because his dreams are deep and don't end, the fish will go on swimming up to the nets for all time, as long as the god stays asleep. The men who go out in the boats are careful to speak very quietly when they're on the water. They don't want to wake the god."

"A heathen story," Devora murmured. "There is no god actually under that water."

"Do you know that? Have you swum down there to look?" Hurriya's voice turned bitter. "You asked me to guide you. Yet you believe this is your water and your land, and me a stranger in it. And you don't believe what I tell you about it. How should I guide you, *navi*? You should have left me to die near my son."

Devora fell silent. Hurriya's words depressed her. They reminded her of how dependent she was on the Canaanite here, and how dependent the Canaanite was on her. She did *not* know this part of the land. Yet she needed to find in it five hundred living men and a great many dead ones. She looked down at the sea—*Kinnor*—and for a while she watched the water and the great white cranes swooping over it. Whatever the sea was called, it was breathtaking when seen from here, so near the sky. As pure and beautiful indeed as a harp's music.

When she did turn her head at last, she found Zadok riding beside her, and gave a start. The man's face was stricken with awe, his eyes moist though he shed no tears; he was staring at the sea. Devora looked away; it seemed indecent to witness such naked emotion on Zadok's face. She hadn't known the nazarite was capable of being moved at such beauty.

***

They climbed farther into the hills and left the cliffs of the sea behind. Following not the Tumbling Water in its deep ravine but a caravan road that wound up toward the heights. They found dusk falling over a land of dark and wooded ridges, cut sharp and beautiful against the sky. After pointing out the wagon track she thought would lead them toward Walls, Hurriya fell into a sleep that was deep and desperate, her head cradled against Devora's shoulder, her mouth open. As the last light faded, Devora tensed and became more alert, listening now for sounds she feared to hear—for they had reached the high Galilee.

They stopped to refill a few of their flasks with water at a small well where a few boys were tending sheep, Zadok asking questions of them. Hurriya opened her eyes long enough to take a look at the boys, then fell back into her sleep. Devora sat her horse near enough to the boys to see the terror etched into their faces, carved there like letters in stone. Their eyes wide. They had seen things, in these hills, recently. They shook their heads when Zadok asked about the dead, as though too afraid to remember. But they did let the nazarite know that many armed Hebrews had passed the well earlier that day.

Devora motioned Zadok to her side and whispered so as not to wake the girl. "We must try to ride at a trot."

"The horses need rest."

"*I* need rest," she said, her voice sharp with fatigue. "The horses can take us until moonrise, at least. At a faster walk, as long as this wagon track doesn't vanish."

Zadok watched her a moment with dark eyes, then nodded. He cast a glance at the boys, who were already beating their sheep away from the water and up toward the slopes. "They saw something, but ran before taking much of a look, I think." He frowned. "These Canaanites are like mice, always ducking behind a wall or into some hole."

"They are boys," Devora snapped. "And they were brave enough not to leave their flock behind."

Zadok gave her a puzzled look, and Devora turned away quickly, nudged her horse back onto the caravan road, one arm around Hurriya to keep from jostling her.

The *navi* had startled herself. Zadok was right: these *were* Canaanites. How strange that she found herself defending them.

HARDLY DARING
TO CLOSE HER EYES

THEY HAD RIDDEN only a little way beyond the well when the day's last faint light was eaten by the sharp ridges rising about them. When Devora tried to press on anyway, Zadok reached out and wound his fingers through Shomar's mane, his eyes dark against the darker night. "This has not been an easy Sabbath day in your husband's tent, *navi*. You cannot ride to confront Barak ben Abinoam or to face the dead, in the dark, so weary that you could lift no hand against them. And you might kill the girl trying."

She knew he was right. Yet the thought of delaying even an hour—

"The dead are out there, Zadok," she whispered. "In these hills. Maybe over that next ridge or behind that stand of trees." She rubbed her eyes with the back of her hand, but carefully, not wanting to stir Hurriya from her sleep. "We have to find Barak's camp. They're on foot, they can't be far. We can't stop."

The nazarite did not relinquish his hold on Shomar's mane, and the horse began to slow his walk. Devora gave Zadok a baleful look, but the nazarite's face was impassive.

"My covenant is to defend you," he said. "We will rest for the night."

"I should have left you in Shiloh," she muttered, yet she breathed easier. Somehow, with all this quiet, dark land about them and somewhere in it herds of moaning dead, knowing that Zadok was with her was a fierce comfort. Glancing around at those dark ridges against the sky, hearing the snap of branches in the wind, her pulse quickened and she admitted to herself the real reason she didn't want to stop.

She didn't want to close her eyes.

She didn't want to face the nightmares. Not out here, without a tent, without Lappidoth's arms to hold her and bind her to the present.

"That looks like a stand of terebinths," she whispered, nodding to the left. "We could take shelter there."

***

In a few moments they were setting up camp for the night in the lee of the terebinths, each tree ancient and creaking in the wind. Zadok chose a spot for a fire pit, then lifted Hurriya and laid her near it. Devora took Mishpat, a waterskin, a small bag of grains to eat, and the wool roll of her blanket and then turned Shomar loose to graze, trusting he'd come at her call. After watching the

Canaanite wrap her salmah tightly about her body, Devora sighed, took up her own blanket, and covered the girl with it. Hurriya's eyes watched hers a moment, but her face could not be read. Devora stepped away, resigning herself to a cold night. Her thighs and rear were sore from riding; she supposed Hurriya must be far more sore. She got the bag of grain; the girl would need to eat something, exhausted or not. Taking one of the waterskins, Devora poured a little over her arms and washed them, though she spared no water for her face. She could feel the dust of travel, a coating of it on her skin, and she yearned fiercely to wash it away, but water on a journey in the hot weeks before harvest was not to be wasted. She took the waterskin to Hurriya and let a little run out into her cupped hands. "Scrub up to the elbows, girl," she said, and Hurriya gave her a look but obeyed.

They ate in silence while Zadok cracked dry branches into kindling, dug a fire pit, and laid the wood within. His rough, powerful hands scooped up dry, fallen leaves, and he covered the wood with them. Hurriya hummed a little of her go-to-sleep tune, the one she'd sung on that Sabbath evening by her child's cairn. Then she fell silent, eating with her head lowered. Devora felt she should say something to the girl but didn't know what. So she chewed the grain slowly—too fatigued to put much energy even into eating—and waited for the fire.

She felt the dark close tight about her, pressing in on her heart. She glanced over her shoulder more than once. The wind-talk of the trees sounded ominous now, a portent of death. For a few moments the old primeval prey-fear of a fierce wind at night overtook her—the fear of being caught, helpless, and swept off the earth, or the fear that the wind would bring something predatory and godlike swooping down upon her as she shivered in the grass. Neither moon nor stars were visible, and the dark beneath the trees was like blindness. Like *hoshekh*, the dark that fills the mouth and nostrils and gets inside the heart until the spirit itself is cold.

She wanted light badly, but considered telling Zadok to stop making the fire. The cracking of branches had been so loud—though perhaps hidden in the cracking the wind was causing in the trees behind them. But the fire—the fire would be bright and visible for a long way. Raiders she didn't fear; they would not trouble Israel's *navi*, and she pitied the raiders who would choose Zadok for a foe. But the dead—what if there were dead near enough to see the fire?

Drawing in her breath, Devora beseeched God silently for a vision of the night to come. She heard wood rubbing quickly against wood and knew Zadok was making fire. Near her, Hurriya had lifted her eyes toward the trees too. For the briefest moment, Devora felt scorching heat on her right side, the side nearest Hurriya, but the heat did not pass into and through her as it usually did. No vision came. Devora sighed. At least that momentary heat was *something*. God had not forsaken her and her People entirely; he was still here, somewhere. She could still feel the touch of that *shekinah*, that desert-heat presence. It just wasn't *showing* her anything.

"There's something in the trees," Hurriya said.

Devora looked up quickly, peered beneath the trees. Glanced at Zadok, saw him setting his spear by his hip, ready to take it up at any sign of movement. For a while they all watched the dark.

But beneath the trees nothing moved, only the branches overhead. Zadok began rubbing the sticks together again.

"What did you see?" Devora asked the girl.

Hurriya just shook her head. "I'm sorry. I must've imagined it."

The fire roared up, and the nearer trees leapt into being. The shadows were dark and strange beyond the circle of light.

"The wind has you uneasy," Zadok said in that low rumble his voice made when he was tired. "Will you sing, *navi*?"

"What?" Devora didn't look at him, her eyes on the wood.

"Sing. There is no *kohen* here to sing to God and to remind the land and the trees and the night that they belong to God. Will you sing?"

Slowly, forcing herself to deepen her breathing, she turned to face him and the fire. On impulse, she decided to do as he asked. Anyone near—or anything near—would hear the song, but perhaps God would hear her better too.

> *Ashirah lahashem ki-ga'oh ga'ah*
> *Sus veroch'vo ramah vayam!*

Devora sang softly at first, then loudly, defiantly, the Hebrew words rolling one into the other and then galloping from her like horses riding across an open place, not to be halted or challenged, free and strong and fierce.

And you, God, you breathed on the face of the waters,
Made a dry passage and we passed through,
Water on our left,
Water on our right.

The stranger said, I will pursue the People,
I will overtake them and devour them,
I will divide up their herds among my men,
I will enjoy their women,
I will end them with a bloody hand.

And you, God, you breathed on the water,
The waves covered the stranger, the deep swallowed him up.

Devora let the words rise from her belly and her throat and her lips, out into the night, in a wailing, exuberant cry, the high, screaming song of a woman of a desert people.

Ashirah lahashem ki-ga'oh ga'ah
Sus veroch'vo ramah vayam!

When she fell silent at last, she lowered her eyes, not wanting to share the pain in them with the others. She had sung that song with Eleazar once, thirty years past when she was barely more than a girl and much of the repairing of Shiloh had fallen to her. She and Eleazar had sung that after the cairns were raised, tossing the words back and forth between them, even as their forebears had done on the lethal shore of the Red Sea. Devora pressed her fingers to her lips. The problem with aging was not that death was near, for death was always near. The problem with aging

151

was that a woman began to carry too many memories within her.

"That's what you sing when you're afraid?" Hurriya's voice sounded small and bitter. "You sing about your God killing my people?"

"No," Devora said wearily. "Not *your* people. It is the *Shirat ha'Yam*—the Song at the Sea. The first *navi* sang it. She and her brother the Lawgiver and their brother the first high priest sang those words on the day of Israel's deliverance from a foe who killed more of our People than the unclean dead ever did." She glanced at the Canaanite. "In Kemet, where we were made slaves."

"Now you are here," Hurriya said, "and you make my people *your* slaves."

"That is not how it's supposed to be." Weariness overwhelmed her. She realized her hands were shaking as if with extreme cold, and she held them between her thighs to keep them still. What was wrong with her? She felt as though she'd fallen off Shomar's back and was tumbling down a long slope. Too much had happened in the last few days. The infant. The raid on Shiloh. Eleazar's death. Too much.

"Zadok, keep watch, please," she said quietly.

"Your will, *navi*."

"Get some sleep, girl," Devora called across the fire. Then she lay down in her own bedding. She no longer cared what dreams might come. Sleep was suddenly its own necessity and its own end that justified any terrors it might hold. Devora tilted her head back and gazed at the sky. There were still no stars—she wished desperately that she could see stars. They would be a reminder of the promise that came with the keeping of the Covenant, the promise God had given their fathers in the desert.

Can you count the stars in the night sky?
Even so will your children and your children's children be beyond counting.

Those sharp points of cold light were a better defense against fear than the bronze points of a thousand spears. The unclean dead never looked to the sky. The dead had no promises, no Covenant. The People, though—they had the eternal promise that their seed would never die in the earth's dark soil, that they would grow and fill the land, planting after planting, harvest after harvest.

The stars would have been a comfort.

Reluctantly she lay down on her back, folded her hands over her breast, and closed her eyes. Reciting to herself the ten conditions of the Pact written into stone within the Ark, she shut out the crack and sway of terebinth boughs, the sound of the wind, the uneven earth and roots beneath her back, even the soreness of her thighs and rear from the day's riding. But she found she could not shut out the fear, so she caught it instead and put it in a little wooden box inside her mind and snapped that box shut and held it there in the dark. That is where you belong, she told the fear. If there was anything in the trees, Zadok could watch it. It was for her to sleep, to be rested when God or her People would need her. She slowed her breathing. Listened to her heartbeats. Recited the Ten again. *You shall have no other gods before me...You shall remember the Sabbath and keep it sacred...You shall not steal...You shall not bear false witness against another...*

***

Her eyes flew open. She could still hear the silence after her mother's shrieks and then the wet sounds of the dead feeding. Could still feel the cool clay pestle in her hand, clenched tightly because her palm was slick with sweat and she had to keep hold of it. Breathing hard, Devora struggled to reorient herself. She was lying on her side with a fire before her. Hurriya sat across the fire, her eyes reflecting back the flames. She was singing softly. That same go-to-sleep song Devora had heard her sing before. The melody tugged at Devora; there was something so wistful about it. Like a woman alone in a boat on a lake singing to another woman walking alone along the shore.

Somewhere to the left, Shomar whickered softly. Zadok was not at the fire; he was gone.

Devora wrapped her arms about herself and bit her lip to hold in a whimper. Anger flashed through her, a heat that didn't warm her. She could not suffer these dreams now. She could *not*. The People needed her.

"Did I cry out in my sleep?" Her tone was sharp, bitter.

Hurriya stopped singing and shook her head. Kept watching the fire. She had a strained look now that she wasn't singing, as though it was all she could do to hold back her pain from overwhelming her.

"Where is Zadok?" Devora asked.

"He heard something."

"What did he hear?"

"A deer. He said."

Devora looked to the trees. The wind had died down and the trees were no longer full of menace but only mournful. Because they trapped the dark and held it beneath their branches even as some men and women trap it in their hearts.

"A deer," Devora murmured.

She thought it unlikely that a deer would have drawn the nazarite from the fire. She shivered, glanced away from the trees, saw the girl watching her.

"He was alone with me," Hurriya said after a moment, her voice holding a faint hint of relief. "He didn't touch me."

"You are unclean," Devora said, irritated. "And Zadok does not take women unwilling. He's a nazarite; he'd hardly need to."

"That's what Hebrew men do," Hurriya said.

Devora felt a rush of anger at her and beneath it a touch of pity that she let the anger smother. This girl had endured things she had never heard of a woman enduring before. But she couldn't afford to think about that. Devora looked away from the girl and watched the fire, wondering where the nazarite was and whether indeed he had heard or sensed the dead moving in the thicket. She shivered, and when she glanced at last at the Canaanite, she saw that the girl was shivering too.

No, she was *shaking*.

Devora watched her with growing alarm; the girl's eyes stared just over the fire into the dark beyond it, and her eyes were those of someone staring at things God hidden before the making of the world and had never intended to be seen by living eyes. Devora rose and went to her side. The *navi* could feel heat rising from the girl as though she were sitting next to a fire blazing as high as the roof of a house. But after a moment the heat was gone, simply gone. Hurriya blinked, then her shaking subsided.

And suddenly Devora understood. She caught her breath.

"You *saw* something," Devora whispered. "Something that isn't here, not yet. And you did earlier too. When you saw something in the trees."

Hurriya glanced at the *navi* but seemed disoriented.

"Answer me, girl," Devora snapped. "Has this happened before?"

"Twice," she whispered. "Twice before this night. While I was with child."

Devora tried to take this in. It shouldn't be possible. Could the girl be imagining it? Yet Devora had felt the heat. She *knew* that heat. God had shown this girl things that usually only his eyes saw. Yet how could this be? She wasn't Hebrew.

"What did you see?"

"A man, Hebrew, I think. He was beating my sister." She began shaking. "I would rather die than see this. I wasn't dreaming."

"I know," Devora said quietly.

"Then I saw you. You were sitting beside a dead man. I don't know who he was. You got up to gather stones." Her eyes were vulnerable. "What does it mean?"

Devora took a breath. "It means you are chosen to be the next *navi* of Israel." Hardly believing her own words. "It means you see what God sees."

Hurriya laughed that cold, bitter laugh she had. "I've been touched by your God, you mean."

156

"Yes." Devora's voice sounded very small to her.

"I don't *know* your God."

For a moment only the fire was speaking.

There was strife in Devora's heart. This woman was *not* of the People.

"It seems *he* knows *you*," Devora said. "This is a very great burden, and a great gift. No veil between you and God. I have to think about this."

Devora got up quickly, paced out to the shadows beyond the firelight. She set her back to the nearest tree and just breathed evenly.

That Hurriya should be chosen, that was a sign.

But a sign of what?

That, revoking his promise, God had chosen another People? Or that the survival of the Covenant and the People depended on strangers? Or something else?

She glanced around the bole of the tree, saw Hurriya at the fire in her salmah. Thought again how inadequate a garment that was. A new and strange thought occurred to the *navi*—what if God had left the People unsheltered because they themselves had given no shelter?

Shelter the stranger in your land...

If Hurriya was the next *navi*, it was because God had something for her to say to the People, something only Hurriya could see, something only she could tell them. Something they must hear. Something about the strangers in their land.

The sickly sweet scent of death assailed her, making her belly heave. With a gasp, Devora turned her gaze away from the fire and gave a start, her heart pounding. A tall figure stood there in the dark, massive and looming over her. Its eyes glinting in the light of the fire.

It was not Zadok.

THE CORPSE

FOR SEVERAL HEARTBEATS Devora stood paralyzed, caught by the thing's eyes, which were empty and cold and only gave back firelight the way metal gives back a dull sheen. The corpse's sides moved in and out as it took quick breaths. Then it snarled, a sound that had nothing human in it, and lunged into her, knocking the breath from her, pinning her to the tree with its weight. Devora lifted her arm to shield her face and throat, felt the thing's neck pressed against the heavy wool of her sleeve. Its breath on her cheek, cold as the air over a frozen lake. The corpse leaned hard on her arm, its teeth snapping a mere breath from her throat; it had lurched right out of her night dreams and into her waking life, it had come for her, she'd always known it would. She found her breath and screamed shrilly. Turned her face to the side, fighting to hold it off with her arm, but the thing was *strong*. Another moment and it would be *feeding* on her—

A flash in the dark, and the corpse's head was severed half from its neck and fell limp against its left shoulder.

The thing's hissing went silent, but still its cold hands grasped at her. Wide-eyed, Devora saw Hurriya standing behind the corpse, naked, Mishpat lifted in her hands.

With a cry, Devora dropped to her knees and threw herself to the side in the dark, heard the corpse scrambling after her as she rolled. A cry from Hurriya, and as Devora rolled onto her back she caught a glimpse of the sword flashing again through the air, and then she was on her belly again and then had her hands and knees beneath her and was pushing herself up to her feet.

The corpse was impaled on Mishpat, the blade driven into its chest; its head hung limply behind its shoulder, and its hands were groping in the air. Hurriya was ducking them.

"The head," Devora gasped. "The head!"

Hurriya wrenched the sword free of the corpse's belly and began swinging it like a wood-axe, chopping the blade into their assailant's head, shoulders, and arms. Again and again. The body went down and she stood over it, lifting Mishpat high and sending the blade shrieking down through the air. Sobbing as she chopped into the body.

For a moment Devora looked on with horror. Then staggered toward her, panting. "It's done," she rasped. "It's done, girl!"

Hurriya didn't seem to hear her; she just kept lifting the blade and chopping. Her face wild with anguish. Bits of necrotic flesh flew through the air. Some of it spattered across her legs.

"God's Covenant, girl! Stop!" Devora cried, her eyes wide.

A sound of crashing through the trees to her left, and

she spun to face it. Hurriya did as well, lifting Mishpat, but then there was a man's cry from that direction: "*Devora!*"

For an instant Devora was startled—Zadok had never used her name before, nor had she permitted it—but relief overwhelmed the brief shock. "Zadok!" she cried.

The nazarite burst into sight, his spear in his hand and three waterskins looped over his shoulder. Taking in the scene at a glance, he cast spear and skins aside and swept Devora up in his powerful arms, startling her. In a moment he'd borne her to the fire and set her beside it. His eyes were hot with fury, but he said nothing. He ducked into the shadows of the trees, and in a moment he returned with spear and waterskins and Hurriya walking beside him, naked and shaking, her legs bespattered with bits of flesh and tissue. She carried Mishpat out to her side.

Devora got hurriedly to her feet. "Zadok, my waterskin—"

He tossed it to her. "*Why* did you leave the fire?"

"Why did *you*?" Devora cried.

Zadok looked at her a moment. "Stay here," he said firmly.

She nodded jerkily. His bronze spear clutched in one hand, the nazarite rose and hurried back into the shadows beneath the trees. Devora looked into the dark for a moment, shivering. Were there more out there, more dead?

But she had a problem here, near at hand, something she had to tend to. Something she *could* tend to.

"Sit," Devora said to Hurriya. "Quickly."

Hurriya lowered herself unsteadily, the firelight showing goose bumps along her arms and on the skin of her breasts, from the cold. She held Mishpat out to the *navi*, and Devora saw now that the girl had wrapped a small cloth about the hilt, so that her skin did not touch it. Devora would have been relieved, but she was too shaken with fear. Hurriya set the blade before Devora and removed the cloth. She did so slowly, as though reluctant to let the blade go.

Devora set the blade aside—it would have to be cleansed—and then poured out the entire waterskin over the girl's thighs and legs. Swept up some dry brush and began scrubbing her legs.

Hurriya gasped at the pain of it.

"Be still," Devora snapped. "You have bits of—of *it*— on you. Be still, girl."

Devora bent low over the girl and looked at her legs carefully in the firelight. Hissed through her teeth and brushed at a spot just above her knee. She glanced at the hair between the girl's thighs, then gave a closer look though her face burned. But nothing had spattered that high on her body.

When Devora was satisfied that none of the unclean flesh was left on the girl's body, she began brushing fiercely at the ground, pushing dirt and offal into a small pile that one might cover with two hands, if one dared to touch it. Devora straightened and turned toward Hurriya, still breathing fast.

"Never do that again," she snapped.

"It stopped moving," Hurriya breathed. "It stopped."

"Yes, it did."

"And it didn't bite you. Or me."

"It didn't." Devora's voice was sharp. She wanted no comfort or help from this heathen girl; now that she was sure the girl had no bits of the corpse still clinging to her, Devora wanted to be left alone, to hold herself in her own arms and shiver. She realized she was still on the edge of panic. A whimper of fear rose in her throat, and she held it back. She bit her lip, hard, tasted her own living blood. Began to breathe more calmly. The girl was right. The corpse hadn't bitten the *navi*, hadn't even touched her bare skin. She was all right.

"You don't know what I saw." The Canaanite stared into the fire. "Coming down from the hills. With my child. The things I saw. I couldn't watch another woman be eaten."

Devora knelt by her and sat back on her heels. She watched the firelight play across the younger woman's face. Then glanced over her shoulder at the dark under the trees. With a shudder, she wondered if she would ever again be able to sleep near trees.

"Thank you," she whispered, and glanced back at the girl. But Hurriya had lost consciousness.

Devora watched her a moment, saw again the leanness of Hurriya's body as she lay naked by the fire. Her breasts rising and falling with her breath. That ghastly pallor to her skin, almost as though she might be one of the dead herself. And now, great bruises forming on her thighs and the beginnings of sores where the saddle had rubbed her raw even through her salmah.

A terrible unease was growing in Devora, as though some beast had given birth in her heart, and its clawed pup was growing, scratching at the walls within her, feeding on all that Devora now saw. Many times Devora had suffered her nightmares and night terrors, seeing again her mother's face and the lurching dead in the camp. Often she had cursed the heathen in her heart, those who would cast the dead into open water, uncovered and unrestrained and utterly without burial, if the Hebrews who possessed the land permitted it. Devora hadn't forgotten the Canaanite cheekbones and eyes of the dead who'd fallen upon Shiloh camp thirty years before. When Canaanites were brought before her seat beneath the olive—which was rare, for cases involving them were easily dealt with, without the *navi's* intervention—but when they *were* brought to her, Devora had dealt her judgment harshly, knowing that only the strictest observance of the Law could keep the People safe. One Law for the Hebrew and for the stranger in the land, and a stoning and then burial beneath the stones if the violation of Law was so severe that no lesser cleansing would suffice.

Often, she had remembered the Canaanite features of the dead.

But never had she imagined having her life *preserved* by one of the heathen.

Hurriya shivered in her restless sleep. Devora crouched beside her, held her hand an inch above the girl's brow. Warmth. The beginning of a fever, perhaps. For a moment the panic rose again in Devora. What if it was the fever of the dead? But no, the girl did not have that look. This was a fever of the living body, some uncleanness that came of having a child and losing it and suffering after. At least so Devora hoped.

She rose shakily and walked about the fire. Took up Hurriya's salmah and brought it back to where she was lying. Draped it over her. Hurriya didn't move beneath it.

***

Devora set to the task of cleaning her sword, with as much care as she had cleaned Hurriya's body. She shuddered as she wiped the flesh and stains from the blade with a handful of grass. She did so meticulously, slowly, careful not to get any of it on herself. "I was right to bring you," she whispered to the blade. Her eyes round in the dark.

Glancing up, she caught a glimpse of movement beneath the trees and gasped. Her heart wild in her breast. She gripped Mishpat's hilt and was about to cry out, but then Zadok's enormous shape emerged from the darkness, and he stepped out into the firelight. He had on his goatskin gloves and was dragging the corpse behind him by its ankle, carrying his spear in his other hand. He gave Devora a grim look and cast the body down at the edge of the firelight. "I think it is the only one," he said.

"You think?" Devora whispered.

He set his spear aside. "I may be wrong. You and the girl must stay by the fire, *navi*."

Devora nodded. She was full of questions, but she glanced down at the corpse, and for the moment her questions choked in her throat.

Now that it wasn't moving, the corpse seemed indeed a pitiful thing. Its left shoulder and the left side of its face had been terribly hacked open by the sword. The rest of it—a husk and only a husk. As though God had sucked out the breath of life that he'd blown into the human body at the beginning of time and left behind something fragile as papyrus but upon which no letters Hebrew or other could ever be written again. In this leathery flesh that remained, no hopes or fears could be inscribed, and even if a man were to pull the unclean bones free from this withered corpse and chisel words into them as if into stone, even those bones would merely crumble away. Gazing at that corpse, Devora felt a horror of the brevity of life and the transience of all lives human and animal, which in the end are eaten or devoured whether by their dead or by some rogue lion or only by wind and soil. Whether God will remember them or not.

"Where were you?" she breathed.

"By the water," Zadok said. "There's a stream downhill, beyond the trees, barely close enough to hear a shout. I heard something in the trees while you slept, and I went that far looking for it." He paused, his regret showing in his eyes. "That was a mistake."

"It *was* a mistake," Devora said hoarsely.

Zadok was silent a moment. "I am used to doing this alone," he said. "When the levites send me out. When there is some corpse in a man's barley or feasting on his flock. Forgive me, *navi*."

"We are not hunting, Zadok." Devora couldn't keep the edge from her voice, and no longer wished to. So the man was grieving. So he felt he'd failed Eleazar. He still had responsibilities to *her*. "Not until we find Barak and his men. We need to *find* Barak. And you need to stay here and defend us until we do."

Zadok gazed into the fire, the lines of his face tense. "There were three sets of footprints by the stream."

Devora was silent a moment. Zadok's words doused her anger like ice water. "The dead?"

"They did not walk like living men." His gaze flicked down to the corpse. "We must hope the other two have walked on."

"Surely my scream would have brought them if they hadn't," Devora said uneasily.

Zadok shook his head. Then he crouched by the corpse. His gloved hands turned its head to one side, then the other. Devora gasped. The body was missing both of its ears. Indeed, now that it lay in the firelight she could see that the right side of its head had been torn open from where the ear should be to the middle of its hair, baring tissue and torn muscle and a white glint of bone.

"Ears are easy to tear away," Zadok muttered. "If one of these is feeding, it is likely to go for the throat or the cheek or the ears. Soft places where the teeth can dig in and tear. This one may have been in the trees all evening, *navi*. Yet it did not moan or approach our camp. It did not hear us." He gave her a grim look.

"So the others could still be in there." Devora peered into the dark beneath the trees.

Zadok didn't answer. His hands were shaking slightly.

"*Don't* freeze on me," Devora breathed.

"Your will, *navi*." The nazarite's voice was hoarse. Without lifting his gaze from the corpse, he pulled out his bronze knife and set the blade against his left palm. Drew it swiftly across his skin. For a moment he closed his hand around the blade. Devora looked on, disconcerted, as blood leaked between his fingers.

She rose to get a cloth, but Zadok shook his head. "Let it bleed a while," he muttered.

She watched him a moment. "This will keep you alert?"

He lifted his eyes to hers. Dark with pain.

She nodded, glanced at the corpse, then at the fire and the girl lying beneath her salmah near it. Trying to gather her thoughts. After a moment she realized Hurriya was awake and watching them. Her face still terribly pale, her eyes cold.

"Is the girl well?" Zadok asked hoarsely. He was gripping his sliced hand tightly with the other.

"Yes," Devora said.

"She must not panic. It's best if we stay quiet tonight."

Devora nodded.

"She took up your blade." Zadok's eyes shone in the firelight. "Brave girl. For a Canaanite."

Hurriya could probably hear their words, though they kept their voices low; she was only a spear's length away. But she did not appear to react to them. She was staring at the corpse.

"She hates them," Devora whispered. "She doesn't *fear* them anymore, not as I do. She just hates them."

"Hers are a strange people."

"Yes they are." Devora glanced back at the trees, peering into the *hoshekh* beneath the branches. Nothing there. Nothing that could be seen. She glanced down at the corpse's ravaged face. It was male, but she could tell little more about it. Neither what color its eyes had been nor its age. "I can't tell if he was Hebrew or heathen," Devora muttered. The uncertainty of it weighed on her. It seemed now vitally important to her to know who had unraveled the roots of the Covenant: the heathen in the north or the uncareful Hebrews. She gave the corpse's face another hard look, then her gaze strayed down its body, settled on its hips. She drew in a quick breath as a solution to her uncertainty occurred to her.

Devora averted her eyes quickly, her face warming. Found herself facing Hurriya, whose eyes seemed to read hers. The Canaanite woman got unsteadily to her knees, one hand clutching the salmah tightly about her. Hollows about her eyes—the day and the night were exacting a fierce toll on her body.

Hurriya crawled near, then bent over the corpse, swiftly tugging its clothing aside. Devora couldn't look. She fought a surge of nausea at what Hurriya was doing, at her closeness to the dead. But the girl was already unclean; it would make no difference.

"He was Hebrew," Hurriya rasped.

Devora said nothing. Zadok watched the Canaanite with that quiet wariness of his.

"You Hebrews mark your bodies," Hurriya said coldly. "A Canaanite woman always knows what kind of man has assaulted her."

Without another word, Hurriya rose and returned to her place across the fire, keeping her salmah wrapped tight about her.

Devora looked after her a moment, thoughts leaping through her, quick as a flight of deer through a wood. She exchanged a look with Zadok, then went to Hurriya. The girl lay shivering. Devora knelt by her, trying to think through what the girl had said. There had been signs enough for her to interpret, but she had to step carefully. She watched the girl's face.

"The child's father. Malachi ben Aharon. You were his slave?"

Hurriya didn't answer.

"He bought you and was cruel to you?"

The Canaanite just stared at the fire.

Devora waited for a while. She heard Zadok digging, for there was a body to bury. The *navi* was just about to give up and try sleeping again when the girl spoke.

"My father couldn't feed the three of us—my mother, my sister, and me. So he sold me to one of the other workers in the olive grove. A Hebrew, who could afford me. He sold me because I was old enough to be—desirable. When that man—" Her voice broke, but she recovered quickly, and Devora felt chilled at the anguish she heard. "When he touched me, I thought I'd die. The way he hurt me—he *liked* to hurt me."

Not knowing what other comfort to give, Devora reached out and gripped Hurriya's shoulder through the salmah. Her breast felt tight. Nothing of which Hurriya spoke was against the Law. None of it was a breaking of the Covenant. But the fear and hate she saw in the girl's eyes—no woman should have to endure that. It was women who gave the Covenant to their children, who bore in their wombs the living sign of the promise. With God, together they made the future of the People. What had happened to Hurriya was not against any words of the Law, but surely it could destroy the Law and the Covenant all the same.

"I tried to hide from him once," Hurriya whispered. "He beat me until I couldn't rise from his bedding for three days. And little Anath had to hear it. Every one of my screams. Malachi only lived a stone's throw from my father's shed. They worked the same presses. When I took water out to him at midday, I would look up and see Anath in the treetops." She fell silent.

"I have erred," Devora whispered. "You have no kin to return to. None who will keep you. I should've found another guide. Yet the things you see—" She thought for a moment, her heart aching. "You must return to Shiloh with me—after this. You must be near, where I can teach you."

Hurriya shook her head. "I'm not going back there." She paused. "I don't care about these visions," she added after a moment. "Or your God. But help me find Anath." She swallowed. "And the dead. If you want to help me, tell me everything you know about the dead. You have so many rules about the dead. So teach me."

"Girl—"

"I am no *girl*. I am Hurriya of Judges' Well. I have lost my child. Those corpses—they *took* my child. My *child*. I have one sister, and that is all I have. I will find her, I will help her stay safe." She was speaking rapidly now, trembling with urgency. "We are going to a camp of armed men. When—when I am *clean*—" She mouthed the word with distaste, "help me find clothes. And a knife. And my sister. That is what I ask of Israel's *navi*."

"I will see that you have clothes. And we will have to find herbs for your fever. If I teach you about the dead," Devora added after a moment, "I must teach you the whole Law. And you must abide by it."

"Your Law." Hurriya laughed coldly, bitterly. "Always your Law, your strange and terrible Law. You would cast a woman from the tents because a corpse touched her, or stone a woman for placing a bowl of fruit before the goddess."

"If necessary, yes," Devora said hoarsely. "The People must be kept clean."

Hurriya turned her face away, shivering in her salmah. "Teach me, then. I don't care."

171

Devora's temper flared. "You *do* care, you impossible heathen!" she hissed through her teeth. "*Damn* you. Filthy, unwashed—you think your gods and the corpses of your dead are both things to keep in your houses! You bring the dead down on us, bring the blight and the curse and barrenness to the land—and then you lie down ready to die and you don't care! You *do* care, damn you!"

"It was a *Hebrew* corpse in the terebinths," the girl whispered without turning her head. "And a 'heathen' who saved you. Now I am so cold—please. Let me be. Please."

The bitterness had left her voice, only weariness now. Her tone doused Devora's temper. The girl was feverish and suffering. Of course she didn't care at times; she hurt too much to care.

Devora sighed. She had a double obligation to this strange girl—as a supplicant and as the next *navi*, who must learn from her. She reached for the girl's waterskin where it lay discarded by the fire pit and held it to Hurriya's lips. "Drink. As much as you can, before you sleep. We have to cool that fever."

Hurriya didn't open her eyes, but her throat moved as she swallowed. Devora tilted the waterskin, and to her relief the Canaanite drank deeply. "We'll talk after we've slept," Devora said, then lowered the waterskin and left it by Hurriya's hand.

A clack of stone behind her, and Devora turned to see Zadok piling rock upon the pit he'd dug in the earth. The body was out of sight, already in the ground. She breathed a sigh of relief. The corpse had unnerved her. More than that, it had ripped loose the already fragile latches on her memory. A glance at Hurriya showed that the girl had already fled back into sleep.

Devora too lay down in her bedding; she was shaking again. She could feel the cold of that corpse's flesh through her sleeves, where it had seized her. She kept her eyes open. All too clearly, she could imagine other dead stumbling out of those trees while she slept, waking her with their low moans only moments before they grasped her and—

She held herself tightly, turned her back to the trees with an effort, and faced Zadok, who was crouching across the fire from her, making a triangle between the three of them. The back of her neck twitched; she couldn't stop thinking about what might creep out of the dark behind her. With that vast, menacing *hoshekh* behind her, the fire was little comfort. She glanced at Zadok's eyes, saw them reflecting back the fire, tried to summon up her anger at him for leaving their fire. But her anger was like damp kindling that wouldn't light; the fear was too great.

After a moment, Zadok lifted his gaze toward the sky, and she followed with hers. Drew in a deep breath, let it out slowly. The wind had died and the clouds were drifting apart; there was a great fissure in the sky, like a ravine cut into the darkness, and in it shone bright stars. Devora found herself calming.

"Bless you, Zadok," she murmured. He must have seen her glancing often at the sky earlier. Must have known what she was hoping to see.

She willed her body to relax.

Closed her eyes.

Immediately she saw her mother's face. Vivid as though her mother were crouching beside her, teeth bared.

Devora's eyes flew open. She clenched her hands tightly around her arms, breathed deep for another moment. If she couldn't banish that memory from her mind, sleep would be out of the question. She would end up weeping through the night.

She watched the stars a few moments.

At last she sat up. Put her back to the fire and reached for Mishpat. She laid the blade naked across her thighs and looked into the dark beneath the trees.

"How many dead do you think are out there, Zadok?"

"Too many."

A stick cracked in the fire.

"Yes," Devora said. "Too many." She shivered, gazing out at the dark. She didn't turn to look at the nazarite. Instead, she watched how firelight and shadow played across the rough stones of the cairn.

It had been long since she'd slept without Lappidoth's arms about her, yet now she was here, alone, without him. Desperately she thought of him, wondered where he was. Was he sleeping that deep sleep of his, or was he standing, perhaps outside his tent, gazing up at the same stars in the same sky, praying for his wife? Devora yearned suddenly for the warmth of his body against her back and for the smell of him. Lappidoth smelled of cattle and wind and heather and wild barley, for he would run his hands through the barley that grew wild in the pasture as he walked toward his herds.

The cold panic was rising in her again. During the day she was in control, she could cut through her fear like her own iron blade. But now, after dark, after seeing that corpse—she needed some way to survive until dawn. With that cairn so near, and the darkness beneath the trees, and no tent over her, no arms about her—she couldn't do this.

She breathed faster. Then an idea occurred to her that was comforting, but it gave her a pang of guilt, too. She didn't know how to ask for it without it seeming like—

She wrestled with it.

"Will you lie beside me, Zadok?" she whispered finally.

She heard him stir slightly.

"To hold me, while I sleep?" Her shoulders alone betrayed her tension. "I know we will both have evil dreams tonight. Yet I would like very much to sleep, if I can." She swallowed. "And not wake screaming."

She felt terribly vulnerable, even naked, asking for this. It meant setting aside her dignity as the *navi*, it meant—too many things. It should be Lappidoth here. She should be asking him.

Yet Zadok had always had her entire trust.

She felt the nazarite settle beside her, sitting by her. A powerful, large presence. She didn't look at him.

"You miss him," his voice rumbled in the dark.

She didn't have to ask who he meant. "Yes." Her throat tightened. "I wish he were here." If he *were*, if Lappidoth *were* here to hold her, he only and no one else, she could let herself cry. She could let herself shake apart in terror, until the fear had passed over her like the angel of death, knowing that he would still be there holding her, without judgment, while she put herself back together again.

"It is a strange thing I ask," Devora whispered, burning with anger at herself for showing the nazarite how vulnerable she felt. "You can refuse."

"I don't." His voice softened.

Devora nodded wearily and lay down, and after a moment Zadok lay behind her, his beard scratchy against her neck. His arms closed about her, warm and strong. She shivered.

"Thank you," she whispered.

He squeezed her gently.

"Don't fall asleep."

"I won't, *navi*."

She lay still in his arms a while, willing sleep to come. The Canaanite had begun to snore softly. Devora could hear from Zadok's breathing that he was still awake, and a calm settled over her. He would watch. It was all right. And if she woke, his arms would hold her to the present, as her husband's did. His arms were strange, more muscled than her husband's. She felt another twinge of guilt, yet it was strangely pleasant being held in them. There was so much of his father in Zadok, so much of Zefanyah. She felt his breath on her shoulder and found her heart beating a little faster.

"Zadok," she whispered.

"Navi."

She paused. "In the trees, you called out my name. My name. Not *navi*."

He tensed a little.

"You called *Devora*. As though my name belonged on your lips." Lying in his arms, she was suddenly alarmed at the intimacies the two of them had taken that night.

"I was frightened for you, *navi*," he said. "I intended no insult to you."

"Don't do it again," she said quietly.

"Your will, *navi*." He sounded weary.

She didn't say anything more. She watched the darkness under the trees warily. She wondered if Zadok *cared* for her. In that way. She'd felt for a moment that she could sense it in his breathing as he held her. And he'd called her name, her own name, freely, even as a husband might call out his wife's name. He'd never done that before. She wondered how she felt about it if he *did* feel that. It had been a long time since she was a girl, and pursued. She was not one now.

And she needed Zadok to be *Zadok*, the Zadok she knew, the man who stood with his spear behind her seat beneath the olive tree. A man she could trust to perform any task without flinching, whether the task was to spear an infant corpse or hold her while she slept. He had always been reliable, as few men were. What if there were passions, longings, in his heart that she did not know? What if, in the uncertain north, he was to become strange to her as well? If she could not trust Zadok—if she could not trust even herself, even her own heart—what was there left in the land that she *could* trust? What stood between her and the moaning in the dark?

She clung to his arm with her own small hands and closed her eyes, forced herself to breathe evenly. Whispered a few words of the *mitzvot* to calm herself—

If a living man touch any unclean thing, a corpse, or the carcass of an unclean beast, or the body of any creeping thing, then he too is unclean.

She thought of the Law stretched like a great tent over the People to keep them safe. She felt Zadok's chest against her back, strong and sure. Felt his breathing. He was still awake, still watching. One by one, Devora doused the fires of the busy camp her thoughts had made in her mind. She could not allow her thoughts to dance madly in the firelight, like the shadows dancing on the cairn. Right now she needed sleep and someone to watch over her during the hours she was defenseless. That was all that mattered. The rest must wait. She breathed slower.

Though she barely remembered it, there had been a time when she had not recited the Law before sleeping. A time when she'd had no nightmares to ward off. A time when she had been young, had not been the *navi*.

Part 2
Shiloh, Years Past

THE GIRL WEEPING

THE FIRST TIME Devora ever glimpsed a thing that did not yet exist, she was twelve years old and only recently a woman. The vision came to her the day before her mother's death. It was just after dawn and there was frost on the heather, one of the last frosts of the year. Devora was carrying a ewer down to the stream outside her parents' camp to fill with water, humming to herself. The frost made little noise beneath her feet, for she'd wound heavy cloth around her sandals to keep her feet warm, and this muffled the sound. Her mind was on the changes and the soreness in her body and the prospect of being permitted to go to the Feast of Tents for the first time later that year. She broke into a run for the sheer joy of it, just to feel the wind in her hair. This was a pure kind of joy, a kind she would rarely experience again.

Without warning, heat blazed within her as though she'd leapt from the frost right into the smoke above a fire pit. She gasped for air and stopped, almost falling to her knees. Even as she did, she glimpsed across the stream, startling her, a young woman who looked identical to her. A woman who had her face. She was running through the grasses, weeping. Devora held her breath and would have called out, but in a moment the other woman was gone. Just gone.

WHAT GOD'S EYES SEE

THE SECOND TIME, Devora was fifteen, and the vision came to her only moments after her first kiss.

At that time, Devora lived in the girls' tent in Shiloh, a vast, four-sided pavilion shielded on one side by a wall of tall terebinth trees, like a green veil between the girls and the tents of the priests. At first Devora resided there as a ward of Naomi's, a waif who had wandered to Shiloh out of the hills, crying incoherently about the dead. The old *navi* Naomi had listened to her and sent the nazarites out to find the camp from which Devora had fled. Several of them returned to Shiloh days later, their faces grim, the wooden staves they carried darkened with fresh stains. Devora had watched them enter the camp, wide-eyed, and then had hidden beneath her blankets in the girls' tent until her trembling stopped.

The other girls had resented her. She was not one of them. No father had brought her to Shiloh to give her to God along with bushels of wheat or a young, unblemished bull. She had no father at all, and no priest had spoken for her, asking for a betrothal, as had already happened with many of the other dedicates. Devora was a stranger in the girls' tent. And she often woke them, screaming, from her dreams. The other girls tormented her, and Devora in her misery struck upon an unusual solution. In the middle of one night she got up and knelt in the middle of the great pavilion and pressed her face to the earth and cried out, waking the others:

Ata adonai, whose hands made earth and sky,
Who breathed life,
I bring you a gift,
a small gift,
the only gift I have.
I give to your service and your use,
this girl Devora of Ephraim tribe,
this girl is yours,
consecrated to you,
kadosh, kadosh,
she serves you.

Hannah, the oldest of the girls, gave an indignant cry when Devora finished and lifted her face. "You can't dedicate *yourself!*"

"I just did," Devora said quietly, and she faced the other girl with a new boldness in her eyes. "No less than you or the nazarites or the *navi.* I am God's."

***

Devora had begun running through the grasses that morning of her mother's death, and though she now lived in a permanent camp, she hadn't stopped running. In those first summers in Shiloh, Devora fought to banish from her memory the death of her mother and the growling of the dead in that camp. Her memory seemed to her a badly woven basket; things obviously were capable of leaking through gaps left in the weave, for she'd forgotten things before. So she packed her mind with the six hundred *mitzvot* the way a farmer packs a basket with grain, leaving no unused space, hoping that the more she filled her mind with the Law and the traditions that kept the People safe, the less space there would be for the terrors of the past.

In the ferocity of her study and her flight from memory, Devora knew she seemed grim for a young woman. The one joy of girlhood that remained to her was to watch the young nazarites on the fighting ground each morning, admiring the way the sun had bronzed their powerful arms, noting the sheen of sweat on their bodies as they danced the spears. Young Devora had a favorite among the nazarites, a man who bested most who came against him. In his strength and certainty, he reminded Devora of the nameless herdsman who had defended his cattle from the dead, that man who appeared often in her dreams.

The nazarite had a birthmark on his shoulder in the shape of a spearhead, and the other young men teased him over it. Devora was drawn to him for that. He was not godlike and unreachable; he was like her. He too was nettled by his peers. Devora admired him with a fierceness in her heart for the way he responded. For the nazarite would clap his brother on the shoulder and laugh. "We will be fighting on some high slope and God will look down out of his wide sky and see us all sweating in the heat, and he will be looking for some man to bless that day. His eyes will notice my shoulder. And God will say, *There is my servant Zefanyah, I will bless him.* The rest of you will all have to find other ways to attract God's attention."

***

To Devora's delight and embarrassment, her nazarite took to watching her in the evenings. He would stand within earshot of the tables where Eleazar the high priest taught the six hundred *mitzvot* of the Law, one table for the sons of priests and one for the dedicates who might become their wives and thus must know more of the Law than the wives of herders or tanners or caravan merchants. Devora would flush when she felt the nazarite's gaze, and one evening, for the first time, she failed to answer one of Eleazar's inquiries correctly. The high priest gave her a prolonged stare, then grunted and moved on to ask a question of the other table, without any reprimand beyond that small, noncommittal noise. But Devora's face burned as though God had placed a sun in front of her. And the other girls whispered quietly about it, which made her burn even more.

That night, Devora stayed behind, feeling an embarrassed need to apologize to Eleazar. The apology only made him cross.

"Get some rest, Devora. You're only, after all, a woman," he muttered, waving a hand dismissively.

Devora's eyes darkened at the comment. It was viciously unfair—she had a better memory than any of those who sat at the boys' table—but she didn't have a response that wouldn't earn her a beating or a week of chores about the camp, so she turned on her heel and stalked away through the tents, thinking dark thoughts about God's appointed high priest.

She had just reached the shadows of the terebinths in their line behind the girls' tent when she felt a strong arm about her waist. The soft laugh behind her, a laugh she recognized, stilled a momentary panic. In a moment she was pulled up against a firm, male body, her heart wild within her. She had just time to glimpse his face and gasp before the nazarite covered her lips with his, and the shock of the kiss rushed through her like fire and flood. A weakness came over her that was almost like drowsiness, but beneath it there was a thrill and a heat tightening up deep within her. She yielded willingly to the kiss, so many feelings rushing into her and through her, like cattle stampeding through a grove, the force of their passage tugging the leaves from the lower branches and sending them whirling about. After a few moments she found herself gazing up at his face, her lips still parted. Hardly enough air.

He smiled.

"You *are* pretty," he murmured. "Sleep well tonight." He cupped her cheek in his warm hand, and she just stared up at his face, blushing, because it was unlike her to have nothing to say. Then he kissed her again and she made a small, soft sound as he did, overwhelmed by the taste and scent of him and the strong, uncompromising way he held her. Then he released her, brushed the tip of her nose with his lips, and moved away through the dusk beneath the terebinths, leaving her standing alone, shaking a little. The cicadas were louder than anything she'd ever heard, and she could see every shadow and every patch of dim light beneath the trees cut as sharp as though the world had been made only moments before. She lifted her fingertips to her lips. Her body still felt warm and weak. This wasn't *anything* like how Hannah had described kissing in her stories in the moon tent.

It occurred to Devora as she stood beneath the terebinths that if this nazarite asked for her, she would be his second wife. She knew he had a wife whom he went to visit each Sabbath, an afternoon's walk from here at the encampment of Beth El. A woman of Manasseh tribe that Zefanyah's father had bought for him after his mitzvah. He might even have children; Devora wasn't sure. She would have to find out; surely the woman would come to Shiloh soon for the Feast of Tents. She felt a little unease, but she had never expected to have a husband. No man in the camp had spoken for her before, and she had no father to provide a dowry. This kiss was new—and unexpected.

She wondered if she *was* pretty.

Even as all of these new joys and anxieties rushed through her like wine and water, Devora lifted her eyes and saw the *navi* walking between the tents with two other women of the camp. A heat rushed through her that was nothing at all like the warmth she'd felt deep in her belly when Zefanyah had held her and pressed his lips to hers.

This heat scorched her and dried her out and left her pale and faint. Then the vision came, and the shock of it was too great. After a moment she slid to the ground, fainting.

***

A touch on Devora's shoulder woke her, and she came to with a cry of panic. Old Naomi was seated beside her, her brown face wrinkled and furrowed like a freshly plowed field.

"Calm yourself, girl," Naomi said. Her voice was firm and had a hard edge to it, though it wasn't unkind.

The *navi* touched Devora's brow, and her hand was dry.

Above her, the cicadas seemed loud as thunder.

Devora drew in great swallows of air.

"Why did you faint?"

"I grew dizzy," Devora said. "And afterward I fell."

"Your flesh was hot as coals when I reached your side. But now you are cool. There's no fever."

Devora moistened her lips with her tongue, for they felt so dry they must crack.

"You saw something, girl."

She hesitated, then nodded.

Naomi watched her a moment, her eyes hard and unrevealing. At last she made a small noise of assent. "Do you know what it is like to be the *navi*?" she asked.

Devora shook her head.

"God terrifies us all. The *kohannim* do not dare to take off their sandals and step onto the holy ground within the

Tent unless they've first washed for seven days." Naomi gave a wry smile. "I wish men in the land might do that before entering into their own tents to lie with their wives. They would smell better. But there, God scares them more than women do." Naomi looked toward the Tent of Meeting, and her eyes hardened. "Yet they do fear *me*. Did you know that, child?"

Devora nodded.

"God sends visions to my own eyes and does not care whether I wash first. In fact, I do not kneel or ask for him to show himself, he simply does. His *shekinah*, his presence, falls on me like wind and fire and nearly scorches me to the ground. A heat almost too fierce to bear. You know what I'm talking about, girl?"

"Yes," Devora whispered, frightened.

Naomi's gaze pierced her.

"What did you see, child? Before you fell?"

Devora shook her head vigorously, and Naomi's eyes narrowed. "You have pluck, girl. Not many people try to hide something from God's *navi*." She lifted a few strands of Devora's hair between her fingers, looking at them as though she might find in them the answer to her questions. That wry smile again. "Very well. You and God may keep your secret, for now. But listen to me, child. I want to know whenever you have one of these dizzy spells. I need to hear about it. And I think you will come visit me in the mornings. We are going to have a lot to talk about, you and I."

The thought of approaching the old *navi*'s tent, alone, to be questioned by her—that would have filled Devora with dread, if the old woman's words had not already given her more dread than she could carry. Naomi helped the younger woman to her feet, and for a moment Devora clung to her, feeling unsteady. The fear of what all this might portend, what it *must* portend, gripped her.

"Please," she cried. "What does it mean? Why am I seeing these things?"

"It means you are the next *navi*," Naomi said quietly. "It means you are seeing what God's eyes see."

CARRYING THE DEAD

THE NEXT AFTERNOON changed everything.

It was Devora's turn at the washing. As she left the white tents to make her way upstream, she hauled a washing board under one arm and carried a basket of heavy, soiled cloth on her shoulder. The sun was late-summer hot, baking away what strength she had, and she moved beneath it in a daze. In the sky behind her, cloud was piling upon cloud, promising thunder.

Doing the washing meant a long walk. The women of Shiloh kept the Covenant and were careful not to soil the stream that ran through Shiloh before rushing east past many camps of the People on its way to the Tumbling Water. Instead, the women took the clothes to small, isolated pools that formed in the mud near the stream. In the early dawn the water in these wash holes was cool and clear, but a little splashing of clothing in them and they became brown and more soiled than the tunics and robes a woman hoped to wash. So as the day aged, the women had to move farther up the stream to find new wash holes, often walking far from the camp. Once the clothes were laid out to dry, there was a brief respite. A woman could lie out on the grass and watch the thunderclouds build on the horizon or stare for an hour at a small beetle clinging to a reed. Or, if she was far enough from the sight of the tents—and if she dared—she might strip away her own tunic and leap into the cold river with a shock like being born. There, swimming between sand and sky, a woman could feel, if just for a little while, completely free and clean.

Today Devora had to walk far; as her feet squelched in the river mud and the tents of the encampment fell far behind, she could see through a haze of green reeds Hannah and Mikal, the women of the shift before her. They were bathing. Devora hoped to find a clean wash hole after passing them. She tried to hasten, but the weight of the basket on her shoulder made her grunt, and twice she slid in the mud, catching herself on a splayed hand but splattering her face and breasts with mud. By the time she reached the bathers, she was livid and in an ill mood. She cast them a glowering look that neither of them noticed. They were enjoying the river and had no room in their minds for anything but the fresh, cool water. Hannah was leaping and diving as though she were part fish.

It was the upcoming Feast of Tents, not only the cool water, that had them in such a good mood. Some of the girls were already considering who they hoped to dance for; a few had even begun quietly sewing decorative patterns into their dresses: flowers, or shapes of people crossing a desert (for the Feast commemorated the time in the desert), or trees.

Now even Hannah called out to Devora cheerfully.

"Come swim with us, Devora! The clothes can wait!"

For a moment she hesitated. The thought of joining them and letting the water wash the dirt and mud from her skin and the terrors from her mind—it was an attractive thought.

But she turned away from them, shouting back, "I will keep to my work, thank you. You can play like fish if you like."

She heard the groans and boos of the girls in the river, but ignored them and moved on through the river mud. She couldn't bear the thought of being among other women just now. Naomi's words resounded in her mind like drumbeats: *The next navi…you are the next navi…you are seeing what God's eyes see.*

Devora had spent the early morning in the old *navi*'s tent, in what Naomi promised would be the first of many talks between them. The old woman had questioned her keenly about the visitations she'd had from the *shekinah*, and Devora had found herself telling the *navi* of her first vision—the one that had come to her when she was twelve. The words had flowed from her like water and blood, until she was nearly sobbing with them. She told of her mother's death and of how she had seen herself grieving—how she had been *warned*—and had said nothing to the elders in the camp.

"They would've thought I was dreaming. That I'd fallen asleep when I should have been bringing water to the camp." Devora's eyes burned with tears. "I didn't want to be beaten. And they're all dead. Because of me. *Because of me.*"

Naomi had listened in silence, her sharp eyes peering deep into the girl, then sighed. "Don't be foolish, girl," she said. "You didn't know better. You do what you must, you trust the rest to God. Some days, a woman can only save one life. That day, it was your own life. Some day yet to come, it may be another's." And Naomi clapped her hands, and a slave came in with hot tea.

But when Naomi sent the younger woman from her tent at last, Devora felt little comfort. She believed old Naomi—she was the *navi*. God was sending her visions. The enormity of it was unbearable. Because she'd said nothing. She'd seen and said nothing. She searched her memory. The fear she'd felt then, of being beaten by the elders for telling lies—that seemed another girl's fear and not her own. She could remember the fact of it, but not what it had felt like. Now as she stumbled on through the mud with her washing board and her basket, Devora burned with anger at herself. The girl she'd been—that girl had been too afraid to do what was necessary to keep her people safe. Devora could never forgive her for that.

She came to a waterhole, one where the water was clean and the laughing of the girls was distant, and she let the basket down with a groan. She cast a glance back at the girls bathing. It must be nice to be Hannah or Mikal. To have never seen the dead. To have never truly suffered or feared. To worry only about whether they would be a man's first or second wife and whether that man would be young or old, handsome or foul. Devora's own hopes of the night before, and the way she'd been flustered at that kiss, all seemed so foolish to her now. Bitterness gnawed at her heart.

You are the next navi.

If that were true, there would be more warnings. What she had seen the day before must have been another warning, and she swallowed uneasily, realizing what the warning must mean. She made up her mind to tell the *navi* of it when she returned from the washing. Naomi the Old was right. She must never again hide anything she had seen. Not if it was from God.

She bent over the basket, reaching for a tunic. She made a face; the water before her was clean, but she had not picked her spot well, for the reeds here *stank*. There was a scent of decay, of something rotting under the weeds—

Something cold grasped her ankle.

A savage pull, and the ground rushed toward her. She slammed onto her belly; her fall shoved the air out of her before she could shriek. She kicked wildly, glanced over her shoulder and saw—*it*. A face half-torn away, its mouth open now in a hiss; eyes gray and sightless, a thin hand clutching her ankle with terrible strength while the other hand clawed forward to grasp a clump of reeds near the roots; with a groan, the creature pulled itself forward, toward her.

Its rotting torso slid free of the brush, and for a moment Devora was certain that she was back in her mother's tent, and the thing that had been her mother was crawling back into the tent after her, grasping at her. The body below the waist was gone, and it trailed entrails and scraps of tissue behind it. The reek of it did violence against Devora's insides. She tried to scream but managed only a breathless whimper. Its cold, dry hands gripped so tightly. Making her unclean.

She kicked at it, but it only snapped at the kicking foot with its teeth, and Devora twisted and writhed in panic. She looked desperately about her, hands scrabbling among the soiled clothes that had fallen around her. She wanted a stick, a rock, anything—she gave a low, keening cry as the thing's other hand seized her calf, and she heard the slither of its body through the reeds. In a moment it would have its head above her leg and would dig into her skin with its teeth. It would eat her—it wanted to *eat* her!

Her hand struck something.

Wildly, she grasped it with her fingers—a hard surface—

The *washing board!*

With a cry she lifted it in both hands and rolled to her side, brought it crashing down on the creature's head as it hissed just above her captured foot. She heard the smack of the wood against soft, rotting flesh. A growl from the creature. Screaming now, the air back in her lungs, she smashed the board down on the creature again and again, putting all her strength and terror into each blow.

When she stopped, the corpse was still, the top of its head mashed. One eye had been crushed by the washing board; the other stared dully at the sky.

Panting, Devora reached down, pried the dead fingers from her leg, then pulled her leg quickly away from its hands. With trembling fingers, she examined her shin and ankle. There were no scratches there, just a developing bruise where the corpse had clutched her. Her lip began to tremble, and she stilled it. She would *not* cry, not here.

Devora got to her knees, shaking. She could hear cries nearby, splashing. Then running feet. The girls from the stream. Hugging herself tightly, Devora looked at the thing that lay still now in the grass, smelling like a cow found dead in a field days late. Though the thing's strength had been terrible, it was small. She looked at the cut of its hair, at the tatters that remained of its garments. A boy. It had been a boy. A small boy.

Then the other girls reached her, their hair wet about their shoulders, dry cloth wrapped quickly around their bodies.

Hannah swayed on her feet, her eyes wide. Her hand went to her mouth. "Oh God, oh God, God, God," she moaned through her fingers.

"It's Nathan," Mikal whispered. "It's Nathan."

Nathan was Hannah's younger brother—gone a few days before to carry a message to the camp at Beth El for the priests.

Hannah moaned and fell to her knees.

"It *was* Nathan," Devora said hoarsely, remembering too vividly her mother's face in the door of the tent. "Now it is unclean. It's not him." She shivered; a breeze touched her cheek, and then without warning it became a wind, driving ripples across the water hole and making the reeds whisper, and the heat was gone from the day. Devora was sweaty and shivering in the wind. "We have to make a cairn," she whispered.

"There aren't any stones here," Mikal said, her face tight as though she were holding back tears.

Devora looked out over the reeds toward Shiloh. The camp was a long walk. They could go to find men, but that would mean leaving the body in the weeds. That would be unthinkable. And in any case Hannah would not leave the body like this. One of them could go. But the others would have a long time to wait, and—she glanced at the corpse. It had been half-eaten; there were other dead near, somewhere. None of them should wait here, where other mangled dead could already be crawling through the weeds. A fire lit in her, and her terror flickered out. She was not shivering, crying, useless in the reeds. She was not standing by while others confronted the dead for her. She was not helpless, as she had been in her mother's tent.

"My skin is already unclean from its touch." Devora stooped over the body. "I will carry him to the camp. The men can make a cairn for us." She kept her hands from shaking as she slid her arms beneath the reeking, broken thing that had been a boy; she lifted it. The corpse was very light—lighter than the basket of clothes she'd carried. Its intestines trailed to the ground beside her as she held it. Devora averted her eyes. "Gather up the clothes, Mikal," she murmured, and then took an uneasy step forward, then another. She tried not to think of what she was carrying; when it shifted slightly against her, she bit back a scream, swayed for a moment, eyes closed.

"Let me help." Hannah's voice was hoarse with crying.

"Touching it means being put from the camp." Devora's own voice was harsh. "That should only happen to one of us."

Hannah stifled a sob. Devora ignored the sound, kept walking. The mud by the river sucked at her feet. The wind, which made waves of purple blossoms in the heather and made the reeds hiss like serpents, kept tugging her hair across her face. She gritted her teeth, pressed on. There had been no opportunity for Hannah to say goodbye to the child. Devora understood her pain, but she had no time for it and could not permit herself to think about it, or she would begin crying as well.

"Maybe we should leave the body," Mikal whispered, her eyes wide.

"We do not leave one of our dead unburied." Devora's voice was cold.

Hannah cast her a grateful, tearful look.

"Run ahead to the camp, Mikal," Devora said. "Tell them."

Mikal bit her lip, then nodded and sprinted through the reeds. In a few moments she was far ahead, running fleet as a gazelle.

Devora gazed ahead, fixedly ahead. The camp seemed an eternity away, as though it were in far Kemet and she had a wilderness to walk across before she could get there. Her arms ached beneath the small weight of the boy. Yet she did not let herself stumble or stop.

***

By the time Devora and Hannah stumbled out of the heather and reached the first of the tents, Devora's rough washing dress was pasted to her back with cold sweat, and despite the wind her hair clung to her cheeks and neck. She feared falling ill, but the grim resolution within her was stronger. She still carried the dead child.

The *kohannim* and some of the other levites had gathered at the edge of the camp, and Mikal was there speaking urgently, tearfully, with them. The high priest stood with them, his sleeves bloodstained from a recent sacrifice, an *olah* in the Tent of Meeting. He'd been listening to Mikal with a grim look. But then one of them saw Devora and Hannah and cried out, pointing. They all fell silent.

The levites parted, making a path for the two girls. Eleazar's eyes were wide with shock, his gaze fixed on the burden Devora carried. She saw Zefanyah, and the look *he* gave her lent her strength, strength she badly needed. Devora held her head high and carried the boy's corpse into the midst of the camp.

As she reached the *navi*'s tent, two nazarites ran up with a woolen cloth and laid it a few feet before the door of the tent, so that Devora could set the body down without defiling the earth within the camp. Then the cloth could be lifted to carry the corpse to the slope where cairns were raised, and the body could be wrapped in the cloth, lowered into the earth, and covered with heavy stone.

But Devora did not lay down her burden. She stopped with her toes nearly touching the edge of the cloth and waited, holding that small, dry weight in her arms, her eyes on the woman who stood in the door of the tent.

Naomi wore the white dress of the levites, and though she had never been tall, in the moonlight at the door of her tent she looked as regal as a queen of Kemet. Her gaze took in Hannah's tears, the corpse Devora carried, the brown stains and gore on Devora's sleeves.

Her eyes grew cold.

"Were any of you bitten?"

"No, *navi*." Devora held her head high, though she wanted to slip away and hide; the hardness of Naomi's face

203

shook her. Devora stood very still. "I was the only one it touched."

She heard a half sob behind her. Hannah.

Naomi searched Devora's eyes for truth. Her face remained hard, her emotions masked. This was not the Naomi who had smiled wryly at God's secrets or Devora's "pluck." This was Naomi the Old, judge of Israel, who had been alive when the People had taken possession of the land. Naomi, who had learned from the first *navi* and whose responsibility was keeping the land clean from the dead.

"I believe you, girl." For a brief moment, Naomi's eyes showed her pain. Devora took in a quick breath, but did not otherwise react. She had to be strong if she was to face the consequences of her choice without tears and without terror.

"Set down the body; a cairn will be built for it."

Devora obeyed, though she felt that any movement might make her collapse in fatigue. She yearned for Naomi to say anything to her, anything personal. Bending at the knees, she laid the corpse gently on the cloth before her feet. Straightening, she looked at it. Lifeless and still, it seemed more pitiful than perilous; a wisp of torn flesh and sinew, a torn-up face without any breath in it. Sunken and small. A thing once made in the image of God and then withered and savaged until nothing left of God could be seen in it.

Devora stood and lifted her eyes. "You wanted to know what I saw," she said softly. "When I fainted."

"Yes." Naomi's eyes were keen.

"I saw you." Devora met her gaze without flinching. "Standing in front of a burning tent. There were corpses in the tent. Then you fell, all at once to one side without bending your legs, and when you hit the ground you were gone. And I saw myself standing near. I saw myself grieving but I had no tears."

Silence.

The men were gazing on with horror. It was the first time anyone but Naomi had heard Devora speak of having a vision. Even Hannah's sobs fell silent, and the girl looked at Devora with wide eyes.

"Were you older when you saw yourself stand there?" Naomi asked.

Devora shook her head, something inside her beginning to quail. "No, I don't think so."

Naomi gave a small, slight nod. Her face giving nothing away, her voice clipped and sharp. "Did you see anything else?"

Devora shook her head.

Naomi made a quiet, dismissive noise in her throat, as though setting what she'd heard aside until its importance was clearer. She looked out over the gathered men of the camp. "This girl is a *navi*. She brings us the *niv sefatayim*, the fruit of God's wisdom. God who sees what has been and what may be. You had best listen to her." She turned her gaze back to Devora, and her voice grew colder. "But she is also unclean. For seven days she is unclean."

Devora lowered her head, blinking moisture out of her eyes.

"Devora of Israel," the *navi* intoned solemnly, "I put you from the camp. You will take neither food nor water nor clothes. You will touch no item in this camp. You will touch no crop nor any well filled with water. You will keep yourself separate from the People, sharing neither nearness nor speech. For seven days."

Devora swallowed. "*Navi*—"

Anger flickered in the old woman's eyes. "*Go.*"

The word was as sharp as a slap.

Devora's face burned. She had tried to plead, to ask for one kind word—whether from the *navi* or the levites or from Hannah or from anyone, she didn't know. She'd been rebuked. She'd deserved to be. For a moment she searched Naomi's face for some compassion or love, but found only that mask, as though her weathered face had been chiseled from stone, immutable law written into it in crevasses and hard lines, even as the Law had been written into stone tablets long ago on Har Sinai. There was in that face no pity or reprieve or farewell, only the cold justice that Shiloh hoped would keep a People from perishing from this earth.

Devora glanced behind her, saw Hannah watching her with reddened eyes and tear streaks on her face. Mikal white as though she were ill. The levites had their eyes on the corpse, and they too looked pale.

Suddenly she needed to be *out* of this camp, away from Naomi's hard eyes. Devora turned and ran. The levites stepped back out of her way, careful not to touch her with so much as a fold of their garments. That brought a fresh sting to Devora's eyes, and her feet pounded the soil as she sprinted, her hair flying behind her.

But as she reached the last of the tents, she heard a man's voice call out her name, not loudly. She stumbled, then straightened and turned. Through her tears she saw Zefanyah approaching at a jog, a waterskin slung over his shoulder. Her face burned with shame and she looked away, furious with herself that the nazarite should see her like this, not only unclean but her eyes tear-swollen and surely hideous.

"Devora, take this with you," he called. She glanced up, and he tossed her his waterskin. Without thinking, she caught it out of the air with both hands. She could feel the weight of it; it was full. Enough water for a few days. He was giving the waterskin to her, a true gift, for she could not bring it back with her, neither to him nor to the camp. She would have to bury it out in the wilderness; her touch had defiled it the moment she had caught it out of the air.

She hugged the waterskin to her breast and looked at him through the strands of hair that her run had left disheveled across her face.

"Thank you," she whispered.

He smiled, and there was such warmth in his eyes that she couldn't bear it. She turned from him and ran again, ran harder, not looking back to see if he was watching her. The city of tents fell behind her, the low voices of the camp fading to a hum like that of bees.

Once she was halfway up the slope, Devora slowed, then bent over, gasping for air, the waterskin still clutched to her breast. The day was getting dim; with the hills looming so high around Shiloh, especially to the east, dusk came early and dawn came late. The cold reality of what had happened fell on her, as sharply as though she'd ducked under a fall of ice water. She sank and sat in the heather, the lovely blossoms swaying about her in the breeze that had replaced the earlier wind. She was cold, and her body itched with dried sweat. She lifted her hands and she could feel the cold of the dead boy's flesh. She was defiled. Unclean. *She had touched the dead.*

Devora clutched at the stems of the heather and tore at them. She let out a long, raw scream, tossing her head back and screaming until she had to gasp for breath again. Yet still her breast ached as though there was a great bruise across her body. She sat for a while in the weeds, just catching her breath. Then she chafed her arms against the cold, trying to think as the night gathered about her. She heard the cries of jackals, but they were far from here. Later, even as the first stars appeared, she heard the low moan of one of the lurching dead. Even though it was far away, she shivered at the sound of it. She had no weapon in her hands, neither knife nor washing board. She had only the waterskin Zefanyah—bless him—had tossed her. And even had she had something lethal in her hands with which to defend herself, she had no desire to see another of the loathsome dead.

Yet.

She had carried that child. She had done what she must, what she feared to do.

The thought gave her strength. She bent and searched among the stems of heather. It took her some time to find what she needed, but at last she pulled a jagged rock free of the dirt, and she held it up before her eyes, looking at it in the starlight. It was longer than her hand, and thinner. And this stone knife had not been handled by any of the People, had been touched by no one but God who had shaped it and placed it here in the earth for Devora to find. And at the end of her seven days, Devora could simply toss it aside.

She forced herself to her feet, her eyes wide in the dark. She had heard the moan; she knew there were other dead in the hills. But she refused to lie crying in fear.

As she moved across the slope to find shelter, the wind picked up again, as if to hurry her. It rushed through the heather, even as it had when she was carrying the body toward the camp; the heather flattened before it as before the rush of God toward his Tent. It was very beautiful— the blossoms moving like a single living creature beneath the stars—but it was ominous too. As though something powerful and unexpected was coming to the valley.

KINDLED LIKE STRAW

FOR THE WEEK of her uncleanness, Devora lived by filling her waterskin from small creeks in the hills about Shiloh and by foraging for berries and roots, which were plentiful this close to the harvest. She kept her waterskin and her stone knife with her at all times, even once when climbing a tall tree to take eggs from a bulbul's nest. Yet she was nearly always hungry. She washed her dress and bathed sometimes in the mornings in streams she found, but by nightfall she felt sweat and dirt caked on her skin, which was a misery to her, and her dress became ragged and stiff, as though it were a part of her uncleanness.

Dutifully she avoided the herds of cattle that ranged farther up the valley, and once when she saw the smoke of campfires on a ridge and caught the scent of roasting meat, she turned and ran through the heather, putting distance between herself and those tents, until her mouth stopped watering.

Several times she heard a corpse moaning, and once she heard two dead moaning, as if to each other, from opposite slopes across the valley. She found it difficult to sleep, and when she did, her dreams were violent and evil. Sometimes she sat in the weeds fingering the edges of her stone knife and looked at the sky or gazed down at Shiloh's tents, and thought of Zefanyah or of the cattle herder who she'd seen fighting the dead years ago. That was far more pleasant than thinking of the dead. She imagined her return to the camp, her reintegration into the People. She imagined the nazarite sweeping her up in his arms and kissing her, having missed her and yearned for her for seven days.

She tried his name on her lips.

Zefanyah.

She decided it was a beautiful name, a mysterious name. Even an erotic one. Zefanyah: "God has hidden him." The word meant hidden like a secret or like a treasure, something you store up to give to someone at the proper time. Devora began to pray softly and silently in the dark. New hopes, strange hopes, were blossoming inside her, and she dared to wonder if perhaps God did not hate her, if perhaps God had forgiven her for her helplessness the morning of her mother's death. Forgiven her enough to have stored up this treasure, this secret for her.

***

On the final night of her exile from the camp, Devora sat near the summit of the hill of cairns where Shiloh buried its dead, with her back to a great olive tree. She had spent the past two nights in this same place; the olive was a comfort to her, something warm and alive and straight at her back, something that reached toward God's stars. Though she was still unclean and outside the Law, she at least felt as though the Law was *there*, a great tent over the valley sheltering the People, and one of its poles firm against her back. It gave her comfort. She gazed up at the stars and thought of the invisible roof of that tent. She thought of telling Zefanyah about it.

Even as she thought of him, the moon lifted above the opposite ridge.

Looking up at it, she stopped breathing.

Most nights, the moon glided gracefully into the sky over Shiloh valley like a great white crane. But tonight the moon shone dark red, a great sore in the sky. Devora shrank against the olive tree; she suddenly felt terribly exposed on this hillside; her instincts screamed at her to hide, even if it meant digging at the earth with her fingers to make a burrow, like some beast of the hills. All thoughts of Zefanyah had fled.

The moon crept higher.

One by one, the little fires of the camp far below went out.

She breathed shallowly; she kept watching that moon. It was unnatural, that color, and the size of it—as though the moon had swallowed up much of the sky around it. She waited for some vision that would warn her or help her interpret what she saw in the sky, but no vision came, no touch of dizziness. The air was cool and clear.

She couldn't sleep; she just watched the moon creep, bloodied, across the sky, until it set.

Then for a long time the night was dark again, and chill. Sometimes the jackals cried in the hills, and Devora shivered, both relieved and frightened that the moon had gone, leaving no hint as to what it portended.

A shriek shattered the night like glass. Devora froze. The cry was distant—it came from the direction of the camp. The cry went on and on.

Then there were other screams, thin and distant. Her eyes grew round in the moonlight.

A deep, deep call—a single rolling note—filled the air, and the hills deepened the sound and rolled it on and gave it back to the air amplified. Devora felt it in her feet and legs, in the slamming of her heartbeat. Someone had blown the shofar, the ram's horn, down in the camp. One long note, now fading to silence except for echoes from the more distant ridges—the *t'qiah*, the note that means *God is mighty, beware, this land is his!*

As if in answer, another sound erupted, quiet at this distance but distinct enough to make Devora shudder in the night.

The moaning of the dead.

The wailing of many, many throats.

She got to her feet, gazing down at the tents, her heart in her throat. There were sharp, terrified screams on the air and, under it all, that moaning. The ram's horn did not call again.

"*El adonai*," she whispered, "*adonai*, help them."

A flame went up in the night, a tower of fire rising over one of the tents, as though some power had spewed fire toward the sky. She watched with wide eyes. She felt a rush of heat across her face, crackling along the skin of her arms. It was the same as the feeling that came when she had a vision of things to come, the rush of the *shekinah* through her mind and body—yet *this* heat was immeasurably stronger, as though someone down in the camp had opened the door to a furnace the size of a mountain. The heat rushed *into* her and through her, and she cried out, every part of her burning; in a moment it might wither her like a dry leaf tossed into a fire pit.

Yet even as the scream left her lips, the heat was gone.

It had passed through her.

The cool air again touched her skin. Thirst parched her; she tasted salt on her lips.

Then she was running.

Below, the fire was spreading through the camp, and still there were moans and screams, a few male voices raised in a psalm of battle and defense. Panting, Devora rushed down the long slope, rushing through the thigh-high heather, feeling it slap against her ragged dress. Rushing as though if she could only get there in time, the camp might live. She knew that she needed to be there, with those she had begun to love. She began calling their names, calling their names in the dark as she ran, the glow of the fire on her face. Her sides burning.

***

Devora reached Shiloh and the tents of the *kohannim* just as dawn reclaimed the sky from the dark, her legs streaked with dirt and sweat from her run. The early light showed her smoke rising from many tents that had been set afire; men were moving about. With heavy gloves on their hands, they pulled charred bodies from the ashes and dragged them out, setting them in long lines. A small girl huddled with her arms about her knees by the lines, rocking back and forth. No one knelt to speak with her or shoo her away.

There were so many bodies. Forty, maybe fifty. Some were missing limbs or had great gashes in their sides. Many had been blackened in the night's fire, skin and flesh baked away to leave only stretched, sinewy things behind, like heathen doll-people made out of sticks.

A small boy of perhaps seven winters stood by the line of bodies. Behind him stood a lone woman, standing straight and silent as though unwilling to let pain bow her shoulders. She was veiled like a heathen girl, her eyes lowered to conceal her private grief from the view of others.

There was something familiar about the boy's face, and Devora watched him, troubled, as she approached the line of bodies. She saw that his eyes were hard; they were not the eyes of a child. In the moans of the dead and the roar of fire, that small boy had learned, in one wrenching of the heart, that the same God gives and takes away.

She also saw something more. Something in the shape of his face.

Feeling as though she had stepped off a cliff of stone and was falling through a great expanse of air, Devora made her way to the boy, until she stood before him and his mother.

"You are Zefanyah's son," she said softly.

The boy didn't answer her. His eyes remained hard, and he kept his gaze on the bodies.

"Your father—he is here among the dead?" She could not keep the pain and shock from her voice.

The boy nodded and looked down at one of the bodies.

Devora shivered and followed his gaze. The corpse the boy was staring at was charred almost to soot, the face unrecognizable, white teeth and eyeless sockets facing the sky.

"Zefanyah," she whispered.

The boy nodded again. The woman standing behind him made no sign that she'd heard, or indeed that she was capable of seeing or hearing.

Devora gazed down at that scorched body. How many nights she had dreamed of being held in his arms, being kissed, being his. How in her dreams he and the man she'd seen defending his cattle by the river—how they had become one, youthful, strong, vital. A rock a young woman might lean on. Now all that strength, all that life, all that fierce will and heat, how it had all been doused in the brief dark between the moon's setting and the sun's rising. She could not understand. She could not. It had been one thing to carry the body of a tiny boy through the reeds, to feel that boy reduced to mere bones and sinew, but that a man she had seen sweating on the training ground, whose muscles rippled in the sun's heat, a man who might wrestle a lion to the earth and whose grin lit such fires in her body—that *he* might now be nothing more than brittle bones within a shroud of ravaged and burned tissue. How could it be possible? She drew a breath, and she turned to the boy. The boy and the silent

216

woman Zefanyah had left behind, with none to pitch a tent for them. "What is your name?" she asked the boy.

"Zadok." His tone was flat. He didn't look at her.

Zadok, the righteous one.

She took his face in her hands, made the boy look at her. Found his eyes. "Zadok." She spoke intently, desperately, and after a moment she could see through her tears that the boy saw her, was returning her gaze. "You must find stones. Heavy stones. Ones that hurt to lift. Help the men bury your father. Whenever one of the People dies, you bury them so they cannot rise. You raise a cairn high, high enough that God will see and remember them." Her voice broke. "Do you understand me?"

The boy nodded. He looked as though he might cry too.

Devora straightened, glanced at the woman grieving. "God will remember your husband." Her voice broke. "God will remember all of them!"

Then Devora turned and walked along the line of bodies, shaking. Forcing herself to look at the faces. Those whose faces were still recognizable—she knew them all. All of the freshly dead.

At the end of the line of bodies, a girl sat on the ground with brown fluid and bits of flesh spattered across her nightdress and a knife held loosely in her hand. Devora knew her.

"Sarai?" she called softly, kneeling by the girl.

Sarai looked up. Her face was smudged with dirt. "They're all dead," she said, without emotion. Her eyes were dazed, in shock.

"What happened?" Devora whispered.

217

Sarai just looked past her, at the lines of bodies. Devora followed her gaze. A young man was moving down the lines with a heavy stave in his hands, and as he passed each corpse, he struck its skull hard.

Devora flinched and looked back to Sarai's face. Her friend's eyes were distant. Devora took Sarai's face in her hands and pressed her forehead to hers. "Don't look," she whispered.

Sarai brought her hands up, placed them on Devora's, but made no effort to draw back from her touch.

"Sarai, it's all right. It's all right." She spoke as softly as she could, though fighting her own horror. "Shh, it's all right," she whispered.

Sarai moaned.

A hand gripped Devora's shoulder from behind, startling her, and then a voice she knew, a man's voice: "Devora, the *navi* is calling for you."

She glanced up. "Eleazar!"

He looked at her numbly. "Will you come?"

Devora nodded numbly, rose, and walked beside him, letting him lead the way through the white tents. Zefanyah, *Zefanyah* dead. So many dead. Where was the *navi*?

"Where did they come from?" she whispered.

Eleazar answered her but didn't seem to have heard her question. His voice sounded dull, hollow, as though he were speaking from the bottom of a well. "I was sleeping. We were all sleeping. Those things were *feeding* in the tents by the river—who knows how long before someone blew the shofar."

"How many?" Devora felt a sense of unreality closing on her, like a fog descending over the camp and shrouding the carnage. Her head felt curiously light.

218

"Fifteen, maybe twenty." Eleazar's eyes were bloodshot. "Herdsmen, still wrapped in their wool. Heathen. Canaanites. They stumbled in from the slopes."

"Canaanites," Devora repeated. Anger bit at her.

"Yes. They bit—so many." He stumbled, caught himself. Devora looked at him, appalled at his fatigue. He seemed to be on his feet only by sheer effort of will. "The nazarites—they saved me. Some of the others. And I got several priests to the Tent of Meeting and we brought out the Ark. We brought out—and the camp—the camp burst into flame. The dead lit as though they'd been doused in oil, yet they walked about still moaning even as they burned—" His voice dropped and he whispered words of the Law under his breath:

The people must not be burned with fire
not consumed with flame
but buried beneath clean stone.

"God's judgment on them was so entire, so complete," he said. "Some burned away until not even bones were left behind."

Devora shivered. She recalled the leaping of flames into the dark as she had seen it from the hill, and the sense she'd had of heat passing across her skin, though the fire was so far away. And how it had felt like the heat that came when she saw things that hadn't yet happened. Behind the leaping of visions into her waking day there rested a Power and a Presence that might burn the world at a touch. The appearance of the visions was the gentlest of its visitations, as though a great mother bear with teeth the length and lethality of knives had chosen to nudge her hip gently with its nose.

"Not even bones," Eleazar whispered. He looked around them at the camp. Men and women were moving past them now, some with bandaged arms or with bloodstains on their robes.

"We will have to watch for signs of fever," Eleazar said, in that hushed voice that was so unlike the exuberance of the priest who taught in the evenings. "Some in the camp may be hiding their wounds. Many people touched the dead last night. We have to find out who is clean and who is not."

"Why are you telling me this?"

Surely Naomi the Old had given orders for everything that needed doing?

But before the levite could answer, they reached the *navi*'s tent. Eleazar drew aside the flap and inclined his head respectfully. With a tremor of unease, Devora stepped through.

***

Inside, the *navi* was propped up on cushions, her face pale and damp with sweat. No one else was there with her. Her eyes shone, and her hands trembled where they clutched at the cushions. Her garment had been cut away from her right shoulder, where a livid bite could be seen in the skin above her breast, a fierce half circle of red marks, the marks of human teeth. Devora sucked in her breath as she saw it.

Naomi looked up, gestured her close. Devora hurried to her side and knelt there. She reached for Naomi's hand, but the old woman cried out, "*Stop!*"

Devora stood still. She could feel the heat from her flesh through the air between them, as though the woman lying on those cushions carried hot coals inside her body.

"I am unclean, girl," the *navi* rasped. "Do not touch me."

"No," Devora whispered.

The *navi* had to swallow twice before she could speak further. "They brought you to me, the priests. I hoped they would," she managed.

"I'm here," Devora said.

"The Canaanites brought this on us," Naomi said quietly. "There will always be strangers in the land, and they will be neglectful of the Law. Until it is too late. You must help the People remember the Law." She tapped a small clay jar at her side. "Open this," she whispered.

Devora did so, careful not to touch Naomi's hand with hers. Careful to touch only the top part of the jar. In a moment it was open, and the *navi* lifted it in one shaking hand. "Bow your head, girl," Naomi said, and then upended the jar over Devora's head. A little olive oil trickled out over her hair and her forehead. Devora closed her eyes as it ran down her face, slick and sweet-scented.

"You have been like a daughter to me," Naomi murmured. "As they all have. But you are the one who sees. I always thought it might be you. The way you remember the *mitzvot* as easily as other women remember the names of their kin. I wish I'd had the time to prepare you. To tell you things first…I anoint you, Devora. I anoint you the *navi* and judge of Israel."

Naomi lowered the jar, lost her grip on it. It rolled aside until it stopped against the side of a cushion.

"Don't die," Devora whispered. She opened her eyes, and took in the sight of the old woman burning up on her cushions. The reddened bite wound. The fever sheen in the *navi*'s eyes.

"Girl," Naomi murmured. "You'll have time to mourn me later. Only be strong, for they will look to you. The *kohannim* know already what you are. I made sure of that. Now we must act, girl. Before this fever takes what's left of me." She lifted a hand weakly, pointing at a pile of furs in the corner. "Bring what you find. Be quick."

Choking back her anguish, Devora hurried to the furs, knelt there, and tossed them aside, revealing a long, narrow box of plain cedar, no jewelry or adornment, just God's own wood.

"Do what needs to be done. With that," Naomi croaked.

Slowly Devora slid the lid from the box. Inside she found a long blade with a hilt of bone. The blade was much longer than her arm. She touched the metal gently, heard her fingernails ring quietly against it. "This isn't bronze," she breathed.

"Iron." Naomi was breathing hard between the words she forced out. "A gift. Sea Coast man—I saved his life. He left me that. Take it, Devora."

In anguish, Devora turned and gazed at the *navi*, whose eyes seemed glassy now. Naomi kept moistening her lips with her tongue, as though to fight the desert heat in her skin the only way she could.

"I can't," Devora gasped.

"At dusk, the *kohannim* will." Naomi's hand twitched on the cushions. "I would rather it were you. Because you are the *navi*. And you have seen the threat. As none of them have, not truly. You took that small boy in your arms—" Her breathing was labored. "It is you, Devora. They will look to you for judgment. Because you see what God sees."

"I *can't*," Devora cried. She had slept little in the past seven nights; now her hold on the waking world seemed tenuous. Her memories crowded upon her, ready to do her violence: the thing that had been her mother looking in at her through the tent flap. Its mouth open in a hiss. The firm, cool surface of a stone pestle in her palm.

She made a little noise, like a whimper.

"*Devora.*" Naomi held her gaze, though now her entire body had begun to shiver violently. "Listen to me. It is kinder for me to die this way than in the lingering fever. I want to know that my body will not stand from these cushions when I am gone. It is kind, Devora. Listen to me. You have seen how God is a father who burns away what threatens his children, and you and I have felt his heat. But God is also our mother. As a woman, I know this. That her heart is a deep, deep lake dousing all wrath and flame. That she kisses us when we are born. Quickens new life within us when we have become women. God made both Adam and Eve, both in God's likeness. And if this is true, Devora, what I tell you, what Miriam who was *navi* when I was a girl told me, then God who is like our mother and has compassion will forgive us the evils we cannot avoid and the lives we cannot save."

Naomi moved her shaking hands, folding them weakly over her breast. "Do this for me, Devora." She closed her eyes, panting softly, her face slick with perspiration. "Do it quickly."

Devora's vision blurred. She had seen this. She had seen a vision of Naomi dying. She had foreseen her own grief at her mother's death. And in neither case had she been able to save either her mother or the mother of Israel. The tears hot on her face. Try as she might, Devora could not think of God as a mother. Distant, delivering visions and then demanding action, and *not* maternal, not one who might embrace or hold a grieving, shattered girl.

Naomi whispered the words of the *sh'ma* and closed her eyes. For a few moments more, Devora stood shaking, the hilt of the iron sword clutched tightly in both her hands. Naomi did not open her eyes or speak.

A great cold settled in Devora's heart.

This could not be avoided. It could not be delayed. She saw so clearly in her mind the face of her mother, distorted and hissing. If she were to see Naomi like *that*, it would break her; she would collapse and never again stand.

"I love you, mother," Devora cried, and lifted the blade.

JUDGE OF ISRAEL

DEVORA STEPPED from the tent, drawing the bloodied sword behind her, the blade's tip trailing in the dust. The levites and the young women parted for her, standing silently to either side, watching her. Devora's face was terribly cold. All the heat had been sucked out of her and out of the world. As she walked by, one of the levites began to weep quietly. She didn't look at him.

"We need another cairn," she said softly.

She walked slowly through the camp, feeling embers crunch beneath her sandals. An occasional metal ringing from the blade as the edge struck some rock along the way. Doubtless there would be some nicks, some damage in the sword; she did not care. She looked about her at the bodies and at the young men already gathering great stones to make the cairns. So many cairns. She looked at them and walked on. Until she stood at the very edge of the camp, gazing out across the reeds by the bank. There were more bodies in the water, she saw, facedown and caught against some rock jutting into the river or dragged half onto the bank. Perhaps some had not caught at the bank but had drifted free, like leaves blown into the water by a high wind. In the confusion of the night, some of these bodies might have escaped, slipping downstream to pollute the Tumbling Water and the fields of their People.

She did not care.

She stared out at the reeds and the heather on the high slopes behind and the dark, rising ridges of the Galilee hills to the north. She smelled smoke and burned flesh and decay. She heard weeping and low talk among the men at their work. For a while she recited in her mind the names of those she'd known who were now gone from the land: Mikal with her laughter and her love of mischief; Tabitha, who had dreamed of love and rich herds in the lower valleys; practical Leah, whose hands were so clumsy, though she worked harder than any of them. Even Zefanyah, who she had so admired on the fighting ground. Zefanyah, who had kissed her. Who had given her his waterskin. He too had been among the night's dead.

They were gone. All gone, for all time. The land on which they'd stood had been defiled and filthied; it might be a generation before the stink of the dead was gone from Shiloh.

She recited some of the Law quietly to herself, seeking calm. Most of the *mitzvot* were stored up in her heart, and reaching for one was like reaching for a memory of a beautiful summer day. She had replaced most of her memories with *mitzvot*; how would she ever be able to replace the memories of this night?

"Devora?" A man's voice. She didn't turn her head. Eleazar. He was breathing hard; he came to stand beside her. "Devora?"

She didn't answer. She kept looking at the heather, which was moving now, softly, in a breeze.

"Devora? *Navi?* Has God shown you what must be done?"

"You must wait," she said.

She said nothing more, and at last the high priest turned back to the camp.

Devora stood there, weak and faint because she hadn't eaten. Still, she stood looking across the heather. As the sun slid to the edge of the hills, she whispered, "You are cruel, *adonai*, but I understand why you must be."

The wind picked up in the heather, but there were no words in it. Just the rustle of weeds bending so they would not break.

She turned her eyes to the hills, saw the way their ridges cut at the sky in the gathering dark. "I will judge the People for you, as she did." Her voice gathered strength. "I will keep the land clean."

It was the only thing she could give Naomi—or any of them. She covered her mouth with her hand and held her feelings tightly within her. Let loose, they would tear at her and devour her as ravenously as the dead.

She must build a cairn over her feelings, a high cairn, so that she could stand before the People.

***

When dawn arrived, Devora turned and walked back into the camp. As she reached the Tent of Meeting she stumbled; two levites caught her by the arms before she could hit the soil. She moaned softly; they brought her unleavened bread and mutton, and after washing quickly to her elbows, she held the bread in both hands and tore at it until she felt like vomiting. They brought her water, but refused to let her drink more than a few quick sips at a time. Her stomach lurched within her. She clutched at her belly with a groan, and they stood patiently by.

When she was able to stand again, she motioned to them and they helped her to her feet. She stood there in the tattered shift she'd worn throughout her exile from the camp, the shift still stained with brown streaks from her fight with the dead boy in the reeds. She drew in a breath; she reeked of death and sweat and unwashed girl. She wrinkled her nose once, then composed her face and lifted her arms, like Moseh in the desert. She called out the words—the words of the Lawgiver that would summon the People to her.

The women came stumbling from their tents and the men from their work; they had piled the cairns high, and all but a few were now finished. They gathered about her in a half circle, their faces stained with blood and dirt, their eyes weary. A few gazed at her with cautious hope.

"I am Devora of Israel," she said, "and I see what God sees." She took a breath, her eyes glancing only once to the tent where Naomi had died.

Then she faced her People and began making judgments, separating the clean from the unclean.

PART 3
THE HIGH GALILEE

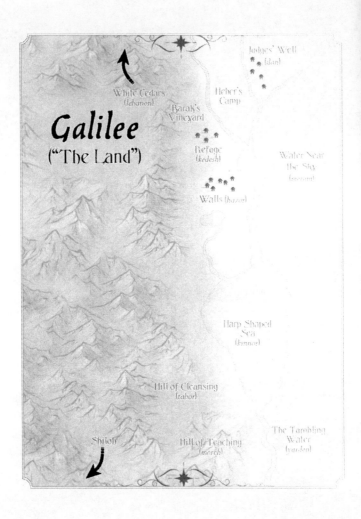

WATER NEAR THE SKY

HIGH IN THE GALILEE, where the Tumbling Water is just a stream one can wade through by brute force, there is a high plateau the Hebrews call *Merom*, Water Near the Sky. There a small lake reflects back the stars; lilies and other delicate water flowers cover its surface near the shore. Shielded on all sides by a bowl of earth and rock, the lake is far more placid than the Harp-Shaped Sea, and the fish there, though few, are fat and slow, and they sleep as they swim. If the fish in Kinnor are like dancing, leaping deer, the fish in Merom are more like lumbering oxen. They are not as pleasing to taste, but the Canaanites in those hills have many ways of preparing them that give delight to the tongue and gladden the heart.

The boats that plied this small lake in that time were flat-bottomed and small, nearly coracles; in each, a single man would stand with a spear and a small net for catching the fish he impaled. In the warmer months, the boats would slip out on the quiet water in the dark before dawn and return as the sun rose, each with its cargo of bloodied fish. Salted and dried, the fish would fill great bins; the people who lived in that earthen bowl were well fed. Once, a mighty town had stood there, with a steep slope at its back and a circle of high walls of baked clay. Walls, the Canaanites had named their town, a boast to others who might wish to seize the lake from them. Now the walls were only a ring of tumbled and cracked bricks; not even a wooden palisade of cedar from the hills had been raised in their place. Hebrews had come there, with spears and cries in a language the Canaanites did not know, and they had brought with them a new God who apparently did not care for walls in his People's path.

Tearing their way through the walls, the Hebrews—the last of the Hebrews, for other tribes of their People had already found fertile valleys in which to pitch their tents far to the south—these weary and hungry and furious Hebrews set fire to half the town and killed many of the men whether they were armed or not, in their fury to possess this place near the sky. Women were dragged from their dying houses and thrown to the dirt streets, where sweating, ragged men forced them even as the slaughter continued on every side.

The Law that had been given to the People of the Covenant in the desert forbade this treatment of captives:

> *When you see among the captives a beautiful woman and you desire her and bring her to your tent, she will shave her head and weep for her father and her mother who are dead, for one full month, and in that time you will not touch her.*

And if you find she doesn't please you, then you will let her go where she will. You will not sell her or make her an item of trade, for you have known her.

Those *mitzvot* the judges had declared in the desert, part of the great Law to bind the tribes to each other and to the God who'd found them thirsting and perishing in the dead-haunted ravines. And often these *mitzvot* had been followed in the south, where the levites had demanded that the men remember the cost of breaking the Covenant. "Our fathers' Covenant, not ours!" some of the men would cry. And the levites in wrath would shout: "Is this then your fathers' land and not yours?

Hear, men of Israel! Our God in the desert made this Covenant not with our fathers, but with us, with each of us who stand here alive this day.

And the men, hearing these words, had held back their hungers and heeded the levites. It would not do to break the Covenant and to spurn the God who gives and who takes away even in the moment of taking possession of the land he'd promised them.

But these last tribes that raged northward after all their brothers and sisters had found land in which to lift their tents—these last tribes were not eager to let any Law restrain them. Few of the women of Walls were given time to mourn their dead. Some were held to the ground, their garments torn from them, even as their husbands or fathers bled to death in the dirt beside them. The screams of the dying and the screams of the survivors tore the air.

The newcomers, however, did keep the *mitzvot* that demanded cairns for the fallen. They dared not break *those*.

In the days after the death of the town, many women gazed out of tent flaps, their faces bruised and tear-stained, the numbness in their eyes replaced for a few moments by wonder as they watched the Hebrew men gather massive stones from the slopes behind the town and pile great cairns above each of the dead, both Hebrew and Canaanite, until a forest of stone monuments stretched along the bank of the Tumbling Water where it emptied into their lake from the north. Never had they seen the dead treated so; their own way had been to weight the bodies and give them to the lake, that in time, through the digestion of fish, they might be taken back into the people. In shock, these women watched as the cairns went up, not knowing what it meant, only that it was strange, wondering that the Hebrews took time to tend to their enemy dead as well as their own, and bewildered that they feared the bodies so much that they would pile heavy rock upon them, nor give them to any fish that might be eaten by a man.

Later, some of the women would weep bitterly for the loss of the spirits of their people, but first there was only shock. The town was gone, the men they had known were gone, their own bodies had been torn and used for the pleasure of others who did not even know their language or their names. Everything was different, everything.

The winter that followed was the hardest Walls had ever known, for the Hebrews were yet strangers in the land and the land did not know them nor did it consent to feed them. The survivors, conquerors and conquered, squatted in the charred ruins of ancient houses or shivered in their tents; the fish stored in the bins had been squandered by the raiding spearmen, and coracles had to set out on the water even in the bitter cold to look for food. Parties of men began to leave the town, pressing north, farther into the hills, to raid the smaller villages of the Canaanites. Some perished, and some settled where they found food; few came back.

In Walls, some of the Canaanite women were killed because they could not be fed, but most were not. And when the first caravans came through on their way from the steppes of the Horse People to the cities of the Sea People on the coast, more women were bound and bartered to them for the goods needed to make life possible again along the shores of Water Near the Sky.

Yet it was just as likely that the desperate men might barter away a Hebrew woman rather than one of the captives, for the Canaanites who had lived uneasily beside the Hebrew women through the winter knew many useful things—including when the caravans could be expected to come through and which goods each carried. So many, indeed most, of the captives remained in the tents of those who'd claimed them. And before a year had passed, the ruins of the town were filled with the cries of infants. These children would grow up with Hebrew fathers and Canaanite mothers, and in them would survive a love of wooden houses rather than tents, and a desire for gods you could hold in your hand, and the wisdom to make the fish taste like a divine gift.

The grandchildren of those children lived in Walls now, and Walls persisted as a town of scattered houses of wood and thatch. In some, little gods carved from wood or clay were concealed; in some, they weren't. In the quiet hours while the lake lay dark, the little coracles set out again upon the water, moving silent as dreams over the lake, and in them stood patient and grim men whose blood was Hebrew or Canaanite or both, wielding the spears the conquerors had brought against fish now rather than men. They were the wealthiest and best-fed settlement in the Galilee, for they had the knowledge of two peoples and the strengths of each.

Yet they had also the griefs of two peoples, the griefs of desert grandfathers and lakeshore grandmothers. They lived fiercely and drank deeply of barley beer brought up from the valleys of Manasseh and stored in great barrels in the town's beer-house. They danced Canaanite dances at the full moon and they kept within their houses on the Hebrew Sabbath. They loved fiercely and faced death grimly, the people of Walls. Rarely did any of them send children to serve God in Shiloh, and rarely did any go to the Feast of Tents, to remember the time in the desert.

Exasperated, Naomi the Old had sent a levite to live among them, to remind them of the Law, and they had tolerated him—it was important, after all, to have someone who could sing the Words of Going after cairns were raised—and in time they even loved him, but they did not listen to him much. Their homes by Water Near the Sky were all the land, and the men and women of their town all the People.

***

As Shomar picked his way down from the ridge toward the camp Barak's men had pitched on the shore of Water Near the Sky, Devora thought the lake very lovely, even lovelier than that larger lake now a day behind them, the one they called a sea and over which cranes flew and beneath which fish apparently swam out of the mouths of gods. Before her on the saddle, in her arms, the *navi* held Hurriya, whose breathing was a little shallow. Devora could feel the heat of the girl's fever even through her salmah. The previous night had not broken the fever, though it had not worsened either; Hurriya had wakened with it, exhausted by a long and restless night. Devora herself had wakened earlier, sore from the previous day's riding, yet strangely relieved of her fatigue; she'd wakened with Zadok's arms about her, strong and sure. His breathing light, for he was awake. He had not let her go during the night. Neither had he ceased watching. And he had let her sleep until daybreak.

She had flushed, finding herself held so. She had slipped from his arms gently, not daring to look at his face. She felt his gaze on her as she washed to her elbows, nearly emptying her waterskin, then chewed on a little bread from the store Zadok carried in his saddlebag. Her tension grew. The trees seemed dim and hostile in the morning light. Hurriya still slept, though fitfully; a look at her face and a hand held a feather's width over her brow confirmed for Devora that the Canaanite's fever hadn't broken. The cairn was an ominous presence, reminding her that the dead were near. And Zadok's gaze made her acutely uncomfortable. What had she been *thinking*, lying in his arms like that, like a wife, no matter how frightened she had been of her dreams? What if he misunderstood, thought she were seducing him? What if—?

But she couldn't spend the morning in turmoil. She needed her strength of mind. She rounded on him, the words on her lips stilled by the amusement in his eyes.

"Intolerable," she muttered, and turned her attention to the girl. "Saddle the horses, please," she called over her shoulder.

"Your will, *navi*." The nazarite's voice was rough with sleep. He made very little sound as he rose and got to work breaking their camp.

Devora focused on the Canaanite, seating herself by her and calling her name until she opened her eyes.

"You're very ill, girl," Devora said softly. "You might as well know it."

"I know it," Hurriya said wearily. "Being heathen does not make me a fool."

Devora paused, then gave her a quick nod, though she didn't know whether she meant it as acknowledgment or apology. "I am just tense, girl. There will be more dead today. And more the next day. May God send one of us a vision with some comfort in it."

"Does he?" Hurriya rasped. "Those he's sent me have been like—like nightmares."

"No, he doesn't. He sends visions when they're needed, and then they are unlikely to be pleasant." Devora cast another uneasy glance at the terebinths. "And they are needed now."

She gave the girl a little water, and as soon as Hurriya had swallowed it she slipped back into sleep, and Devora gazed down at her in dismay. She hoped they did not have far to travel this day to catch up with Barak and his men. Who knew how the girl would survive another day on horseback.

She went cold inside at the thought of Barak ben Abinoam and what he had either commanded or permitted. But as she gazed down at the sleeping girl—the sleeping *navi*, she reminded herself—she knew that she had a more pressing matter to attend to than her fury at Barak.

She rose and went quickly to where Zadok was readying the horses. The nazarite had just lifted Shomar's saddle to his back; the horse whickered softly. Devora stepped near enough to speak for his ears only. Yet standing so near him—she was more aware of him today than she had ever been before. His strength, his solidity, the way the muscles in his arms moved, the masculine scent of him. She suppressed the shiver this sent through her, felt her face burning again. She forced her thoughts to the matter at hand.

"Zadok, I want you to watch over the girl's safety."

Zadok stopped, his hand still on the girth strap. "You care for her," he said in a low voice. Devora could hear the disapproval in it. "I know. I have eyes. But she is *heathen*."

"She is the next *navi*," Devora whispered.

Silence.

Zadok's eyes showed his bewilderment, as though she'd told him the sky was made of tree leaves and she expected him to gather them up for her.

"She is the *navi*, Zadok. God sends visions to her."

"How can that be?"

"I don't know." Devora pressed a hand to her temple. "I really don't know. God's ways are strange."

Zadok's face darkened. "She is heathen. I will make no covenant with her. You, I will defend."

"You'll defend who I ask you to defend," Devora said sharply.

Zadok just growled and turned back to the horse, which flicked its tail.

"Damn it, Zadok, it's strange to me too. But the life of the next *navi* must be preserved. Even if—" Devora swallowed. "Even if I should die. The younger *navi* has to make it back to Shiloh after this."

Zadok moved around the horse, checking the saddle and the bags.

"Do you trust me, Zadok?"

"I trust you, *navi*." He gave her a pained look, and Devora was reminded sharply that he'd spent the night holding her.

"Then *trust* me. This girl is the *navi*. I don't understand it either, or like it. But God has chosen her."

A pause. "Your will, *navi*." His tone heavy with reluctance.

"Thank you," she said. "I need you, Zadok." *I need you to stand at my back*, she thought but didn't say aloud. *I need you to enforce my will when I make decisions. I need you to trust me. I need you to not mention last night, not act as though I am any other woman, not try to speak to me of it or—or kiss me. I need you to be as reliable and unbendable as that spear you carry, as reliable as you've always been.*

"You had better wake your Canaanite again," Zadok muttered after a moment.

Devora nodded and watched his face a moment before moving wearily to stir Hurriya from her restless sleep.

***

They spent much of the rest of the day in silence, and Devora sorrowed over it. It was as though someone had planted a thicket of willows between them, and they could hardly see each other through the veil of hanging leaves.

It was also a day of delay, for they stopped often to give Hurriya rest or to grant Devora a few moments to look through the grasses for some herbs that might calm her fever. She found only a few leaves of mint, had hoped for ginger root. She made do with what she had, but it did little good, and she wished bitterly that she had some of Hannah's knowledge of herbs. Even as girls, Hannah had never been good at remembering *mitzvot*, but she had always known where to find a particular blossom or a particular root and what to do with it once you found it. For Devora, there had been only the Law.

In the end, she and Zadok walked their horses, easing their way through the last miles. Perhaps there would be herbs at the camp or at that settlement on the lakeshore— surely at Walls Devora could find a midwife with knowledge of herbs and fevers.

They had spent the day tense, their eyes on the slopes about them, watching for the dead. Once, only once, Devora saw three human shapes moving along a distant ridge, walking in file like living men yet swaying from side to side like trees in a wind. She rode on without mentioning the corpses to the others, though she suspected Zadok had probably seen them too. It was more important to find Barak's camp than to pursue a few straggling dead across the hills—but it was long before Devora could tear her gaze away from those distant, ominous figures.

The fact that they didn't see more was unnerving; after the attack in the night, Devora had been ready to see herds shambling toward them, moaning and hungering for her flesh. The emptiness of this country, the constant vigilance, Zadok's tense silence, the shallow, feverish breathing of the Canaanite girl in the saddle before her—all this made Devora so jumpy that she was nearly nauseous. And the saddle rubbed her thighs terribly raw, adding an acute physical discomfort.

***

Now dusk was falling and Barak's tents lay below them by the water. The *navi* saw the open sky reflected in the lake, and when she glanced to the side she saw the lake reflected in Zadok's eyes.

"Few tents," the nazarite said quietly.

"Fewer even than I thought," Devora agreed.

The tents were pitched tightly together, like a flock of birds eyeing with dread the sharp hills surrounding them. Ready to spread their wings in a moment and leap back into the sky, leaving the land to its own horrors. Quiet in the dusk ran the Tumbling Water, which the lake fed but which didn't start tumbling until after it flowed out of this narrow valley and began descending out of the hills. The smoke of cookfires wafted across the water toward the cedar-and-thatch houses of Walls, a half mile around the edge of the lake.

But only silence wafted back.

Some of the men of the camp were standing at the shore, tiny at this distance. Perhaps they were gazing across at the eerie town. Towns were loud. So were encampments of tents and flocks—but towns were louder, and the men knew this. The beer-house at least, even at this hour of dusk, should have been boisterous and awake with firelight.

This town, however, was utterly still, utterly silent.

Devora didn't like it.

"Zadok, ride ahead, please. Tell them the *navi* is here. That she wishes to speak with Barak at once. And ask for herbs for the girl."

"Your will, *navi*." Yet Zadok cast her a glance that showed his reluctance to leave her side; Devora wondered at it. She did not think she would be in danger riding into the camp. She was *kadosh*. And she and the Canaanite girl were unlikely to be attacked by any dead on this open slope as they neared the tents. Devora cast an uneasy glance over her shoulder at the ridge behind them, half expecting to see corpses silhouetted against the sky. But there was nothing there. Not even a bird. As though the entire land had gone silent, waiting.

Like that settlement across the water.

Perhaps it was only that Zadok was uneasy leaving before speaking whatever words he'd hidden in his heart since the morning. For a moment Devora both dreaded and hoped that he would say something. But the nazarite only turned and gazed down at the camp grimly, then nudged his horse into a canter.

As he rode ahead, Hurriya whispered, "I don't have to fear him, do I?"

"No. Other people do."

"What is he?"

"You must have heard stories. Everyone in the land knows about the nazarites."

"I know they fight."

Devora watched Zadok approach the tents below and felt sorrow and a strange kind of possessiveness for the man. Zadok was hers. Had been, ever since he took the nazarite's vow, swearing it to her and God. Even before then—ever since she gave him words of comfort that day he stood by his dead father. It was right that she should speak for him. "Fighting is *all* they do," she said. "They do not tend the land, they say no prayers and perform no priestly duties. They do not trade or barter. They defend those who keep the tablets and the Tent of the Law. They give up everything for that. No, girl, you don't need to fear him."

Hurriya started shuddering. Devora felt the tremors against her body and tightened her arm about the young woman. "What is it, girl?" she whispered.

"The faces," Hurriya whispered back. "The faces."

Devora was suddenly aware of an intense, familiar heat emanating from the woman she held. Her eyes widened.

After a moment the heat flickered out as abruptly as a candle's flame. Yet Hurriya kept shaking. "The town is full of lost things," she whispered. "We have to go there."

"You saw something," Devora murmured.

"Only for a moment. A glimpse. Faces. There was a fire and all the faces were burning."

"I don't see any smoke over the town." Devora thought for a moment. Had God sent a vision of what had happened there, of what would happen, what might happen?

"The gods are cruel," Hurriya said, her voice thick. "Do they think I'll hate them less for taking my child because they bless me with knowledge they keep secret from others?"

"It is no blessing," Devora said dryly. "The *navi* brings words men need to hear, visions they need to see, not visions they *wish* to see. You see what God sees, but men don't want to see what God sees. It's not a blessing."

They were nearing the outskirts of the camp now, and Devora heard a horse coming toward them. It was not Zadok's horse. After a moment the rider cantered away from the tents and approached them, and Devora saw a scarred face and braided hair. She knew this man, and her lips twisted in distaste. Omri, the Zebulunite.

"You are here," he called as he approached. "Where is Nimri?"

"Ask him when he arrives," Devora quipped. "Where is Barak?"

Omri's eyes narrowed. "Have a little respect, woman." He drew his dun-colored horse up alongside Shomar. "You were supposed to come with an Ark," he muttered.

"Barak will have to settle for me," Devora said icily.

Omri grunted and rode beside them a moment. Then he leaned near, attempted to glance down Hurriya's salmah. Devora felt the girl tense.

"A Canaanite," he said. "And a curvaceous one. Is she for sale?"

"No, Omri." Devora's voice was winter. "She is not."

"Still." He leered at the girl. Hurriya stared fixedly ahead.

"She's unclean, Omri." Stressing each word, Devora added, "For seven days." Actually, only six days of her uncleanness were left, but this northern savage didn't need to know that.

The man recoiled and rode just behind them, his face unreadable. Devora turned her shoulder to him, speaking in a low voice to Hurriya. "Because you are unclean, your feet must not touch the ground within the camp."

Hurriya glanced over the *navi*'s shoulder, and her eyes flickered with hate.

"Ignore him. Don't even look at him. Think of him not as a Hebrew man like the one who owned you but as a small boy watching a dragonfly to see what it will do. Now imagine the dragonfly not moving, not even a flicker of its wings. The boy pokes at it. The dragonfly still does not move. So he loses interest and goes to trouble some other."

"There are no other dragonflies," Hurriya murmured.

"What?"

"No camp followers. Didn't you see? You and I are the only women here."

Devora gave a start. She halted and heard Omri halt a little way behind her. She gave the camp ahead a hard look, and considered what she *hadn't* seen, riding into the valley. Hurriya was right. There was the camp, but there were no camp *followers*. None of any kind. Devora knew enough about the raids that plagued the land to realize that any camp of armed men always had followers. Thieves ready to pick the unclean bodies of the dead. Carpenters and weavers who might be called upon to mend a broken cart or a torn tent or coat. Old Canaanite women with packets of herbs, ready to tend to fever or foot rot. And young women, Hebrew and Canaanite and mixed, women without husbands or fields to glean, who in the final extremity of their hunger would barter their bodies for food. Usually there were far more camp followers than there were men in the raid. But not this time. There were none. Not when the men were going to seek out the dead.

That made her uneasy—it meant she and Hurriya were alone in a camp of men. Already others in the camp were gathering outside their tents, not near enough yet to shout to, but near enough to watch Devora and Hurriya ride in. Omri wasn't the only one who was famished enough for sex to cast an eye on the *navi* and the woman who was with her.

"It doesn't matter," Devora murmured. "I am the *navi* and can't be touched. And you are unclean and can't be touched. These men are bound to the Covenant and the Law."

"I have seen how they keep it here," Hurriya said coldly.

Devora straightened. She didn't want to think about that just now. About how the keeping of the Law may have decayed in these hills. She cast the men an uneasy glance. Remembered Lappidoth urging her to take the other nazarites with her. "*We* will keep it," she said. "And so your feet will not touch the ground within the camp.

249

Stay in this saddle until I can arrange for bedding and a tent outside the camp."

"Where I'll be defenseless," she said quietly. "Your rules are ridiculous."

"And necessary." Devora's voice was sharp. She was keenly aware of Omri's eyes on her back. "We don't know what kind of touch allows the uncleanness to pass from one body to another. So we must assume any touch may defile."

"But this fever isn't—it isn't *that* fever." A sharp intake of breath. "It isn't, is it?"

"No." Devora softened, and started Shomar toward the tents again at a walk. "No, I don't believe so. It is all right, girl. But the words of the Law remain. The Lawgiver in the desert demanded seven days. He wrote that into the Covenant. To make sure the People would never become too hasty, never endanger the camp by bringing someone unclean back into it too quickly. Our Covenant holds the living together and gives them hope, and keeps the dead buried and still. Look around at the terror in these hills, and see the consequence of neglecting it."

Omri interrupted then by nudging his horse alongside Shomar. His grin showed all his teeth.

"Where are the dead, Omri?" Devora asked, cutting off whatever the man had intended to say.

"God knows. We've been waiting here for Nimri since early morning."

"I see. Have you sent men to scout the hills around? Why is the town so quiet?"

"Why doesn't God send us visions to tell us?" Omri muttered. "Why else have you come?"

"God may send warnings," Devora said, "but I doubt our God intends to do the work that the men of this camp can do."

"He didn't send us warnings that the dead would be eating tribesmen up by Judges' Well. So what good is he?"

Devora stared at the Zebulunite in disbelief. "You northerners marry heathen, allow heathen gods to be worshipped in your tents and your houses. Someone up here leaves dead unburied, untended. And the dead rise and begin eating, and you want to blame *God* for not forewarning you? Your actions, your—callousness toward God and Law—these are warning enough!"

"You're the one with a heathen slut on your horse," Omri grinned. For some reason he didn't seem rattled by Devora's outburst, and with a shock she realized that she had diminished herself in his eyes. Just a woman getting upset and railing at a man, like any other who didn't know her place. That's what Omri must be thinking.

"There's too much God in you," he told the *navi*, then looked her over as he had on the hill. Devora's jaw tightened.

"A lot of woman too, though," he grinned. "I am glad you are with us."

Devora said nothing in reply; her unease grew. Hurriya was tense in her arms. Perhaps the girl had a point about the men of this camp.

"I saw the nazarite," Omri said as he nudged his horse closer, "but not your husband. Why didn't he join us?"

Devora's throat was tight. She couldn't say that she had begged Lappidoth to remain behind, for this would diminish him in the eyes of the northern men, making him seem a slave to his woman. Yet anything else she blamed his absence on—his age, or fear, or a devotion to other duties—would make him seem no less small to them. She kept her lips closed and held down a flash fire of fury at Omri for the question. And truly, she wanted—needed—Lappidoth here. He had always been the tent over her, the shelter for her when her fears were fiercest.

"Huh," Omri grunted. "At least I have something to look at that's prettier than Barak's old face."

Devora felt her face burning. The Zebulunite was *flirting* with her. Yet she was the *navi* and had a husband, and if she'd had a son when most Hebrew women had their sons, that son would now be Omri's own age, or older. What was he thinking?

Devora nudged Shomar to a slightly quicker pace, but Omri stayed beside them, complimenting her eyes, the line of her jaw, the cradle of her hips. Devora's face burned hotter.

Hurriya shifted as though about to act or speak; Devora clenched her hand tightly around the girl's arm through the wool of her salmah, forbidding it.

"I like the way you ride that horse," Omri crooned. "Would you like to ride something else?" As Devora refused to look at him, Omri sidled close enough to place his hand on her thigh, his fingers gripping her in the most nauseating manner. She turned on him as quickly as a serpent. "What are you doing?" she whispered fiercely. "Do you think I won't cry out and have you stoned for trying to possess another man's woman?"

"I don't see another man here," Omri grinned. "He seems to have lost you."

As if she were a sort of misplaced trinket that had rolled out from under her husband's watchful eye and might now be picked up! Lappidoth had taught her that men were capable of valuing all of a woman, not only her thighs or her womb. This oaf apparently wanted only to rut with her. She was the *navi*; who did he think he was?

"Get your hand *off* me," Devora hissed.

Omri's fingers dug into her thigh as his face flushed with anger. Perhaps he had not heard that commanding tone from a woman since he was a small boy in his mother's tent.

Devora's eyes went dark. She reached for Mishpat.

Just then there was a clatter of hooves, and glancing over her shoulder Devora saw Zadok riding toward them from the tents at a clip that was just a little too quick to be casual. Relief swept through her like a summer wind.

Omri followed her gaze and scowled. "Does that dog always heel you?" he muttered. His hand left her thigh.

"Only when the *navi* needs him to," Devora said quietly. "I am *kadosh*, Omri. Holy. Not to be touched."

He sneered. "You are still a woman."

"Not your woman."

"Huh. The Galilee is a long way from Shiloh."

Devora's insides went cold. How dare he. Did he think distance lessened her husband's claims on her, or hers on him? Or did Omri mean to threaten her, to indicate *he* could claim her as he pleased, here in the north, among his own people?

Zadok was nearly up to them. Omri whispered, "If you find your need is hot on you, woman, and you need a man between your legs, my tent is easy to find."

"Shouldn't you be making plans for dealing with the dead?" Her hand clenched about Mishpat's hilt, a fact that Zadok's eyes didn't miss as he reined up beside her. Massive and brooding and watching Omri with his cold, dark face.

"Omri," Zadok grinned—though the grin did not touch his eyes. "Is there any beer in the camp?"

Omri bristled, as though expecting a challenge. But Zadok offered none.

"Ride with me," the nazarite said. "There's a lot we need to talk about." He said that with a bit of an edge to it, and in a moment he'd grasped the pommel of Omri's saddle and was steering the man's horse away from the women. Devora let out the breath she'd been holding, but her hand did not lift from Mishpat's hilt.

"You still think I should sleep alone at the camp's edge?" Hurriya asked quietly.

"*I* will be sleeping at the camp's edge," Devora said firmly. "I am *kadosh*. My tent will stand apart. Zadok will be at hand. You will have bedding outside my tent. Be alert and cry out if you need to. But you won't need to. No one but a fool would cross Zadok."

Hurriya looked ahead, at the men standing outside their tents. "I see nothing but fools," she said.

Choosing not to answer that, Devora watched Zadok and Omri cantering ahead, then lifted her eyes, looked again at the placid lake and the too-silent town on the farther shore. Cold clenched about her heart. She didn't know what Hurriya's vision meant, and the younger *navi* was untrained, unable to interpret the things God showed to her. But Devora did know this. Whatever was to happen here in the north would begin there, at that lake.

At the town of Walls, which no longer had any. Among houses silent as cairns for the dead.

***

As Shomar followed Zadok's horse among the tents, Devora began to notice how *odd* this camp was. Not at all what she might have expected—but then, her experience of fighting men was largely limited to the nazarites, who were well-armed, disciplined, and who acted as though ferocity were an essential, if unspoken, part of their vow. This camp was *not* a camp of nazarites. It was something else entirely.

For one thing, the men were barely armed at all. Only a few with shields, some without even spears, just farming implements or sharpened poles. These were northern men; their fathers hadn't taken any lions' shares of the loot from the cities whose walls had tumbled in the south where the Tumbling Water stopped tumbling at last and moved lazy and wide through green fields. And the glances of desire they cast at the two women riding past could not disguise their underlying fear. Devora saw the way their hands trembled, the pallor of their faces. Was it *these* men she had come north for? These were only children, fearing the dark.

The men gathered near as she walked Shomar through the tents, and the horse shied, having never been among such a press of people. Devora patted the horse's flank to calm him. Feeling the shiver that passed through Hurriya,

Devora said softly by the girl's ear, "My husband's horse will not drop you."

Hurriya gave a terse nod.

"Anath loves horses," the Canaanite said after a moment, keeping her eyes on Zadok's horse ahead of them, refusing to glance at the men who crowded close to either side. "She even found one, a wild horse by the river. She tamed it and used to ride it in the early morning. She thought none of us knew, but *I* knew." Again the shiver. "I need to tell her horses hurt. They hurt. Why does she always look happy after riding?"

"A horse doesn't always hurt," Devora smiled. "We just haven't ridden much, you and I. We will heal." Privately she wondered if that was true of the girl. It was perhaps a miracle that she was still this lucid. Would herbs help, or was this journey in the north consuming the girl's last strength? She cursed Barak in her heart for making such a journey necessary.

She tried to ignore the fear in the many faces around her. But what good would a camp filled with terrified men be to her or to God?

"*Damn it*," she whispered.

She kicked Shomar to a gallop, startling a cry from Hurriya. Then a shout from Zadok, who had turned in his saddle at Hurriya's cry. Devora made for the center of the camp, pulling up her horse where the tents were thickest. Men gathered in a half circle about her, and she lifted one hand high, her other arm about the Canaanite.

"Tribes of the north!" she cried. "Put away your fear! Bury it. Raise a cairn over it. Shun it as you would the dead. It will do you as much harm, or more. Remember that you are men. And men of Israel, whose fathers wrestled with God in the desert and wrung blessings from him!" Her voice rose nearly to a scream. "God gave you this land of promise, took it from others who were here before you and gave it into your hands. Now defend it!"

The men looked at her, but none raised their voices to affirm her words. Their faces were still pale with fear. Devora faltered. She was used to men listening attentively when the *navi* spoke, before springing to action. But these men had never stood before the *navi*'s seat. In their faces, Devora saw that her words neither shamed them nor inspired them. In their eyes, she saw that they were merely listening to a woman because a few moments ago there had been no woman in the camp, and she was strange to them.

"Listen," she told them, trying to keep her voice steady. Their gaze unnerved her. "Everyone fears the dead," she said. "I do too. But the dead are weak, and the God of your land is strong. Do you fear to face the dead without spears, shields, with just a fence pole in your hands? The dead don't even have that. They are just stumbling, clumsy bodies. Taking them down," she chopped her arm through the air, "is like cutting trees. Our fathers broke a strong wall at Yeriho. The dead are not stronger than a stone wall."

The men stared at her in silence.

"Be strong and courageous," she urged them. "Show our God that you do not doubt, that you are not less than your fathers were." She faltered. "Do you not know who I am?" she asked at last.

"You are from Shiloh," one man called out.

"I am the *navi* of Israel," she said. "I see what God sees."

"God has turned his eyes away," another man called. "We passed an orchard—it was blighted."

A murmur rose from the men, an angry, despairing sound. Hurriya shuddered, and Devora's arm tightened about her. She understood; the men had seen the *malakh ha-mavet*, even as she had. And the only vision of victory she had to share was an image of a woman driving a peg through a corpse's skull. She'd told Barak that women would protect Israel. But if she told these men that, these cruel northern men, they would surely only laugh at her with that cold, bitter laughter that she knew all too well. What could she tell them? These were not supplicants waiting on her judgment beneath the olive tree—yet they *were* waiting on her judgment. They were waiting to hear what God might say to them, what accusation God might make to explain the presence of the walking dead, or what defense God might make for the removal of his protection. All their eyes on her. So many eyes filled with dread.

"God will defend us," she said hoarsely. "He fights with us." The inadequacy of her words shook her.

"Let's go," Hurriya whispered, turning her head so that her lips were not far from the *navi*'s ear. "Please, let's just go."

"Be still," Devora whispered back. She gazed out over those despairing faces and understood the Canaanite's panic. She had miscalculated. All it would take was the wrong word spoken, and these men might take their despair and terror out on *her*. She could feel Zadok's tension behind her, as though all the air around the nazarite was stretched tight, ready to snap. Omri at least had slipped away, no doubt uncomfortable around the nazarite.

Lappidoth had wanted her to take all the nazarites with her. Swallowing, she conceded that he might perhaps have been right.

But her anger was stronger than her fear. These men would *not* wilt like a dying crop and leave her and this Canaanite girl and the other women of the land to face the dead for them. "Where is Barak ben Abinoam?" she cried.

Mutely, several of the men gestured toward the shore, and Devora glanced there and saw by the water one tent larger than the others, a great pavilion dyed in earth colors, rich browns and reds. Devora lifted her eyes, caught Zadok's gaze, nodded toward the pavilion. Then she turned her back on the scared men, coldly, deliberately. Keeping her arm tight around the Canaanite, whose breathing was quick and shallow, perhaps from fever, perhaps from fear.

Devora gave the tent a grim look.

She would make sure this was a meeting Barak ben Abinoam would never forget.

KADOSH

BARAK WAITED, cross-legged, on the rug-covered floor of his pavilion. He could hear the *navi*'s voice outside, speaking to his frightened men. He cursed Nimri in the silence of his heart for failing to bring him the Ark, that he might burn the unclean dead from the land. As a child sitting between his grandfather's knees, he'd heard of how the Ark had burned dry the Tumbling Water itself, which south of Kinnor Sea was not the stream it was here but rather a roaring, crashing river falling out of the high hills. He'd heard how the tribes had crossed over on dry ground. Of how the Ark had brought drought to their enemies or kindled their tents like straw. He glanced at his spear where it rested against one of the four poles of his tent. A spear was enough for a man to carry against raiders from the sea—but against the dead?

Barak heard the sounds of horse and saddle outside of the door of his tent and straightened. She was here, the *navi*, just outside.

He dreaded this meeting but had determined that Devora would come to *him*, here. He would not argue with a *woman* where his men could see and hear. Especially *this* woman.

She was *kadosh*, set apart. Which meant she couldn't be understood, no more than God. She was a woman; when he'd faced her on her hill above Shiloh, he'd seen the fineness of her features, her smallness, the shape of her body within her dress. She should be in her husband's tent, pleasing him or mending his garments, or preparing stew and warm milk for him. But she was not in her husband's tent. She was here. And it was to her, out of all the men and women of the land, that God chose to speak and reveal what was to come. She and the Ark were both vessels to carry words spoken by God. One vessel of wood, one of flesh, both were reminders that God was at hand.

He took a small breath; he didn't know how to handle her.

***

Zadok entered Barak's pavilion first and moved aside to stand by the door of the tent, tall and glowering, the light from Barak's small fire playing off the hard, unforgiving edges of his face. A moment later Devora swept in with a swish of her long, travel-stained white dress and fury in her eyes.

The *navi* did not do anything Barak might have expected of a woman entering his tent. Devora did not kneel before him on the rug nor did she sit. She strode across the tent, giving him hardly time to lean back from the intrusion before her hand whipped across his face, striking him hard enough to black his vision for an instant.

He caught her wrist even as she drew it back, held it tightly. Her eyes were dark as the midnight at the bottom of a lake.

"Release the *navi*'s hand." A growl from Zadok at the door of the tent.

Breathing hard, his pulse pounding in his temples, Barak gazed into those midnight eyes a moment before glancing past Devora to see the nazarite standing like a tower, filling even the war-leader's voluminous pavilion. Barak's own growl was deep in his throat. But this was the *navi*. She was *kadosh*. Forbidden to touch her. He let go of Devora's hand, his teeth bared from the effort of holding in his rage. His cheek stung.

"How *dare* you," the *navi* hissed, standing before him. "Israel *needs* you. How *dare* you betray the Covenant so."

He rose slowly to his feet, breathing deep. "Where is Nimri?" he growled.

"Dealt with." Devora nearly spat the words, and the threat in them took Barak aback. His anger flickered down like a fire growing cold; he was bewildered. What had the *navi* done to that belligerent herdsman of Naphtali tribe? What *could* the *navi* do?

"Give one reason, one, why I shouldn't deal with you likewise." Though Devora's head barely came to Barak's chin, her presence filled the tent. "God is not an idol of wood you can cart about, wine-drinker. You think God is a—a weapon for your hand!" Her face was flushed with fury, those eyes darker by the moment. "But you are a weapon in *God*'s hand, Barak!"

He bristled. He would *not* be upbraided by this woman, like some boy come late to dinner with unwashed hands. "I am no god's weapon and no man's," he growled. "I am a vintner who has been eleven days from my vineyard while dead prowl about it, and I fear for the harvest." He lifted his hand when she started to speak, and to his surprise she stopped and listened, though her eyes flashed. "I do want the Ark. I see it isn't coming." For some reason he found himself needing to persuade her. His voice had an edge to it. "Some of the men in this camp want to thieve our few horses and ride after the dead now, this night, and be done with it. Men of Omri's sort. Others wish to slip away when I'm not looking. It is only by a *hair* that I hold this raid together, *navi*!" He was shouting now but could not stop. "These men *need* an Ark. Something holy, something *kadosh*, something they can keep their eyes on, that will tell them where they are supposed to stand and where they are supposed to walk, in what direction, whether to fight or flee. Something they will trust more than they trust me. They need an Ark. I sent Nimri for it—" He took a breath. "I had little time, and I hoped he would deal with the high priest in my stead—"

"Nimri *slew* the high priest."

A silence brittle enough for a single word to shatter. For several moments, no word did. Barak's face went completely white. The tent seemed to tilt toward him, and he could hear every beat of his heart.

Unthinkable.

He fought to breathe.

"I—did not mean that it should come to that," he whispered.

The silence stretched until it was taut and tense. Devora's face grew colder. Zadok loomed by the door of the pavilion with his arms folded across his chest, like some monument in fertile lands on the other side of the desert. Their eyes were on Barak with an intensity that shook him. His palms were sweaty, his throat too tight for words.

The *high priest*. Slain.

Nimri—what had he done? A scream was rising somewhere in the back of his mind.

"You're more heathen than Hebrew," Devora said at last. Her voice was like the winter wind through a door. She turned with a dismissiveness to her movements, as though she had no more time to waste with him. Zadok drew aside the tent flap and preceded her, and in a moment she was gone and the tent was too full of thunderous silence. Barak swayed on his feet.

The high priest was *dead*. The blight in Barak's vineyard appeared vividly before his heart. He had taken up the spear, pleading with God to shelter his vineyard while he defended the vineyards of other men. What wrath had that ass Nimri brought down on them all? Barak's covenant with God was already a fragile, provisional thing.

He burst into motion, sprang from his tent. Outside, dark was falling.

"Navi!"

She was already on horseback, with a young Canaanite in the saddle before her. Zadok was mounting his black gelding. Men stood at the egresses of nearby tents, watching with wide eyes.

"You can't leave!" Barak shouted, his voice pitched in a way that shamed him. "The men—"

"I am not leaving." She nodded toward the lake. "I am riding to that settlement."

Barak shook his head. "Not alone—"

"God has something to show me there. There was a vision as we came down from the hills." She nudged Shomar forward, turning her head enough that Barak could hear her speak over her shoulder, though she did not look at him. "There's something in the cedar houses I need to see."

Barak glanced at the lake and the silent houses. "I'll get men."

"I'll hear God better without them." She and Zadok spurred their horses to a trot.

Aghast, Barak called to the men outside their tents. "Stop them!"

Several men sprang before the horses. Even as they did, Devora unsheathed Mishpat and held the blade ready at her side, where it shone in the starlight like an invitation to death. Clean and white and unanswerable as an act of God. Barak gasped, for the blade was clearly iron, not bronze. Once only in his life had Barak ben Abinoam seen with his own eyes an implement of iron; the heathen champion who'd led the coastal raid Barak had repelled years ago had carried such a blade, and it had cut through the bronze shields of Barak's men as easily as if Barak were defending his vineyard and theirs with only sticks of wood—as though a heathen not-god lived within the metal, thirsting with the need to sever and kill.

Whether at the sword or the oncoming of the horses or the fury naked in the *navi*'s eyes, the men fell back. The *navi* and the nazarite sent their horses into a brisk canter. In a moment they were gone from the camp, riding out toward the shore.

"*Damn it!*" Barak yelled. "Omri, Laban!" The war leaders were already near, drawn by the shouts and the hoofbeats, and they ran toward him. "You each gather up ten men, your best. Follow me!" Barak shouted the words as he ran for his own horse. As he saddled Ager and then leapt astride, his heart pounded fiercely. Women and God always brought trouble to a man's house. This woman and her God more than most. "*Ya!*" he roared, wresting Ager's head up and digging in his knees.

THE SILENT TOWN

DEVORA AND ZADOK had a good start, and Barak didn't catch up to them until their steeds had carried them into the town, past the settlement's cistern and up a long street between two-story houses of cedar and fir. No voices called out from the houses, either to greet or challenge these strangers in their town. Nor did Barak call out to the houses. The gaping holes of the upper-story windows opened on lightless rooms as dark as though God had never created light. *That* kind of dark.

Fears rose in Barak's mind that he hadn't shivered under since he was a small boy—when he'd cry out for his mother, and her soft words would drive away the unclean, lurching things with which his imagination had peopled the night. His mother was not here now. And the irremediable dark within these deserted houses might conceal anything. Bodies, whether still or in motion. Bodies rising from the floor, mouths open and hungering, silently approaching, arms outreached to grab at him. His blood was loud in his ears, loud and demanding as God's voice at Har Sinai. It took everything in him not to turn his horse and bolt from this strange town.

But there was no scent of death. Just stillness.

There was no sound of hooves behind him; the other men he'd called for were no doubt riding to catch up but hadn't yet reached the settlement. He glanced down at his saddlebag. There was a curved bulge where he'd packed the shofar he carried. If he needed it. He made the sign against evil quickly with his left hand. He had lost the Ark; he intended to keep at least the *navi*.

Barak caught up with her, his horse wheezing, even as Devora slid from her own steed's back where she and Zadok had halted outside a tumbled ruin of rafters and soot. One of those houses of cedar—a very great one—had burned to the ground; heaps of charred wood rose from the ashes the way lost kin rise from the mists in our dreams, fragments of our past demanding attention. There was no smoke rising from the cinders and no glow of embers—the fire must have been out a few days—but the scent of burned wood remained thick in the air.

Barak pulled Ager up before the ruin, a few steps from Devora. "What are you doing?" he whispered fiercely, glaring down at the *navi*, ignoring the tall nazarite who stood by her. "There could be dead here."

"There most likely are."

"Then what are you doing here, *navi*, without more men?"

Devora glanced at him, her eyes still dark with anger.

Zadok's voice was a cold challenge in the dark. "If the *navi* says there is something we must see here, then there is something we must see."

Devora glanced at the nazarite. "Even if there wasn't," she said quietly, "we must find an herbalist, or her supplies. For the girl."

Barak gave the Canaanite an uneasy glance. The girl was gazing about, frowning as though looking for something she might recognize. Her eyes were a little glazed, and she was very pale. With a start, Barak realized she was ill with fever.

"That girl," he said hoarsely. "Is she—"

"It's not that kind of fever," Devora said. "But she has touched the dead." With her gaze fixed on the charred ruin before them, the *navi* unstrapped a waterskin from the side of the saddle and handed it up to the girl. The Canaanite took the skin and held it, but didn't drink.

"Wait for my men," Barak said.

"Are you afraid, Barak?" An edge to the *navi*'s voice.

He didn't know how to answer that. Admit his fear to a woman? He turned his head and spat on the hard-packed dirt of the street.

"So am I," the *navi* said. "Let's take a look." For a moment the *navi* turned her attention to her horse. The gelding's eyes were showing their whites, and Devora scratched under his chin a moment. The gelding whickered softly, but his eyes stayed round with fear. Leaning in, Devora whispered in the horse's ear. Then she stepped away from her horse, with Mishpat unsheathed at her side.

"Zadok, watch over the girl, please."

"Your will, *navi*."

Devora left her horse, and the nazarite sat his with an uneasy look that Barak could well understand. As the *navi* walked slowly to the ruin, Barak looked at the charred timbers, then his gaze darted to the houses at either side, which were solid and intact. Only one house had burned. There must have been no wind. Still, a fire in an encampment or a town was a furious thing; there must have been men here to put the fire out before it devoured the other homes. But how had they salvaged nothing of this one house yet kept it from the others? It was as though this one house had been struck by a firebolt of divine judgment from the sky, or as though the people had stood about it with water and blankets, keeping the fire contained. Watching it burn. It made no sense. *Nothing* about this town made any sense. He had been here before, twice, years ago. Once when he met Hadassah as she drew water from the town's cistern, once when he came to speak with the town's elders at the gate, during the worst raids from the Sea People. It had been a grim settlement but a thriving one. Now these silent houses—it was as though the settlement he knew had never existed. Or as though he were no longer even walking in the waking world—as though somehow he had ridden Ager right into the dream country. He shivered.

"That fire was not accidental." Devora kept her voice low. "Look. There's wood piled against the wall that fell, and fragments of a broken oil jar."

Barak gave a start and took a closer look at the ruined structure. Yes, he could see the woodpile now—a great heap of embers and charred ends of boards, hidden half from sight under the collapsed wall. And a few pottery shards in the ash. He glanced at Devora, noting the confidence and rigid certainty of her posture, the cold in her face. *She sees what others do not*—that's what was whispered of her in the land. *She finds justice; the defiler and the defiled cannot hide from her.*

"Why would someone burn an empty house?" he murmured.

"It wasn't empty," Devora said quietly.

Barak's pulse quickened. He took another look, a careful one. There. His throat tightened. Crushed beneath the fallen timbers, a body charred and blackened, only its legs visible. One shred of cloth wound about the left leg had somehow escaped the fire as if by an act of God, who loathes above all deeds a murder committed in silence without eyes to witness. The betraying cloth was white, though smudged now with ash and soot.

Devora stepped with an old woman's care through the ruins. Barak watched her without dismounting. The white cloth gave him an uneasy feeling in his belly, like nausea, but weaker than that; he felt that he knew what kind of cloth the man had worn and what it must signify, but he would not look at it in his mind. It was like the dead in his vineyard—he knew the horror was there, he could hear it rustling among the vines, but he could not see it without stepping closer to peer between the green leaves—and that he would not do. If some man had been murdered here in his own house, his shelter burned down about his head by his neighbors' malice or fear, let God whisper the secret, if he would, into the ears of his *navi*; Barak would not go digging among the cinders to find it. He had trouble enough.

In the saddle, the Canaanite began humming softly to herself. The sound of it was very lovely, and the tune was simple and familiar, though it was a moment before he knew what it was. Barak felt his eyes burn and scrubbed the back of his hand across them quickly, and only then realized it was the same go-to-sleep song Hadassah had used to sing while holding her belly, when she was with child.

"Be still, woman." His voice was hoarse.

The song stopped. Hurriya looked at him.

"We're all going to die here," the young woman whispered.

Barak jerked. "I said be still," he snapped.

"Something's wrong here. All wrong. Some of the people didn't leave. And the ones that did left parts of themselves behind. And now we won't be able to leave."

Barak lifted a hand to slap her, to bring her out of whatever fit she was in or merely to silence her. But at that moment Devora turned back toward them. Barak lowered his hand.

"Something very wrong *did* happen here," Devora murmured when she reached them, and her face was cold.

Hoofbeats interrupted her, and Barak snapped his head about to gaze down the street, the way they'd come. Several horses turned the corner—eight, maybe nine horses. All that the camp had left, since Nimri had not returned. He recognized Omri at the front and Laban right behind him, a man nearly as large as Zadok, with his great axe strapped across his back. Both of these chieftains bore torches, the firelight revealing their faces in the dark. As they rode nearer, it was clear the others were men of Laban's, hardy men of Issachar. Barak breathed a sigh of relief. He could bear the silence of this town better if he had men at his back.

"Chieftain!" Omri called as the men pulled up beside the ruin. "More men are coming. On foot."

Laban gave the ruin a dark look. "What is this?"

"They burned the house," Devora said, nearly trembling with fury. "These half-heathen. They *burned* this house and him in it. He needs a cairn." Her voice rose, something near panic. "They *needed* to give him a *cairn*."

"Why kill him at all?" Barak asked. "He was a levite. I saw the robe."

"He was already dead," Devora said. "They locked him in his own house. His body likely stopped breathing long before the fire was lit. His neighbors boarded up his house, shutting him in. They could hear him thumping against the walls inside. They could hear him moaning." Her eyes had a distant look, and Barak wondered suddenly if she was *seeing* what she described, not as a woman imagining it or deducing it, but as a *navi* witnessing it, witnessing events that were already past as clearly as he himself might witness some event in the present. He felt a chill.

Then the look passed from her eyes and she drew in a slow breath. "It took them a long time to gather up the courage," she murmured. "They stood there praying and weeping in the street. And finally they burned the house."

"God," Barak whispered. "Holy God."

"They *spat* in the face of Holy God when they set fire to a body made in his likeness," Devora said coldly, turning from the ashes and striding back to her horse. "Only God has any right to burn lives from the earth. Bodies belong beneath clean stone, with raised cairns so they can be remembered. Who will remember this man?"

Hurriya, still in the saddle and shivering a little from her fever, was gazing on the ruin with a fascinated, focused look.

"Men are different in the towns," Laban said, his voice deeper even than Zadok's. "We believe we are twelve tribes, *navi*, but we are really two. Men of the tents, men of the cedar houses. Issachar still lives in tents. Here, in the hills of Naphtali tribe, men have raised houses or live in houses the Canaanites raised. Men of the tents hold to the Law. We know how fragile our tents are. Men of the houses—" He shrugged. "The houses are large. They like to have many people in them to share bread. They learn strange ways, are quicker to do strange things."

"This is no Canaanite custom," Hurriya called faintly, "to burn our dead. We take our dead to the water."

Even as Devora climbed into the saddle behind the girl, Barak glanced down the empty street, pondering what commands to give Laban and Omri.

They were here. They might as well do this right.

"My men and I will look around." He looked to the nazarite. "The women stay here."

"Zadok," the *navi* said, her voice cold and authoritative. Without another word, Devora got her horse moving and walked him down the street, with the Canaanite breathing shallowly, her head resting on the *navi*'s clothed shoulder. The nazarite gave Barak a warning look and followed.

Barak cursed. "Laban, search the west end of the settlement. See if you can find any of the people who lived here. Take the men. Omri, with me."

He turned Ager and rode after the *navi*, overtaking her. He heard the clatter of hooves from Omri's steed close behind him and, more distantly, the hoofbeats and the voices of the men moving off in the other direction. Seeing that woman riding ahead with that wild blade unsheathed, fury and confusion burned in his breast.

Barak moved his horse alongside Shomar and pressed the gelding's side aggressively, his leg brushing Devora's a moment. "Do you think you can ride where you will," he whispered fiercely, "like a man?"

"I think I can ride where God sends me," she said.

Omri drew up alongside Barak on the left, holding his torch away from his horse, and he gave Barak a look that made it clear the young chieftain would enjoy beating this woman and teaching her her place. Barak held up his hand to forestall any fool's speech from the younger man. He pitched his voice low. "*Navi*, you are not in Shiloh. You are in my camp, among my men. You will go where I tell you and stay where I put you."

The *navi*'s eyes flashed. "This is Walls, this is not your camp," she said.

"If you leave the *navi*'s side, you will die tonight." The Canaanite kept her eyes lowered in the way of a northern woman, with respect, but there was a bite to her tone.

Barak's eyes widened.

"What have you seen, Hurriya?" Devora asked quietly.

"The dead." The Canaanite gazed ahead with that same, glazed look. "They filled the street."

"And you saw Barak fighting them," Devora murmured. "So it was not a vision of what has already happened. Hurriya has visions, as I do, Barak. She sees what God sees. You can trust what she says."

Two women who were *kadosh*. Two of them. But Barak

275

didn't have time to dwell on it, for the girl's words seeped in past his anger and unease. His palms began to sweat. "There are dead in the houses or somewhere near," he said.

"I saw them in the street," the heathen girl said faintly.

They walked their horses slowly, watching and listening. They had kept their voices low. Their horses' hooves seemed too loud against the hard dirt. The street grew a little wider around them, and instead of houses there were now low shops, structures with three walls and thatched roofs, open to the street. Walls had been the largest settlement in the north, and there were many shops on this narrow market street that ran the length of the town. In most of them, the wares still hung, exposed to any thieving hands, as though their owners had fled without tarrying to pack away their livelihoods. Barak saw pottery, lovely in its beauty but with a thin sheen of dust settling over it. He saw dyed cloth brought in by camel and caravan from the coast, he saw beads and jewelry from the Horse People east of the Tumbling Water. One shop sold small gods and goddesses. Devora hissed through her teeth as they passed that one.

At last the *navi* stopped beside an open shop where dozens of small leather pouches hung on cords from the roof, and bound sheaves of leaves and herbs hung beside them. She rode Shomar right into the shop without dismounting and talked with Hurriya in a voice too quiet for Barak to hear her words. The *navi* brushed her fingers across the leaves, sometimes bringing her hand to her nose to catch the leaves' scent. She opened some of the pouches.

It seemed to take a long time, and Barak's palms kept sweating. He peered down the street at the dead market and the empty shops. Omri fidgeted beside him, drumming his own saddle with his fingertips. "Why do women take so long at everything?" the younger man muttered. "Take half a day to a market, come late to a meal, come late to bed. When I own a girl, I'll—"

"Shh." Barak held up his hand again. Omri subsided with one last mutter, then kicked his horse and rode ahead a little. Barak waited by the shop. He wondered suddenly if he should muffle the horses' hooves by winding cloth about them. He felt wary of making any unnecessary sound. Even the crackling of Omri's torch sounded too loud to him. He glanced at the grim nazarite and saw in Zadok's eyes that he too was anxious, though he sat very still in his saddle. Barak lifted his head and took the air's scent, but could detect no decay in it. He looked about at the emptiness of Walls with wide eyes, his heart beating fast. The girl's words kept echoing in his mind. The dead were here. Or somewhere close.

After a moment he thought he heard humming, and caught his breath again. The Canaanite; she hummed only a few notes, then stopped. The loss of it wrenched at him; for a moment she'd sounded very like Hadassah.

"What is that song?" he whispered as loudly as he dared. He'd never asked Hadassah what the words meant, but hearing the melody now, with Hadassah dead beneath her cairn and forever lost to him, the strangeness of the tune and the heathen words of it haunted him.

When Hurriya spoke after a moment, her voice was cold and distant. Devora kept looking through the herbalist's wares, appearing to ignore the girl.

"He grows tall as a cedar tree," the girl whispered, and Barak had to strain to hear her. "He will have fine things to delight him. Olive oil and perfumes for his body. And a woman who is scented and lovely for him. And when his mother has died, he will hear her voice whenever he walks by the water where her body is. I—I sang it to my little one, walking out of the hills. Until he died. Afterward, when I tried, he—it—the moaning—"

She fell silent.

Barak gazed at the girl in horror.

Devora held a few leaves in her hand, and now she plucked a few more from their sheaf by the roof above her head. Barak recognized the first as mint but had no idea what the other leaves were. The *navi* handed them to the girl and said softly, "Chew these, girl. We'll brew some into tea later. Chew, it'll help."

The girl took one leaf and nibbled on it, her breathing shallow.

Devora backed her horse out of the little shop. "That song. Why do you Canaanites promise soft lives to your children?" she asked, her voice quiet and bitter. "You make it too easy to forget the desert. You give them lies to hope in. Life is—brutal. It might be given to us or taken from us. Painting your eyes with kohl or wearing dyed cloth from the sea does not change this." Her face darkened as she gazed about at the abandoned shops. "You heathen will never be as vigilant as we are. You have not suffered as we have."

For a moment, only the sound of hooves on the hard, packed dirt.

"*I* have suffered," Hurriya said, biting off a little of the leaf.

Devora flushed and said nothing.

"And you are wrong. Maybe my mothers and fathers never had to fear being eaten in the *desert*. But, knowing the danger, we might be as careful as you! And we *know* things, useful things. Walls—our fathers *built* walls, but yours tore them down. Walls could have saved my—" She choked and fell silent.

"Walls couldn't have saved this town," Devora said. "Whatever happened here happened inside the houses."

Down the street, Omri began to thump the butt of his spear against the packed earth, and Barak bristled. Did he have to make such noise?

"Look," Zadok said sharply.

Barak and the *navi* both followed his gaze and saw, far down the street, beyond the shops, where another street lined with houses crossed this one, there stood a mighty house, much larger than any other they'd seen, an elder's house. This house also had gone up like a torch. The walls still stood, but they were charred and blackened from fire and there were great holes in their sides. The roof appeared to be entirely gone. More than anything, the house reminded Barak of the way blackened cedars sometimes stand on the hills for years, their insides hollowed out by lightning and the wrath of God.

His throat tightened. This town, like his own small homestead, had been prosperous. It sat by a lake filled with fish, a day's walk from plentiful fields, a land of rich vineyards and soft rains. The land they'd been promised, milk and honey. Grape bunches large as a man's chest. Hadassah, her body warm in the soft night. Where were those promises now? Burned out, blighted, ash and cinders.

Cold sweat. His tunic stuck to his back.

They cantered slowly past the shops toward the house, and Omri joined them, lifting his spear. He looked a little pale. As they rode closer, Barak thought he saw movement in the shadows before the door of the house. With a shock, he realized there was a figure on its knees, bent over another figure that lay still on the earth. Barak gasped. That figure supine on the ground was a corpse, an unburied and defiled corpse. All the flesh and muscle had been stripped from the legs, which were only bones. Only the torso still resembled a living person. The body was small—a child or a dwarf; its face had been torn and gnawed, making it impossible to tell. The belly had been gouged open, and the thing leaning over it had its fists full of entrails, lifted slickly from the torn belly to its hungering mouth. As Barak halted his horse, the thing glanced over its shoulder at him, its mouth and chin dark with blood, its eyes—*terrible* eyes—dull and sightless in the starlight. It snarled, teeth bared, like an animal warning scavengers back from its prey.

The eater was a woman.

A sound of hooves behind him, then Devora was beside him on her gelding with the Canaanite riding before her. The *navi*'s face was hard and cold, the Canaanite's twisted in a hatred that blazed like a flame no amount of water could put out. Together they gazed at the hissing thing, which gazed as fixedly back.

Lightheaded, Barak gripped Ager's mane, fearful that he might slide and fall from his horse, like a boy only just learning to ride.

Slowly the thing that had been a woman rose to its feet, the entrails on which it fed still clutched in one hand, like a tether attaching it to the other corpse's belly. One of its slack breasts visible through a rent in its garment, swaying as it moved. It bared its teeth at Barak and Devora, took a lurching step toward them, dragging one foot behind it. A sudden breeze brought its reek to their noses.

Barak saw Devora lift her blade and held up his hand to stop her. Though his hand shook. Yet it was he who defended the tribes and their women. He would not send one of those women against the dead—not even a woman carrying an iron blade.

Grimly Barak hefted his spear.

"Be careful," Devora said. "It's stronger than it looks. Cut into the head. And remember it is unclean—both the one feeding and the body it feeds on. Don't let it touch you."

Barak nodded and raised his arm, readying the spear, then rode hard at the shambling corpse, a scream rising in his throat that he held back and would not loose. His palm was slick with sweat where he gripped the haft of his spear. As he hurtled toward it, the corpse opened its mouth as though to offer a kiss, lifted its arms as though to embrace him.

THE MOANING DEAD

BARAK'S SPEAR took the corpse in the shoulder, spinning it about and nearly unseating the chieftain from his horse. Then his spearhead ripped free of the necrotic flesh. The haft remained in Barak's hand. Suppressing an urge to keep on galloping until he'd left the corpse far, far behind, Barak wheeled Ager about, and horse and rider threw themselves at the corpse again, though Ager let out a panicked squeal that no man should ever hear his horse make. The thrust of the spear into its shoulder had turned the corpse about, and now it was facing Barak again as he came at it from the opposite direction. It hissed and lifted its arms again. Barak roared in defiance of his fear. The warm wetness down his leg and the sharp scent of urine warned him that he had unmanned himself, but he didn't care. All that mattered was getting that horrible, lurching corpse to *be still*.

His spear took it in the jaw this time, and caught; his own velocity tore him from the saddle, and as he fell Ager reared and squealed again and then tore off down the street. Omri wheeled his own steed about and hurried to catch the fleeing horse.

Barak landed hard in the grit of the street, which had been packed firm by generations of sandalled feet. The wind was driven out of him. He rolled to his side, gasped for air. Saw the corpse staggering closer, splayed hands reaching down at him, the gaze of those murky eyes fixed on him. His spear had caught in the thing's jaw, and the haft was dragging behind it along the ground. The corpse stank, a negation of all life and breath and every touch of God's fingers on the land.

His heart wild in his chest, Barak ripped his knife free of its sheath on his hip, but even as the walking corpse closed on him, its face burst apart, bits of its head and scalp splashing aside like something half-liquid. The corpse slumped to its knees. The bronze head of a spear protruded through what had once been a face. Barak's knife dropped from his hand and he clutched his chest, gasped for air.

Zadok rode up, his face grim, and his gloved hand took the haft of his spear and wrenched it free of the corpse with a sound like a foot coming free from clinging mud. The dead woman fell backward to the ground.

Then Zadok stepped his horse over to the lifeless body the woman had been feeding on and stabbed its head with his spear too.

The nazarite swung the spear up so the point jabbed toward the sky, and his dark gaze held Barak's. "You have never faced the dead," he said. "Only the living. I see it in your eyes, Barak ben Abinoam. I have faced the dead, and the *navi* has faced the dead. Now you have also. Render the *navi* of Israel more respect." Then he turned and trotted his horse back to where the others waited, leaving Barak heaving for breath on the ground.

Barak found his hands were shaking. He had never known fear like this.

He'd been afraid during the great raid from the west, facing the warriors of the Sea People with their iron blades and bejeweled ears, but usually he'd been afraid only *after* the battle, when they lay dead around him and he'd turned and retched into the grass, trembling with reaction.

But this—this corpse. It had been a *woman*. And it—it had come after him like a lion or a wolf, something hungering and mindless, its hands grasping. The way it had *moaned*—

Still needing more air, he got shakily to his feet, looked for his horse, then remembered that Ager had bolted and Omri had ridden after him. Such was his own terror that he did not think even to be angry at the other chieftain for his flight. Nor did he even flush dark with shame when he saw Devora and the Canaanite girl looking on. Panic still rushed in his blood like winter water.

Suddenly every house in the street to either side held a menace in the dark. Barak stilled his hands, slowed his breathing. He was a chieftain of Israel. He could not afford panic. He swallowed, several times, moistening his throat enough to speak again. "Let's get out of here. Now."

"We came here to find the dead, Barak," Devora said. "Not hide from them."

"They *devoured* Walls," Hurriya breathed. The girl's hands were trembling where they clutched Shomar's mane.

"And maybe other settlements too." The moon had risen over the thatched rooftops, and Devora's eyes shone in the light. "But take heart, girl. Your sister has *not* been eaten. You had a vision of her."

"Not a good vision." The girl looked faint.

"She was alive in it."

"Yes, she was alive," Hurriya whispered.

Devora looked at the corpse a moment, then her gaze moved to the door of the burned house behind the corpse. A great bar of wood had been locked across it, holding it firmly shut. The door was charred, but it stood. "Everything has gone wrong," she said softly. "Something has torn the Covenant."

"Who?" Barak said. "Who has broken the Covenant? Who is God furious with?"

Devora shook her head wearily and slid from her horse, leaving Hurriya in the saddle. The Canaanite's eyes widened; she looked as though she didn't trust the horse not to bolt away with her alone in the saddle.

"You don't simply *break* the Covenant, Barak ben Abinoam," Devora said sharply, gazing at that door. "You loosen it. Think of the roots of a crop field, intertwined beneath the soil, strong. A hundred tiny acts each day loosen the weaving of those roots. Untruths, betrayals, infidelities, cruelties, blood spilled without cause, bodies left unburied—all of these eat at the roots like the gnawing things you find when you dig up the earth. The roots are the People, the soil is the land of promise, the weaving of the roots is the Covenant." Devora glanced at him in the dark. "Then a wind comes. A storm. If the roots are loosened, if they aren't bound tightly together, the wind

285

tears away everything, soil and crop." She approached the door, touched it a moment with her fingers, drew them back as though she'd been burned. Her voice became distracted. "You won't find just one guilty man somewhere in these hills, some man we can stone and be done. It is a thousand small evils that bring this emptiness upon us."

She placed her aged hands beneath the bar and tried to lift it. Barak heard her breath wheeze.

"What are you doing?" he called, alarmed. He didn't want to know what was in that house—or any of the others. He didn't want to see anything more. He wanted to get back to the camp, regroup, gather his men.

"Taking a look," Devora said. "Help me please, Zadok."

The powerful nazarite dismounted and moved toward her. His face was calm, which staggered Barak, and shamed him. Yet he understood it. The nazarite had work to do, had a task, something definite that could be done in this town whose silence mocked all possibility of action. Zadok gripped the cedar bar and lifted it for the *navi*, then opened the latch on the door and swung it open; part of the door, soot-blackened, crumbled away as he did.

They gazed into the interior. Moonlight came through a high window and through a great gap that had been burned in the roof. It was a great house, two stories; the window was on the second, and there were no windows on the lower story, though the fire had burned away the far wall. All across the floor were dark shapes, and a lingering scent of charred meat. Barak sucked in his breath.

Devora peered in, one delicate, bony hand clutching the jamb. Her eyes glinted faintly, and her hand tightened around the doorframe as though she were dizzy. Zadok gave her his arm to steady her. Barak held his spear in both hands across his chest, reassured by the solidity of its wood.

"Burned," Hurriya whispered, gazing over their heads at the interior. "Like the levite's house. They burned this house, with the dead in it." A touch of awe in her voice.

"Twenty-three." Devora was tight-lipped. "We do not burn the bodies of the People, we bury them."

Barak could not count the shapes in the faint light; his eyes could not pick out one from another. But he did not question Devora's sight. "God of our fathers," he breathed.

"It *is* terrible," Hurriya said suddenly. "But the people of this town found a way to protect their kin from the dead. What right have we to judge them?"

Devora spun to face her, her eyes livid. "And where are those people now? Are they here? Do they live? Do you know?"

Hurriya didn't answer.

"Did—did *this*—help any of them?" She waved her hand at the house. "Shut the door, Zadok."

He did, and replaced the great wooden bar over it, locking the bodies within. For just a moment the nazarite leaned against the door, as though overcome by what he'd seen. Barak just sat his saddle, overwhelmed.

"Look," Hurriya called softly.

The others glanced up. After a moment Devora saw what Hurriya meant and pointed. Barak saw that a narrow strip of linen hung from the charred window on the house's second story. By some miracle a little of that linen had escaped the flames, and he could see that it was dyed scarlet; against the charred timbers it seemed garish and utterly out of place. As though someone had decided to hang up fine clothes to dry in the heat of a burning house.

Devora exchanged a look with Hurriya, then gazed at the cloth steadily. "A brave act," she whispered.

"I don't understand," Barak muttered. "It's a scrap of cloth. What does it mean?"

Devora's voice was soft in the dark. She sounded awed. "Someone—someone living—led twenty dead inside, so that her kin could slam shut the door and bar it behind them. She must have escaped to the upper room and pulled up the rope ladder behind her so that no dead could follow." For a moment Devora only gazed up at that window, her face pensive as though struck with thoughts that had never occurred to her before.

"Think of it," Hurriya breathed. "Just think of it. She stood up there alone. With twenty dead hissing beneath her. Their hands reaching for her."

"It is not only men with spears who have courage," Devora said.

"She?" Barak's eyes had widened in horror. "How do you know it was a woman?"

"Not a woman, a girl," the *navi* said. "Don't you recognize the linen?"

"It's just a scrap of cloth."

"Nothing is ever just a scrap of anything, Barak ben Abinoam. Everything made bears the shape of its maker's hands and can betray who its maker was, even as every hill and thicket in the land bears the imprint of God's shaping fingers. Everything is clay, everything is marked."

"It's a maiden sash," Hurriya said. "A girl wears it beneath her breasts when she wishes to beg Astarte for her breasts to grow full. For her blood to come. A girl wears it when she tires of being just a girl."

"Yes." Devora gazed at the window and its limp linen, and her voice hardened. "This town, also, is more heathen than Hebrew."

"But brave," Hurriya whispered.

Barak gazed up at that linen, struck with horror. He tried to imagine standing alone while twenty of those—those *corpses*—waited below you for your foot to trip. And the flames licking up the sides of the house. "She didn't burn," he said, looking at the window. "She jumped out. Led them in, then leapt from the window."

"She did," Devora said quietly. "It *was* very brave. Though she died for it."

"Died?" Hurriya gasped.

"That rock in the earth there, by the wall—it is smeared with old blood. She cracked her leg there, or her head."

"Maybe she rose to her feet, and lived," Barak said grimly.

"There is a wide swath of soil, like a furrow, leading away from the rock. She was dragged away, eaten. Not all the dead were in the house. And the dead caught her right after she leapt—otherwise the neighbors would have come for her first."

The desire for this to be wrong gripped Barak's heart so fiercely it startled him. "No, a neighbor saw her wounded—one of the men who barred the door. And came to pull her away. That's what the marks in the soil mean."

"Would he have dragged her body along the earth between the houses? He would have lifted her and carried her in his arms. What she did was holy, Barak. God gave her a great task, and she leapt for him. You do not carry an injured holy one to safety by dragging her body through the dirt."

He winced at the thought. The scene Devora suggested was too terrible. That a girl—a child—might risk so much, and achieve such a victory, only to fall to her death: it was an injustice that blasphemed God and mocked the Covenant. He could not bear it, or accept it. A *navi* Devora might be, but she did not have that look in her eyes now, the look that meant God was showing her visions. And these were only marks in the dirt. They might mean something else. They might mean anything. It was only dirt.

A cough in the street behind them interrupted, and Barak turned to see Omri walking his own horse toward them, with a tether about the neck of Barak's steed. In the light of the torch he still held, Omri looked pale. As he drew near, his gaze flicked to the corpse in the street and the body it had been eating. He stopped and sat his horse, staring down.

"Rare for there to be just one," he murmured.

"Yes," Devora said. "It is rare."

Omri stepped the two horses in a wide circle about the body. Their eyes rolled, and Barak's horse shied, nearly tearing the tether from his hand; at last he was near enough and he tossed the tether to Barak, who caught it deftly out of the air. "Horse nearly galloped back to Shiloh," Omri said, tearing his gaze from the horror in the street. "I should ask you to barter that breast-piece for him."

"He's worth more than a breast-piece, Omri."

"Then trade me her." Omri attempted a smile and gestured at the *navi*, who swung about with her eyes dark and fierce. "She'd be pleasant. Worth the loss of a horse."

"She's *kadosh*," Barak said, taken aback.

Omri seemed to notice how they were all looking at him: Zadok, Devora, Barak. The Canaanite's eyes were lowered, but her shoulders were tensed.

"She'd do," he muttered.

"Touch her and die," Zadok said quietly.

Devora just gazed at the Zebulunite coldly, which seemed to bother him more than Zadok's threat.

"You needn't act like I tried to lift your skirt," Omri said in a subdued tone. "If a man doesn't break this silence with a jest, it'll madden him."

Barak gestured at a cache he'd spotted to the side of the burned house, a great pit dug into the ground, likely walled with stone, concealed now beneath a great wooden cover. "Break open that cache, Omri. May be supplies we can use. Supplies this town won't need." He cast a grim look at the burned house.

The Zebulunite walked his horse toward the cache, grumbling beneath his breath. Omri had challenged Barak for the leadership of the camp while the men were still gathering, days ago. Barak had bested him; now it seemed Omri wanted to show Barak he was still a man. But Barak had no time for this. He stepped beside Devora quickly and growled, "Don't entice him, woman. I'll not have the two of you bring shame on my camp."

Devora flushed dark with anger. "*You think*—"

"You must have glanced at him," Barak muttered irritably.

Devora hissed through her teeth, but Barak was already moving, mounting Ager. Stroking the horse's neck to calm him, he nudged Ager into a trot around the corner of the broken house toward that cache. Even as he did, Omri pried beneath the lid with his spear and levered it up, then tipped it over. That great cedar lid fell back and slammed down against the earth, a sound that echoed up the street between the empty houses, revealing a great hole in the ground. A sickly-sweet stench rolled out, and Barak gagged a moment, cursing silently in his heart. Fool townsmen had stored *meat* in there. But it had gone bad; surely they'd *salted* it, at least. He'd hoped desperately to find vats of grain, unfouled grain.

"Whoa," Barak murmured to his horse, which was shying nervously at the reek. The animal whickered and stood breathing hard. Barak leaned down over its neck. "Good, good," he whispered in his horse's ear.

"*Navi.*" Zadok's voice was urgent.

Barak glanced over his shoulder at the nazarite and the *navi*, saw Devora's eyes widen. A small figure was climbing up narrow steps out of the cache, a silhouette against the shadows. A dull sheen of eyes in the moonlight. Several other shapes were coming up the steps after it. Lifting its foot from the last step, the first moved out of the cache and staggered across the trampled earth toward them. It was small—stood no taller than Devora's belly. Some of the others climbing out behind it were even smaller.

Children.

These were children.

He took a breath. Something unsettled him, but he felt a flood of relief that drowned any uneasiness. Children. The promise of the Covenant, that the People would live and thrive and fill the land, no matter what came. A rush of faith into his heart such as he had not felt since he was a small child, sitting at his grandfather's knee hearing stories of their People's escape from the brick pits of Kemet and their taking of the land. This was surely a mighty sign. During the raids a few years ago from the fortified settlements on the coast, it had been common enough for encampments to hide their children in pits or caches concealed beneath thick brush, to be retrieved later once the threat was past. This town had been eaten by the dead, and perhaps its last men and women had fled into the hills with the dead close behind, after first ensuring their children's safety in that cache.

"Children!" he called to them, the joy in him nearly choking his voice.

At the sound of his voice, the children—so *many*, climbing out of the cache—lifted their arms in the dark. And with a shock, Barak knew that something was wrong. Badly wrong.

Those dull, glinting eyes.

High, wavering moans as the children lurched out into the street.

Devora let out a wordless, anguished cry, and Hurriya made a small, choked noise. The *navi*'s cry fell upon Barak's heart like the stone that triggers a landslide. He lurched into motion, wheeling his horse about. "Back!" he called hoarsely. "Fall back!"

Zadok swore and lifted his spear, moving his horse between the *navi* and the advancing children. Devora just sat her horse, gazing at the children with a horror as though she were watching the entire land burn. The children were lurching toward her horse; in a moment, they would close about Zadok's horse and hers like a tide about a rock.

"*Navi!*" Barak's voice was too high, like a child's. "Ride! Ride!"

She didn't move.

Omri too sat his horse as though frozen.

Zadok let out a battle shout and sent his horse into the dead, laying about with his spear, using it more as a staff then an impaling weapon, knocking the small corpses from their feet with the force of it. It took them a moment to get back up, and Zadok wheeled his horse, spinning his mighty staff as easily as he might a child's toy. But there were too many. Their moans filled the air, drowning out all thought and hope.

Barak saw two small girls lurch past the nazarite, toward the *navi*'s horse—he could almost hear words in their moans. He was certain—he could almost hear words. The moans tore at his mind. Barak screamed and drove his own gelding between the *navi* and the children. His heart beat, cold sweat stung his eyes; he lifted his spear but froze, those tiny, glinting eyes gazing up at him; he didn't know what to do. Children. Children of the People. He couldn't spear children of the People.

A hand grasped his calf, closing about the bronze greave, the fingertips digging into the exposed skin at the back and pulling. Panting, Barak of Israel gazed down into

294

a hissing, livid face, a face gashed and darkened with dried blood, the eyes scratched and unseeing though fixed in the direction of his thigh. The thing that had been a small girl hissed like an asp, its teeth stark in the night, gums drawn back.

"El," he gasped. "El, El, El—" The name of God, over and over and over, like a child's syllable chanted against some groping terror in the dark. He couldn't move; he felt the tug on his leg, so strong. The face bending toward his calf, even as the other girl reached and took his foot. Other children—such small, small beings—staggered against his horse, their little hands reaching up at him. The animal trembled violently, its back rippling beneath Barak, but it was well trained. This horse had carried him in a charge against raiders from the coast. The horse shook as with fever but did not bolt.

Devora's high voice startled him from his paralysis.

"Run, girl! Move! Now!"

Hurriya slid from the saddle and fled, stumbling, for the far side of the ruined house.

Then Devora cried out in a screaming ululation that rose in pitch like a shriek of steel, then fell into words, a battle song, old Hebrew, the dialect of their grandfathers in the desert, when every hand, living and dead, had been raised against their tribes. Devora rode at the children. Her white horse slammed bodily into the crowd of dead, beating aside the small bodies with his great flanks; in a moment the *navi* was at Barak's side, her face stern, her eyes cold fire, her hand white about the hilt of that iron blade; her arm swept down, and the weapon scythed through small bodies, cutting away arms, shearing flesh and bone. The girls fell away from Barak's horse, cut open, hands and arms severed from them—but even as they fell beneath Shomar's hooves, there was no blood. There were no screams. Only those keening moans of hunger all about them.

Then Devora had ridden past, taking her wide-eyed gelding in a wide circle through the street, her blade slashing and cutting. Zadok fought his way to her side, and the two rode together, spear and blade. Even as Barak shook away his panic and hefted his own bronze spear again in his hand, he saw the two girls lurch back to their feet near his steed. Their arms were gone; one's chest had been crushed by the hooves. Yet their dull eyes were fixed on him; their mouths gaped in wordless hissing. The stench of them was vile, worse by far now that their bodies had been carved open. They were unclean. They were reaching for him.

With a shout, Barak lunged to the side, driving the spear into one child's brow. The small, decaying body went limp, but the spearhead had caught in its skull and could not be pulled free; the child's corpse hung as a dead weight on the end of the spear, nearly pulling Barak from his horse as the girl's knees buckled. The other came at him, and Barak drove his sandal hard into its face, driving it back a few lurching steps as he fought to pull his spear free. He was drenched in cold sweat; his heart hammered within him.

Devora's song rose into those high, desert wails, then fell again and again into words, as she rode among the dead. Numbly Barak lifted his eyes to her, saw her bound hair shining in the moonlight, her sword an arc of white in the air, never still. Behind her galloping horse, a trail of bodies, shattered and reeking. A few staggered to their feet or crawled along the ground after her; the rest were still, their heads carved open in terrible wounds. Zadok had ridden now to the edge of the cache, was spearing the corpses as they stepped out. Omri had joined him there and lent his spear to the fight, though he looked ready to be violently ill.

The body by Barak's horse hissed, and with a curse the chieftain plucked out his knife and drove it hard into the thing's forehead. He shuddered as it twitched and went still, sliding off the blade and dropping to the earth, on its back. Panting, he gazed down at it in cold horror. It was a girl. Just a small girl. It still wore the dirtied remains of a woolen dress; the cloth had been torn away from its right shoulder, baring a breast as flat as a tablet of stone. Barak ducked his head to the side and vomited, his midday meal rushing up his throat in a steaming flood. He choked and coughed, drew the back of his hand across his lips. His other hand gripped the haft of his spear, rigidly, a child's body still impaled on the bronze head.

Barak the vintner, war-leader of the northern tribes, sat his horse shaking. He drew from his saddlebag the shofar Laban had brought to him when he first formed the camp. The ram's horn Othniel himself had blown when he fought the first raiders from the sea, when Barak had been just a boy. Now Barak lifted the shofar to his lips and blew a long blast. He needed his men. He needed God. He needed someone, anyone, to share with him the terrible responsibility of fighting these walking corpses that had once been breathing, laughing children. The call of the horn echoed through the town.

THE OLAH

THE CHILDREN tried helplessly to reach up and grasp at Devora's feet as she rode through them. They strove to catch her, to pull her from her horse, but their small bodies were no match for either the strength or speed of the gelding Lappidoth had given her—or the savage reach of the *navi*'s blade. Behind her by the cache, Zadok and Omri jabbed their spears downward again and again, like Canaanites on the lake spearing fish. The light from Omri's torch shone on the hissing faces.

A few moments more and it was done. Devora turned and cantered back, taking out the few that were still staggering or crawling along the ground. The blade cut through scalp, skull, and brain. In the end, there was only a street filled with bodies, strewn across the packed dirt from where Barak's steed stood shying to the open cache.

She rode to the cache and glanced down the steps into it. Small bones lay scattered at the bottom. Bones of children. Bones picked clean and cracked open for the marrow. In the deaths of so many children of her People, whether mixed with heathen or no, Devora could see the death of the Covenant. She could see the touch of the *malakh ha-mavet*, as though its mighty wing had swept over the town and all those touched by its shadow had died, regardless of promises made or promises kept or promises broken.

She made a high-pitched, furious sound like a beast discovering a trap about its paw, then rode back. None of the children lifted themselves from the begrimed earth to challenge her. Beside her, Zadok dismounted and left the cache and walked slowly among the bodies, making sure each of them had been speared or cut through the head, making sure all were still.

Hurriya made a choked sound from where she watched from the corner of the charred house. Her eyes were round and dark in the dim light. Omri walked his horse away from the cache. For once he did not even look at the women. He had eyes only for the bodies in the street.

Barak still sat his horse in the middle of the street, in shock, the shofar now held in one limp hand. Devora cantered toward him until she was near enough to address him without lifting her voice.

"Do not hesitate again, chieftain of Israel." Devora's voice was a shard of winter. "These were not children. These are the dead. Look at their eyes, not their bodies. Whether they wear a levite's white or a young girl's sash, whether their face is that of a spearman or an infant, the eyes of the dead hold nothing. They are only bodies to bury." She kept Mishpat carefully extended, though it tired her arm—for the blade was spattered with unclean gore. "Did any of them touch your naked skin?"

The look Barak gave her was distant, distracted, and her heart skipped a beat. "Barak?" she asked harshly.

"No," he said after a brief hesitation. "None."

"Are you sure?"

"They touched only my greave," he said hoarsely.

She held his eyes a moment, then accepted this as the truth and looked back at the stillness in the street, the unholy stillness. She could not think about what she had seen and done; there were judgments to make. "Before you enter the camp, you must cut a strip from your cloak, Barak ben Abinoam, and wrap that wool about your fingers. Then pluck away the greave and cast both bronze and wool to the earth. Do not touch the bronze with your hand. In this way, you can enter the camp clean and under no judgment."

"It will be as you say, *navi*." He seemed hardly to hear her; his voice was a croak.

She turned from him, holding back her own dread. What had happened this night would rattle any man. Barak seemed frozen with horror now, almost like Zadok had often been, though his eyes flicked from the left to the right; he did not seem unaware of the bodies at his feet or the charred house before him. Dismissing him from her mind, Devora began walking Shomar away.

Omri rode up alongside her, still clutching his guttering torch, his eyes round with fear and wonder. "That blade," he said.

"Yes, I can wield it," Devora said sharply. She had no patience right now for the man.

"It—it really *is* iron," Omri breathed. His gaze was fixed on the *navi*, as though wondering if she too were made of some strange, foreign substance of which other women were not. Devora ignored him and walked her horse back down the street. Shomar stepped nervously over the corpses, and the *navi* caressed his neck softly, whispering in his ear. She met Zadok's eyes as she passed him; the nazarite straightened and gave a weary nod. It was done, then. The nazarite drew his knife and cut his hand grimly, then sheathed the knife.

She led Shomar to the corner of the burned house and glanced down at Hurriya, who was shaking. After a moment Devora dismounted to stand before the shuddering girl. The girl's horror pulled at her heart.

"Close your eyes," Devora said softly.

Hurriya gave a small shake of her head. She stared at the children in the street.

Devora took a saddlecloth and pressed the cloth to the young woman's eyes. "No, girl," she said. "There is no ruined house, no town. You are in the olive grove, and there are no dead. You are watching your sister play in the branches."

"The town," Hurriya whispered, without trying to remove the cloth. "The whole settlement. Like my child."

"No." Devora glanced at the dark hole of the cache. Her body felt cold, everything inside her was cold. "Not the *whole* town. They probably locked the children in to keep them safe, then lured the dead away, all that they could. They must have meant to circle back."

"Only they haven't," Hurriya whispered. "They haven't circled back."

Devora was distracted from answering by the sound of hoofbeats. She glanced over her shoulder. The other men

301

were riding down the street toward them, summoned by the sound of the shofar. Laban rode at their head with that massive axe of his ready in his hand, held as lightly as though it were only a hatchet. They stopped near Barak, looking down at the shattered corpses, their faces stricken.

"It is all right," the *navi* called, raising her voice in a shout. "There were dead in the cache, but—"

The door of the nearest house across the street jolted hard in its hinges, then shuddered again, a sound as of bodies thrusting against it from within. Devora swung to face the door, her face white with shock.

The dead. Roused perhaps by Devora's battle song or by the shofar to stumble about within the house, looking for the living. Perhaps they had been on the second floor and had finally tumbled below. Now, alerted by Devora's shout to the direction in which they could find her, they had thrown themselves against the door.

"Spears!" Barak rasped. He dismounted and tugged his own spear free, and several of his men left their horses and ran up, one with a spear like Barak's, the others with poles or rakes or whatever they'd improvised along the journey.

"Break the door," Barak gasped, unable to find enough breath to make the order any louder. "Let it out where we can slay it."

The men were as pale as he. Devora heard the breaking of cedar, the sharp crack of the door coming apart; the door splintered and wrenched aside, and dead lurched out into the street, their teeth bared. Their arms reaching for warm flesh. Barak's men were between her and the corpses, and they shoved their spears hard into the corpses' bellies and thighs, pushing them back by brute force. But the dead still groped for them and moaned, not heeding the wounds.

"Their heads!" she cried. "Strike them between the eyes! Between the eyes, men of Israel!"

As if wakened by her cry, Barak surged into action, leaping forward and driving the bronze point of his spear into one skull, driving it in by the ear, the flesh parting at the metal's touch like a rotting apricot.

Devora moved toward the house, but Zadok stepped near and took her arm in a firm grip, peering into her face. "*Navi?*"

"There are dead in the houses," she said numbly.

Her hand tightened about Mishpat's hilt, and she tried again to step toward the door, but Zadok thrust her behind him with one powerful arm. One of the dead had pushed a pole aside and now grasped one of Barak's men by the shoulder, pulling him toward its jaws. Zadok's spear drove into its open mouth, and he lifted the corpse free of the door; it jerked helplessly in the air, impaled and writhing with the cold metal driven into its throat.

Devora gasped as Zadok spun, his spear sweeping through the air. The incredible strength of the man! The corpse came loose and was flung through the air, slamming into the ground. A snap of bone. The corpse got to its feet, one arm limp at its side, and lurched toward them again. Others were still pushing out at the door, being barred only by the long-shafted weapons and the desperate strength of the men. Those men were ashen-faced, panicked, screaming as they held the dead back, the long fingers of the dead catching at their hair, their cheeks, their arms. One man was pulled in close, and a hissing corpse bit down on his ear and tore it away with a long strip of tissue and flesh.

She saw Barak leap away from the door, screaming orders. While Zadok and Laban and a few men held the dead back at the door, four others ran with Barak to the cache and wrenched its massive lid up from the ground. They brought it swiftly to the house and pressed the wooden lid against the door, pushing the dead back into the house by sheer might and barricading the door with it, holding it in place with their own living bodies. The massive lid shook as the dead pounded against it from within.

The house had two stories, one window for each; the lower window was barred with wood, but now Devora could see gray, half-eaten hands reaching through cracks in the wood, some of them missing fingers, tearing chunks of wood free, ripping away the covering over the window. Devora lifted Mishpat and stepped near even as the wood slats came away and a corpse's face appeared at the window, pale against the darkness behind it. The left side of its face that of a young woman, the right side eaten away almost to the bone. It hissed at her, and Devora thrust Mishpat at it, cutting across its cheek. The corpse fell back from the window into the darkness of the house; she could hear it hissing and spitting.

The men at the door were screaming, Barak roaring louder than any. The door was rattling.

There was a cracking of wood above her; she glanced up, caught the glimpse of another torn and half-chewed face gazing down at her out of the dark frame of the second-story window; then the thing was coming through, climbing out. It toppled and fell toward her with a slow and terrible grace, as though falling through dark milk instead of air. Devora screamed, then something else slammed into her side, knocking the breath from her. She sprawled in the dirt, glanced up, wheezing. Saw Zadok ben Zefanyah standing over her, his eyes cold as though there had never been warmth in the world. The corpse had fallen almost at his feet and was staggering upright when the nazarite drove his spear into its face. The point passed through the thing's skull and out above the base of its neck. Zadok pressed his boot to the body's shoulder and shoved it free of his spear; it fell back and crumpled to the earth as lightly as though it were only a heap of clothes.

"Get back, *navi*," Zadok growled. "Away from the houses. Into the market. These are for me to fight."

But now, as Devora looked about her, she saw the doors of the nearest houses bucking and shaking as well; there must be dead in most of the houses on this street, corpses locked inside. She could hear moans muffled behind the wood, and she shivered. She heard the clear, deep voice of the shofar lifted, louder than the wailing of the dead, louder than the slamming of their bodies against the doors. Barak had his shoulder pressed to the great lid, his other hand held the ram's horn to his lips. Living men came running through the market shops toward them, perhaps twenty, thirty men. As though the shofar had called them. But they were on foot and must have left the encampment moments after Omri and Laban did, and then taken this long to reach their chieftains who'd ridden in on horseback.

Devora backed up and stood in the midst of the street

with Mishpat gleaming in her hand. She saw the cracks appearing in wooden doors up and down the street. Whatever dead had waited concealed within, the battle and the voices outside their doors had stirred them. The lid that Barak and the men held to the first door leapt like a living thing, and one of the dead within forced its arm out. Then the corpses were pushing the men back, with a strength born of unstoppable hunger, a strength that would not give out, for the dead felt no fatigue, no hopelessness.

With a roar, Zadok threw himself hard against the door, lending his weight to that of the shorter men, and the lid slammed back into place so sharply that its edge severed the decayed arm. It fell to the ground and lay there like a piece God had discarded when shaping men at the beginning of time.

Another corpse began climbing out through the lower window, and Devora impaled its head on Mishpat. Breathing raggedly, she realized that the men could not contain the dead in these houses. More corpses would spill into the street at any moment. And though other men were now running to join them with staves and knives and makeshift spears, they would not be enough.

Omri had let his torch fall in the midst of the street when he had taken up the lid with Barak and the other men; the torch still lay there, blazing in the dirt. Now Hurriya ran from the corner of the burned house and took up the torch, panting as she staggered toward the house, toward where Devora stood at the window the dead had torn open. Realizing her intent with a shock, Devora leapt in her way, seized her arm, wrested the torch from her.

"No!" the *navi* cried. "Not with fire! These were the *People*! Not with fire!"

The Canaanite tugged wildly to get her arm free, her eyes intense. "Let me go!" she cried. "We *have* to! This was my vision. What the gods meant me to see!"

Devora looked at her in horror, holding the torch away from her, out of her reach. The Canaanite woman's face was translated in revelation, in sudden, awestruck belief that the gods hadn't abandoned her, that the blessing or the burden they'd given her was more than just a caprice.

"We have to burn the houses," Hurriya shouted. "We have to burn them! As the people here did."

"No," Devora breathed. She glanced suddenly at the torch she held in her hand, at the flames. Words of the Covenant rang in her ears in the deep, calm voice of Eleazar ben Phinehas ben Eleazar ben Aharon:

> *The people must not be burned with fire*
> *not consumed with flame*
> *but buried beneath clean stone.*

And, faintly, the rasp of Eleazar's dying words: *Don't let the People be—eaten—or—or burned…*

"We have to!"

"We are *not* heathen," Devora cried.

Hurriya took her arm wildly, clutching her through the thick wool of her dress. Her eyes alight. "So you Hebrews have ways to keep the dead from rising. Your cairns, your graves, your Covenant. But the dead *have* risen, *navi*. And the people here have found ways to deal with them *then*!"

"It is a heathen way!"

"Yes!" Hurriya screamed. "Or we die!"

Suddenly Devora's own words from earlier that night were recalled to her mind as clearly as though spoken to her this very moment by God:

> *The navi brings men words they need to hear, visions they need to see, not visions they wish to see.*

Hurriya too was a *navi*, and she'd been given a vision of faces burning.

A man near her screamed, a shrill cry like a doe when a lion tears into its shoulder with his teeth. Devora looked up in time to see a corpse-gray arm wrapped around the man's breast and a ghastly head tearing flesh raw from the man's throat. For the briefest of breaths she met the walking corpse's eyes and saw nothing there; then the thing had pulled Barak's man through the window, and his legs were disappearing into the house. Devora leapt for him; her fingers brushed the bronze greave on his leg, then he was gone. Not even another scream. Just gone. She made her decision and with a shriek she thrust the torch through the window and dropped it there before springing back. Other gray faces filled the window, hands reaching out; men sprang past her on the right and on the left, their spears thrusting at the window, shoving the dead back, the way boatmen shove long poles against a riverbank. Then the dead faces were backlit by bright flame; something had caught within.

"Torches!" the *navi* cried. "More torches! Burn them! Burn the house!"

***

Men improvised torches using bits of wood from shattered doors or from whatever they could find, and Laban swung his torch from one to the next, lighting them. Hurriya retreated to lean against the wall of another house; she took a crumpled leaf—all this time she'd clutched the herbs in her hand—and began chewing on it. She was very pale.

Devora didn't watch either the men or the Canaanite; she had eyes only for the burning house, her face twisted in grief. In this place where she could not tell if the living or the dead were Hebrew or heathen, where the *mitzvot* were hardly kept, where no tithes were sent to Shiloh nor any young men or young women sent to the Feast of Tents, the Covenant had been hacked through and shredded, as though a mad harvester had attacked the crop of the People with a sickle before the crop was ripe. And now she had hacked through the Covenant herself, burning bodies rather than burying them. Yet what else could she decide? The Covenant demanded that she keep the People safe from the dead, keep the land clean—yet the land was now so defiled that sword and clean stone were not enough to mend it. Only fire could cleanse the unclean death from this town.

Dark smoke poured from the upper window and then flame, licking its way up toward the roof, hungrier even than the dead. The sight of it seared her mind. A burning, an atrocity, this smoke they were sending into God's sky, the sharp scent of meat burning. Like a perverse, horrible *olah*, a burnt offering, an atonement for the breaking of Covenant, an atonement for their failure to keep the land clean and undefiled. But this *olah* must surely reek in God's nostrils, must surely make their God vomit and heave in revulsion at what was happening in the land he dwelled in.

Then the men were lighting the house to the left, and Devora could hear the moans of the dead within. The dry cedar cracked and sang its fierce death song as the fire spread faster than tears or prayer. The roof of the first house cracked open with a clap of thunder, then crumpled inward, and the moans within fell silent, buried beneath the broken timbers that crushed them down and covered them like a cairn of wood and charcoal rather than stone.

Devora spun in a slow circle, taking in the gray, filthy ash drifting down from the blazing rooftops, dark against the firelit air. Some of it fell on her arm and burned her, and she cried out, not knowing whether the ash had come from a burning bed or from one of the bodies of the People. She gazed in horror at the sky, dark with smoke.

"*El!*" she shrieked. "*Elohim! Adonai!*" Anguish tore at her, stripping pieces away from her mind. She screamed for her God. Begged for his mighty hand to return and cover this town and the land.

The ash fell from the sky. More of it now. Everywhere the cracking of roofs and walls giving away. The shouts of desperate men, the low moaning of the dead who did not feel any pain of fire or spear but only the pain of being unable to feed, unable to fill their hunger.

The smoke spread out above them, unfurling across the sky like dark wings, like the *malakh ha-mavet*.

Devora stopped screaming, her throat hoarse and on fire. Barak was gripping her arm and shouting something, but she could not hear him. Then, after a long moment, sound returned to her world, and she heard the fire and the rattling of doors up and down the street, other dead trying to get out, trying to get at them. The sound clasped her heart in a cold grip.

"Burn everything!" she hissed. "Burn it all!"

Then she shook Barak away and ran, her feet pounding over the ground, the ash still drifting down. She reached up and beat it from her hair. She glimpsed Shomar turning in circles in the street, terrified but unsure where to bolt. She cried his name, ran to him, seized his mane and sprang to his back.

Even as she mounted, she heard a scream that came to her ears piercing above all the rest. Hurriya!

Devora saw where the dead had broken free of one of the houses and were stepping over the body of a fallen man. Hurriya had taken up the man's spear in both her hands and was stabbing at the dead. She speared one in the brow and the corpse dropped to its knees, but before the young woman could pull the spear free, another of the corpses grabbed the haft and used it to pull Hurriya close. With a cry, Devora sent Shomar galloping toward her, the smoke stinging her eyes. Leaning from her saddle, one hand wrapped in Shomar's mane, Devora caught up Hurriya in her arm and with a desperate strength that would have shocked her on any other night than this, in any other place, she pulled Hurriya up into the saddle before her. The spear was ripped from the Canaanite's hands and left in the grip of the dead. "I'm getting you out of here!" she cried in the girl's ear, and Hurriya clung wildly to the horse's neck.

"Run, Shomar! Run!" Devora cried, digging her knees in hard. The horse leapt beneath her with a ferocity like something being born. Dead moaned behind her, and dead spilled from a shattered door into the street before her, and Shomar rode them down, permitting the Hebrew and the Canaanite only the briefest glimpse of their sightless, ravenous faces, the white of cheekbones through torn and missing flesh. Then they were riding out of the town, Hurriya bent low over Shomar's neck, her hair in Devora's face. Hurriya kept sobbing, "They took my baby, they took my baby—" The *navi*'s heart pounded as she urged Shomar quickly out along the shore of the lake, everything in her tight and desperate and ready to unravel in grief. Her nostrils seared with the scent of flame and smoke and decay.

IN THE SILENCE OF GOD

DEVORA DID NOT let Shomar slacken his pace until they had ridden some distance across the shingle. Then she halted and gazed out over the water, her heart still racing. The town burned behind them, and Devora could hear the distant crack of wood beams breaking in the flames and the shouts of living men. There were no longer any moans from the dead.

Suddenly she couldn't hold it in any longer—the doubt, the anguish, the fury at what she had done and at God for letting it be necessary.

"*God!*" she screamed.

Hurriya tensed in her arms.

"*Ata adonai!*" Devora's rage and despair echoed across the water. The reflected firelight on the lake was strangely beautiful.

"Where are you?" she screamed. "This—this burning—is not an answer to our need! *It's not an answer!*"

Hurriya whispered, "The dead will hear!"

"*Let* them hear," the *navi* snapped.

She urged Shomar back to a canter, heard the splash of water under his hooves as he bore them along the shore. She was riding away from the town and away from the camp, out into the dark and the silence. She could not bear to see the *malakh* spreading across the sky, hiding God's stars with its dark wings. She could smell the smoke in her hair.

"None of the gods are listening," Hurriya said.

"God *is* here," Devora cried. "He is *still* here. He is still covering us. He sends you visions." Lifting her voice, she shouted across the water, "Send *me* a vision! Send *me*!"

"What if he doesn't?" Hurriya said, her voice brittle with pain. "What then? Will you crawl back to Shiloh?"

Devora brought Shomar to a halt again, sat breathing hard on his back, felt the horse's sides moving as he breathed between her legs. Something soft and powdery touched her face, and she looked up in the dark and realized flakes of ash were falling, even here. She shuddered.

The town behind them was not only silent, it was dead. And she could do nothing, had done nothing. She had barely ridden from the burning houses with the one other life her horse had carried into the town. She had saved no one but Hurriya.

Vividly she heard Naomi's words in her heart—*Some days a woman can only save one life*—but those words seemed empty to her, a riddle without an answer or without any answer she could bear.

"There were children," Devora whispered.

No visions came to her over the water. No answer.

Hurriya was gazing back at the fire far behind them. She was shaking more violently now, and Devora could feel the heat from her body, a heat that was not one of vision.

"Chew your leaves, girl," the *navi* muttered.

"I lost them."

Devora's heart sank. Perhaps the leaf the girl had been chewing before the dead attacked would be enough to calm her fever for a while. But she didn't know; she was no midwife or herbalist. They would have to get more. At that, Devora's momentary fury flickered out, and exhaustion fell over her like a collapsed tent. She slumped a little. She felt old.

"Those houses," the girl murmured. "Those houses full of dead. The people—they couldn't bear to kill the sick. They couldn't do it. So they locked the sick into the houses on that street. Trusting the doors to hold. That's what happened. I can see it. No vision, but I can see it."

"A corpse is stronger than a living person," Devora said wearily. "They don't hold back. They don't hesitate. They don't doubt. They don't care if they destroy their bodies to break a door. They just kill and eat. The People, who are living, are capable of restraint. Of weighing choices and consequences. Of judgment. The dead are not." She glanced at Hurriya. "To be without restraint, to be without *Law*, is to be like one of the dead. Without the Law to hold you back, you may break a door, you may shatter some obstacle, but you will break yourself too."

"They couldn't let their dead go," Hurriya rasped, as though she hadn't heard. "You can't either. You aren't grieving for the dead, you're screaming out your guilt to them. That's what was in your voice, when it echoed over the water. You want your God to give you a vision of the next day, or the next, but you're gazing at the past. Ever since you took me from Shiloh. You're gazing at the past, and so no visions come to you."

The words shook her. Only Lappidoth had ever touched that bruised part of her heart, and he had never done so with words. No one else had ever seen this in her—her guilt, the sense of crushing responsibility, the conviction of all those she'd failed. Zadok's pain. Her mother's death and, later, Naomi's. The many deaths in that burning town. All of them her burdens to bear—and only holding herself and her People strictly to the Law had kept their weight bearable.

Until now. Glancing up at the smoke that had taken the stars from her—taken even that visible sign of God's presence and God's promises—she felt as though even the Law, even the Covenant, had been stripped away, like the roof of a tent torn aside in the wind of a violent storm. She had torn some of it away herself, turning the bodies of the People into ash and dust.

"You can't carry the dead with you," Hurriya whispered out of the dark, and her voice was that of a feverish, suffering woman with a heathen accent. But her voice was also that of the *navi*, speaking of things she and God had seen that for others remained unseen. "You can't. If you can't take some part of them back into your heart as sustenance, take joy in having known them—if you can't hum a sleep-song to them or talk to them quietly in the evening—if they cannot sustain and nourish you in the water you drink and the fish you eat, then you have to at least do it the Hebrew way. You cannot bear them; you have to bury them."

Devora knew Hurriya was right. The dead from her past were like corpses she'd hefted onto her shoulders and now struggled beneath, carrying them in search of a cairn rather than laying them down and going to gather stones. But she did not know how to gather stones for the dead whose presence she felt within her. She didn't know how. She gazed out over the water and wondered if God too was watching the reflection of the flames on the lake.

"If God is silent," she said, "I will act as though he is not. When God sends no visions, when we don't know if he is with us or if we are left to die in the ash among the corpses, we must still act as though his hand *does* cover us. Our responsibilities are unchanged. Nothing else will suffice." Under her breath she added, "*I* will not demand assurances."

She guided Shomar back toward the fire and the distant settlement and, farther along the shore, the tents of the northern men. In the firelight, she glanced at Hurriya's face and gave a start.

Hurriya's cheeks glistened with silent tears.

Devora felt a pang of remorse. The girl was exhausted. Shomar, huffing softly in the dark, was exhausted too. This was no time to be riding along the shore in the dark, fleeing her night terrors. She put her arm about the girl's waist and pulled her back against her breast, holding her tightly. "Shh," the *navi* whispered.

"Further north," Hurriya whispered back. "I have to get further north. I have to find Anath. I have to find her."

NO SURVIVORS

THE RISING SUN found Barak walking with the other war-leaders through a strange land of falling ash and ash underfoot and ash in the air they breathed. Omri and Laban spoke in low tones about what to do next, where to lead the men, where to seek the dead, but Barak walked in grim silence. He could not stop thinking about the hours of flame and heat and sweat. His men had worked right there amid the flames, shoving the flaming dead back into the houses, fighting to contain them as they burned and withered.

Those *faces*, melting in the flames. Hissing and snapping their jaws even as they burned.

"How many men died last night?" he whispered.

The others fell silent.

"Five of mine," Omri muttered after a moment. "And eight others."

"Mordecai ben Enoch was dragged into the fire." Laban turned and looked back up the street. "He was a strong man, and he killed twelve of the Sea Coast raiders when they came through the Galilee. Four wives will be watching at the window of his house, but he won't come home to them."

Thirteen. Thirteen men.

"And how many unclean?" he said.

"Eight men bitten and lived," Omri said.

"Show me," Barak said.

Omri and Laban exchanged a look.

"I know," Barak growled. "Show me."

***

The eight knelt in a line in the street where the children had died, with two armed men standing guard behind them. As Barak approached with the other chieftains, he saw the *navi* moving along the line with slow but unfaltering steps, with that wild blade unsheathed and held out to the side. The nazarite, for once, was not at her side. Devora's face was grimmer than Barak had ever seen a woman's face before, and she stood straighter and fiercer than any woman he'd known, her posture one of uncompromising duty; she might almost have been a man.

"Is it right that a woman should do this?" Omri muttered.

Barak held up his hand, and the Zebulunite fell silent, though his body was rigid with tension.

Some of the eight knelt in the ash between the tall houses of their own free will. Three were feverish and trembled where they knelt, one of them barely conscious. Four had been bound, their wrists lashed together and then secured with short cords to their tied ankles. One had struggled until he'd toppled to his side, and one of the men assigned to guard them had moved to him quickly and, gripping his arm with a gloved hand, pulled him back to his knees. "You shame your kin," the guard hissed in his ear before stepping back.

As the *navi* stopped before each of the kneeling men, she asked the man's name, repeated it after him, and then met his eyes with hers. "You fought to defend the People," she said. "The Words of Going will be sung for you."

A few of them thanked her. One did not look at her, and she placed the tip of her blade beneath his chin, gently lifting his face until he did. Barak saw that she was careful not to touch any of the men, though she stood near them. She did not shrink away or scream. She did not do anything he might expect a woman to. Her face remained hard as stone.

With each man, once she had heard his name, the *navi* lifted Mishpat and the blade swept down through the air with a sound like a bird's wing. When the ash at her feet was soaked dark, she stepped away and stood before the next of the men.

One of the Hebrews down the line wept, but none of them screamed as the sword fell. Not one. There had been screaming enough during the night. Perhaps they had screamed so much that they had lost the ability to, like singing until you're hoarse. Or perhaps the horror of what could await them was greater than the horror of the swift, delicate blade.

Looking on, Barak shivered and felt again the touch of the dead on his leg. In the hour before dawn, Barak's pavilion had been moved near the edge of the town, and he had gone to it once he could hear no more moans of the dead. He'd cast aside his spear and fallen to his knees inside his tent the moment the flap fell back, plunging him into a warm, comfortable darkness that was utterly different from the cold night within the town. The floor of his tent was spread with rugs of Canaanite design, many of them woven even here in Walls, others to the north in Judges' Well; he felt the weave of them against his knees. He'd fallen to his face, pressing his brow to the rugs, moaning, praying, begging, though he didn't know for what. He could not rid himself of the sight—in his mind— of that little girl impaled on his spear.

With a groan he'd rolled to his side and lifted his knee to his chest, his hands feeling quickly along the skin of his leg. There was no bite there, no scratch or wound. But his skin felt to him like ice. Like dead skin. He breathed raggedly through his teeth, exploring his calf with his fingers. He kept moving his fingers up and down along his skin, gasping for air. He was alive. He was alive, but they had *touched* him. Those things—those corpses—unclean corpses—they'd touched him. He squeezed his eyes shut against the sudden rush of tears. "Make me clean," he moaned, "make me clean."

He wanted then the wine of his vineyard, not to drink but to wash his leg, even as he might wash out a wound. He had clutched at his leg, breathing hard, trying to grapple with what had happened this night. The silent town. The children. The dead girl's touch. He felt almost as though he were in the grip of a fever; he shook and twisted on the rugs. Called out once for his wife. Hadassah, whom God had taken. As God had now taken an entire town. An entire *town* of the People.

***

Now, as Barak ben Abinoam stood watching the holy woman take the lives of eight of his men, his leg remained ice cold and the ashes on the ground warm against his sandalled feet. He lifted his eyes and gazed bleakly at the burned-out husks of what had once been great houses of cedar. He had known this town; he'd met Hadassah here. Now everything here was unfamiliar to him. He did not know how to act, what to decide, what traditions either of his People's or his wife's might apply. He had burned her mother's gods that the God of his own fathers might keep his crop and his land safe and unstrange to him. But everywhere he turned, he saw all that should have been safe now contorted and burned.

At last the *navi* finished her dread work. As Barak watched her she glanced up, and for a moment their eyes met. Hers were cold as the lake. Barak looked away. When he lifted his gaze again, the *navi* was already a long way up the street, leaving the dead. The two men who'd guarded the bitten now stood by their bodies, which lay like bundles of clothes on the ash-covered ground. Looking more like some child's joke than the bodies of dead men.

Omri and Laban stood silent beside him. He could sense their horror. There were no words for this, there had never been and never would be. The bodies lay very still. A little way beyond them, Barak could see the crumpled corpses of last night's children, all of them covered with a fine layer of white ash so that they no longer looked like the bodies of the dead but like the monuments of Kemet where their fathers' fathers had toiled to make brick. But the statues in Kemet were said to be forms of beauty, while these statues of ash were the forms of children that appeared as though they'd died in terrible torture. Chewed and bitten, some with their bellies eaten. Their scalps cloven by an iron blade. Their faces distorted, frozen for all time in expressions of abominable and unanswerable hunger. Suddenly and for the first time, Barak was grateful that his seed had borne no lasting fruit in his wife Hadassah's body. Had it done so, he might have had to see his own flesh become one of—one of *these*. He was a man of the north; he had survived blight and bad harvests and raids from the coast. He had survived many things. He did not know if he could survive that.

"How did this happen?" Omri whispered. He had his face averted, as though he could not look directly on the bodies.

"The *navi* may know," Laban rumbled.

Barak shook his head. He did not need a *navi*'s vision or any words whispered out of the dark by God to guess. "The men of Walls concealed them in the cache," he said quietly, "then most of them left. They must have hoped to draw away the dead, lead them away from their children."

"But we found the dead here," Omri said.

"Only some—those that died in their houses, perhaps even after the others left, the living who had no fever and could still walk. They locked all the houses, and they closed up this cache. All we've found are the men and women they left behind. The unclean ones."

Omri looked pale.

"We only found one of the dead that wasn't in a house. That one must have burst out somehow—something drew its attention before we even came here. It was—feeding." Barak swallowed uneasily. "Maybe someone came to the town before we did. One of the men coming home perhaps. Or someone from another village visiting kin."

"*Elohi*," Laban breathed.

Barak lifted his eyes toward the stark, surrounding hills. The groaning dead who were in the streets of Walls must have groped their way over the stones and up the slopes after the settlement's men and women, pursuing them with a hunger that would never rest, never halt. It had been a good plan, whoever among the men and women of this town had devised it, when they realized there were too many dead to burn. But for the children, it had been too late. Maybe one of the children, or several, had been bitten, had become unclean. Had fallen and lain still and then risen and sought to devour the others. Secured in the cache with their small flasks of water, waiting for their parents to return bringing safety and food, the children had no way to flee or hide from an enemy that was locked inside with them. Those who were not entirely eaten had succumbed and risen also, until the entire cache was just filled with those small bodies with sightless, waiting eyes, silent in their decay.

Had the parents returned, they might in their despair have been devoured by their own children when they lifted the cover at last from the cache and reached down to pull them out.

But the parents hadn't returned.

"How long has the town been silent?" Laban said quietly.

Barak shook his head. Long enough, certainly, for the ashes of the houses the townspeople had burned to grow cold, the smoldering of embers to cease. Long enough for all the bodies of the children in the cache to stir. A day? Several? He wondered if any of their parents still breathed. The men of Walls might have had spears to fight with, but Walls had not suffered a raid since the coming of the Hebrews to the land, and those spears had likely only been wielded against the fish in the lake since the time of their grandfathers. And they would have had women with them, and old men. What chance could they have had, fleeing the dead on those slopes?

A cold, choking guilt settled in his throat to match the cold touch on his calf and the cold fear in his belly. He had arrived too late for this town.

Barak turned and began striding back toward the tents. Omri and Laban followed. "We will build cairns over each body," he growled as he walked. "Even the burned ones. Dig them out of the ashes if you have to."

"Are you serious?" Omri exclaimed.

"I am, and you do not want to argue with me, Omri of Zebulun. I am not in an arguing mood."

"But *every* body—there must be dozens—"

"At least. See that it's done. Laban, will you make sure none are missed?"

"If you ask it," the somber giant said carefully.

Barak gave him a brief, grateful look. "I do ask it."

"Do you have *any* idea how long that will take?" Omri snarled.

"It is what the *navi* would wish."

"Since when does the *navi* command the spears?"

Barak turned on him, and his face was lit with such wrath that Omri fell back a step. "The Covenant says to build cairns, we will build cairns!" He was shouting. "Look around you, you fool. Do you want to question God's ways in this field of ash?" He glanced at Laban. "We will not leave one body unburied! I want none of them left! Am I clear?"

"You are," Laban murmured. Omri merely gazed at him in shock.

"Gather stones!" Barak shouted. Spun and strode back up the street. Enough of this ash and smoke.

***

Zadok stood still as a cairn himself amid the ashes and fallen timbers, his spear fallen at his feet. Devora approached wearily until she stood at his side. After a moment she set Mishpat aside near her feet. Straightening, she scrubbed at her face with her hands, trying to smudge away the dirt and ash. Then she just stood there. She watched his chest rise and fall. His eyes were dark pools that gave nothing back when she looked in them. All around them, men with gloves and rolls of tentcloth gathered bodies and shrouded them, bearing them to where Barak was having cairns raised on the shore of the lake. Sometimes the men cast looks at Zadok, and their faces held awe or bewilderment. Those who had seen him the night before had seen how he fought.

"Zadok ben Zefanyah," Devora said after a while. "I need you."

Devora reached for the small bronze knife Zadok wore sheathed at his hip. She tugged it free and reached for the nazarite's hand. Gently she opened his fingers and drew the blade across his palm, making a slit deep enough to bleed for a while. His breathing changed a moment later; it must have taken his body a moment to feel the pain. Then his head turned, and those dark eyes focused on her.

Devora placed the hilt of the knife in Zadok's hand, pressing it against the cut, then closed his enormous fingers around it. "If there was ever a man of our People who needed a wife to look after him," she said, "that man is you, Zadok. Why don't you have one?"

"I could not defend both Shiloh and a woman." His voice was deep and hoarse. Hearing it was a relief to her. "A day would come, *navi*, when I would have to break one covenant or the other."

She nodded and looked out over the ashen street. Saw the men bearing away the last bodies of children. It was too much; she felt as though she were drawing in death through her eyes, aging and crumbling away like ash as she watched. But she couldn't close her eyes; what waited in the dark behind her eyelids would be far worse.

"What do you see, Zadok? When you close your eyes."

He watched her for a moment. "They were in the tents." His eyes shone a moment, surprising her with their moisture. "I ran out to look for my father. They were everywhere. The stench—" He shook his head. "They were crouching over my father, four of them. Outside the Tent of Meeting. They were eating him. Behind them, Eleazar took up the shofar, blew the call. My father had saved his life. I tried to get his body away from the dead, tried to *fight* them—"

He fell silent.

"I'm sorry," Devora said.

"I failed him. Every time I face the dead, I fail him."

"No," Devora whispered. "Zefanyah would have been proud of you. You are the kind of man he would have liked. The kind he would've wanted at his side. I know this, Zadok."

He just looked bleakly out over the ash.

"I need you, Zadok," Devora said. The pleading in her voice did not shame her; she had to lean on someone, if only for a moment, or fall over. "I am barely holding it together. Those—children—" She swallowed. "I understand your suffering now. Why you stand still, the way you do. I encountered the dead as a girl, you as a boy. But since, you have gone out time and again to hunt them and raise cairns over them, whenever one has been seen in the land. Wherever Shiloh has sent you. How do you stay on your feet, Zadok? Tell me."

"I remember who I have to protect," Zadok said.

Devora laughed coldly, bitterly. Something in her heart cried: *But I am a woman! I am the one who is supposed to be protected.* But she knew better. She was the *navi*. Judge and mother of Israel. It was her burden to bring God's visions to the People and keep them safe. Her eyes hardened, and she stifled her laugh.

"Did you see it, last night, Zadok?" Devora asked, forcing the words out. "The *malakh ha-mavet*? Did you see it over the settlement?"

"I saw smoke," Zadok said grimly.

For a moment they both listened to the sounds of the men laboring by the lake.

Zadok wiped the blade of his knife on his cloak and sheathed it. Then bent and took up his spear. "I have taken the nazarite's vow. It does not matter if God is here or not." His voice was rough. "Or if the angel of death is here or not. *I* am here. I have taken the vow."

Devora let out the breath she'd been holding. His words sounded so much like her own words to Hurriya during the previous night. "All right. If anyone made it out of here alive, where did they go?"

"Kedesh. The town of Refuge," Zadok said. He was quiet a moment, and when he spoke again his voice was softer. "…I did want a wife once."

Devora glanced at him, jarred out of her thoughts.

Zadok nodded, his tone strangely subdued. "A woman who lived in Shiloh, who would always live there. I thought—" He glanced at her eyes, then looked away. "I thought that any act of mine would defend both her and the tribe of Levi. Nimri's raid taught me differently."

Devora's eyes widened.

"Me," she gasped. "You wanted *me*."

He just looked at the lake.

Devora recalled Zadok crying out her name as he rushed toward her through the terebinths. She recalled the way his breathing had changed as he'd held her. Yet—she had known him so long. And she had never known this.

With a sudden blush, she wondered if other women in Shiloh camp had known. She who saw what God's eyes saw—might she have been blind to what other women might see? Had her husband known of Zadok's heart? Had *she*? Her head spun and she felt a great urge to sit down, but there was nowhere to seat herself that was not covered in the ashes of the dead.

"You chose Lappidoth when I was a boy of eight," Zadok muttered. "When I was a young man, Lappidoth seemed to me to be very old. I thought he might die, and I might ask you then, after your time of grief. I had a fool's heart. Forgive me, *navi*, so that I will be released of this burden I endure."

She watched his eyes a moment, saw the suffering there. How like his father he looked in this moment. The hard lines of his face, the depth and uncompromising purpose in his eyes. The only thing different was the anguish. Zefanyah had died before he could know pain like that.

She shook her head. "You've broken no covenant, Zadok, none with me. There's nothing to forgive."

"If you wish me to relinquish my vow—"

"Stop," she cried softly. "By the tribes, stop, Zadok. Just—be quiet a moment. Let me think."

She lowered her head. She could feel his gaze on her, and it was warm, undemanding. Yet she wanted to flee. The feelings in her heart and the feelings in his—whatever they were—it was too much. Everything she had encountered in this dead settlement was too much. She needed to go up into the hills where the wind was loud and the People were quiet. She needed to find some place to kneel and weep and pray.

But what did she fear? Zadok was younger than she, but he was not a boy. She lifted her gaze and saw him looking on her with concern. The anguish beneath it was deep but faint, like old coals after a fire had burned down all night. She sighed and stepped nearer to him, took his face between her hands, the scratch of his beard warm against her palms. He didn't move either to hold her or draw away. A tenderness welled up in her like a spring. She was conscious that the men dragging the bodies from the street could see them, but she didn't care. This moment was between the *navi* and her nazarite, and she would not let watchful eyes or any rumor they might start disturb it.

She looked up at him. "Who do you protect, Zadok, now that the high priest is gone?"

Zadok met her gaze without flinching. "Israel's *navi.*"

"Then keep protecting her," Devora whispered. "And Devora, the woman, loves you for it. I am my husband's, I cannot be yours. But you do not *offend* me, Zadok. You are so important to me. You have to know that."

Zadok caught her hand in his, held it in that firm, unyielding grip. His eyes searched hers. Then he nodded. "I know it," he breathed.

"Thank you for sharing your heart."

"Thank you for sharing yours," Zadok rumbled.

A smile touched her lips. "We've grown old, Zadok."

"Maybe the *navi* has." He returned her smile. "But I can still outrun or outfight any man in Israel."

"Beast," she murmured. She was grinning now. His boasting cheered her. Zadok bore deep pain, but nothing—neither the rising dead nor the hard burden of slaying dead children nor his yearning for her—nothing could still the fire he carried within him. That cheered her.

Even the *malakh ha-mavet* seemed no more than a shadow cast over sunlit ground, in the face of Zadok's enduring fortitude.

"It's good that you never took a wife, Zadok ben Zefanyah," Devora told him, lowering her hands from his face, regretting the loss of that warm beard against her palms. "You would be too much for her. You and Lappidoth are the only men I have ever met of whom that is true. Other men, women can work with." She smiled again and turned to glance up the ashen street. Men toiled there, but if they had been watching her, they were not now, and whatever judgment each of them had made on her was locked for the moment within the silent Ark of his own heart. There would be cairns by the water, new ones. She must go and sing over them. She must resume her burdens. She took Mishpat up from where she'd set the blade aside.

Zadok set a powerful hand on her shoulder. "*Navi*," he said. His voice had grown stern again, but it had lost some of its grimness, and the sound of it was a comfort to her.

"Refuge is where we'll find any from the town who still live and breathe," he said. "But we will not find any survivors, *navi*."

BREAKING CAMP

THE MEN HAD moved some of their tents to the edge of
the burned settlement, raising a forest of canvas around
Barak's pavilion; this had allowed the men to take the work
of cleansing the town and raising cairns in shifts. After
singing the Words of Going over the cairns, Devora's
mind and heart were so full, so turbulent, that she
stumbled toward these tents without a word to anyone.
She wanted only to throw herself to the rugs and sleep
until the men broke camp and she had to get to her feet
again. Devora hardly even noticed the looks men gave her
as she stumbled by with Mishpat still clutched in her hand.
Their eyes held awe or fear—she had become strange to
them. They were not looking at her as they had the
evening before when she rode into the camp with a
feverish heathen girl before her. Gazing at her now, their
eyes still said *woman*, but those same eyes held alarm rather
than desire. They did not know what to think about her or
what to do with her. She was *kadosh*, set apart—as alien to
them as God.

Even the glance Omri cast her as she passed held this strangeness, yet his gaze roved over her body. He stood, stroking his jaw with his hand, his eyes thoughtful and dark.

Laban was standing at the edge of the tents, sending men this way and that, and he saw the *navi* and directed her to a massive white tent. It had been his, but it was the levites' color, and he gave it to her. She didn't know where Laban meant to rest and did not have the energy to care. Nor did she know where Hurriya or Zadok were; neither was by her tent.

Inside, Devora stumbled to her knees and held Mishpat upright before her, the point resting on the earth, the hilt before her eyes. Before singing over the cairns—while waiting for the last ones to be raised—she had cleaned the blade and then polished the metal to a sheen; no trace of the unclean dead or of those bitten remained on the immaculate, though dented, metal. Now she stared hard at the blade. And felt things hardening within her.

She could still feel the slight resistance of each man's neck against Mishpat's blade, she could feel the tension of it in her hand. A night of terrible judgments. Not all of them hers. She spoke quietly to God in the dimness of her tent.

"Where are you?" she asked. "Have you truly lifted your hand from us?" Anger tightened her throat. "How have we offended you so greatly? Is it that our People mixed with the heathen? Yet—in that town—many of them fought to live with such strong hearts. Did all they could to preserve their *children*. As Hurriya did. They were not strangers to the Law—they could not have been strangers to it in their hearts. Why didn't you bless their acts? Why were those for nothing?"

Her tent flap drew aside and she glanced up with a sigh, expecting Hurriya or Zadok. But the man who stepped into her tent was shorter than the nazarite, his face hidden beneath a hood, one hand holding a heavy wool cloak closed, the other at his side carrying a bloodied knife.

She gasped, but the man murmured, "Do not scream, *navi*," and she recognized Barak's voice.

"What is this?" she hissed, her eyes wide.

Devora pressed a hand to her breast, waiting for her heart to stop pounding from her moment of fright.

He could not mean violence against her. That didn't make any sense. She watched in puzzlement as the war-leader tossed back his hood, revealing a wan face and haunted eyes. She drew in a breath; the man's hair had grayed. His hair—it had streaks of gray in it, gray as Lappidoth's hair—but there had been no gray in it before. She gazed at him in horror. "Barak?"

"I have come to your tent and the men will gossip," he said quietly. "But in here it must be. I will have no prying eyes for this. Do not cry out; I don't mean you ill."

The man opened his cloak and with his left hand drew out a dove, clutching it by the legs, the severed neck dripping blood onto the ground. "I will make a covenant with you, *navi*," he said. Breathing raggedly, he crouched across the tent from her and began carving into the bird with his knife, cutting the feathered body into two halves with a brutal, quick efficiency. Devora rose unsteadily, watching him, her heartbeat back to normal, her mind catching up. A covenant? A covenant to do what?

Barak separated the two halves as far apart as his arms could reach, then set them gently on the ground. He glanced up at her then, his eyes fierce. "I will promise you something you desire," he said. "You see further than men's eyes. And you are unshaken by the dead and know much about them, that is clear. I will hear you before the decisions I make. I will let you strike down my word if you know the decision to be wrong, and I will trust you as God's *navi*, holding back only those decisions that safeguard the lives of the men."

Devora looked at him, assessing him. The man was sincere. However reluctant he had been to acknowledge her or afford her respect, he was sincere now.

"And what promise do you ask of me, Barak?"

He glanced down at the two halves of the dove, then back at her. "Can you look, *navi*, and see whether I will survive the cleansing of the land?"

"It doesn't work like that. I can't answer your questions. God sends what he knows I need to see, to preserve what he wishes preserved."

He was silent for a moment. "But it's going to get worse."

"Yes," she whispered.

"Then I ask a simple thing, *navi*," he said quietly. "If I should be taken by the dead, my body defiled and half-eaten and rising unclean from the ground—" His hands began to shake as he spoke, and he set the stone knife carefully aside and got to his feet, facing her, his eyes filled with fear such as Devora had rarely seen in a human face. Her throat tightened.

"If my body should rise," he repeated, low and intense, "ride after me, *navi*. Ride and find my body. Pile clean stone above me, with your own hands, even if I have been dragged far away." He took a slow breath. "I have no seed, no inheritance in the land. If I live, I will take another wife and ensure my seed persists. But I may not live. And I will not wander the land unclean."

She gazed at him, and it seemed to her that the tent filled with the scent of ash and smoke.

"Do this," Barak said, without any quiver in his voice, though he passed his hand over his brow. "Make covenant with me. And any strife between us is at an end." His eyes were so terribly earnest, so desperate, it was all she could do not to look away. "You are the first judge of Israel, and you are the *navi*. Where you tell me I must ride, I will ride. Where you tell me to cast my spear, I will strike. Make this covenant with me."

She glanced down at the two halves of the dove. This was no small thing, to make a covenant. What they did here, God would watch, and remember, even if they should forget. Yet she had always been quick to make her decisions. Delay threatened life.

"I will," she said.

The relief on Barak's face was so naked that she looked aside.

They passed between the parts of the bird seven times. Each time they recited—first Barak, then Devora—the ancient, simple words of the rite:

> *Let it be done to me*
> *as it was done to this bird, and more*
> *if I break this covenant*
> *or fail to keep it.*

When her voice fell still the seventh time, Devora felt the responsibility of this covenant settle over her shoulders like a heavy wool cloak; it was an almost physical feeling. The bond of responsibility between her and the war-leader could not be severed, not by death nor by anything that might happen in life. It was as sacred and as real a covenant as that which she had made with Lappidoth her husband many years ago. It was as real as the covenant the tribes had made with each other, and the covenant they had made with the remnants of the heathen peoples at the vale of Weeping, and the covenant they had made with God on the mountain in the desert. Upon its breaking would follow a curse.

One did not make a covenant lightly, and Devora wondered what consequences this covenant would have that she could not yet see. Yet she did not regret her act. Barak was bound to her now, and surely what he had asked of her was no different than the responsibilities the Covenant between God and the People had already placed upon her. She was accustomed to being bound to a duty; this one did not frighten her.

Barak stood, and to her relief, he took the remains of the bird with him. He gave her a nod, then left her tent as abruptly as he'd come. Devora breathed softly in relief and sank to her knees in the silence of her tent. Alone once more. She couldn't bear having to speak with another person right now. She could not bear the thought of having to carry one more burden.

Her need for rest fell upon her as savagely as a growling bear, but she shrugged it off and got to her feet. No. She would pace and think. She would *not* close her eyes, not until she was very far from this place. Not until the moans of the dead were less near in her memory, less loud in her ears.

***

When Devora left her tent a while later, the air still smelled *burnt*, and a film of ash had settled on the surface of the lake, turning the lilies on the water to pale corpses of themselves. All around her, men were breaking camp and preparing for the half-day march toward Refuge. Devora went to Shomar and curried him, then saddled him for the day's ride, though she winced at the thought of that saddle between her sore thighs again. Barak and the other chieftains appeared to sit their horses without discomfort; riding must be something a woman could get used to. She talked to Shomar softly and listened to him whicker softly back. She began reciting the words of the Law under her breath, to calm the edge of her anxiety:

> *And these words, which I command to you this day, will be in your heart: and you shall teach them to your children. You shall talk of them when you sit in your house, and when you walk by the way, and when you lie down, and when you rise up.*

"We have raised the cairns," Devora murmured to God as she patted Shomar's neck. "We will *not* forget our promise. And I trust your promises hold true also."

She didn't know if God was listening.

A sharp crack of wood disturbed her thoughts, and she glanced toward the last wooden houses that stood, their roofs bearing blankets of ash. Devora caught sight of Laban at the door to one of the houses, swinging back his great axe and slamming it into the wood. Three other men stood behind him. Large, lithe men of Issachar with makeshift cudgels ready in their hands. Devora nodded, approving from a distance what they were doing: breaking into the last houses to check for any lurking dead before abandoning the camp and the town. She turned back to her horse, checking his hooves, then giving him water to drink and grains to eat from her small store of them, for this was no time to turn him loose to graze. His eyes were soft and liquid in the midmorning light.

She listened without watching as Laban and his men went from one house to the next. Once, she heard a man's scream, followed by the wavering moan of a walking corpse. Devora shivered.

Then the moan was cut short. Perhaps Laban's axe had done its work.

She strapped her waterskin and Mishpat to the side of the saddle.

She glanced about for Hurriya and at first didn't see her. Then she glanced toward the burned settlement and was startled to see the Canaanite approaching out of the town, coming from the houses the men had already checked. Zadok walked beside her, and as he looked toward Devora, for the briefest moment she surprised a look in his eyes of yearning and regret that battered at her heart. She looked away, embarrassed to have caught that look. He *did* want her, then, as a man wants a wife. She sighed. It was clear that he would continue to treat her with great respect. But how was she to treat *him*, knowing what she now knew?

The sight of Hurriya distracted her. The girl was carrying a fistful of green leaves that must have come from the herbalist's shop in the market, and she was no longer wearing her stained salmah. Instead, she wore a thick woolen gown, dyed green. It must have belonged to one of the wealthier wives of the town, and it reflected a Canaanite's sympathies: a love of bright colors and things that draw the eye in the sun. Devora found her own gaze held; though Hurriya walked with discomfort and though there were dark bruises about her eyes from nights without rest, she looked suddenly beautiful. And little trace remained of the unease she had once shown around the nazarite. Then the girl stumbled and leaned heavily on Zadok's arm, and a flame of jealousy lit within Devora's heart so sudden and so fierce that it shocked her; she damped it swiftly, furious with herself.

"Those clothes are unclean," she said as Hurriya approached her with a wary glance at Shomar. Zadok gave the *navi* a nod without looking directly at her and departed to help the men with the tents. And Devora breathed easier.

"So am I," Hurriya said wryly. Her left cheek was full of herbs, and she chewed them slowly. Her eyes had lost their glassy look, but she was still deathly pale. "Why does it matter?"

Devora sighed. "I'm glad you found clothes," she said after a moment. "And you look lovely in them, Hurriya."

The young woman glanced at her, perhaps surprised to find Devora calling her by her name.

Everything was strange now. The problems over which she sat in decision this day were very different from those she had judged when men of the People came to her olive tree with broken pacts or broken in spirit. Her own decisions were strange to her—hard necessities that were driven not by the Law but by the panic she saw in men's eyes and the bursting of the dead through wooden doors. The very sky above her was strange, darkened by ash and by the burning of lives and the burning of the work of men's hands. Zadok's heart was strange to her, concealing within it things she hadn't suspected. Even Hurriya was strange to her, in this green gown. She looked—whole—in it. As though not only the edge of her fever but also some of her weariness and her grief had fallen away, even though her body showed where it had been ravaged by fatigue.

"I don't know how to restore the Law," Devora whispered. "In this place."

"By giving me a waterskin," Hurriya said. "By helping me find my sister. By helping these men protect their houses and their kin from the dead."

Devora looked at her. She took Hurriya's waterskin from its strap on the side of the saddle and passed it across. Hurriya took a small drink.

"I think I understand your Law better than you do," Hurriya said, passing the waterskin back with both hands. She held it almost reverently, and Devora wondered how often she had gone without water on her long walk from Judges' Well to Shiloh.

Devora gave her a sharp look but said nothing.

"You say your God gave you this Law in the desert when he looked at you, when your Lawgiver looked at him. When they faced each other on Har Sinai."

"Yes," Devora said.

Hurriya leaned forward, her eyes intent and far more lucid than they had been the night before. "When you see another's face—the face of a child, or another woman, or the face of the goddess, or the face of someone hungry or hurt—their eyes, they look back. They look at you. They ask your love, they ask you to hear their crying and know that you and they are both alive, and some day you may be hurt, you may be hungry. It may be your child carried dying in your arms." Hurriya choked a moment, then went on. "When I look at you, you look back. Only the dead don't look back."

Devora thought about that as she bent to tighten Shomar's girth straps.

"You think the Law is a pact with your God, a pact with others of your People. But it's not just a pact."

Devora just listened, thinking hard.

"It's an answer," Hurriya said intensely. "You have rules for everything. But it's not the rules that matter. It's that you *want* to make them. You want to answer the suffering you see in another woman's face. You want to give her safety, or justice, or comfort. That's what matters. That's why you have your Law, why you love it. But when you sit in decision at your olive tree, or on this horse looking at the burning town, you have to find the right answer to the suffering you see. Your fathers in the desert found the Law, found that answer. So it guides you, like I guided you into these hills. But you still have to find the right answer to each face you see."

Devora rose, looked at her over Shomar's back, swallowed. Suffering could give a woman insight, she knew, and surely few women had suffered as this Canaanite had. "I misjudged you, Hurriya. I treated you as only a child. A bruised, grieving child."

Hurriya's smile was only a little bitter. "I am the *navi*, remember."

"I remember," Devora said softly.

Hurriya gazed at the ruin of Walls. "Both our Peoples suffered there," she said quietly. "Do you still blame mine? For the dead?"

"God sits in decision over us all," Devora conceded. She swung into the saddle, wincing briefly at her soreness. "Come," she said.

"You are a stubborn old woman," Hurriya said. Devora helped her up with a grip on her clothed arms.

"As an aging olive," Devora agreed as Hurriya settled before her with a groan at her body's pain. "Come, girl. Let's talk about your visions, since only you are having them."

Canaanite the girl might be, but there was no denying what *else* Hurriya was. Or what duties Devora had to her, to teach her and prepare her.

Shomar whickered as Devora nudged him forward.

"Let's talk about being the *navi*," she said.

ZADOK'S RUN

A FEW HOURS later beneath the hot sun, Devora received a fresh shock when she and Hurriya and all of Barak's men reached a ridge overlooking the town of Refuge. Gazing down into the valley, Barak cursed. Hurriya shivered once. Devora merely stared; even the nightmare at Walls had not prepared her for this.

The town was no longer a refuge but a trap.

With the valley of the Tumbling Water before it, a high cliff at its back, and strong walls on its east, south, and western sides, Refuge conveyed strength. It was one of three such settlements in the land, walled towns that Yeshua the war-leader had wrested from the Canaanites and established as safe places the People could go to in time of need, or that a fugitive could flee to in search of justice if pursued by one who wished to kill him. Perhaps that fierce chieftain, Yeshua ben Nun, who had torn down so many walls in the river valleys of the land, had one day gazed up at some sheer stone fortification and realized his

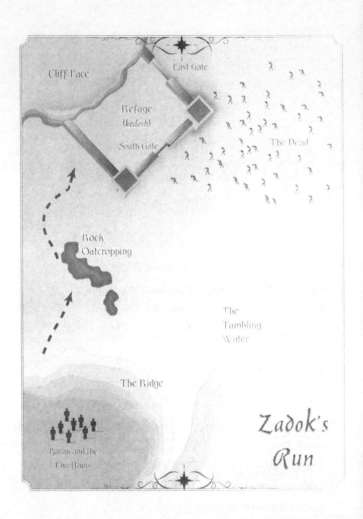

Cliff Face

East Gate

Refuge
(kedesh)

South Gate

The Dead

Rock
Outcropping

The
Tumbling
Water

The Ridge

Zadok's
Run

Barak and the
Chieftains

People might eventually need such a defense themselves. Or perhaps he had foreseen how divided the People would become and realized that there would be a need for neutral cities, places where it would not be permissible to kill for any reason, even the execution of justice.

> *Let there be three towns of refuge, where a fugitive may flee his enemies who would devour him. And one of these shall be in the north.*

Whatever Yeshua had been thinking when he declared those words, he surely had not anticipated this.

For there were indeed enemies now in the north who sought to devour the People.

And they were here.

Hundreds of corpses pressed against the south and east walls, and others behind them pressed forward, crushing the first line of the dead against the stones in their mindless, urgent hunger. The wind carried up the reek of them and their eerie moaning, a sound that crept inside Devora like shivers from extreme cold, until her hands were shaking and she had to clasp them behind her to still them. Beneath the moans, another sound: like the rattle of a landslide but softer, like a hundred drums that were not keeping rhythm together. Or like hands, many many hands, beating upon stone.

The men stopped on the ridge and let their packs slide to the ground. The chieftains on their horses gazed down with mute horror. Vivid in Devora's memory was her vision beneath the branches of the olive tree, her foresight of great herds of the dead lurching through the land.

For a long while, no one spoke. They just watched the hundreds of dead slamming their decaying flesh against the stone walls below.

"They need bows," Hurriya whispered at last.

"What?" Devora whispered back.

"Bows. Like the Sea People have. Look. A few of the dead lie still. They've been throwing things from the walls at them. But they need bows."

Devora had heard of bows, of course, but had never seen one. Yet she saw how they might be useful. If one had the ability to kill at a great distance, greater than a spear's cast, and more accurately—if one had that, one could simply slay the dead from the walls, then issue out to build cairns once all the dead were still.

To his credit, something had hardened in Barak during the afternoon's march. He sat his horse a few moments watching the horror below, then turned and called out, "We are men of Israel, and that is a settlement of Israel. Let's relieve that town by nightfall, men."

Some of the men shouted, lifting their spears or whatever implements they held. Others just gazed down at the walled town, learning new fears.

"Omri, Laban." Barak strode up toward a promontory of rock that jutted out from the ridge, and the other two men strode to join him. Devora did not. She had no interest at this moment in the plans of men. She listened to the thudding of those hands and bodies against the walls of the settlement below and realized with a dull inevitability that this ordeal of facing the dead in this strange hill country would go on, and on. That God alone knew how many dead they would have to bury, how many valleys they would have to search, before it was done.

Even as she struggled with this, Hurriya's body grew fiercely hot against her breast, and Devora gasped, for the flash of heat nearly scorched her. Then it was gone, as quickly as it had come, and it was again a mere heathen girl who leaned against her in the saddle and not a living torch.

"They're going up the river," Hurriya breathed as she came out of the vision. "All of them, right now. They're fleeing, but the dead follow. Men and women from Walls, many of them."

Devora caught her breath. Suddenly it was clear to her what had occurred. Those fleeing Walls had come here, to Refuge, only to find the dead waiting outside. So they had kept running, going up the river. Taking some of the dead with them.

"Stay here," Devora whispered, and she slid from Shomar's back, wincing at the stiffness of her body. She took a breath and broke into a run toward the outcropping of rock where Barak and the other war-leaders stood, debating how to attack the dead below. "Barak!" she called out. "Barak!"

The man turned.

"We have to go!"

"What?"

"We have to go! The refugees from Walls. They're fleeing up the river. Hurriya has *seen* them. A vision—a vision from God!"

Barak swung down from his horse and strode to her, his breast-piece clinking. Omri looked on bewildered, Laban looked pensive.

"What are you talking about, *navi*?" Barak growled as he neared.

"We have to hurry north. There are men and women in the open field, in the vineyards, with the dead close behind."

Barak's eyes widened, he shot a glance to the north. Nothing could be seen there because of the curve of the river valley between the steep hills.

"My vineyard is up there," he breathed. Then shook his head. "We have to relieve those in the city. Then their strength can join ours."

How could she convince him? "No. We must first preserve the lives of those of the People who have no walls."

Omri nudged his horse closer. "What is this woman's talk?" he muttered. "The dead are here. Sound the shofar, Barak, before these men feel their manhood wilt. Before they slip away into the hills."

Barak looked from Devora to Omri, his face pale.

Devora rounded on the Zebulunite. "Hurriya had a vision!"

"She's a Canaanite," Omri sneered.

"She's a *navi*! She sees what God sees! What God needs *us* to see!"

Barak gripped Devora's arm, his eyes intense. But she did not flinch. "If your girl has seen a true thing, we will have dead before us and dead behind," he whispered fiercely in her ear. "And if the dead have overwhelmed the vineyards and homesteads along the Tumbling Water, then going up that river we will have dead to either side." His eyes glanced toward Refuge below. "And I have *kin* in that town."

"All the People are your kin, and the safety of their

houses and their tents is your responsibility. These at least are safe behind a *wall*."

"For how long?"

"We have a covenant." Devora leaned close. "This is *not* where you will cast your spear, Barak. *God* shows the way to victory, Barak. *God* shows us how to clean the land. Not our own wisdom, which is small. If you break covenant with me, Barak ben Abinoam, if you ignore the visions he sends, I swear to you, every last one of your men *will die*. Do not do this."

He cursed and gazed at Refuge, a muscle twitching in his cheek. For a moment Devora had doubts. This was a war-leader who'd sent men after the *Ark*. Why did she believe he would respect a covenant with her any more than he had one with their God? Would he hold true?

"We *cannot* leave them to die," Barak growled, releasing her arm and pacing furiously.

"They have a wall," Devora cried. "We'll come back for them."

"*They* don't know that!"

"Barak, don't listen to her," Omri hissed. "Look at her. She's just a woman. And she wants us to listen to the fever-rambling of that heathen slut? Don't be a fool, Barak! Look at the men. We have to fight *here*."

Barak glanced at Devora, his face pale as a fish's belly. "We'll have to get them some message. The people in Refuge. Those men and women, those children. They have to know we'll come back for them."

Devora let out her breath. He was listening to her. She looked down at the town and something clenched inside her. The dead slamming their hands and their bodies

STANT LITORE

against those walls—who could make it through *that* to
bear any message to the town?

"Who do I send?" Barak breathed. "Who do I send?"
Wide-eyed, he glanced at the other war-leaders. "Omri,
you or I might do this thing, but none of the men could.
They're farmers—they couldn't get through that—they'd
have to go around to the far wall, they'd have to get to it
without being seen. Fight if they are seen. They'd have
to—" He stopped, helpless.

"I'm not doing it," Omri grunted.

"Nor you, Barak," Devora whispered. "The men need
you."

"I will make the run," a deep voice said behind her.

Devora turned slowly. Her face went very pale. "You
can't," she breathed.

Zadok stood there, his face set, a fire in his eyes. The
men looked on Zadok with fresh awe, and Devora could
see reflected in their eyes the fierce legend of the nazarites.
"No," she whispered.

"This could mean your death," Barak said. "An unclean
death."

"I have known since my seventh winter that I will die,"
Zadok said firmly. "And I chose *how* I will die: in service to
the Ark, or to the *navi*, or to the sons of Levi. The day of it
is God's to choose."

Devora met Zadok's gaze, saw the fire in it, saw
deeper, saw the certainty and the devotion and the fierce
glorying in the task, the knowledge that if he ran to that
town, in that act his failings would be forgotten both by
himself and by God. The knowledge that he would at last
have fulfilled his vow.

"Zadok," Devora said, "you don't have to do this." She couldn't lose him.

"None of Barak's men have my stride or my skill. I am the only one who can." He smiled grimly. "And I *can* do this. God's hand is on me; I will reach the walls." He met the *navi*'s eyes. "I can finally do a thing worthy of my father."

Devora's throat tightened. She stepped near him, so near their bodies nearly touched. What she had to say other men mustn't hear. She whispered fiercely in his ear, pleading. "I've seen the *malakh ha-mavet*. Twice. God's hand is *not* on us."

He looked at her, his dark eyes above hers. "If we leave these people with no message, you will suffer. I know. You know too how bad it will be. I *can* do this."

She sucked in breath between her teeth, her panic rising. Before she could speak again, Zadok nodded to the plain below and said, "*Navi*. That outcropping of rock. To the west. It'll hide me most of the way. It can be done."

Her gaze followed his nod. She could see the outcropping, almost a low wall of stone rising at a slant from the land, as though God had driven a massive stone into the soil like a spearhead. Beyond it, a stretch of open grasses, then the west wall of the city, the only wall with no corpses beating against it.

But she saw something else, too.

"Zadok," she said, "there's no *gate* in that wall."

It was true. The walled settlement had two gates, one in the east wall and one in the south—both had dead beating against the timbers, which must surely have been reinforced heavily from the inside. In fact, the reason there

were no dead pressing against the west wall was likely
because no one had fled into the city through it when the
corpses had first descended on the valley.

"The men of Refuge will lower a basket for me,"
Zadok said.

"You don't know that. They're terrified. Who knows
what they'll do."

Zadok smiled grimly. "When I make it past those dead,
navi, Refuge will want to speak with me." His smile
widened, showing his teeth. "I promise it."

"Zadok—" But her throat tightened, choking off her
words. So much she didn't know how to say.

He gripped her shoulders in those powerful hands, held
her gaze a moment. Then he glanced over her shoulder at
Barak. "Keep and preserve her life, in my stead. The
Canaanite too."

Barak gave him a brisk nod, his face drawn.

Zadok nodded back, then stepped away from the *navi*,
releasing her. Quickly he unbuckled his breast-piece and
cast it aside; it would be too heavy, a hindrance rather than
a defense. His greaves, too, he slid from his legs. His tunic
he pulled off over his head. He stood a moment in his
loincloth and his sandals, his body muscled and bronzed
by the sun, his dark hair long and uncut. He took it up in
firm hands and bound it in several knots near to his scalp,
where it would be less easy for the dead to grasp. Then
knelt on one knee at the *navi*'s feet, lowering his eyes. His
fingers moved quickly, tightening the laces on his sandal.
"Bless me, *navi*," he asked.

She didn't want to bless him. She wanted to keep
pleading with him not to go. She wanted to ask him to stay

with her. Slowly Devora set her hand on his head, felt the thick curls of his hair. For a moment she didn't speak. When she did, her voice sounded frail to her.

> *Adonai bless you and keep you,*
> *Adonai make his face shine on you and be gracious to you,*
> *Adonai look on you with favor and give you peace.*

She didn't lift her hand from his hair. Another, she was going to lose another of her tribe, her family. She'd lost Naomi. She'd lost Eleazar. She was going to lose this man too. "Zadok, you—" She tried again, managed to keep her voice calm. "Tell them where we're going and why. That there are people with no walls and no refuge, and we go to shield them. Tell them we will be back and that as long as they remain within their walls, God will be their shield and their tower. Tell them the *navi* is with Barak's men and that she promises them this. Zadok—" She paused, gathered herself. Her voice low and intense. "You make it to those walls, Zadok ben Zefanyah. You *make* it there."

She lifted her hand, and Zadok got to his feet. His eyes met hers, and they were unveiled. The passion in them she had only seen before in Lappidoth's eyes.

"*Navi*," he said with another duck of his head, and then he turned and bolted into a run, flashing past Barak and the gathered men, darting down the slope. Devora found she couldn't breathe, watching him move. He was fast, fleet as a deer, leaping and ducking through the brush.

Almost absently Barak gave the chieftains commands, calling to ready the men for the march upriver. But his gaze never left the valley below, and the other tribal leaders walked away slowly, looking over their shoulders.

At last, only Devora, Barak, and Omri stood on the high rock. Omri's face was pale with horror, Barak's awed. Devora, however, felt that she had been struck through the breast with a spear and was now in shock and waiting to feel the pain of it. She glanced once back the way she'd come. Shomar's head was down; he was grazing among the rocks. Hurriya sat huddled on his back, watching Devora with eyes glazed with pain and vision.

"Holy God, the man can run," Barak breathed.

Devora swallowed and turned her eyes back to the valley. Had she been a young woman, she might have offered to run herself, hoping that God would bless her and shield her as his *navi* and bring his words through her to the settlement.

Once again, Zadok carried her burdens for her.

The nazarite was sprinting along the outcropping now, keeping the low stone bulwark between him and the dead; there were perhaps only a few spear casts between him and the southern wall where the dead moaned and beat on the stone. He would have to run northwest along the stone, then round the far end of the outcropping and make for the west wall, hoping either that the dead would be too preoccupied to see him or that his legs would carry him so swiftly to the wall that he could be hoisted up before they reached him.

It was desperate.

And wondrous.

She watched Zadok's powerful body race along the rock. In him she saw his father, Zefanyah, who had danced the spear so furiously on the training ground that none of the other nazarites could best him. Zefanyah, who afterward would stand laughing among the other men on the packed dirt, sweating, his chest heaving, until he would glance over to where Devora watched with the other girls and smile at her.

And she saw her husband, Lappidoth, as a young man, slaying the corpses that had come for his cattle, his bronzed skin shining in the sun, his blows powerful and sure. His eyes full of purpose and will and the determination to hold firmly to what was his.

"I have never seen a man move like that," Omri muttered.

"Until this last night and day, you had never seen a nazarite," Devora said, her heart swelling with pride even amid her fear.

"He is one man," Barak said. "There must be four hundred beating on that wall. At least."

"He is Zadok ben Zefanyah," Devora said.

"He's rounding the end of that rock," Barak said quietly.

Below them, Zadok came clear of the rock, but even as he did, several figures lurched out of a fissure. Eight, nine of them, barring his way. Devora found she couldn't breathe. There had been dead hiding *in* the rocks. Possibly someone working the fields had taken refuge in some den within the rocks and been followed and eaten, and the dead had stayed there until stirred by the sound of Zadok's footsteps and his breathing.

Now they were upon him.

A hush fell over the hill. Devora's blood was loud in her ears. She could have forbidden him to go. She was the only one whose forbidding he would have heeded. Yet she knew that this would have broken him.

The moaning of the dead was faint but terrible in her ears.

She watched helplessly as Zadok leapt among the dead, his spear flashing in the sun. Two figures lay still on the ground. He spun and danced—he *danced*—darting forward and back, leaping over one corpse that had tumbled to its knees, landing on his feet and bringing the spear up, stabbing with the bronze head, wielding the butt end like a weapon itself, knocking corpses back. Then he wielded the spear one-handed—though its weight was not light—and his other hand plucked out his knife, and that too flashed in the sun as he leapt and fought.

"He's going to make it," Omri breathed. "He's actually going to make it."

Zadok fought in utter silence. No raiding cry, no prayer, no voice that came faint to Devora's ears. Just focused, silent discipline.

"*Navi!*" Barak gasped.

"That does it," Omri muttered.

Some of the dead were breaking away from the south wall, lurching out over the open grass, their attention drawn by the moans and snarls of the corpses that had closed on Zadok. Devora bit her lip and prayed silently, her palms damp with sweat. Below the ridge came the sounds of men shouldering their burdens, unaware of the grim battle the nazarite was fighting.

But now Zadok thrust his knife into the face of one of his assailants, and it appeared to stick in the corpse's skull, for he shoved the corpse aside, abandoning the blade, and broke free, bolting out over the grass. The way he'd run before had stirred the admiration of his watchers, but now he *truly* ran. It couldn't be less than two hundred strides between the rock outcropping and the west wall, but he tore across the ground like a stallion in full gallop. Veering north to buy time as the lurching corpses moved toward him, a reeking herd flowing along the wall and over the grass.

"He won't make it," Barak said softly.

Omri just shook his head.

"He will," Devora said forcefully. "He *will*."

Run, Zadok. She mouthed the words, without sound. *Run, Zadok. Run, damn you.*

He had perhaps eighty strides to go—but there were dead all around him now, and dead between him and the wall. He dodged and darted between them, sometimes knocking one aside with his spear, then spinning past. Devora saw the dead thicken about him, and she felt almost dizzy.

"*Run!*" she cried aloud.

She saw the sunlight on his shoulders and back where he shone with sweat. He dodged and the point of his spear cut the air. Then the dead were thick between him and the wall, and he didn't hesitate, didn't turn back or flee. The nazarite ran directly *into* the corpses, wielding his spear and using the sheer force of his run to shove the walking corpses aside.

Omri cursed. *They say a nazarite fights like ten men*, Omri had told Zadok when the two of them met, both taunting him and questioning.

No, Zadok had answered. *I fight like twenty.*

Now Zadok proved it. He spun on his heels faster than Devora had ever seen any man move, ducking and thrusting among the dead, his lethal bronze slicing and piercing scalp and face, throwing corpses to the earth. Still they closed on him, hands grasping for his shoulders, his arms, uncaring that he was armed. Their fingers brushed him, defiling his skin, yet he struck with both blade and shaft of the spear, as though it were only heads of summer wheat touching him and the spear he held a scythe. More corpses fell. But now he could not move forward farther, so he stood and fought. The moaning dead pressed in on him, the ones behind shoving those before them, and after a moment Zadok went down beneath the sheer weight of their bodies, and Devora let out a low cry; she couldn't help it, it tore its way up her throat. She saw the corpses bending over that piece of earth where he'd fallen, only thirty strides from the wall. She wanted to look away, but she couldn't. Something was tight and hard in her breast. She remembered the scorched, unrecognizable face of Zefanyah as he lay stretched out on the ground in a line of dead.

"He *rises!*" Barak yelled. "He rises! *Navi! I can see the sun on his spear!*"

Devora gasped. It was true; she could see it too. The flashes of light as the spear thrust up from the ground, twice, then again. And then with a roar she could hear even from here, even over the wailing of the dead, Zadok ben Zefanyah, nazarite since he was seven, burst to his feet, the dead still clutching him, one of them even with its jaws about his left arm, blood running down to his left hand. Yet Zadok stood, screaming hoarsely, thrusting against the dead with the shaft of his weapon. His hair had come loose and it swept about him as he fought and turned, hair longer and more flowing than any woman's, hair that had never been cut. Bloodied now about his shoulders. Dead grasped at it, pulling his head back; a corpse tore into his left shoulder with its teeth. Still he remained on his feet as they ate at him, still he roared and battered at them with his spear, using it more now as a pole and shield than as a thrusting weapon. Bodies lay still about his legs, dead he'd silenced, yet others clambered on top of the fallen to clutch at him. He drove the butt of the spear back, crushing the face of the corpse that had his shoulder, destroying its head; he shook his arm and shoulder like a man shrugging off a cloak, and the body fell away. Blood ran down over his chest from the deep bite in his shoulder. The dead still held his hair and his left arm, yet he turned, and gripping his spear near its head, he drove the point like a dagger into the eye of a corpse behind him. He was bleeding, he was unclean, still he fought. Still he fought to get the *navi*'s message to that settlement.

People had come to the west wall now and were hurling shards of pottery and ewers and even beams of wood down on the dead who moaned between the wall and Zadok, though with little effect.

"He is still fighting," Barak breathed. "He is still fighting."

"He is a nazarite," Devora said again. Everything in her numb.

Then the dead tugged Zadok beneath them a second time, and on the ridge Devora and Barak and Omri waited, but there was no flash of sun on Zadok's spear nor any surge of the man to his feet. Only the dead, bending over that spot and feeding, covering Zadok so that his body could not be seen through them. A pain sharp near Devora's heart. His body. Zadok's body. It would be left down there, to be fed on, to *rise*—if the dead left any of him intact.

With a cry, Devora turned and moved as quickly as the her soreness would allow, running for her horse.

"*Navi*, no!" Barak tore after her.

In a moment Devora felt the man's weight slam into her, bearing her to the ground on her belly, driving the breath from her. Wheezing, she kicked wildly, but he crushed her to the earth.

"We have to get his body!" she screamed. "We have to get his body!"

"It's no good! Be *still*, you fool woman!" His growl in her ear.

"No! We have to!" She shrieked and thrashed under the chieftain's weight and heard him cursing wildly as he fought to hold her. All she could think of, the one terror in her heart, was that Zadok was down there being torn and eaten, that she had sent him to die and could not leave him there, not like that. Zadok, who had loved her and sworn to her, who had been her defender and her right arm and her strong cedar to lean on, these last days of their nightmare journey into the north. She could not leave his body there among the dead. She could not betray him so.

Sobbing breathlessly, she kept fighting, and Barak wrenched her wrists over her head, pinning them in a grip that she could not escape. With his other hand he wound leather tightly about her wrists and knotted it; a strap perhaps from the leather beneath his breast-piece or from his greaves. She spat and bucked but could not dislodge the man. Felt him lifting her, carrying her over his shoulder as she kicked and pummeled his back with her bound hands.

"Stop fighting me," Barak whispered fiercely. "There's nothing we can do. Nothing."

She kept struggling, barely hearing him. The ground moved dizzily beneath her as he strode, carrying her toward her horse. And still she screamed with the moaning of the dead in her ears. Screamed her throat raw in protest, screamed to Zadok and to Barak and to God who was watching somewhere in his terrible silence.

Part 4
Along the
Tumbling Water

THE WITHERING LAND

THE MEN MOVED north, with Devora tied to her saddle, her wrists thonged to the pommel. Hurriya clung to her waist from behind her. North of Refuge there was no road and no town—just the broad valley of the Tumbling Water, a strip of well-watered earth a quarter mile wide, nestled between steep hillsides. The land leveled out for a while as they followed the water north, and the river here flowed slowly. On the west bank there was a cart track that led them past small vineyards that drank in the hot sun, between water and hill. Behind each vineyard could be seen a low house of cedar or pine, like a tired bear with its back to the steep rising of the land.

In any other year, this might have been a cheerful place. At this season the vines would have been green and lush for harvest, with fat clusters of grapes almost too heavy for a man to lift.

But Devora felt no cheer. She sat her horse rigidly. She was uncomfortable and sore. But that was nothing compared to the humiliation hot in her breast. She rode beside the men, tied to her horse, like any slave. With her wrists bound, she could not lift her hands to cover her face, though she felt their eyes on her. She felt naked. Any grief she might show would be terribly public.

And as she'd told Barak, in all things made or done by God or by men there was a message that could be discerned. The message in the strap about her wrists was clear to her. Surely she would not be respected as the *navi*, not here, not among these men. Not now that Zadok was gone. Zadok's presence too had been a message, a sign of her authority, a sign that she was set apart. That sign was gone. The men might look at her now and see only a woman in a dirtied, stained white dress. Once Omri even rode to her and sneered, "Just a woman." She didn't move or look at him, and she dreaded for a moment that he would grip her thigh as he had done once, but at that moment Barak's voice came sharp from where he rode a little ahead. "Omri!" And cursing under his breath, the man let her be.

As she watched him go, Devora felt the bite of anger. Only another woman. Prone to tears or hysterical screaming, of value because her body created life, but not to be trusted outside a man's tent. What if, seeing her so, the men stopped listening to her? Certainly Omri had; his brief moment of awe that night in Walls had not survived seeing her screaming like a slave girl as Barak tied her and tossed her onto her horse. How could she help her People if her words to them were no longer the words of one who sees what God sees, but only the words of a woman who rides without a man beside her?

Her gaze flicked down to Mishpat, which was still strapped to the side of her saddle. The blade had not been taken from her—for she was *not* a slave. And though she could not reach it, the sight of that sword hardened her. She was still Devora of Israel, whether free with a nazarite and the mighty presence of the Law behind her, or trussed to her saddle like a raid captive.

And even her humiliation, even her grief, were small things compared to her dread at what she now saw before her and behind her and on every side. For this was *not* a lush valley ready for harvest. The dead had been here first. And with them, its sere wings scything through the vines, the *malakh ha-mavet*. Where its shadow had fallen, the vines were withered and dry as brambles; there were no lights in the houses.

Barak grew visibly tense as the slow tread of the men brought them farther upriver, and Devora recalled his words at the lakeside: *I am a vintner who has been eleven days from my vineyard while dead prowl about it, and I fear for the harvest.* This was Barak's country: the vineyards of the north Yarden, famed in Israel. The people of Walls, Hebrew and heathen, had led the great herd of the dead straight up this valley, where the vineyards awaited them like a long row of riverbank blossoms to be trampled. There would be no harvest.

As they passed up the cart track beside the dying fields, silent as mourners, they came upon strange sights. A walking corpse that crouched amid the vines and dug at the ground with its fingers, with relentless, slow movements that seemed utterly without purpose. The corpse did not even glance up as Omri approached it from behind and drove a spear into its skull.

369

After that, they found a corpse pinned, half-crushed, beneath a wagon with a broken axle; perhaps the man had died there. Now he lay on his back, the wagon holding him at the waist. The corpse writhed and growled at the men who passed, twisting to the left and to the right, struggling helplessly to get on its belly and crawl toward the living. The men at the head of the line stopped and stared at it a few moments. For once Devora felt nothing seeing the corpse twist and strain to get at them. It was only one more corpse in a land that was itself becoming a corpse.

It didn't really matter.

After a few moments, Laban strode forward with his axe and took off the thing's head. The head rolled away from the wagon and stopped with its face toward the sky. The jaws didn't move, but the milky, dead eyes did. Laban growled and brought the axe down on its brow, swinging like a man splitting wood. Hurriya glanced away with a shudder; Devora just looked numbly on.

As the line of men began to shuffle uneasily past the wagon and the still corpse, Barak detailed five men to make a cairn. Then he rode to Devora's side and drew a small knife from a sheath he'd strapped to his shin. With calm, measured movements, he set the knife to her bonds and cut them; Devora felt the cold of the bronze against her skin, but Barak was careful and he did not cut her. When her hands were free, she lifted them slowly, rubbing her wrists, wincing as life came back to her numb hands, hurting them.

"I am sorry," Barak said quietly. He had the grace at least to look ashamed. "He died bravely."

"He died." Devora's voice sounded small to her, and hopeless.

Barak said nothing.

"His body will rise."

"I know." The war-leader coughed. "When we return, we will end that and raise a cairn for him."

"I should never have let him go." Devora closed her eyes.

Barak rode beside her a moment, as though he were trying to think of words to say. Then he sighed and kicked his horse into a canter and left them. Hurriya squeezed Devora slightly, her arm about Devora's waist, and whispered, "He died serving those he loved. The gods will remember him. Your God will too."

***

They stopped briefly about two hours before dusk, and the men shared some of their diminished rations without fires or means of heating them. Sore and exhausted, Devora passed Hurriya's waterskin to her, then lay down in the weeds by the riverbank and looked at the sky. She didn't want to eat. She couldn't cry, couldn't sleep.

After a while, someone settled in the grass beside her, and she felt a hand stroking her arm gently through her sleeve. Soft humming. That go-to-sleep song of Hurriya's. Devora didn't turn her head to look at the girl, she just listened. The grief and terror and fatigue of the morning and of the previous night hit her all at once. Withered fields. An entire settlement, gone. That girl who longed to be a woman, leaping to her death. Zadok, her Zadok, dead.

Beneath all those feeding corpses. Tears stung against her eyelids; she rebuked them. She yearned suddenly for Lappidoth, for his strong arms about her, holding her so that she could sleep without fear. Letting her hide her face against his chest so that she could weep without shame.

But here she had only Hurriya and her melody and the soft touch of the girl's hand through her sleeve.

"Thank you," she said.

Hurriya stopped humming. "We Canaanites don't let a woman grieve alone," she whispered.

"Neither do we Hebrews." Devora reached and gripped the girl's own arm through her dress, returning the touch. "Did you really see them, girl? Survivors from Walls?"

"Yes. With the dead behind them."

Hurriya and Devora were silent for a while. Then the Canaanite said, "Tell me about this God of yours, who sends these visions."

Devora opened her eyes and gazed at Hurriya's deathly pale face and the empty sky above her. In her dress the girl looked nearly skeletal. Her eyes were weary and glazed with the slow return of her fever, but they held no hatred, only concern. A tenderness for her touched Devora's heart. The girl was ill and fading a little, yet she had come to where Devora lay and had hummed that song for her. This was a woman who had already walked the length of the land once, bleeding and carrying a child. Her fever and illness were unlikely to keep her from doing what she felt she needed to do for those who needed her.

And Devora *did* need her.

They were two women alone. And they had been through fire and death and terror together. Only

Lappidoth had ever seen Devora's heart as naked as this girl had seen it.

She should be caring for and comforting and guiding this new *navi*. Instead, she was being comforted *by* her. Devora sighed and sat up, drawing her responsibilities back about her even as she had often seen Hurriya draw that salmah about her thin frame. "We know little of God, even we who see things that only God sees," she told the girl. "We only know that he's made promises and that when he's made promises in the past he's kept them."

Hurriya was quiet a moment. "What promises *has* he made?" she asked.

"That we will possess the land always," Devora said wearily. "That we will have children, as many as stars in the winter sky. That he will dwell here among us."

Those promises seemed so empty to her now. The land they possessed was reduced to withering fields and ash. An entire settlement had lost its children. And her own womb was barren. Sarah had borne a child out of the aging desert of her body—but that was only a story of the past.

Maybe Sarah had been right to laugh bitterly.

"That your people will always possess this land," Hurriya repeated, an edge to her voice. "Your God doesn't love my people. Why then does he curse me with visions? Does he think I haven't suffered enough?"

Devora could hear the tremor in Hurriya's voice. She shook her head. "I don't know."

Before they could say more, a short call on the shofar interrupted, summoning the men and the two women to their feet. It was time to move on. The sun above was hot and lethal in the sky, and it was all Devora could do just to get to her feet. Yet she turned and took Hurriya's arms in her hands, feeling the fever warmth of her through her sleeves, and lifted her to her feet as well. The woman almost fainted from the effort of rising. Devora didn't think she could have stood on her own. For just a moment Hurriya leaned against her, and Devora allowed it, a protective fire in her heart.

THE VINEYARD

BARAK KEPT the pace quick, leading the men in their long file along the rising riverbank past fields of barley and vineyards that were dying away like weeds in a fire. His shadow stretched out before him to his right now, long like the shadow of a tree. It was late, yet somewhere ahead there might be refugees fleeing the dead—if that heathen girl really *was* seeing things God saw. They had covered a lot of ground this day, and unlike any men and women fleeing Walls, they'd had no need to hide from the dead; they'd slain those they'd passed. No doubt the survivors of that burned settlement had traveled slower, hiding when they had to and always watching for some chance to shed pursuit and double back toward Walls. They might even be within reach this very night.

And Barak had another reason for haste. They were very near now to his own vineyard. And still all the land about them showed evidence of blight and death. His anxiety clawed at him. He had to know. He had to know for sure. As he took note of whose fields they passed, he ceased to think any more of the heathen girl or her refugees or of the *navi*, or of how Zadok had fought as though he had no fear of any corpse. His whole mind was bent on his vineyard, nearer with each step.

When they reached his vines at last, the sun was already kissing the hills with fire. Though Barak had always loved the sunsets of the Galilee—had often stood outside his door with his wife to watch them before taking her inside to his bed—he did not love this one. The burn of it along the ridges made him think of the fire at Walls. Made him think of the fire that had devoured the gods Hadassah's mother had cherished. Made him think of the nights afterward when he sat silent by his hearth, watching the coals, grieving for his woman. Made him think of things lost and never recovered.

And what Barak saw now in his field, he did not know how to bear.

He rode Ager out into the vineyard a way, then slid from his horse and staggered toward the first row of his vines like a drunken man, swaying on his feet. Behind him he heard Laban riding up and down the line of men, urging them to keep moving. Omri just sat his horse, watching his war-leader and shaking his head grimly. Devora nudged Shomar past him, and Barak heard Omri growl at her, "Your Shiloh God has abandoned us, woman."

But none of this made much impression on Barak ben Abinoam. He stumbled on toward the heart of his field.

Nothing lived in that field, nothing at all; the ground was dry, the earth itself drained of color and richness. The shriveled remains of vines limp upon the dead earth like weeds upon a shore, or hanging brown from their straightening poles like the skins serpents shed and leave behind. Barak lurched through this wasteland of his crop like one of the dead himself, then stopped and just gazed at the dead rows. Only when he felt the dry, brittle soil against his knees did he realize he'd stumbled. For a time he just knelt there in the midst of his desiccated field.

"Barak? *Barak?*"

A woman's voice, coming through the roaring in his ears as though from a great distance. Barak ben Abinoam turned his head, saw Devora standing near, and behind her Omri and others of his men. Her lips moved, but this time he did not hear her words. He should get up, he should go to find his house, his beautiful home of cedar and thatch. But he didn't yet have the strength. The dryness of his vineyard had crept inside him the way a desert wind can creep through the flap of a tent that's been poorly fastened.

He reached down, took a handful of gray soil. It felt more like sand against his palm than dirt. A moan rose in his throat.

"You," he groaned. "You are more like a heathen whore than the God of the Ark, the God this fool woman prates of. I left this field, I went to lead your People, I took down the spear." His voice rose, he was nearly shouting, venting his fury and despair without rising from his knees. "I stood in that burning settlement, I stood at Walls, I fought. How can you let my harvest wither? Are you not God of planting and of harvest? You took my Hadassah, you took the harvest I expected of her womb. And this—

you take this." He lifted his eyes to the silhouettes the hills made against the darkening sky, that dark, unknowable expanse from which came rain and day's heat and which the evening's first stars did so little to light. "What covenants do *you* keep, you whore?" he cried.

He saw the *navi* step before him. Saw her lift her hand. Then the left side of his face rang from the slap.

"Be silent, you fool," the *navi* snapped.

Barak just looked at her a moment. Then he began to laugh, loudly, the laughter building from deep in his belly. He just knelt there and laughed until tears poured down his face.

Devora watched him, aghast, and when he fell silent at last, gasping for breath, she hissed, "Get *up*. Barak, we can't stay here. Grieve tonight in your tent, not now."

He shook his head. His hands clenched in the soil.

"Barak!"

"You cannot ask that of me," he breathed. "You cannot. This is my land, these are my vines. This is my house, my land." He would not look up at her. "Omri can lead the men."

"Omri can lead the men of Zebulun. But who will lead the men of Naphtali? Issachar? If not you?"

A long silence.

"Find another," he whispered.

"Barak ben Abinoam!" Strain in her voice. "Whether God and you keep covenant or not, you have made a covenant with *me*, and I call you to fulfill it."

He met her gaze. "Why? Why ride when I have neither field nor wife to defend?"

"Defend the *People*," the *navi* cried. "Defend the Covenant!"

"I have no Covenant," he said. "God keeps no Covenant."

"Then defend *me*. Help me, Barak. Help me take these men against the dead."

Barak gave her that same empty look. Then a shrill cry tore the air—a woman's scream of panic. Barak felt his breath catch in his throat. His body stilled, listening. The air erupted with moaning, the distant wailing of the hungry dead.

Barak stirred at last, rising to his feet. He stared hard across the vineyard. "That came from the house," he whispered, going cold with horror. "*Hadassah.*"

It seemed impossible to him in that moment that only half a year ago he had stood in this vineyard toiling beneath the sun, near where he stood now, and one of the field slaves had run to him, calling his name. The man had been out of breath, and it was a few moments before Barak could grasp the man's message—that something was terribly wrong with his pregnant wife. Barak had tossed his pruning tools and his gloves to the dark soil and bolted for the house, charging down the long row between the vines, panting for breath. That had been the day God had taken his wife from him, the day he had arrived almost too late. The fever had burned through her all too quickly; when he stood in the door gasping for breath, she had turned her glassy eyes to him and whispered, "I'm glad you're here."

The last words he'd heard her say.

Now Barak leapt to Ager's back and swung the horse about so hard the gelding nearly foundered. He sent Ager galloping hard between the rows of shriveled vines, his blood cold. He *had* to know who had screamed, what woman had cried out from his house.

He heard Devora's horse galloping behind him, heard her cry, "Quickly, Shomar!" but paid her no heed. In moments he could see a long house of cedar above the dead vines, and then he was out of the withered stalks and riding toward the door of the house, but others were there before him. The stench of them ripe in the air. He caught a glimpse of a living figure slipping through the door of the house and slamming it shut. Corpses staggered after it, throwing themselves at the door. Others beat at the walls of the house with their hands or hurled their bodies into the wood. Thirty or more. Some of them naked, their bodies torn and chewed, terrible wounds. Others disheveled, their clothing rotting on their backs, their bodies rotting within their clothes. Another shriek from within the house. Roaring, his whole mind filled with Hadassah's memory and Hadassah's death, Barak ben Abinoam lifted his spear and rode down the dead.

HEBER THE KENITE'S STORY

THE NEXT FEW moments were the most terrifying Devora had known since childhood. There were shouts behind her, but her whole mind was fixed on the man riding hard before her, out of reach. And on the dead slamming their bodies into that house. She heard the shriek from within, and Devora herself screamed silently as Shomar bore her toward the ravenous dead at a gallop.

Ahead of her, Barak leapt from his horse, landing on his feet with his spear clutched in both hands, and then he was at the door, wielding that bronze weapon with a ferocity Devora had never seen him display before. The butt of his spear slammed hard into one corpse's belly, sending it flying from the door; then the sharp bronze point drove into another corpse's skull. Devora slowed her horse, and Shomar reared with a shrill animal scream as several corpses turned from the wall and lurched toward her, their hands reaching for her, for the horse, for them both. The stench of them ripe in the air.

"Hold on!" she gasped to Hurriya. Unsheathed, Mishpat whined through the air.

Another shriek from within the house, then an abrupt end to the cry.

Heart pounding, Devora took off one corpse's scalp, and the little circle of hair and flesh spun through the air. Still the unclean thing came at her, growling like an animal. Its brain exposed and pulsing. Then there were dead all about the horse, grasping at her legs and Hurriya's. All those murky eyes staring up at them from faces that had been bitten or chewed half away. The Canaanite took up a waterskin, nearly full, in both hands, and brought it smashing down on one corpse's head, using its weight to knock the corpse away. It staggered back, then caught its balance and came at them again. Devora lifted her voice in song, shakily, but felt no desert ferocity, only raw, pounding terror as the corpses' fingers caught at her dress, tearing it, trying to pull her from the saddle. Mishpat slashed across faces and hands.

A glance showed Barak standing in his door, having forced it open, and spearing the dead as they came at him. He kicked one hard in the belly, driving it back as he wrenched his spear free of another corpse.

There were shouts behind them in the field, men running on foot. And a horse's hooves, galloping hard. Then Laban was with them, his axe swinging in the air, splitting one of the faces that had been snarling up at Devora and Hurriya. Hurriya bent low, slamming the waterskin against the hands that grasped at her; then one of the corpses got its fingers in her long hair, and with a scream she was wrenched from Shomar's back. Devora reached for her and caught only a fistful of green dress that tore away in her hand. "*Hurriya!*" she shrieked.

After a panicked heartbeat, the *navi* slid from Shomar's back into the dead, their hands on her flesh, her gown, making her unclean. Screaming, she carved with her sword, cutting away the terrible dead faces. Hurriya. *Hurriya!*

Cold breath on her throat and the cold of a hand clutching one side of her neck, pulling her toward the corpse's teeth.

Devora spun into the corpse, saw its eyes inches from her own, her sword trapped between her body and its cold flesh; panicked, she brought the hilt up and smashed the hard bone into its face. She shoved the corpse back with a strength that only terror could give her. Another cold hand on her shoulder, pulling her back, wrenching her from her feet; she fell. For a moment she lay on her back and saw their two faces above her, and screaming she brought Mishpat up and cut into them. Quickly she rolled to the side and got back to her knees, barely keeping herself from vomiting. One of the dead she'd cut stumbled after her, and she drove her sword into its head like a spear. Its toppling weight tore Mishpat from her grasp and she scrambled to the corpse's side and retrieved her sword with a desperate pull at its hilt. Heaving for breath, she looked up and saw Laban with his arm about the Canaanite, pulling her up onto his horse, her dress torn open at her left side. The girl was shaking and weeping; four dead lay still, their heads cloven by Laban's axe. Drawing in a ragged breath, Devora realized it was over.

Laban rode to her and leaned half out of his saddle, extending his hand to her.

Devora shook her head. "No, unclean—" She glanced at the weeping girl. "Did any of them bite her?"

"No." Laban's voice was a deep rumble. "Take my hand, *navi*. Uncleanness doesn't matter now, not up here where the dead have touched everything. Another week and we will all be unclean, whether we live or die."

Devora gazed up at him. The deep brown of his eyes, his weathered face. Once before a man had offered her help when she was unclean. She remembered Zefanyah tossing her the waterskin when she'd left Shiloh, that time the old *navi* had banned her from the camp. She remembered the warm leather of the waterskin in her hands, how she had cherished it those days and nights when she was alone in the heather.

Laban's face too was kind.

"I can't," she whispered. Pleading. "The Law is all we have. Our only tent. Without it, we are only leaves in a high wind." She pressed one hand to the earth, splaying her fingers, and forced herself to her feet. Hurriya's tearful eyes gazed at her as she rose.

"Are you all right?" Devora asked her.

The Canaanite nodded shakily.

"Thank God." Devora yearned suddenly to hold her, to pull her close. Instead, she turned toward the house, saw Barak still standing in the door, leaning on his spear, his chest heaving as he caught his breath. The dead lay about his feet in a heap of reeking flesh and tattered cloth. His gaze met hers and there was a look about him that she had never seen in anyone but Zadok.

He cast his spear aside with a bitter expression and turned to go into the house, and Devora stumbled toward the door, stepping with a shudder over the bodies strewn about it. She heard Laban's deep voice and Hurriya's faint, exhausted voice behind her, and then footsteps, and she waited at the door for the Canaanite. Hurriya was as white as if she had no blood left in her body. Her legs shook within the remains of her dress. Devora caught her arm, pulled her near, put her arm about her to steady her, and they went in. Behind them Laban turned and rode back toward the men approaching on foot over the field.

The interior of the house was dim, with the day's fading light coming in only through a few untended gaps in the thatch between the stout cedar boards that made up the walls and roof. There was a large window in the far wall but it had been closed and barred with wooden slats. To the left, a wall with a few bundles leaning against it and a ewer for water. A few clay bowls. To the right, some bedding left in a corner and a doorway covered with a heavy, hanging rug, likely leading to the room where Barak used to sleep. In the center of this main room they found a short man with a sun-weathered face, aging but still lean with muscle, crouched over a woman whose face had gone still with death. The man was clad in leather armor. For a cloak he wore a once magnificent gazelle pelt, now dirtied and stained. He held a bloodied knife in his hand; there was a great gash in the woman's left breast.

To Devora's horror, the woman's womb was round with child; she was pregnant, and the man had killed her. The *navi* drew back with a gasp, then saw the livid bites on the woman's arm.

The man held out his hand as if to ward them away. "I had to kill her," he said quickly. "She was bit. I only killed her because she was bit!"

Barak stared at the corpse for a long moment. "She's not Hadassah," he said softly. The rage went out of his eyes like a doused fire, leaving them cold and dim.

"Of course she's not," Hurriya said softly. "Our dead don't come back to us, Hebrew. Not unless they come back in hunger."

Barak didn't answer; he just gazed at the corpse. Hurriya stepped past him, gave the man with the knife a wide berth, went to lean against the open doorway at the other end of the room. She lowered her head as though to seek what privacy she could as the fright of her near escape took hold of her. Devora watched her, worried, but did not go to her. Her heart had not stopped pounding.

"Who are you people?" The man with the knife looked from one of them to the other. A flicker of recognition in his eyes when he glanced at Hurriya's face, though the Canaanite didn't appear to notice.

Devora turned her gaze away from the Canaanite. "I am Devora, the *navi*. I see what God sees."

The man sneered. "God doesn't see anything anymore. She's left us. Left the land. She's gone."

Another day, Devora would have rebuked him, would have had sharp words. She had none today. Not with that corpse on the floor and so many of them outside, lying in the blighted field about the house. "That might be," she said. "But if God does have anything to show us, I will see it. Or she will." She nodded toward Hurriya.

The other man followed her look, but Barak cut in. "Where are the dead?"

"Everywhere. Hills stink with them. You can't do anything but run."

"We didn't come here to run," Devora said quietly. "Are you bitten?"

"No," he muttered. "I'm likely to end up the only man in this forsaken land who isn't." He considered her with that look the northern men gave her that meant she was strange to them, a woman but something else as well. That look that meant they didn't know how to speak to her.

"I'm Heber," he said.

"You're a Kenite." Devora recognized his accent.

One side of his mouth curved, half a smile. "I am."

The Kenites were desert men. Rare to see one west of the river. They were not of the twelve tribes, but had bound themselves to the Hebrews with many covenants in the wilderness years, and had sheltered vulnerable Israel out where the wind screamed in the rocks. The Lawgiver himself had taken a Kenite wife, and the Kenites had sworn to live by the same Law, worship the same God. The Kenites were known in the land as a wild tribe, hot-tempered and skilled with bronze.

"You have a camp nearby?" Barak asked.

"Up there." Heber waved his hand vaguely upriver. "Had four men with me. Dead ate them. Ate my horse. Ate theirs. I crawled through the river a while and lost them. Fell a few times, then got up and went on. No use dying in the water, unburied, for anything to eat. Two nights back. So dark, those clouds, no moon even. Couldn't see anything. Even God must have been blind in that. Finally find a little place to get out of the water, up onto the high bank. Can't get back to my camp—too many between here and there." He shook his head. "We'd had a good raid," Heber said. "Against the heathen," he added quickly, seeing the look Devora gave him. Hurriya must have heard him, but she didn't look up from her grief. Impossible to know if she was even listening.

"I don't care to get the blood of the People on my knife," Heber went on. "A good raid, though. Loaded most of our goods on horseback. We meant to trade at Refuge and hear who had seen the dead and where. Set out that way, didn't make it. Our horses. They ate *our horses*."

"Your camp. How large is it?" Barak asked. "Is anyone left there?"

"No, just my goods. Some woven rugs, a slave girl. And my other horse, Ira." He scowled. "I did not come easily by that horse, and now I'm on foot, with the dead on every side."

Devora gave him a sharp, appalled look. His *other* horse. When she and Zadok had left Shiloh, they had taken with them two of the only three horses in the camp. Barak's camp had only eleven. And this *raider*, who lived by taking the possessions of other men, spoke casually of his *other* horse. She glanced at Hurriya, but she was still leaning against the doorway, silent in her grief.

"At dawn, there were dead along the bank, just wandering there," Heber muttered. "So I lowered myself over the edge before I was seen, and there was a wolf's den under the weeds, in the wall of the bank. I slipped in. No wolves now. They don't like the dead either, they don't. Nothing living does." He glanced up at Barak and Devora, and his look was haggard with memory. "Had to stay there in the dirt all of the last day and this last night and most of this day too. No food. Didn't dare crawl down to the river for water. Didn't dare sleep. One of the dead fell from the bank once, right into the water, made my heart nearly stop. Waited for it to get up—where it was standing it would have seen me—but its body broke in the fall, its back maybe. It just moved its head from the left to the right, facedown in the water. Couldn't even moan with its face in the water like that. Probably still there. Hope it rots there." He lowered his voice fiercely.

"Sometime this morning, the dead wandered on, all but that one in the water. So I got up, climbed quietly as I could onto the bank. Walked downriver a bit, climbed back down for water, then up. Kept moving. Have to keep moving now. Found refugees coming up the river to meet me. From Walls."

"They're alive!" Devora cried.

Hurriya looked up quickly. It had been her vision of survivors that had sent them here.

Devora felt a surge of sudden hope. If this were true—if there were truly refugees from Walls, men and women who still lived and breathed and had survived the death of their settlement—if Barak's men could find them and protect them—perhaps everything would be all right. If they could save some of the People, surely they could cleanse all the land. Surely it would mean God had not forsaken them. Whatever reason God had for sending no visions to his servant Devora since their coming to the north, for sending visions of what might come only to a Canaanite girl who did not worship him—whatever it all meant, if they could save these people, they would know, they would *know* God was with them. And all these deaths—the children in that town, and this pregnant woman who lay dead on the floor of Barak's house, and *Zadok*—these deaths would not be without meaning.

389

Heber nodded. "Fifty, sixty of them. Fleeing the dead. Said Refuge was besieged. Said I could join them, they'd be grateful, they would, for another knife and a man who knows what to do with it. But I wasn't going to try going north again." He shuddered. "Thought I'd be able to slip by the dead, if I was quiet. I'm used to being quiet. Then I met her." He nodded toward the corpse behind them. "She wanted to try getting back to Walls. Made a pact with her—"

He stopped. His face went ashen. He was staring past them at the corpse.

HURRIYA

DEVORA GLANCED over her shoulder and froze. The corpse was *moving*, its fingers twitching against the cedar floor. Though it had a knife wound in its breast.

"*El kadosh*," Heber breathed. Holy God.

"*El adonai*," Devora whispered. She lifted Mishpat and turned toward the body. By the door, Hurriya's face twisted into an expression of loathing and hate.

Even as Devora stepped toward the corpse, its eyes opened. Devora gasped. There was nothing in those eyes, no emotion, no awareness, no life. The woman's eyes did not reflect back either Devora's face or the blade lifted over her. Devora recalled Hurriya's words to her amid the ashes of Walls—that in the eyes of anyone living, be she Hebrew or heathen, you could see her life and her need and the reflection of God in whose likeness she was made.

But not in these eyes. These eyes might drink in what the corpse saw, but they gave nothing back.

The corpse's lips parted and it drew in its first breath, lifting its heavy womb. Then it let out the breath not in a wail like a new life being born, but in a long, slow moan, a sound that swept into your ears and inside your mind and under your ribs and into your heart, the voicing of a need so great it could never be met, not even if the one voicing it should devour all the world.

The corpse rose up on its elbows and rolled to its side, those dull eyes turning toward Devora's legs, the moan dropping to a hiss.

"God!" Barak choked. "Slay it!"

Heber stepped near, his bloodied knife ready. "Step aside, woman," he said.

Devora could not look away from the corpse's eyes. She felt cold throughout her entire body. Then the thing's arm lifted, fingers curling to grasp. It reached for her leg.

"Damn you," Devora breathed.

She brought Mishpat down. The iron sank into the corpse's head as easily as a keel sinks into water. One shudder and the corpse went still. Devora's blade held it up on its elbow for a moment, then the body slid from the sword and fell back. Its hands hung limp. A great gash in its head, cleaving it nearly to the eyes. Those eyes were open and unchanged.

It did not bleed.

After a moment they heard the sounds of anxious voices outside, the men talking. And a scratching against the wooden floor in the other room, probably the flight of a mouse.

"God," Barak breathed again. "God."

"It's what happens," Heber muttered. "Seen it before. Never get used to it, though."

Devora just stared at the corpse's womb, so large and full. This woman had carried life for the People, had carried within her own body the survival of the Covenant and of her tribe. Now she lay dead and unclean. Devora could see no movement against the skin of the corpse's belly, but still the sight of that distended belly struck her with horror. What if some small, waiting life yet moved in there? She had an almost overwhelming urge to bend and press her hand to that unclean flesh, to feel for some movement or some beating of a tiny heart.

"Get it out of here, please." Devora swallowed.

Barak nodded, his face stunned, and he stepped toward the outer door, then through it. They could hear his voice lifted outside.

"You did it right, girl," Heber said. "Went for the head." He lifted his gaze from the body, gave Devora a bewildered look. "What are you doing with a man's blade?"

Devora ignored him, stepped away, and looked to Hurriya. The girl still leaned against the edge of the inner door. Her eyes still glassy from the lingering fever, yet intent on the body.

"How many have to die?" the Canaanite whispered.

"Some days a woman can only save one life," Devora muttered. Glanced at Heber. "It looks like today we saved yours."

"The men with you did," Heber said. He nudged the body contemptuously with his foot. "Not that I'm not thankful for it, Hebrew." He looked around at the dim room, glanced up at the rafters. "May be enough room for the men in here. Could wall up the door, be safe until dawn if we're quiet."

"There are five hundred men by the river," Devora

said. She gave the walls of cedar a look of distaste. "We'll sleep in the tents."

Barak stepped back in, and two men with him. They had gloves. Grimly the two took up the corpse by its feet. Devora stepped aside as they dragged it out through the door. Hurriya stared at the corpse until it was gone.

"Cairns," Devora whispered.

"They gather stones already," Barak said.

"Thank you."

Heber glanced from one of them to the other, the bewilderment in his face growing. He sucked in his lower lip, chewed on it.

Barak's face was drawn with pain, and Devora remembered that his fields and his very house had been defiled. Devora stepped beside him. "We will cleanse the land," she said for his ears only. "And there will be another vineyard."

"I will keep my covenant," the man said wearily, and Devora realized that though she'd meant to comfort, Barak thought she was doubting him.

Before she could say anything more, she heard that scratching sound from the inner room again, louder now. Frowning, Devora glanced at the rug hung over the door to the inner room, then gasped. The rug had been pulled aside a little, and a corpse was looking through it. A mangled body on its elbows, most of its face chewed away, only one eye intact, both ears gone, a thing deaf and nearly blind and no longer bleeding or feeling, yet still moving, crawling and scratching its way across the floor in terrible purpose. Even as Devora glimpsed it, the death-stench filled the room, pinned back previously by the heavy rug and now freed to warn them all, though too late.

It happened fast. Too fast. The thing's rotted hand reached out, grasped Hurriya's ankle, and tugged sharply. The Canaanite fell to her knees hard, then slammed down on her face with a startled cry. The corpse tugged Hurriya half under the rug as it pulled itself forward, climbing onto her. Ripping her dress open and gouging into the woman's side with its fingers and teeth. Even as Devora leapt at the corpse with Mishpat in her hand, she saw the rush of blood, red and thick, and torn meat.

With a scream Devora swung the blade, slicing through the corpse's face and carving the top of its head away. The body fell to the side and did not bleed or stir. Devora cast her blade aside and threw herself to her knee beside Hurriya. The wound in the girl's belly was lethal; the blood coming out was black and sluggish, and her face was pale, so pale. The girl was breathing in shallow little gasps, but she was aware, and her eyes looked helplessly up at the older *navi*.

"You didn't tell us there was a corpse in that room!" Devora cried over her shoulder.

"I didn't *know*!" Heber sounded shaken. Perhaps realizing that it might as easily have been him leaning against that door.

"Get out. Both of you."

The men hesitated.

"*Get out!*" Devora screamed.

Footsteps. She heard Barak take up her blade and wrap a cloth about it—as though to signal her that he would make sure her sword, her waterskin, and her horse were seen to. But Devora didn't turn or acknowledge him. Another moment, and she and the Canaanite were alone.

Heber's knife lay on the floor near them, forgotten. Devora took up a fold of Hurriya's torn dress and pressed the fabric to the wound, but the blood welled up, soaking it. There was nothing she could do. Even if Hurriya could survive such a fatal wound—even then—Hurriya looked up at her, kept her gaze on the older *navi*'s face.

"I—I'm dying," Hurriya choked. Her eyes wild with the sudden, terrible knowledge of it.

Devora reached for her hand, gripped it, brought it to her breast. The girl's hand was unclean, but Devora was unclean also. Even if she weren't, in this one moment she could not care. What did it matter?

"Can't die," the girl gasped, her eyes wide. "I didn't find Anath. I didn't find her."

"Hurriya—" Helplessly, Devora gave the cloth over the wound more pressure. Without effect. She didn't have long.

"Please," Hurriya whispered, "find her."

"I'll try." Devora could hardly speak through the tightness of her throat. Her promise to try was all she could give.

"Oh gods." Hurriya's face was white, and the pain in her eyes was terrible, like a reflection of the pain in the eyes of God. She gasped for air a moment. "I'm sorry. I'm sorry I—hated you. Blamed you."

Devora's eyes moistened. "I'm sorry too," she whispered.

Something passed between them, something for which there were no words and would never be. Hurriya squeezed the older woman's hand once, and Devora returned it.

Then Hurriya's gaze flicked toward the dead woman. "Don't want to be—like her."

"You won't."

"My body—should go to the fish—"

"I can't," Devora whispered. "I can't do that. I'm Hebrew."

"I know. Hebrew." A plea in her eyes. "Devora, we are both women."

"Yes," Devora whispered.

"Your Law," Hurriya said faintly. Blood pooling beneath her. "Made to shelter, preserve your People. Your People weren't—weren't made to preserve it."

"Don't talk. Just breathe. Just breathe." Devora moaned. She was losing one more woman she loved. She couldn't bear it.

"You'll lift stones above me?" Hurriya rasped.

"Yes."

"And sing over my body?"

"Yes."

Hurriya's eyes glistened. "I wish I could—could hold him again. My baby." Her hands were shaking.

"I know." Devora lifted the girl's hand, pressed it to her cheek, holding back her tears. "I know."

"He was so small," she whispered. "So small."

Hurriya's eyes closed, and Devora could hear her body fighting to breathe now, in little gasps.

"Hurriya," the *navi* whispered, but the girl didn't open her eyes. With a shock she realized Hurriya's eyes would only open again if she rose from the dead.

Her chest tight, Devora hummed the first few notes of Hurriya's song, in a desperate hope that hearing it, she might come back. But she didn't. Instead, her breaths grew shallower and shallower. Lifting her hand from the bit of dress she'd pressed uselessly over the wound, Devora took the girl's hands gently in hers, feeling their warmth. She held them a while. They were so small, like a child's.

"Sleep, then," Devora whispered, sniffing back tears. "You sleep now, daughter. Sleep."

One last, small breath. Then Hurriya's chest no longer moved. She was still. Devora held the girl's hands fiercely, but there was no longer any pulse in them. A quiet, keening noise rose in her throat. Hurriya was gone. Her daughter was gone.

Shaking, Devora folded the young woman's hands over her breast, then reached and caressed her hair softly, tucking it behind her ears and laying it smoothly about her shoulders. Her tears cooled on her cheeks. "No," she kept whispering. "No, no."

She bent low over Hurriya's body and kissed her lips, gently. Hurriya's lips were soft but dry. Devora kissed the girl again, and a third time, and felt that if she were to try and stand and leave the girl's side, she would break apart, frail as clay.

Yet she had to. She glanced at the knife Heber had left on the floor. There wasn't much time. Still she gazed down at Hurriya's still body. On an impulse she unwound from about her own waist the scarlet cord that she had used there as a sash, the same cord that had once held the furs wrapped about Mishpat and that had come with her all this way into the north.

Gently Devora wound that faded scarlet cord about Hurriya's wrist. The cord looked lovely on her, even in its lack of color—as though Hurriya had been wearing it like a bracelet for years, while she gleaned in the fields or picked

olives from the branches of the orchard by which she'd
lived. As though she'd carried it with her all the way from
the north, then all the way back again. It was weathered; it
had endured, even as she had. And like a cairn, the cord
was a covenant, a promise. The cord bound them both to
each other. Like her iron blade, that cord had a history. It
had belonged to the *navi* before her, who had been given it
by Rahab herself, the Canaanite girl who had preserved the
lives of two Hebrew spies during the taking of the land
and who had then hung the scarlet cord from her window,
a sign that her house was inviolate and sheltered when the
Hebrew raiders burst at last through the walls of that
settlement.

It was not only that the cord had bound Rahab to the
People and brought her into the tribe; it also bound the
People to her. So that their men would know that Rahab
was one of theirs, not to be harmed, and to be treated as a
woman of their own People might be treated. A sign that
the People had a responsibility now to those women who
had survived the falling of their towns' walls. Devora had a
responsibility. Hurriya had tried to tell her that, tried to
show her.

"Unseeing," Devora whispered, "I permitted
injustices." She had sat in decision so many years with the
Law at her back and the People before her, both Hebrew
and heathen; perhaps she had not looked often enough
over her shoulder at the Law, and so had forgotten what to
look for when she gazed out on the People. She had
forgotten to look for justice for the strangers in the land.
Though it was the Hebrews who possessed the land, a land
of promise, a land they held to be theirs and held as theirs,

yet the Lawgiver had declared that there must be one Law alike for the stranger and for those born in the tents of the People. *Shelter the stranger, for you also were strangers in the land of Kemet.*

Yet her People had not done so. How many women had been left unsheltered, with only a salmah to clothe them? How many?

But Devora had no more room for thought or for anything but the deep, wrenching grief that assailed her. The house had darkened until she sat beside Hurriya's body in deep shadow.

She caressed Hurriya's hair once more, whispering her name. Then reached for Heber's knife.

***

The evening light outside the house seemed bright and harsh to her after the dimness inside, though in fact the sun had now slid behind the ridge to the west and dusk was upon them. Barak stood there talking with Omri in a low voice, and he turned at her footsteps.

"*Navi,*" Barak said.

"I will camp here tonight," Devora said numbly.

After a moment Barak nodded. "I'll set a watch and tell the men to keep silence." He looked as though he wanted to say something more but could not find the words he needed.

Devora simply stepped past him, ignoring his gaze on her and the lustful gaze of Omri the Zebulunite. She had no time or space in her heart for either.

Walking as though asleep, she moved to the place at the edge of the field where the men were raising the cairns. Laban was there; he took one glance at the *navi* and then turned grimly toward the house. As he left, Devora sank to her knees by the cairns, her face drained of life. The other men glanced at her but did not disturb her.

Devora gazed out over the blighted field.

"She was the *navi*," Devora whispered to God. "Your *navi*. How could you."

No answer came to her out of the withered vines or the wide sky, and Devora knew in that moment that none ever would. Even if God were to show her a hundred visions more, there would never be any vision that would give a reason for Hurriya's death. Devora's eyes glistened, but her grief was too sharp for any moisture to wash it out. Her breast felt tight and it hurt almost to breathe. She watched dully as Laban came out of Barak's cedar house carrying Hurriya's body in his arms, tightly wrapped and shrouded in a blanket, neither face nor feet visible. Devora saw a red area in the cloth where her head must be and knew it for blood from the knife wound she had inflicted. The *navi* moaned softly and covered her face with her hands.

***

Devora worked the men hard, raising Hurriya's cairn. She made it the highest one in that line of silent promises to the dead. When Laban lifted the last stone, it clacked into place nearly level with his head. The other cairns were already done, and only a few men remained there to see if the *navi* needed help. The other men had left quickly, not wanting to spend longer than they must in the presence of the dead.

"Go," Devora whispered. "All of you."

Laban hesitated, one hand resting on the top of the cairn. "She was not of the People," he said.

"She is of my tribe," Devora said softly. "I accept her as one of my tribe. Please go."

Laban looked at her another moment, then turned without a word and began walking away through the dead field.

Devora leaned on the cairn, her eyes cold as a winter sea. Then she lifted her voice. Though hoarse, she sang with such beauty that men raising tents in the field stopped and stood still, turning to face the cairn and the *navi* beside it.

As the darkness fell, Devora sang her farewell to a woman of her People.

***

Barak offered a room in his house to her, but Devora could not bear the thought of sleeping there. She staggered out into the withered vines in the dark, moving toward where the other war-leaders had set up their tents with hers nearby. The tent Laban had offered her. She wondered a moment if Mishpat and her saddle and her waterskin were there in the tent and whether Shomar had been well cared for, but her mind was too weary to hold the thought. It was dark now, but she did not walk with any alertness. She felt like a vessel with its oil poured out and left to dry in the dust.

Walking so, she nearly collided with a man, and he called out sharply in the dark. Looking up wearily, she saw Heber's hard face in the starlight.

"Covenant and Law, woman," he growled, "watch yourself."

"I am sorry," Devora said. Her gaze took in the man—he had a bundle on his shoulders and a waterskin slung at his hip. "You're leaving," she murmured.

"I'll not stay to wait for the dead," he said.

"There are five hundred men here, Heber," Devora said. "The land will be clean in a few days, and there will be rebuilding and replanting. Raider or no, a man with a strong back will be honored here."

"Clean?" he said. He looked at her intently, then laughed, hard, a laughter eerily like Barak's when the chieftain had knelt in the ruin of his vineyard. A laughter devoid of any joy, just mirth at the savage futility he saw. The Kenite wiped tears from his face, wheezing with laughter. "You don't. You don't understand." His sides shook. "I've been hurrying south for weeks. Weeks, woman. After raiding in White Cedars. There are thousands. Thousands in White Cedars."

All sound left the world, everything but the beat of Devora's heart. She just stared at Heber, the night terribly dark around them.

His mouth was still moving, but it was several moments before she could focus on his words. Then: "All of them moaning and staggering toward us, every last one of those heathen corpses. These you're seeing are just the first. The first few."

"Thousands?" It came out in a whisper.

"Or tens of thousands. Even God has never seen so many dead." Heber laughed again, shaking his head. The sound chilled her. "I'm going to keep moving, *navi*. I don't plan to stay with your camp. You're dead already. All of you. You just haven't stopped breathing yet." He glanced away to the south, his mirth dying out, the haunted look returning to his eyes. "Make for Kemet, most likely. Get a vast river between me and those walking dead."

"Kemet!" Devora was struggling to collect her thoughts, still the racing of panic inside her. "But this is the land of promise. Kemet—our fathers were slaves there!"

"*Your* fathers. What should I care? They feed laborers well in the dark land. Here, we'll be free and eaten. God keep you, *navi*." And he walked away into the shadows. After a few steps he called back without stopping: "If you reach my camp upriver and my slaves haven't been eaten, you're welcome to them."

Then he was gone.

Devora stared after him into the night.

Thousands.

"Merciful God," she whispered. "Cover us. Let the *malakh ha-mavet* pass over us."

***

Pale as a corpse, Devora made her way back to her tent, which Laban had pitched for her a little apart from the others, for she was *kadosh*, and apparently to him at least that still meant something. The tent was just barely within earshot of the others, and now Devora looked over the night wasteland of the withered field and drew in her breath sharply. Maybe it wasn't a good idea for her tent to stand apart. No nazarite stood watch outside the tent's door. If the dead came lurching across the field, only a thin wall of canvas and the possible protection of God's hand would stand between her and their grasping hunger.

Thousands.

She shivered in the dark.

Shomar was tethered just outside her tent, sleeping on his feet. Devora saw that someone had placed a basin of water within the gelding's reach and that he'd drunk half of it. A little relief touched her; her alarm at Heber's words had cracked the numbness about her heart like the shell of an egg, and for just a moment she stood leaning against her horse, putting her arms about his powerful neck, breathing in his scent. This had been a hard journey for him too. And he was a little part of her husband, here with her. The two of them strangers together in a strange camp. She rested against her horse, not letting herself think of Hurriya or Zadok. There was moisture on her cheek, and she rubbed it away against his sleek hair. She permitted herself no more tears than that, and after a bit she straightened, knowing that if she did not go into her tent now, she would fall asleep right there, standing on her feet like a horse herself.

She didn't know what nightmares she would endure

tonight with neither Lappidoth nor Zadok beside her, nor what the next morning might bring. The refugees they'd been pursuing might have been eaten already, or not. Barak might stand and lead the men, or he might crumble in his own grief. God might protect them, or not. She didn't know. She couldn't even find the strength to care. She wanted only sleep.

Drawing aside the door flap of her tent, she stepped in where it was dark and warm.

She had the briefest sensation of not being alone—then someone grabbed her, a powerful arm pulled her back, crushing her against a firm body. Her eyes flew wide as she felt naked skin against her, breathed in a man's sweat scent. Even as she sucked in a breath to scream, a hand, rough and calloused, covered her mouth. Smothering her cry.

A fierce whisper in her ear. "I don't see any nazarite dog heeling you here."

ALL FALLING APART

DEVORA BREATHED in desperate little gasps, through her nose. Omri's breath was hot on her throat. His lips brushed her neck and she jerked in his arms.

"Shhh, hush, woman," he growled in her ear, his hand pressing down more cruelly over her mouth, bruising her lips. "Hush now."

Fury and fear pounded through her, like fire and ice. Every inch of her body wildly alert. She could feel his rough palm against her lips, his belly pressed into her back, and something swollen pressed to her hip. He couldn't be doing this—she was *kadosh*, not to be touched! She was married. She was *unclean*, though she had yet to tell the camp that. This couldn't be happening.

She tried to bite his palm, and he jerked her head back hard against his shoulder, his mouth moist on her throat. Kissing her. He was kissing her. He did it roughly, bruising her neck. She screamed again into his palm and twisted in his arms, but his arm crushed hers to her sides. She dug her nails into the skin of his hips, but he only breathed louder by her ear.

"That's it, woman, that's it," he groaned softly. "I knew you were baiting me that day. Riding here alone with that nazarite and no husband. Did he enjoy you, that dog? You're going to enjoy this a lot more."

He dragged her back, pulling her with him toward the bedding at one side of the tent. She fought him, but he was *strong*. She kept crying out into his hand, hoping men in the other tents would hear, but the sounds were small and muffled. And she couldn't get *loose*. Panic rushed through her like cold water. He was doing as he pleased, and she couldn't stop him.

She was forced down onto her back, his weight on her. He pinned her upper arms with his elbows, leaning into the hand he held pressed over her mouth, hurting her. His eyes fierce and dark, just above hers. She struggled but was hardly able to move, unable to get him off her. She cried out as his knee forced her thighs apart.

"I can smell your cunt," he breathed, and bit her ear.

She thrashed under him, shoving at his sides with her hands. She had to get him *off* of her. Her eyes shot to the door of her tent, but Zadok was not outside. Zadok wasn't anywhere. Her eyes flicked to the small bundle of her garments and her waterskin, to her left, the length of a man's body from where she lay. She could see the glint of her blade beneath the clothes.

She couldn't get enough air.

"You hush," Omri whispered in her ear.

Devora squirmed, nauseated, as he began thrusting his hips against her, through her dress.

"You don't get to talk tonight. You had us all so convinced you were the *navi*. That you heard *God*. Well, fuck you. Anyone with eyes can see that the Covenant is falling *apart*." The man licked her throat—the animal *licked* her. She shook with rage and fear. "You saw what happened to Zadok," Omri whispered to her. "And so many others. You saw the *dead*. God isn't in the land anymore. God isn't here. If he was, he'd have sent the Ark. Do you hear me? He would have sent the fucking *Ark*. It's all falling apart. So what should I care?"

His hand left her lips, then his mouth was on hers and she screamed into his mouth. Felt the grasp of his hand at her hip, gripping her, then tugging her dress up. She kicked, her knees hitting against his hips. She threw herself to the side; his weight held her in place, but she twisted her left arm free and went for his face. Dug her fingers into his right eye.

Omri reeled back with an anguished yowl, his hands lifted to his face. A hard shove with her hip and he was off her. She rolled away across her bedding, reaching. And as quickly as she might draw a breath, she'd swept Mishpat up in her hand and rolled onto her knees. Brought the sword up in one smooth movement even as Omri came at her, and the blade severed his neck as cleanly as though he were made of thin cloth rather than flesh and bone. His head hit the rugs flooring the tent and rolled toward the door; his body fell to one side of her.

On her knees, holding her bloodied sword to the side, the hilt cold in her hand, Devora screamed in anguish and rage. Panting, gazing down at the headless body. It lay completely still. Devora took in great gulps of air, sobbing for breath. Her heart loud in her breast. She worked her tongue in her mouth a moment, then spat on him. Spat out the taste of his mouth.

He'd meant to defile her. Use her. As though she were some girl he'd taken in a raid and not the *navi* and the mother of Israel.

"The Covenant *is* falling apart," she whispered.

Men were shouting outside, in the other tents. Men who'd heard her cry out. Shaking, Devora forced herself to her feet. Stumbled to the door of her tent, Mishpat bloody in her hand. She glanced to the right, where the head lay faceup, still contorted in that last expression of shocked fury. The eyes already glassy, emptied of life.

Breathing hard, Devora hurried from her tent. Shomar was still tethered just outside. She leapt astride him, not bothering with saddle or any bags, just laying the blade across her thighs. Men were running toward her. Barak was there. "*Navi*, what has happened?" he cried.

For the briefest moment she hesitated. The night around her was strange and dark and there was no moon yet. Behind her in the tent, a slain man, his blood dripping from her sword. Somewhere out there in the blackness over the fields, lurching dead. Thousands.

And no moon yet.

Her right hand tightened around Mishpat's hilt. Her left gripped Shomar's mane.

Everything was falling apart. They could not delay for a night, nor even for a moment.

"We end this tonight!" she called to Barak. "We are not staying here! We *end* this! Bring the men and follow, Barak!"

410

Then, trusting him to follow and knowing she must ride whether he did or not, she dug in her heels and drove Shomar galloping into the empty vines.

FEAST OF THE DEAD

NOW SHE WAS alone. Entirely and utterly alone. There was only the moaning of the dead in the hills on every side, the warm reassurance of Shomar's mighty body between her knees, and the dead bone of Mishpat's hilt in her hand, slick with her sweat. She was panting. She didn't even know if *God* was here. Perhaps the words Omri had hissed in her ear had been true. Perhaps even God was gone. There was only her.

She could still feel Omri's touch loathsome on her thighs, and she wanted to find a quiet place to sit and grieve, but she held herself together. She had to. She had no idea where the dead were; she had to be alert. When she glanced behind her, the camp was just a glow of fires in the distance. For a moment she thought she could see movement on the bank, perhaps Barak following. She didn't know. Out in this dark, she might as well be riding through a land already dead, the Covenant nothing more than torn and discarded scraps of roots, the People a once-green olive tree wrenched from the earth and cast aside. Heber's words dug into her mind: *Thousands, thousands in White Cedars.*

And Hurriya's words. *We are both women.*

"Yes," Devora whispered again, "yes we are."

She made it to the riverbank, discerning it by the faintest shimmer on the water, the only thing that passed for light in this darkness. Shomar galloped hard along the edge of the water. Abruptly she heard faint screams ahead, somewhere in the night. Many of them cries of pain and terror. Then the moaning of the dead, as though the dark itself had taken voice. Devora's fingers tightened in Shomar's mane.

A sliver of moon appeared over the hills, and glancing up, Devora cried out. The moon held her eyes. She stared at it, her heart pounding in her breast. She had seen such a moon before, over Shiloh, that terrible night. The light felt *wrong.* She felt it like a scream beneath her skin. The shine of the moonlight on the dark river to her right was like blood on the water. In horror, she saw its light on her hands and felt it beating on the nape of her neck, the way the sun beats on you on a desert day, that kind of insistence, that kind of draining of energy and strength. But this was cold, so cold.

Then Shomar took her past a stand of dark oaks, and spread before her was a field of trampled barley. In her first wild glimpse of that field, Devora saw things that afterward she would pray and beg to forget, and never would.

There were dead in the barley, hundreds, the stench of them overwhelming. Some shambled through the tall crop

413

by the water, pursuing a small group of living men and women who ran and stumbled before them, likely the last survivors of Walls. Other dead crouched over their victims in small groups throughout the field, and their eyes shone red, luminous in the moonlight.

One corpse was dragging a flailing woman through the barley by the hair, while four other dead lurched after her, bending, their hands grasping, trying to clutch at the living woman, who was young, too young. Nearby, a man had been torn apart, drenching a patch of the field in his blood; one of the crouching dead was chewing on a hand, another on a foot, a third had an ear. One corpse was seated with a pile of entrails in its lap like a nest of dead serpents. It lifted the glistening intestines to its mouth with a slow grace, like a dignified grandmother at a banquet.

The living by the river did not scream as they ran; many of them fled half bent over, as though winded. One, a woman Devora's own age, had cast aside her robe or her salmah and now ran naked in the barley, forsaking dignity for speed. Even as Devora looked, the woman stumbled, and three of the dead fell on her. One grasped the woman's leg in its hands and tore strips of flesh from her thigh with its teeth. The woman kicked with her other leg and screamed, shrill peals of pain and terror. The other two corpses tore into her breast with their fingers, ripping her open and reaching in for those parts of her that God had hidden within her body before birth. The corpses' arms were bloodied to the elbows; one reached low and pulled out the entrails, and the other corpse snatched at them; the first turned on the second and hissed like a cat. The woman's shrieks went on and on, terribly similar to the screams of Devora's mother. But gazing at that woman dying in the barley, this time Devora did not see her mother's face in her mind, her mother dragged screaming out the door of her tent. She saw only Hurriya's face. Hurriya, her life bleeding out, dying helplessly where Devora could not reach her or console her. Fury rushed through Devora like flame roaring from one tree to the next. She held Mishpat out to the side, ready, though her arm felt the strain.

No more of the People must perish.

"*Ride*, Shomar," she whispered fiercely, and sent the horse surging beneath her in a gallop that tore up the dirt.

Faces of the dead turned toward her. A song of metal in the air, slicing down as her horse carried her into this rot in the tall barley in the Galilee night. She rode down upon the woman being eaten amid the trampled plants, and her sword took away first the top of the woman's head, silencing her screams. Then she wheeled about, and Shomar's hoof took one of the dead in the face, sending it sprawling. One corpse still gnawed at the woman's leg, the other rose snarling and lunged at Devora, its gray hands grasping for her sandal, her leg. Mishpat cut away the hands, then carved through the thing's head, and the body fell like chopped wood.

Then Devora was riding about the field, slashing. With her knees she kept a tight hold on her horse, her heart hammering, her mouth hot and dry, her mind gone in one long scream of horror.

The terrible, half-unfleshed faces of the dead—

The moonlight dyeing the grasses the color of blood—

Her own screams reaching her ears—

Her frantic glances about the field showed just moaning, lurching figures and a few dying men and women twisting on the ground, the others in the distance fleeing. Her horse had carried her through to the other side, where the hills rose again and there were fewer dead. She grasped Shomar's mane and dug in and wheeled him about once more, riding back at a canter into the dead. Her body was covered in a sheen of cold sweat, she was shivering. She fought for focus, rode at the first standing corpse she saw and took away its head with her sword.

Another corpse was devouring a boy who struggled weakly under it, and she stopped her horse, and as it reared she carved down into the creature's head. After the corpse fell to the side, she leaned over and drove her blade through the boy. Then she was trotting her horse through the moon-red field, and tears were hot on her cheeks, and she was fighting and killing in a blurred world. She heard sharp cries and deep, hungry moans; she rode through the midst of them, brushing tears and sweat and dirt from her eyes and gazing into faces as she passed, but none of them were her mother, none of them were Naomi, none of them Zadok or Hurriya. And she could save none of them. None of the bitten. Just a chop of the blade she held, butcher's work.

***

Barak rode hard, and Ager wheezed under him. He could hear the *navi*'s hoofbeats ahead of him, though distant, otherwise there would have been no way he could have followed her in this terrible dark. Yet he rode blind; trees rushed by on one side or the other like grim presences, brief touches of some dark heathen god on his mind, looming large and horribly close, then gone as he rode deeper into the night. He was panting, his eyes wide, straining for some glimpse of light; he rode in terror of losing the *navi*, in terror of his horse stumbling. He had not paused to look in her tent but had run for his horse; as it was, he had barely saddled in time to pursue her. Behind him he could hear the faint hoofbeats of a few horses following. Laban perhaps. A glance over his shoulder showed him torches and their reflections on the water, and the dark silhouettes of armed men hurrying after their chieftains on foot. When he heard the screams ahead and the low moaning, it shook him. This was not how he'd wanted to come upon the dead. No plan of attack, no hiding of men in high places where they could rain spears down. Just a headlong gallop into a valley of corpses with his men far behind and leaderless. He cursed under his breath and drove Ager to greater speed.

Then the moon rose, and it rose the color of blood, and he heard the screams in the moonlit field ahead. Everything turned cold within him, and he saw the corpses bathed in the red light, their eyes blind and unblinking. He saw their feeding, saw the People being violated and devoured, heard their shrieks in the barley. Saw the *navi* ride into them as though into a field of wheat, her sword flashing in the moon. Ager carried him into the field after her, in a rush; the reek of decay slammed into his nostrils, stronger than he'd ever encountered it, powerful enough that he nearly slid from his horse.

One moment the dead were far out in the field; the next he was among them, attacking two-handed with his spear, a thrust to the left, a thrust to the right, their faces crowding near, hands reaching for him. He struck at them desperately as his horse surged past them. He was too panicked, sweating, to look and see if his blows had any effect. He tried to keep his eyes on the *navi* ahead; he called out to her, but the moans of the dead overwhelmed his voice.

He was wrenched backward and off his horse, and he landed with a cry in the tall barley, his spear flying from his hands. His stallion sped on, but he could not hear Ager's hooves above the noise of the dead. A hand grasped his ankle, others clutched at his throat, hands cold like water in a pool at the bottom of a cave, but dry as soil baked by the sun. A face swung over his, a face with no eyes but with a gaping mouth filled with teeth. Howling, he shoved his hands against the creature's chest, toppling it over. He reached down, plucked from his hip the small bronze knife he kept there, but others were on him. He kicked and fought, slashing with the knife, his heart pounding wildly in his chest, too much terror to think of where to strike the creatures. He laid open one's belly—it made no effort to defend itself, a thing that had once been a plump woman; its organs spilled from it now, and it still reached for his throat with fleshy fingers. He hacked away another's hand—his knife was sharp—and still it bent and dug its teeth into the leather strap covering his shoulder. The world, the unclean faces, the bright harvest stars and the waving ears of barley between them and him—it all vanished in a white fury of pain and terror. A shriek went on and on—his.

Then he could see again, he was shoving the ravenous corpse off him, pulling his knife free of its skull. He rolled, gritting his teeth, his shoulder on fire. Hands were grasping at his armor; he hacked them off and stumbled, crawled through the barley. Somewhere nearby now he heard the cries of living men. And above it all those long, wailing moans, a sound that was a rape of the mind, a sound that took away all his senses and battered him with unreasoning, animal fear.

He found himself on his hands and knees and he crawled swiftly through the barley. A shape loomed over him. He rolled to the side, somehow got on his feet. His knife found its home in the creature's throat, and he felt hands wrap about his own throat as he sawed, cutting away its head. The body fell lifeless, the hands slipping from Barak's throat. The head fell to the side, and as Barak glanced down at it, he saw the eyes—those murky eyes— *still moving*, tracking him. The jaw still working silently. With a cry he sent it away with a kick of his foot.

He gazed around the barley field, wild with terror, his shoulder burning. Other figures were stumbling toward him, arms outstretched, eyes bright in the moonlight. He cast a frantic look ahead—he could not see Devora anywhere. Only the stumbling dead, so many. A glance over his shoulder showed him the glow of the torches of his men on the edge of the field. Gasping, he staggered toward them, then caught his breath and burst into a run.

No man could face this field of dead alone.

Tall ears of barley whacked across his skirt of leather and his bronze breast-piece as he ran. Sweat poured from his brow. There were dead all about him, but always he looked for where they were thinnest and darted through before they could seize him. His sides, his shoulder, his very lungs burned with fire.

He stumbled over a body and nearly cried out, but then he saw the eyes and saw that she was a woman, one of the living, her mouth open in silent pleading, and he reached down to take her hand and pull her to her feet, panting as the dead closed in. Yet when he pulled at her arm, she was strangely light and her eyes rolled back in her head. He glanced down and screamed, for her belly was torn open and nearly hollowed out, her entrails fleshy and half chewed away, and as he pulled, only the top part of the woman came with him. He dropped her and fell in his horror and shock. Then he scrambled away through the barley, lurching figures all about him, reaching down for him.

His mind, his breath, his whole being was taken up in the effort of flight. Ducking low through the barley, hoping to avoid being seen by the dead. There were too many between him and his men now, but at last he reached the riverside edge of the field and collapsed behind a stand of terebinths. He threw himself into the shadows behind one of the trees, dropping his knife to the ground. There he shook and sweated, certain they were following him, their dark shapes staggering through that field. But he was unable to get up. He clutched his shoulder and cried out. With a need fiercer than he'd ever felt, he longed for his own house and for the cool taste of the grapes from his vines. He clenched his eyelids shut and breathed in through his teeth, losing himself in the throbs of pain, agony that beat like a drum in his shoulder with every pulse of his blood.

He had seen what had happened to the woman in his house. Had seen her eyes open, heard her low wail. He remembered clearly the bite in her arm. He was unclean, unclean, and the wounds the dead left were lethal.

Not daring yet to look out into the field, he set his hand against the bole of the terebinth, forcing himself up onto his knees, baring his teeth against the pain and fear. His throat felt terribly dry, his body seized with thirst. He unstrapped his bronze breast-piece and cast it aside. Tore the leather jerkin beneath it up over his head with frantic, fumbling hands. Ran his fingers across the tender skin of his shoulder, wincing. His shoulder was one great bruise; the leather had been mashed into his body by the force of that corpse's jaws—but when he lifted his fingertips to his eyes, there was no blood on them. Panting, he clutched the jerkin, explored the leather with trembling fingers. He found impressions there, but the leather was tough; the teeth had not cut completely through it. Clutching the jerkin to his chest, he closed his eyes and moaned.

He had *not* been bitten.

Not bitten.

He was whole.

Tilting his head back, he sucked in great breaths of the night air, filling his chest. Alive. He was alive.

On his knees beneath the terebinths, his chest bared, he clutched the leather and just breathed. He could hear water; glancing up, he saw that the ground disappeared into a ravine perhaps a spear's cast from where he stood. Below must be the Tumbling Water, or whatever trickle would later become Tumbling Water farther south; up here on the high, cliff-like bank, the roots of the terebinths likely dug deep toward that enticing water.

Breathing fast, Barak began to shrug the leather back over his head and shoulders. Then strapped the bronze piece back on above it. It had saved him once this night; he might need it again. He cast about him; the knife he'd dropped by his feet seemed a pitiful blade to carry against the dead. After a moment he found a long branch, nearly straight, that had fallen from the tree overhead. He bent and took it up, skinning twigs from it with the knife and then hacking desperately at the narrower end, improvising a spear point. The branch was dry and he feared it might break, but at any moment a corpse might stumble in under the trees and see him. He wanted something with more reach than that knife in his hands.

"Get out," a voice hissed softly.

Startled, Barak nearly leapt up from his hiding place. Glancing sharply over his shoulder, his heart pounding, he found two eyes peering up at him amid a face smudged with dirt. A young man—hardly more than a boy—was hiding in a hollow beneath the terebinth. He'd blackened his face with dirt and was lying with his belly to the ground; he'd drawn the year's first fallen leaves over his body to conceal himself.

"Go!" the youth whispered fiercely. "This is my place. You'll bring them!"

Recovering from his shock, Barak muttered, "Who are you, boy?"

The boy lifted his head just a little, trying to peer out into the field. "Yehoyakim. From Walls."

"What are you doing down there?" Barak said sternly. He felt revulsion clenching up within him. "Your kin are dying out in the barley."

Yehoyakim met his gaze. The whites of his eyes showed. "What are *you* doing here?"

The words struck Barak like a slap. Shame burned through him. He caught his breath, swore bitterly. Cast a glance out at the field. Several lurching dead were very near now, moving toward the stand of trees. He could still hear distant screams and the low moans and nearer, the trickle of water over stones in the ravine below. Stiffening, Barak tested the heft of his makeshift spear.

Something went cold and hard inside him. His breathing calmed. He was Barak ben Abinoam, and no boy to hide behind a tree.

"Fear would devour us all, even as the dead," he muttered. He looked at the youth. The boy had lowered his chin to the ground again. "Stand and have courage, Yehoyakim. Hope that God is no woman to weep or gloat while we die, but a strong man, mighty and furious, as some of the levites say."

"So let *him* fight the dead," the boy whispered.

"Why should he? If God is a man, he will scorn you for shivering so. If God is a woman, she will not admire you or desire you. Either way, your submission to your fear makes you alone." Barak's anger was fuel and fire in his breast, and he straightened, his back to the tree, the spear ready in his hands. The dead were near now. He could hear one of them dragging one foot behind it. He took a steadying breath. In a softer voice, he added, "A day ago I saw a man take on four hundred dead by himself."

"Did he live?" the boy whispered.

"No. But we will never forget him. Neither will God." Barak's hands tightened about the haft of the spear; its weight was reassuring. He could do this. Out of the corner of his eye he caught a glimpse of flame. Looking carefully around the bole of the tree, he saw torches moving through the barley. "Look," he breathed. "The men of the north fight the dead, Yehoyakim. Come with me."

The youth shook his head, but Barak could not see him. After a moment's silence, the chieftain said, "Fine," and then he leapt around the tree and *ran* at the approaching dead. Lifted his voice in a great roar, even as his father's father must have roared at the walls of Yeriho and the burning of Ai, when the People were still newcome to the land and were strong. His blood burned; he lifted the terebinth spear high and drove it hard into the face of the nearest corpse, then swung hard to his right, wrenching the corpse to the side and down. It slid free from the sharpened wood and fell, and the wood did not break. Barak slammed the butt end of his spear backward to his left into the chest of the next corpse even as it closed with him. The corpse sprawled into the grass hissing, and two more were upon him, their milky eyes gleaming in the moonlight. He leapt back and brought up the spear, thrusting toward one's head, even as the corpse that had sprawled to the side a moment before scrambled back to its feet.

The air smelled of smoke. In the field near at hand Barak saw fire rising and the figures of his men and of the lurching dead dark against the flame. Barak fought with a ferocity he had never before felt. He did not know anymore if God was male or female, weak or strong, reliable or fickle. But he had seen how Zadok fought before the walls of Refuge. He had seen the nazarite fight as though possessed by a god, as though he were no mere man but whirlwind and fire in a man's body. Whatever God Zadok had known, whatever that strange God was like, Barak hoped to catch that deity's attention now. And he knew that whatever God might be watching, that God would respond only to courage.

TO SAVE ONE LIFE

DEVORA HAD NOT seen Barak ride into the field and hadn't seen him unhorsed. She rode now along the rising cliffbank of the river, dealing grimly with those dead who were pursuing the refugees. She grunted and panted with the exertion, the burn in her arm as she swung Shomar about again, and again. Whenever she had breath, she screamed at the living. "Downriver!" she screamed. "Circle around! Downriver! There are tents. Downriver! Go downriver!"

Some listened and bolted to their left, darting into the field to try cutting through and heading back the way they'd come, trusting her. Others kept moving north, up the rising slope of the land. In their panic they were no longer men or women but only frantic, darting animals, deer being chased by wolves.

Then there were dead all about Devora's horse, and she was sweating in the cold and her arm nearly giving out each time she brought the blade down. Shomar reared in terror, his belly and flanks covered with splatters of decayed flesh. His hooves struck out, but the dead, who did not fear horses, only grabbed at his legs. Without success, for the horse was quick, its body massive and powerful. Yet as Shomar came back down on all four hooves, gray hands reached up, clutching at Devora's skirts and at the horse's mane. Devora screamed and carved away the hands, but there were many, and now they were all about her, more of them pressing in, so many eyes red in the moonlight. In a moment, a breath, a beat of her heart, she and her horse together would be tugged beneath them, even as the refugees had been.

A man's shout rose above the moaning, a deep-chested roar. A horse with spotted flanks was driven into the dead at her left, and Devora glimpsed Laban's face. The chieftain of Issachar had his great axe lifted high, and he brought it smashing down, the head of a corpse splitting beneath the bronze. The man held to his pommel with his hand and lifted his right foot, kicking the faces of the dead with a giant's strength, knocking corpses from their feet.

"*Navi!*" he bellowed. "To me!"

Laban forced his way through the moaning dead, and Devora cut her way to his side. Then they were riding among the dead together, chopping with axe and sword; Devora's skirts were stained with bits of gray flesh and tissue. In a moment they were free of the clinging press of corpses, free of the intense reek and the clutching of hands at her garment. Their horses took them far out into the barley; then Devora wheeled about. "No!" she cried, and sent Shomar galloping back toward the bank, where there was still a great throng of dead and a few refugees trying to elude them northward.

"*Navi!*" Laban roared.

She glanced over her shoulder, saw him gesturing downriver with his axe. She turned, then she saw it too. Some of the panic eased from her heart.

The men of Barak's camp had come.

They were on foot, and they had lit torches and were now charging into the field, shouting. Devora realized they could see her over the barley—in her white robe on her white horse, with her sword uplifted like a slice of the moon. They were charging into the field for her, because seeing her there, they believed at last that God was here in the field, ready to fight the dead with them.

The men of Israel drove against the dead, waving their torches before them, and the corpses fell back hissing before the flames. Perhaps eighty, ninety men had come. Devora didn't know where the rest were—perhaps shaking in their tents. Parts of the field went up in flame as the barley caught, for the men were desperate and they swept the torches before them wildly, their eyes showing their whites and reflecting back the fire as they confronted the snarling faces of the dead. Sometimes one of the corpses went up in flames too, its ragged clothes catching from the barley or from a torch slamming into its head and setting its hair afire. The dark above the faces of the living and the dead was alive with sparks and strangely beautiful.

Without a word to Laban, Devora sent Shomar into the fray, cutting fiercely with her blade. She kept Shomar moving, rushing among the corpses, some of which turned toward her but too slowly to grasp the fast horse, others of which went down beneath her blade without ever knowing she was there, their faces fixed on the men who were advancing with flame. She heard a scream as one of the men was pulled down, and she turned Shomar toward the cry. One of the dead had fallen, its leg crumpling beneath it. Though the corpse's back and buttocks blazed with fire, it had dragged a living Hebrew down, its arms wrapped about the man's legs. The man's scream rose in pitch as the corpse crawled over him and bit into his face. That scream!

Riding in, Devora clove the corpse's face in half, then turned again, and even as several corpses lurched into her horse's flanks, she grasped Shomar's mane tightly and leaned out to the side and took away the top half of the Hebrew's head, cutting off his scream.

One of the dead got hold of her skirt in both hands, and she clung to Shomar frantically. The cloth tore, but now the dead were pressing into the horse like a wall of cold flesh. Devora heard a shout and knew Laban was beside her, and in another moment he was among those dead with his axe. To her horror, the corpses grasped his axe and pulled the great man from his horse. There was fire in the field all about them now, and the smoke stung her eyes and throat, and she tried to force Shomar through the press of dead to where Laban had gone down, but he was covered with corpses. She heard him roaring, still struggling and fighting beneath the weight of the bodies, even as Zadok had.

But when Devora finally fought her way to him and struck down at the dead, screaming as she slew, when she cleared enough of a space to look down at the corpses that lay cut and spattered over the ground, there was little of Laban left. His face was gone, his chest torn open and emptied, the dead having pulled everything out of it. One more person she had seen die and been unable to help.

Devora stared down at his remains, but no scream would come. Wild-eyed, she lifted Mishpat high and wheeled Shomar about, though the horse's flanks and sides were flecked with sweat and bits of decayed flesh, and the gelding was half-mad with horror. Yet he obeyed when Devora sent him rushing back against the herd of shambling corpses. The *navi* no longer saw anything about her, not clearly; it was all a fever of screams and moans and hissing, inhuman faces, the faces of the true strangers in the land. She cut and thrust and slashed, and backed her horse free with the dead following her, and cut down and slashed again. And in her mind she saw crowding about her not the actual faces in this field but the faces of *her* dead: Eleazar the high priest with his eyes turned sorrowful in the moment of his death; Laban roaring as he went under; leering Omri, as she swung her blade toward his neck; Naomi the *navi*, her eyes glazed, pleading for a swift end and a high cairn; Zadok, her own Zadok, his eyes caring and intense, binding his long hair back before starting his run; her mother, shrieking and clawing at the rugs with her fingernails as something pulled her from the tent; a small infant with only one arm voicing a long moan; Hurriya, lovely Hurriya, frail and thin yet so beautiful in her green dress, dying with her face inches from Devora's own. The *navi* screamed and hacked wildly at the dead.

***

At last there came a moment when Devora lifted her blade and looked about and there were no more dead on their feet. Just men, living men and women, moaning and crying in the trampled and withering barley. And fires blazing all about them, lighting up the night. The smoke stung her eyes and she shivered, recalling the destruction of Walls. Panting, she walked Shomar across the field, listening to the groans and screams of the wounded and the bitten. Shomar's breath heaved beneath her; even her husband's magnificent horse was tired and near collapse. It took all Devora had just to stay upright on his back and withstand the reek of the field.

She halted and gazed down at a patch of crushed barley. There lay the body of a girl, one who could not have seen ten winters before she began hungering for flesh. Half the girl's scalp was missing, chopped away. It might have been Mishpat that cut her; the blade, slimy with gore, hung limp from Devora's hand. The *navi* gazed at the girl and had no tears. She sat her horse. Breathing. Just breathing. She brushed sweat from her eyes with the back of her hand. That girl who lay dead had never been to the red tent, never heard the laughter of the older women, never learned the secrets they would tell her. She had never grown breasts, never known love or the kicking of a child inside her. Yet she was gone, like wheat cut from its stalk before it had an ear, like the infant whose body Devora had buried on the hill above Shiloh, like Hurriya closing her eyes in that cedar house.

Another girl, a little older than this one, had once shivered in her tent while the dead fed on her mother just outside. She had not even dared to cry, for her body hadn't yet learned that tears could be silent. She just hugged her knees and rocked, back and forth. After a very long time, a bloody hand drew the tent flap aside, and a face looked in, a face that was like her mother's yet torn, one ear chewed away and the eyes gray and empty. Her mouth gaped and she *hissed* at the girl.

Devora glanced down at her aging hands, remembered the heft of the pestle she'd lifted, her mother's own pestle she'd used to prepare meal. She remembered bringing it down, her arm rising and falling, bits of flesh and droplets of dark fluid staining her arms and her nightclothes; she had washed all of that ruin from her body and her clothes much later, in a shallow pool far from the camp. Then she'd huddled in the tall grass by the water while her clothes dried. Her knees drawn up to her chin, her arms about her legs. Her sobs beside that pool had been the last time she had ever let herself weep fully, without any restraint.

A girl had died in that tent as the pestle struck again and again. Devora had never carried that girl's body to any wide field within her mind, had never piled any cairn of heavy stones above her.

With her sword tip, the *navi* lifted a little of the dead girl's soiled hair and dropped the strands across her eyes, hiding them. In a hoarse voice, she whispered the Words of Going for them both—the girl who lay here in the barley and the girl who had died long ago in that tent. Sitting her horse in this gore-drenched field, Devora missed that young girl with a yearning that *ached*.

She glanced about the field, saw the men dragging bodies through the barley. There was grieving and ugly work to be done yet tonight, for none of the wounded could be permitted to live. And she could not bear it. Where was Barak? She longed to hand this night to him and rest. She wanted to lie down. She wanted Lappidoth's arms, or Zadok's. She wanted somewhere warm to sleep where there was no moon and no reek of the dead—she could smell it now even in her hair—and no memories but ones she chose to recall.

Men began to gather about her, weary but their faces flushed, because this night they had faced the moaning dead and silenced them. Farmers and carpenters and tanners and herdsmen, they stood with their hands clenched tight around the handles and hilts of implements spattered with flesh and decay—hastily fashioned spears, shovels, hammers, fence posts, a few bronze blades. She looked out over their faces and knew that these men looked to her for judgment or affirmation, or for some vision from God to confirm what their hearts hoped—that their work was now done, and after these fires burned down and the sun rose over the smoke, they could return to their homes and rebuild and replant, and lie with their wives and give the People new children to replace the ones that had been lost. Devora saw in their eyes no contempt for her as a woman, only awe. She was the *navi* to them now, truly, the messenger of God, strange and terrible and holy and set apart. A sword in her hand. She wanted to laugh bitterly, for she had never felt less like the *navi*. She was covered in grime and sweat, her body was unclean from the touch of the dead, and her dress hung off one shoulder, torn and disheveled after her struggle with Omri and after the grasping hands of the corpses. Yet the men needed her now, and she didn't know what to do. The tent of the Law was in tatters; the younger *navi* was dead. What was still holy? What still mattered?

A few of the men around her began to chant, their loud, deep voices opposed to the darkness and filth of the night and the work ahead of them:

> *Urai! Urai! Devora!*
> *Arise! Arise! Devora!*
> *You have shielded your people,*
> *You have cut apart the foe,*
> *You have taken earth and sky from him,*
> *Urai! Urai! Devora! Arise, arise!*

They chanted Devora's name, and she listened but could not speak. She lifted her blade high, though her arm ached from the weight of it. They needed her. Yet she knew she had to tell them that their work had not ended, that there were more dead to come. And how was she to do *that*? If Naomi the Old stood here in her place, she would have had something sharp and strong to say that would put hearts of hard stone into the men's chests and stiffen them against what must come. But she was not Naomi the Old. She was only Devora the Old. And she was unclean.

The men who were chanting fell silent. For others were emerging now from the barley and the smoke, and these others were sunken-eyed and wasted thin and carried no weapons. Exiles in their own land, these last refugees from Walls had lost their homes, their kin, their ability to sleep or sing. Their haggard faces were haunted by an anguish greater than any Devora had ever seen. Yet their ordeal had only begun. It would not end. Even if the thousands of dead coming down out of White Cedars were stilled and buried, for these men and women it would never be over.

We will find those who still breathe, Zadok had told her, *but we will find no survivors.*

One of them—a woman Devora's own age, but so *thin*—reached and clutched at her skirt, and she found she could not look away from the demand in the woman's eyes, a demand made without hope but with only the utter necessity of hearing its answer.

"Yes," Devora said hoarsely. "I have been to Walls." In those few words, in her tone, in her eyes was everything she had to say and couldn't. The deaths of the children. The ash in the air. The line of silent cairns by the lakeshore.

The old woman let out her breath, and something seemed to flicker out in her eyes. She understood.

"I—I'm sorry," Devora whispered.

"Night has fallen," the old woman rasped.

"Night's already here."

"A blood moon," the woman said, looking past Devora toward the sky. "When God turns his back."

Devora shivered, then reached down for the woman's hand and clutched it tightly. The *navi* was unclean. Perhaps the woman was too. It no longer mattered. "You listen to me," Devora whispered fiercely, leaning close enough for the other woman to hear her. "You listen. God has not turned his back. I promise you. He will lift this blight from the land. *He will.* Tonight is a sign of it. If we do not lie down and die, he will lift the blight."

"A few seedlings may grow out of these ashes," the old

woman murmured. "But I am old, so old. I have no seeds. Why should I stand like an old tree in an empty field?"

"Who else will give the seedlings shade?" Devora asked.

The woman laughed. It was not a bitter laugh, only a very tired one. "I am going home," she said, and she turned from Shomar and began walking across the dying field with small, painful steps. Devora watched her go, in anguish.

One by one, the other refugees followed her. The men of Barak's camp fell silent, then set down their burdens and parted to let the exiles pass. The starving men and women walked south along the riverbank, back toward the camp, back toward Walls. They stumbled away under the red moonlight, exhausted, spent, the ghost of a people. Perhaps they would make it to the camp and collapse, and those of Barak's men who had lacked the courage to march tonight against the unclean dead would creep from their tents and bring food and water to these, the barely living. Or perhaps they would not stop. Perhaps they would go on walking, with those same slow, anguished steps. They would walk through the night and on into the next day and on until they came at last to the cinders and ash and the few standing houses and shops that had been Walls. Perhaps they would not stop even then, but would go on, down out of the hills and down the whole length of the promised land, following the steps of Hurriya before them, a silent witness to the violence and the misery in the north. They might pass through the entire land, past Hebrews and heathen who had never seen the dead and who would watch them with wide eyes, uncomprehending yet unable to look away. They might pass out of the green fields into the wide desert and come at last even to the dark earth and the high monuments of Kemet itself, the land of their fathers' slavery, as though to say with their shambling gait and their sunken eyes and their slack, thirsting mouths, *The People who went out from here have perished; only we have come back.* Perhaps even then they would keep walking, until they died on their feet and their emptied corpses still moved slowly over the wide earth, moaning their anguish, their grief, their hunger for all that was lost.

***

When the exiles had gone, the Hebrew men stood silent in the barley. Devora caught the eye of a young man, one of Barak's. Motioned him close. He ran to her side. He was a youth, really. Perhaps he had not even lain with a girl before, but tonight he'd fought the dead, taking up a torch and a sharp-bladed shovel to fight with, while other, older men shivered in their tents.

"Where is Barak?" Devora demanded once he stood by her horse. "We need him."

Pale, the youth pointed toward the ravine and the water in it. "I saw," he said. "The dead had him backed against the water. I saw him, *navi*, he fought like a nazarite! But he fell from the bank, and the dead went over the edge, following him."

Devora's heart sank. These men needed their war-leader. Omri was dead, Laban was dead. If Barak was gone, who was to lead these men? Wasting no time in replying to the youth, she drove her knees into Shomar's powerful sides and sent her horse galloping toward the ravine. She pulled him up almost at the last moment, then peered down at the water and the damp earth and sand. There were several broken, moaning corpses in the water or at the water's edge, and wherever sand rose above the low water it was covered in footprints. She glanced upstream, but the creek curved too much in its deep bed for her to see far. She thought she could hear distant moaning coming down the ravine, but that might be no more than the sound of her terror.

Devora sucked in a breath through her teeth. Clearly in her mind she could hear Barak ben Abinoam's voice:

If I should be taken by the dead…ride after me, navi. Ride and find my body. Pile clean stone above me, with your own hands, even if I have been dragged far away.

Those footprints. The dead had not remained here; something had drawn them away. There was a chance that Barak was alive, that he'd fled upstream, pursued by the dead. Perhaps injured from his fall.

The *navi* glanced over her shoulder at the men in the barley. None to lead them. She could perhaps hold them together. She was *kadosh*, and tonight had proven that being *kadosh* might still mean something—even to men who were kin to Omri of Zebulun tribe. She could urge them toward Judges' Well, where there might be a wall they could get behind. Or south to Shiloh, to plead again for help from the other tribes. Surely if Devora the *navi* spoke of her visions and shared the warning of Heber the Kenite, surely men of Manasseh and Ephraim and Gad

438

would hear her. Surely they would gather with strength to face what was coming. If she had to go to every encampment herself, with nazarites beside her, to speak with the chieftains—! Surely they would come!

These men needed her.

Yet.

She gazed up the ravine. She was certain she heard moaning now. How many dead? And Barak alone, limping and splashing up that stream, with corpses in pursuit. *Ride after me, navi. Ride and find my body.*

She'd made a covenant with the man.

In the tents of the north, the Covenant with God was uprooted and torn apart—but she still had her own covenants to keep. If she were to turn now from this riverbank, if she were to leave Barak to the teeth of the dead, how would she be any different from Omri or Nimri?

Still she hesitated. This was a terrible choice.

She thought of Hurriya gazing up at her, her eyes glassy with fever. *We are both women.*

The decision of one man or woman to stand between another and harm or injustice: that was the foundation of the Covenant. It was the one essential act on which *shalom*, peace, depended. Without it, there was no Covenant, no Pact between people or between people and God. Hurriya's eyes had told her that. She had learned it, not in her mind but in her heart, deeply, as she'd sat watching Hurriya die. She could not unlearn it now. She could not betray Hurriya's memory that way. And she was done with leaving her own dead behind her, unburied, moaning in her memory, driving her to panic and tears at night.

She made her decision.

***

"What is your name?" Devora asked the youth, who had followed her to the riverbank. Other men were approaching a short distance behind.

He drew himself up. "I am Gideon," he said.

That made Devora smile slightly, even in her haste, for the youth was arrogant to name himself without mentioning his father's name or even his tribe—as though his name might be known in and of itself—but it was an arrogance she liked. If a youth could still be arrogant after tonight, he was strong enough for the task before him. "It's a good name," she said. "Gideon, tonight you must lead the men from here, though I have no oil to anoint you." She saw his eyes widen. "Be strong and courageous, Gideon. Gather the men and raise cairns. Then go to Shiloh; I will follow when I can. Make sure you don't camp too near—they will not be pleased there with the men of the north. The high priest is a boy; you want to talk to his mother, Hannah. Ask for messages to be sent to every encampment in Israel, both Hebrew and Canaanite. Have messages sent to the Kenites and to any friendly chieftains across the Tumbling Water. Tell them what has happened. Tell them there are more dead, thousands, coming down out of White Cedars. This is the word of the *navi*."

"Your will, *navi*," the young man breathed.

She hesitated, taking the measure of this young man. "There is one more thing. The men must be checked for bites, all who fought in this field tonight. You remember

Walls? The clean and the unclean must be separated. Check them all."

The young man went white. Seeing this, Devora leaned close, lowering her voice. "Gideon, we won tonight. Don't forget it. Check the wounded. Keep the men clean. Shelter the stranger and the fatherless. Any covenants you make, keep them. Live by the Law, and God's hand will be on you."

He nodded.

Devora turned her attention to the river below, while Gideon watched her. Her face became grim. If Barak had indeed fled upriver, she might find that she needed to get down there to help him or to retrieve his body. The thought of standing between the high, closed walls of the riverbanks, perhaps dragging a dead man with her through the water while the dead lumbered after her like a trapped herd of water oxen—the thought made her dizzy with dread. Clambering down that bank would be like descending into some other place, some dream country that was without Covenant and knew only teeth and blood.

In any case, she didn't see how she could get Shomar down that bank. With a sigh, she slid from the gelding's back. She turned to Gideon. "This is my husband's horse," she said quietly, "and the finest in Israel. Take care of him and receive a *navi*'s blessing. Lose him or endanger him, and receive a *navi*'s curse."

"Your will, *navi*!" He looked with awe on the horse, as though the animal had been touched by God.

Leaning her sword against her hip, Devora took the gelding's head in her hands gently and kissed Shomar's nose. Shomar, who had borne her so far and through so many perils. "I will see you back safe to Lappidoth," she whispered, looking in the damp pools of the gelding's eyes. "I promise."

Devora gave the youth a stern look, then patted Shomar once more on the neck, took up her blade, and stepped away. She began to walk, as quickly as she could, ignoring stiff muscles. She did not look back. Mishpat she carried unsheathed at her side as she moved along the edge of the bank, watchful of both the water below and the barley grasses about her. Not all the barley had blighted, and some patches of it here by the bank were still full of life; the brushing of it across her arms was strangely comforting as she walked.

For a moment she felt that she was again that small girl fleeing her mother's camp, leaving behind her a field of bodies and hoping against every fear in her heart that somewhere ahead of her was a refuge and a tent to rest in. After a few moments Devora halted and bent with a moan at the ache in her body. She took up a handful of dirt and rubbed the soil into her palms, grimacing. She didn't need to be any filthier, but her hands were sweating, and if later she had to climb down that bank, she did *not* want to lose her grip halfway down. And, with a little satisfaction, she noticed that the dirt on her right palm gave her a better grip on Mishpat's hilt. Straightening, she resumed her walk and set her mind firmly on her task, on the fulfilling of her covenant.

She could hear old Naomi's voice as truly as though the woman were walking beside her. *You do what you must, you trust the rest to God. Some days, a woman can only save one life.*

GOD RISING
OVER THE WATER

EVEN BEFORE Barak opened his eyes, he knew he was in trouble. It wasn't just the pain in his right leg or the ice-cold of water under his back.

It was the moans.

They were many. He forced his eyes open, saw his feet first, one bare and without a sandal. The water, cool and dark. The embankment he'd slid down, perhaps only moments before. He looked up farther, saw the starlit sky and dark silhouettes against it, at the edge of the bank, gazing down at him. Moaning in such persistent hunger that he began to shiver violently where he lay in the water.

Even as he watched, one of the dead leaned out, its hand clutching as though to grasp him, and the corpse toppled down the embankment. There was a crack of bone, and with his heart pounding, Barak saw the thing lurch to its feet perhaps a stone's throw from him, one arm limp at its side. Two others were already standing in the middle of the creek, lurching toward him.

Panic shot, violent and cold, through him, as though he'd been speared to the riverbed. For a moment he lay there in the water, watching them approach. Then with a cry he leapt to his feet, glancing about wildly for the spear he'd fashioned from a terebinth branch, but it was gone— either left up on the high bank above him or borne downstream on the water, though that seemed unlikely, as the Tumbling Water here looked to be only knee-deep in the middle. Nor did he have his knife.

The dead closed on him; others now were falling from the bank or being shoved by those behind them. Barak stumbled out of the water, half-dragging the leg he'd injured in his fall; his right leg was torn and bleeding, but it was not broken. Vaguely he remembered a desperate fight at the bank and then being shoved over the edge by the press of the corpses. He could hear distant screams and more moans of the dead and a crackling like flame. He couldn't have been out for more than a minute or two.

He stumbled along the edge of the water, staggering upriver, stubbing his good foot hard against a rock. Pain shot up his injured leg at each step. He could hear the dead splashing behind him, *close* behind him. Cast a glance over his shoulder, saw them reaching for him. Hissing in pain, he fought to push himself to a run, but his leg felt like giving out. With his hands he tore at his bronze breast-piece and tossed it aside as he lurched on. It landed in the water and shone there, would shine there perhaps for years until a patina of green caked to it. It would not have protected him against the dead, and he needed to shed any extra weight. He had to get out ahead of these corpses and climb back up the bank and fight his way to his men. He knew that was what he had to do, but panic coursed through him, urging him to just run, *run*, until he could find some place to hide. He was unarmed, he was injured. And his next glance over his shoulder showed him twelve dead lunging after him in the water, and more falling over the edge, and still more following him along the line of bank above, shambling along in a grim mockery of his flight and of human movement.

Barak left his leather jerkin on—it had saved him once before—and he forced himself to greater speed, still nearly dragging his right leg behind him, as though he were himself one of the dead. The water was cold about his feet and shins. The muscles of his neck and shoulders tensed, expecting the touch of cold fingertips behind him. He had felt the cold, dry touch of the dead before; if he were to feel it again, he was certain he would start screaming and wouldn't be able to stop. He tried to remember his words to Yehoyakim, remember the momentary strength he'd felt in his blood as he'd fought the dead in the barley near the bank. As though he'd been a nazarite himself, blessed by his people's strange God and knowing no life but sweat and the spear and the fall of emptied bodies about his feet. But now, with the river icy about his ankles, he was only Barak the vintner again, a man without woman or child or even any growing field ready for harvest, a man with nothing left but the body he wore. He held back whimpers of fear as he staggered up the river.

He fell once, his face and chest plunging into the water. Sucked in the river through his nose and then heaved himself up on his hands and knees, coughing and spewing out water, shaking with cold. He felt the brush of fingertips across his sandal and the lightest touch on his heel, the first of the corpses behind bending to grasp at him, and he sprang to his feet with a sobbing cry. On he ran, forcing his body on against the pain in his leg.

Once he glanced at the sky. The red moon was not visible between the two cliffs of the bank. There were only the cold stars, the sign of the promise, the sign of the Covenant. Breathing raggedly, he gazed at them a moment, head tilted back as he ran. They had never seemed so beautiful. This might be the last time he would see them; there was a violent stitch in his side, and his breath and strength were giving out. He clung to the sight, needing it, needing that hope. He'd been stripped not only of kin and land, but also of all his certainties; they'd been cast aside as abruptly and completely as that breast-piece. He had tried to command and own the women of his house and the women he needed to use, but with Devora this had proven impossible. He had learned that at Walls. He had hoped to command God also, to control what God might do, or not do, using his keeping of the Covenant, even to the burning of the small gods in his house, to hold God to terms. But God too was ungovernable. Now he had no assurances from God, he had no spear in his hand. He had nothing to lean on nor any weapon. All he had was that sight of cold stars, stars that no blight or unclean death could touch. Those bright points of light gave him the hope he needed to keep his legs moving, to keep running despite the low moans of the dead behind him. Because those stars were one thing at least that could never be removed, and though Barak himself had no seed in the land, perhaps the

promise—that the seed of the People would be preserved—would never be removed either. Even if all else he
might trust or hope in was gone.

Stooping, he took up a jagged branch from the water,
wrenching it free of the silt and river stones. The sand on
the bark gave his hand a good grip on it. The wood wasn't
strong or green; it would break. But it was something in
his hand. He felt calmer. He looked over his shoulder
again; there were no longer dead on the high bank, but
there were perhaps thirty corpses in the stream behind
him, strung out, those along the edge of the water moving
faster, those knee-deep in the river moving slowly and
falling behind. Barak fought for breath. He was a little
ahead of the corpses, but was no longer any faster than
they. He didn't know how far he had run—far past the
barley field, he was certain of that. He could no longer
hear screams or the roar of fire. He clutched the branch
tightly, certain that his running scramble was at an end. He
could press on until his limbs gave out and he lay gasping
and helpless at the water's edge, like a wounded gazelle. Or
he could stop and turn to face them.

Whatever God had pierced the sky with those stars and
hung promises on them admired courage. He was certain
of that at least.

He turned toward the dead and bent, leaning over and
panting for air. He drew in heaving gulps of it, sweat
pouring down his face even though the water about his
feet was cold. Keeping a tight hold on the branch, he
watched the dead stumbling toward him, their eyes like
small, luminous stones in the starlight. He bared his teeth
and straightened, lifting the branch in both hands like a
club.

Then it happened.

A warmth on his skin, gentle like the touch of a linen that had been heated by a woman's body. Then the warmth was inside him, a sense of comfort, the way a man feels when the sun has risen on the Sabbath and he is half-awake but restful in his bedding with his woman still asleep and naked, her head on his chest. Barak thought he heard a whisper, and he turned his head, gazing again upriver. There was a little mist farther up the ravine, concealing the walls of the riverbanks only as much as a thin veil might. Even as he looked, it lifted, and Barak let out his breath in a low sigh, for from one bank to the other the ravine had filled with that pleasant warmth, and he could feel someone whispering to him, though he could not make out the words. But with a certainty as potent as Moseh's when the Lawgiver looked upon the bush that burned and yet did not blacken or crumple to ash, Barak knew that God was there in the stream.

Slowly, as in a dream, the vintner lifted his weaker foot and tugged his remaining sandal free, then dropped it into the water.

"*Kadosh,*" he whispered. Holy ground.

In that moment, he was no longer aware of the splashes of dead feet in the stream behind him, or of the sharp and brutal cold of the water on his skin, or of the sweat running like oil down his face and back. There was only the lifting of the mist, and the nearness, the impossible nearness of God. He let his breath out slowly, standing still, arms limp at his sides, watching the mist rise. The God who filled the space between one slippery embankment and the next was other than he'd imagined, other than he'd believed. Not a cold, aloof woman planting or scything crops, but a warm *shekinah*, a presence. Like hands cupping his face, like a scent of blossoms from a distant grove, like a strain of pipe music almost too faint to hear, like a whisper carried to him on the wind, like love and light and a woman's kiss, thrilling everything in him. He cried out suddenly, a raw shout from his throat, a wordless sound of awe and praise.

Then, as gently as it had come, the sense of that nearness, that *shekinah*, that warm feminine embrace, was gone. And even as his eyes lifted, he saw several tents with a stand of oaks behind them, above the high bank, perhaps twenty feet above him. He stared at them for a long, focused moment. Tents. People. The living. The tents could mean help—a waterskin to drink and other men to stand with him against the shambling corpses.

He heard the moans of the dead close behind him. A glance over his shoulder showed them less than a spear's cast away, their arms lifted to take him. Casting aside the branch, he bolted, splashing through the water and throwing himself against the far bank, which had a little slant to it; he grasped for roots, rocks, any handhold he could, began pulling himself wildly up the bank. Damp soil crumbled and slid beneath his feet; with a gasp, he pulled himself furiously up the cliff, digging in with his toes and his fingers. The burn of pain in his torn leg became a shriek of fire, and he was screaming in the agony of it. The dead were beneath him now, he could feel the thud of their bodies against the bank below him, felt a fingertip graze the underside of his foot. With a howl, he reached his right arm up and found a tuft of weeds to grasp, began pulling himself higher. He gasped and sobbed with the effort. Glanced up, saw the bank and the overhanging oak boughs and above them now that wild, red moon. Only a few feet more, and he could grasp the edge of the bank, if it didn't crumble beneath him. He clung helplessly to the cliff; only a few feet more, but his legs and arms were shaking. If he moved, he'd fall. He knew this. He'd *fall*. The snarls and moans beneath him made him feel as though he were made of water.

Reaching, he grasped a root and gripped it, pulled himself up just within reach of the bank. But the root tore free of the soil and began to swing his upper body away from the wall of the bank. With a desperate cry, he took the root in both hands and pulled himself along it back toward the comfort of earth. But more of the root was pulling out; his heart beat with panic. He reached for some other handhold, grasping desperately, his fingers brushing the wall of the bank.

Suddenly a hand grasped his own, and he gasped, a shiver running through him. But the small, delicate hand was warm with life, and lovely and dark in his own. He gazed up and found a girl leaning over the edge, young, perhaps just old enough to bear a child. A dusky Canaanite girl with the high cheekbones of her people, her dark eyes only a few feet above his own. She was so unexpected, the warmth of her hand and the depth of her eyes so different from the cold, moaning death beneath him, that for a moment he just held completely still, awestruck, as he had been when he'd felt the living presence of God rise over the water.

The girl's grip on his hand tightened.

"Come on," she whispered.

450

WHO GIVES AND TAKES AWAY

A HEAVE, THEN Barak fell onto the weedy bank, coughing and gasping. He grasped a root and rolled onto his back, straining. Took deeper breaths. The pain had become acute; white fire shot up his leg to his hip, and his breath hissed through his teeth.

The young woman who leaned over him was lovely in the starlight and naked as though she were his lover or his purchase. Her face had the Canaanite cheekbones and that cast to the eyes. He found he couldn't take his gaze from her; she was so like Hadassah, though younger and smaller. Her own gaze flicked over his body and she muttered, "Not bitten." She got to her feet.

The moans of the dead at the water below were loud.

Barak scrambled up onto his knees. The girl was walking toward the cluster of tents. A horse was waiting there by a cold fire pit outside the largest pavilion, a small, sleek desert horse so black its hair shone. The girl held in one hand by her leg a wooden *teraph*, a goddess charred by fire yet recognizable as an Astarte, the goddess of planting and birth and harvest and love. Her other arm held a wolf pelt. There was no breeze, and the girl's hair hung lank about her face and shoulders, caked with dirt. There were bruises on the girl's cheek, her breasts, her thighs, her legs. To see her so bewildered Barak, who could not understand why a man would beat a girl so severely, especially this girl. To Barak she was beautiful, lush as the wooden Astarte she held, and the bruises on her body as wrong as the red moon in the sky.

"Wait!" Barak cried.

The woman turned, her fingers already curled around a clump of the gelding's mane. She stood and stared at him. Her eyes caught at him; they shone in the terrible red moonlight. After a moment she swept the wolf pelt about herself, concealing her body.

"Whose tents are these?" he called.

"Heber's." He heard the hate in her voice and suddenly understood. She had been a raid captive. "The men are gone," she said. "A boy was left to watch me, but he is gone too."

"Who is your mother?" he called softly. It was the traditional call of a man to a village girl he wished to court. "What is your tribe?"

He could hear the branches of the oaks tossing.

"I have none," she said.

He gazed at her, and in his wonder he realized that she was not the only young woman he had seen these past days who had reminded him of Hadassah. He realized where he had seen this girl's eyes and cheekbones before. "You're that girl's sister," he gasped. How strange that he should find her here. It seemed miraculous that it should be so, as though this moment had been touched by God. These past days he had seen so few signs of God's touch, only signs of her absence. Until that mist in the ravine below. Until this bruised girl had reached down her hand to help him up. "You're Hurriya's sister."

Her reaction to the name was immediate. She turned with her eyes bright and her face alight with hope. "You know her?" she cried. "My sister—you've seen her! Where is she?"

"She took refuge with my camp," Barak said, and stopped. The light in the girl's eyes was beautiful; to see it go out would break his heart. That light—that *hope*—how long had it been since he'd seen that in a woman's face? In anyone's face?

He saw the light start to fade as she guessed the worst from his silence. Everything else had been torn from her; even her goddess had been charred and burned, perhaps tossed carelessly by some raider to the edge of the fire. He could not take this from her too. "No," he said quickly. "She is well. A few of my men—they led her, and others, west toward the Wide Sea. There are walled settlements there, where she'll be safe." Where this girl might be safe too.

The light blazed again. He saw the girl shaking. "Tyre?" Her voice was breathless. "Or Sidon?"

"Sidon," he said.

"I'm going to find her," the girl said. Clutching the gelding's mane, she leapt onto the horse's back. She winced, for her body was badly bruised, but still she clung tightly to the horse, and her eyes had in them a fierce determination Barak had only ever seen in the eyes of one woman before: the *navi* of Israel.

"Wait!" Barak stepped closer. "Tell me your name!"

"My name," she whispered. She looked distracted, as though searching for the answer to his question. She hummed a few notes of a melody, very quietly, recalling something to herself, something from before her bruises and her pain.

Barak knew the melody well. It was Hurriya's song, and it was Hadassah's song that she used to sing to their unborn child, holding her belly. His throat tightened.

"There were standing dead beneath the olives," the girl said softly. "I found my sister's hovel empty, blood on the walls. But no bodies. Just—my sister and her baby were gone. So I went to find her. And these men found me. And hurt me." Her eyes burned with hate. "In their tents I was Ya El. A joke of theirs. I carried the name of a goddess of my people, so they made me carry the name of their God instead. I hope they are all dead, all of them. I hope they were *eaten*."

"Then I'll not call you Ya El," Barak told her. "What should I call you?"

She bent low over her gelding's neck and kissed the horse's ear. "Anath," she said after a moment. "When the sun comes up, I will be Anath."

Then, before Barak could say anything more, the girl Anath was riding away, past the tents. He watched her, thinking of that hardness in her eyes, thinking of Inanna riding down the gates of Sheol to rescue her lover in the story the Canaanites told. Half expecting the woman and her horse to crumble away on the still air, a thing of ashes and dreams, not flesh and blood. But still he could see her, galloping away from the riverbank and out over the tumbled, unplowed landscape in the red of the moon, riding up the rising land and into the hills.

***

When she had gone, Barak listened a few moments to the moaning of the dead in the river below. He hoped the girl found her way safely to the gates of Sidon. She might barter the horse for food and a room. He hoped so. The thought of it made him strangely calm—that there might be escape, for someone, from this long night of the dead.

The low wailing in the ravine seemed suddenly sorrowful to him. So many people had died up here. He could still hear Anath's song in his ears, and he yearned again for Hadassah, remembering the warmth of her in his arms, how she had taken his hand in hers and pressed his palm to her belly the night before her death. She had told him she could feel the baby kicking, and though he couldn't feel it himself, he had laughed and kissed her ear and told her he could, told her that he was glad she was bearing him such a strong son.

Forcing himself to take deep breaths, he glanced about at the tents and the oaks behind them. He was far now from his ruined vineyard and the camp of his men, and he didn't know how his men and the *navi* had fared against the dead. He hoped the corpses in the ravine below would move on if they could not see him or hear him. He could follow the bank back and look across at that barley field, and if he could do it unseen by the dead, climb down this bank and back up the other. Find and regather his men.

He considered the tents.

He needed meat, something to give him the strength he would need to get back. He could hardly stand, he was so weary. And water. He needed water. Yet he was hardly prepared to climb back down to that corpse-filled stream to get it.

He moved toward the largest of the pavilions grimly. When he drew the flap aside, he could smell the reek of death—that same smell that had surrounded him in the field. But nothing moved within. Nothing shuffled toward him. Nothing moaned at him out of the dark. After a moment, he let the flap fall closed.

A few unsteady paces took him to the little fire, which was just dead coals now, but there was kindling there and dry straw and flints. In a few moments he had a small blaze and was able to make a torch by shoving a short branch into the fire and letting the dry leaves kindle and burn until the fire reached the wood and began to sing and crackle in its joy at sating its hunger to devour all things. Lifting the branch, he returned to the tent. He paused for a while with his hand at the flap, unable to bring himself to open it; he shook and sweated as with a fever. He had seen too much tonight. He did not think he could bear to see one more of those—those *faces*, lifted toward the torch, gray eyes and a bloody mouth opening in a hiss or a low moan.

Bracing himself, he laid the branch at his feet—he could not bring it too near the fabric of the tent. The whole thing would go up in flames. He drew the tent flap aside, peered within.

One of the dead was there, but it was not moving. A bronze peg, a tent peg, had been driven through its skull. Its mouth was open in a hunger that was both silent and eternal.

Slowly Barak let out his breath.

There was nothing else in the tent but bedding, which smelled of urine and semen—but the scent of decay overpowered the other smells.

It took great control not to retch, but covering his nose and mouth with his hand, he stepped into the tent and crouched by the body and waited for his senses to adjust to the offensive smell of the tent.

The tent flap settled behind him. Outside, the branch flickered and burned; its glow passed through the gap between the flap and the tent wall, and the faint red light fell across the dead face. The face was intact; the brow and the skull above it had burst open like an overripe fruit at the passage of that metal peg.

He crouched there a long time, breathing shallowly through his fingers. Once he reached out and touched the blunt end of the peg with his fingertips. He withdrew his hand quickly.

He thought of Hurriya's sister, who looked so much like his wife yet was so fierce-hearted. She was the only living person he had encountered in this camp. And her horse had awaited her by the door of this tent. It must have been her hand that had slain the corpse. Barak thought of that girl lying naked and beaten on these very rugs until that hungering corpse drew aside the flap and peered in at her. He shuddered. He thought of her wrenching that peg from the earth.

Devora's words came back to him. *You must understand this, Barak. The God of our mothers and fathers will deliver the dead into the hands of women.*

Barak laughed quietly. A woman with a blade no man of the People had ever held. A naked slave girl with a bronze peg. Women had always been strange to him, strange as God herself, unreliable and unknowable. To be wooed, perhaps to be possessed and placed in a man's tent where they would hopefully stay a while where he put them, where they could be enjoyed and used. But the women he had seen these past few days and nights were stranger than any he'd known. Or perhaps all women were stranger than he'd known. The levites who kept the Law taught that God had made woman to be an *ezer kenegdo* to man, a help, even as God herself was an *ezer*, a help to the People, her arms surrounding, embracing, comforting, lifting up whom they held. Barak felt suddenly a yearning to know what an *ezer* truly was—to know what the levites actually meant. For if a woman could ride at the dead with an iron blade flashing in the red moonlight or drive a bronze peg through a dead man's skull—and yet weep and lie as weakly as the *navi* had lain in the weeds during their halt that afternoon, then he did not know what a woman was or what a woman was meant to be.

And he did not know anymore what a man was.

He watched the silent face, and a sorrow grew in his heart. He found he could not stand; those lifeless eyes held him. They looked like little river stones with a film of some gray slime stretched thin across their surfaces. His grief for his vineyard and his anger at God suddenly seemed small. *He* seemed small, his complaint and his fear the cry of a small mouse in a wide field. That face—that face, and the faces he'd seen in the barley and in the riverbed—what was happening to the land, to the People? This creature with the peg driven through its brow—he looked at its lips, saw the blood there. It had been feeding shortly before that girl slew it. He shuddered. This broken thing had moaned with a hunger for flesh that could never fill it, never sustain it, never nourish it. It consumed everything it encountered with a hunger like a god's hunger but made no covenant with anyone it fed on. It would use the flesh it consumed to make nothing, grow nothing, produce nothing. It would not have any young. It would not grow any vineyards. It would only feed and devour, and give nothing back. It didn't live: it merely craved.

Yet this had been a man once.

A man who'd tended his vines or his herds, then died. A little circle of tooth marks on his arm told the tale of that death. He was not elsewhere chewed; perhaps he had beaten off the corpse or stilled it, then run into the hills to hide from the People. He had been unclean, defiled; he would have known what his fate would be if the others learned of it. Perhaps he had even hidden his arm beneath a heavy robe for a few hours or a day, even in the heat of the Galilee summer; perhaps he had shuddered each time someone brushed against him as he moved about the tents. In the end, the fever would have grown fierce, burning him from within. He would've had to flee. And here, in these hills, perhaps in this very valley, he had lowered himself among the stones or in the wild grasses, and shivered and vomited until he was done. Then he'd lain still, completely still, under the wide sky. His eyes empty, his chest sunken in on itself. Time had passed, a wind moving over him through the weeds. Perhaps a small antelope had grazed near him for a while.

But at some point his chest had moved, filling slowly with air. Beginning to rise and fall. The body had begun to breathe. Then the mouth had begun to move or the fingers to twitch. Only the eyes remained entirely the same, dull and dead. No spirit returning to look out through them at these hills that had known the footprints of God.

How long had the creature lain there, just breathing? How long before it had climbed to its feet and lurched slowly away through the tall weeds?

That could have been him. Fleeing the dead tonight, only a few strides ahead of their grasping hands, their teeth—that could have been him.

Barak was shaking. "The land has become strange to me," he whispered, gazing at that lifeless face frozen in its moment of famished need. "I wanted only evenings in my house and Hadassah in my bed, her breasts in my hands. I wanted only my vineyard, only the ripe grapes, the coolness of them beneath my feet, the taste of wine. The long battle with soil and worm is enough for any man of Naphtali. God, you give and you take away, and we are only ashes. We are only ashes."

SH'MA YISRAEL

THE MOON must have set and the fire must have died down again to coals, for no light fell now on the dead face, and the dark within the tent became oppressive. Barak didn't know how long he'd sat there. He was numb inside, hollowed out. He tried to recall the comfort he'd felt when the mists rose over the water, the nearness of a God who did not loathe him, a God who might nourish him. He got to his feet and stumbled toward the door of the tent. He had to get back to his camp, his men. It did not matter how bruised and overcome he felt or what kind of God might heal him. There was work to be done and no one else to do it.

He pulled the flap aside, then caught his breath. A figure was standing there in the dark, a little shorter than he was. It must have been listening right at the door of the tent. Even as Barak realized it was there, the corpse grabbed his wrist in its hands, lifting Barak's hand toward its lips and ducking its head, biting quickly. The pain was

461

deep and sharp. Barak roared and tried to pull his hand back, but he only pulled the corpse with him.

With a shout, he turned and pulled the corpse toward the fire pit and slammed it down on the ground, crushing its chest down with his knee. The unclean thing held his wrist tightly, kept tearing at his hand with its teeth. Screaming from the pain, Barak took up one of the fist-sized stones from their ring around the fire pit, and he brought the stone down on the corpse's skull. And again. And again. Its snarling fell silent, and the thing grew still, one side of its head flattened. Its dead eyes did not change; it simply stopped moving.

Panting, his back bathed in cold sweat, Barak dropped the stone and grasped its fingers, breaking two of them as he pulled its hand free of his wrist. Then he tore his hand from its jaws, leaving some of his flesh between its teeth. His face gone the color of maggots, Barak fell back on his rear and sat there by the corpse, gasping. He caught a glimpse of its face; the left side of its face had been chewed almost entirely away. The right side had been the face of a youth, no more than a boy—doubtless the boy Anath had mentioned, the one left to watch Heber's camp, the one she thought was gone. Barak groaned and leaned back, lightheaded; he glimpsed the stars high above his head. His hand and his arm were pulsing, and he lifted his hand before his eyes, stared at the red gash where a chunk of flesh had been torn free; he supposed that piece of him was still held in the dead boy's mouth. For a long moment he stared at his hand. Then he began laughing, shaking his head and laughing, as the blood poured down his hand from the bite and ran warm along the length of his arm. It was all too strange, and life too fragile a thing to understand. He kept laughing quietly until he felt too weak to. Then his vision went gray.

***

Barak heard the sound of sticks cracking and opened his eyes. It was a moment before he could focus. His face felt dry and hot, and his insides were baking. There was coarse cloth wound about his hand. His heart lurched; he could see a human form sitting in the dark by the cold fire pit. Barak was on his back near the pit. The figure glanced at him, and in the dim starlight he recognized her graying hair and the flash of her eyes.

"*Navi*," he murmured. Not one of the dead.

"You've been bitten," Devora said. Her tone one of cold resolution. She was taking up sticks from a little pile she must have gathered while he lay senseless. She cracked the sticks and arranged a little tent of them over the coals.

Barak lifted his hand, saw that it was swollen and dark. He laughed quietly, then coughed from the pain the laugh brought him.

"Some days a woman can only save one life," Devora said. "The old *navi* tried to teach me that, Barak, but I didn't understand. I do now. When you save one life— when you keep Covenant and save even one life—you save the People." She paused. "I am sorry I was too late to save yours."

Barak just breathed for a few moments. He didn't know why he'd thought he was baking; now he shivered with the greatest cold he had ever known. "Stay with me," he rasped.

Her eyes gazed down on him, unreadable as ever. "I will," she said.

All about him were the raiders' tents and the leaves of the oaks dark against the sky. He yearned for his own vineyard—to die beneath his own vines, amid the scent of grapes and growing things. But his vineyard was already gone; it had died without him, and he was left here lingering in fever like a last cutting from it tossed aside to wither on its own. He kept watching the oak leaves and listening to the quiet fire. He had imagined dying at a spear's thrust or of old age, not of the bite of the dead on strange soil. But the *navi* was here, waiting while he died. She would raise a cairn over him. He would be remembered. He took comfort in that.

"I felt the *shekinah*," he whispered. "It rose over the water. And God was neither judge nor wife to me. I do not know what God is."

"You were feverish," Devora murmured.

"No." He shook his head, panting. "This was—before. We think we know what God is, but she is entirely strange to us. Stranger than the land, stranger than the heathen. We lie to ourselves when we say we know God, when we judge God or fear God or speak of God. Maybe God can be loved, as the priests do. I don't know what God is anymore." He shook from the cold, and his teeth chattered, but he forced the words out. "God gives and takes away. Blessed be the name of God."

"*Selah*," the *navi* whispered. *Always.*

He felt the touch of a waterskin to his lips, drank a little, choked and spluttered most of it up.

"The dead," he rasped after a few moments, his throat sore and violent. "Must put them all—beneath cairns. God has not forsaken the land."

"He has forsaken only his *navi*," Devora said. "No visions come. No seed I've planted has borne fruit." She gave a small, bitter laugh. "Nor any seed planted in me." She was quiet a moment. "I violated the Covenant. I killed my mother, twice. Now my daughter too. There is no longer any way to keep the Law. God has forsaken me, Barak. If he has appeared in some way to you, I am glad for you. But all my joy is gone, and all my hope."

"Not all," Barak rasped. "Your girl—the Canaanite. Found her sister. Alive." He was finding it difficult now to speak, his throat was so dry.

Devora glanced at him sharply, then her eyes softened. "Oh, Hurriya," she whispered, then said nothing more.

Barak coughed a little, then gazed past the oak branches, at the sky. At those same distant stars he'd seen from the bottom of the Tumbling Water's ravine. He barely heard Devora's words. He was just focused on those bright stars. His body kept shivering, but he felt again the warm touch of that holy presence in his heart. He was glad there were no sandals on his feet. He wished Hadassah were here, and even her mother, whom he'd sent away to Refuge when the dead came. But especially Hadassah. The things he would tell her. He would hold her, kiss her, and have her, if there was no other way for him to tell her, if he could find no words. All the deeds of his life seemed suddenly trivial to him, but this brought him no despair, only a yearning to hold Hadassah in his arms again, to feel her warm belly swollen with life. And a skin of clear water in his hand to share with her.

"Didn't tell her. I didn't tell the girl about Hurriya," he said.

There was silence for a while.

"I'm glad," the *navi* replied at last. "Where is she now?"

"She rode away. Toward the sea, where it's still safe. She was so *hopeful*. So beautiful."

"Thank you for telling me that." The *navi*'s voice was softer. Even a little vulnerable.

Barak could feel himself slipping beneath the fever. Everything blurring, even himself. He closed his eyes. "*Navi*, tell me the stories of our People. I want to hear them."

He felt a damp cloth against his brow. Then Devora's voice, cool and calm in the heated dark. He caught the stories in bits and pieces, moving between waking and sleep, between the world that is real and the world that isn't. But it didn't matter. He knew all the stories. His grandfather had given them to him when he sat between the old man's knees as a child. It was a comfort, though, to hear them again. To call them to mind. All these stories that made him more than just a vintner and more than just a man who carried a spear whom other men were willing to follow. More than just a man who lay dying. The stories made him one of the People, who would never die.

Devora's low voice told of his fathers Tubal Qayin, who first discovered the shaping of metal, and Yubal, who made the first music so that the *malakhim* themselves came out of the sky to listen. And Yabal, who began the keeping of sheep and goats, the herding of cattle, the pitching of tents. He heard of the brothers Qayin and Hebel—how Hebel was beaten across the head with a great stick, then thrown into a narrow ravine, there to starve until he died. How he rose to his feet some days later, hungering and rotting, until he found and devoured his brother.

Devora told of how the dead filled the land, every land, until God looked down on the hunger and the violence in the earth and was grieved. How a vintner like himself—a man with a wife and three sons, who enjoyed wine as much as any Canaanite—had built a great box of wood, an Ark. Not to carry stone tablets but to carry human lives, which to God's eyes were no less sacred. Rains fell while Barak ben Abinoam tossed in his fever. Rains fell, and the parched and hungry earth drank them until it could hold no more water and vomited the water back up, and there was mud, then flooding, then a great sea that drowned everything beneath it, and the dead floated in the sea moaning. Waves drove the corpses against the sides of the Ark, and their decomposing hands beat upon the wood. How terrible for the few living hiding within—to hear the thunder and the fury of rain on their roof and the slamming of many hands against their walls. And always the moaning, louder than rain or wind, the ceaseless voices of the dead.

"God overwhelms us," Barak rasped, interrupting the tale. "Whatever we do, God is too vast, too deep. I wanted to command God, as I might command a woman." Barak moistened his lips with his tongue; it was so difficult to speak.

"You should lie quiet, chieftain of Israel." Devora's voice, unexpectedly, held concern. "The fever is burning you up."

"God is like—like the *land*," Barak whispered. "You can cultivate the land. You can grow fine things on it. You

467

cannot command it or control it or say, Bring me a fine harvest. You have to work it. God is like that. I didn't understand."

He lay shaking for a few moments, unsure if he was speaking to the *navi* or to Hadassah or to Hadassah's mother. There was a woman here, he knew that much. "I am sorry I burned your gods." His whisper almost too quiet to hear. "I thought I could hold God to her promises. But the land makes us no promises. There are no promises."

"There *are* promises," Devora said sharply.

"I am sorry," he breathed, not heeding her. "Sorry I tried to take the Ark. That I sent Nimri."

She looked at him dispassionately.

"Laban," Devora said after a moment, "would have been the better choice. You should've sent Laban. He might have talked Shiloh into it."

No time left. He lifted his eyes, hoping to see that mist between him and the stars. There was nothing. Yet he knew—knew the God of his fathers was near. He was not afraid. Not anymore.

"*Sh'ma—*" He had to stop. His voice was but a dry croak. He tried to wet his lips, tried to swallow. There was nothing. Then the rush of cool water over his lips and into his mouth, like water from the rock in the desert. Someone was leaning over him, between him and the stars. Someone was pouring water into his mouth. He swallowed, and again, until the water stopped.

"*Sh'ma!*" he gasped. "*Sh'ma Yisrael adonai eloheinu, adonai echad…*"

Then the heat in him was too fierce for words and he moaned as he slid into the grip of it, burning, burning, nothing left but the fire. Breathing was too great an effort when his throat and his insides were so scorched, so after a while he stopped doing it.

DEVORA'S VIGIL

IT TOOK DEVORA a long time to gather the stones. The windstorm had returned to her heart. When she closed her eyes, meaning to rest for only a moment, she would see her mother's face or the contorted face of Hurriya's infant. She'd hear Heber's words. *Thousands, thousands in White Cedars.* Then she would jerk awake with a gasp and move on to gather more stones. There was no rest for her in sleep, no safety. There would probably never be.

Gritting her teeth, she lifted the last great rock to the top of the second cairn (for she'd buried the slave boy first, then Barak), letting the stone fall with a hoarse cry. Then she leaned on the pile of stones, panting. Her eyes stung with salt; in that moment, remembering how Zadok had once placed the stone at the top for her, Devora felt Zadok's loss keenly.

All the strength left her limbs, and she wept for a while. It wasn't that here, alone, she could afford to, but that here, at the utter limit of her strength, she could no longer hold any of it back. The winds within shook and battered her like an old tree in some violence of the air out of the desert. She had raised so many cairns. In a few generations, the stones of these two new cairns would topple or crumble or be overgrown with weeds, and those lying beneath them would be forgotten by all but God. With terrible clarity Devora grasped that the tribes were a transient People, whatever promises they clung to. Transient not only because they lived in tents or remembered living in tents, but because all peoples are transient, and once they move on, the land does not long remember them, even if God does. Even the Canaanites' walls and cedar houses were a transient thing, a vanity. Canaanite, Hebrew, living and dead, they were all strangers in a strange land.

A hasty search of the tents and belongings of the raiders revealed little of use to her—a little bread, a few empty waterskins, many items of luxury that a Canaanite might enjoy but that she refused to, and a corpse, another corpse for her to bury. But she did find one thing she took—a small bag sewn from a goat's bladder, full of small things that clacked together as she lifted the bag and set it by the fire pit. Not coins, but smooth, polished river stones, not yet engraved with any names. She went to sit with her back against Barak's cairn and emptied the bag of stones between her feet. They were beautiful, not as gems are but as stones are when the river has kissed them, and they were many colors. After a moment she picked out one that was a pallid white like the moon grown old, and another that was dark like Shomar's eyes. She held them both in her right palm. Her hand was unclean; perhaps the stones would bring her no true sign. Yet perhaps soon no one's hands would be clean.

"You showed Barak Hurriya's sister," Devora whispered to God. "She lost everything, even her child. But her sister lives. That has to mean something.

"You gave me an answer in Shiloh. I ask for another. Does your hand still cover the People?"

She cast the stones.

***

In the quiet that followed, she sat with the cairn at her back and looked at a sky so full of stars that it made her eyes ache. She still held the dark *urim*, the "yes" stone, in her hand. She recalled her words to Hurriya by the shore of the lake. *In the silence of God, I must act as though he is not silent.*

Yet perhaps God had not truly been silent at all. He had sent visions to her through the Canaanite, had spoken to her through Hurriya. Devora had been bewildered— what message was it that only Hurriya, only a Canaanite, could bring to the People? Now she realized that Hurriya *herself* had been the sign, the message. Some part of her had known this since Walls, since tossing that flaming torch into the house of the dead.

No. Some deep part of her had known it earlier than that. She'd known it from the moment she had seen Hurriya struggling her way up the hill toward the olive tree, naked within her salmah, bruised, carrying the half-eaten remains of her child. Even then, Hurriya's presence at the olive tree had been a message, a demand for justice, for the strangers in the land no less than for those born in the tents of the People. And the suggestion that even tribes who were strange to each other could teach one another something about preserving life and withstanding the unclean dead, something about God. That even a woman who did not know the Law, a woman who feared the Law, might teach an older *navi* more about the nature and the demand of the Law than she had ever before known.

Hurriya had delivered her message. She had done so merely by suffering in Shomar's saddle and by speaking of her grief and anger. And by dying with her hand clasped in Devora's own.

Devora glanced at the stars. She had to believe that God was still watching. That the tent of the Law still covered the land. Otherwise why had Hurriya had visions, and why had her longing for her sister's safety been answered? Why had the *urim* stopped rolling before the *thummim*? Why was Devora herself still breathing?

Devora leaned her head back and breathed deeply for a few moments. She could not stay here, but she could not stand yet; the grief was too violent within her. After a while she took up a small rock with a jagged edge from beside the fire pit and began to carve hard, deep Hebrew letters into the river stones, one after the other, while she sang the Words of Going hoarsely. She did not sing for Barak only, and his name was not the last that she carved into the stones. She carved *Zadok*, on a stone the color of fertile earth, and *Naomi*, on a stone the color of the sky. Then *Hurriya*, on a stone whose purple hue, though faint, suggested blossoms of heather. Her grief choked her voice when she carved the letters of that strange, Canaanite name that had become so dear to her. The thought of Hurriya's sister riding somewhere in these hills comforted her a little, enough that she could carve the letters without her hand trembling; something of Hurriya still lived.

Devora took her time, making sure the letters were well-carved and deep.

The last stone was simply *Am*, mother.

She wished for needle and thread, some means to sew the stones into the shoulders or the sleeves of her garment—for that was how levites carried name-stones, even as the high priest carried the names of the tribes in his breast-piece—but having neither, she settled for taking up the empty goat-bladder bag. But she did not put the five stones away immediately. Instead, she sat looking at them, reading the names again and again; she put them away, one after the other, until only *Am* remained. She could hear Naomi's words: *God will forgive us the lives we cannot save.*

She scrubbed the back of her hand across her eyes and looked to the sky; it was no longer so dark. In fact, the sky was nearly the blue of morning, and the stars were going out. And the scab-redness of the moon was long, long passed, as though it had never been.

"Forgive me for my mother and for Naomi," she whispered, not lowering her eyes from the heavens. "This time I do not ask you for a child. Only do not forsake me now. Forgive me. For her. And for my daughter, whose life I couldn't save." She bit her lip until she tasted blood.

Holding the *Am* stone in her hand, she closed her eyes

but did not sleep. The memory sprang upon her and this time she did not flee it. She faced it and mourned.

***

The pale light before sunrise found Devora still sitting with her back to Barak's cairn, still awake, with Mishpat lying unsheathed across her thighs. Some of the death-reek had faded from the camp, and a gazelle now walked gracefully among the tents, nibbling here and there at a patch of heather. She was a doe, her striped sides moving gently with her breathing. Devora watched her with the kind of hushed fascination a girl might feel, a child who has never seen a doe before. Amid the horrors of the north, Devora's heart had nearly forgotten such grace and beauty could exist. She had nearly forgotten there were such things as gazelles in the world. Once, the gazelle lifted its head and looked at the *navi*, its gaze focused and unblinking. Devora hardly dared breathe. At last the gazelle looked away and walked past the fire pit, almost within reach, looking for more heather blossoms to eat.

Devora rolled her shoulders back, breathed deeper.

The land was not dead yet.

She watched the gazelle for a while, but then the doe straightened sharply and turned to stare at the stand of oaks. Her ear twitched. Then with a few quick bounds the doe sprang away between the tents and was gone.

That alerted Devora to the danger. Without taking her gaze from the oaks, she took up some soil from the trampled ground by the fire pit and rubbed the dirt on her palms. What she wouldn't give for a bath and a safe refuge in which to sleep…

With a grim look, she rose to her feet and stretched her arms and legs thoroughly, ignoring the protest of her stiff muscles and her soreness from the saddle. She lifted Mishpat and swept the cold iron once through the air, letting her arms feel its weight, letting her body get used to it again. She let her weight rest on the balls of her feet and loosened her hips as though she were preparing to dance before her husband.

She recalled how Lappidoth had fought the dead that day, when they came for his cattle at that stream that was now so many desperate miles to the south. How he had ducked and darted among the corpses, swinging his hatchet about as though it were part of him. Devora gazed at Mishpat, recognized the cold necessity of her blade, a thing lethal and cruel, yet a thing as balanced, as beautifully designed in its own way as the Covenant itself. "I intend to see Lappidoth again," she whispered to the sword. "So you and I must dance together, whether we like each other or no."

***

When the dead lurched out of the oaks, arms raised, their skin ashen gray and their eyes wide and unblinking, the *navi* was ready. She watched the dead stumble toward her. Four of them. Great strips of flesh hung loosely from one's chest; another still carried a man's hand in its grasp, chewed off beneath the wrist. One had been male and in life had been a large man and one of some wealth; the tatters of a woolen cloak of many colors still clung to its body. The others had been women. Two were naked, and the third wore a faded green dress and about her waist the blue sash of a midwife. Her gray face was wrinkled; she had lived a long life and had likely brought many lives screaming into the world. Now she took them screaming back out again.

Devora spread her feet a little, crouching slightly, ready to spring to the side or leap forward or back. She held Mishpat before her, both of her small hands on the hilt. "You are unclean," she called to the dead. "An abomination. We do not want you walking in the land. Lie down and be still."

The dead midwife made a spitting noise like a furious cat and lurched toward her, with the others close behind.

"Come, then!" Devora cried, her throat dry. Without hesitating, she leapt forward, spinning on her toes and bringing Mishpat gliding through the air with a hum of wind and death; the cold, dispassionate blade sheared through the midwife's head just above the ears, and the body toppled lifeless to the earth. Devora brought her blade back before her just as the other dead closed on her. They did not fear her blade as the living might; they did not hesitate or slow their lunge toward her. Devora sliced away an arm that reached for her, and as it fell cleanly from its shoulder, no blood spurted, though the stench of rot and uncleanness worsened. She sprang back even as one of the other corpses grasped for her, its fingertips sliding for an instant along her wrist.

One of them opened its mouth in that terrible moan, that wordless, mindless cry that spoke of a hunger that would devour all life and all creation and yet still be famished. The other two took up the moan, and the sound filled the space between the oaks and the tents.

"Shut up," Devora said coldly.

She ducked low and brought her blade cutting through their legs, first one, then the next. Two of the dead fell and lay moaning and twisting their torsos on the ground, and the other loomed over Devora, its hands fastening on her shoulders. The corpse pulled her up toward its mouth, and even as it ducked its head to bite at her throat, Mishpat slid between its breasts and carved upward, releasing stench, cutting right up through its throat and then through its face, carving the top part of the body in two equal halves. It jerked a moment, then its grip on the *navi*'s shoulders went limp, and with a cry of revulsion and fury Devora lifted her knee and drove it into the corpse's chest, knocking it away.

The thing that had been a woman seemed to fall as slowly as a body in a dream. When it hit the earth at last, faceup, its back splattered open and it lay lifeless and tragic in a pool of its own insides.

Devora walked back to the other two, stood over them, sweat running thick as oil over her face, her hair lank and hanging before her eyes. She stayed just out of reach of their flailing arms. They twisted, trying to writhe nearer to her. She felt empty, looking down at them. They were not people, whether Hebrew or heathen. They were not even alive. Their hands and faces were stained with fresh blood, and she thought of Hurriya's tale of how her child and its father had died. These dead spat and hissed and reached for her, their gray eyes dull but their faces twisted in hunger and hostility and loathing and a longing to end life.

"There is no place in the Covenant for you," Devora told them quietly, and brought Mishpat, the Judgment, scything down.

***

The burn of noon found Devora exhausted from raising the new cairns. Yet she did not lie down, she did not sleep. She took up her sword and a bit of cloth from the raiders' abandoned bags and began cleaning the blade.

She knew what she must do.

She was alive and she had covenants to keep. She would follow the remnant of Barak's men south. She would make her way as Hurriya had before her through the strange hills where the dead were. Listening for God in the silent places, she would make her way, night after night, toward the heart of the land. Wherever she was forced to halt by an onset of the walking corpses, she would raise cairns over the Hebrew and the heathen dead. She must be hard and silent as the blade, yet not blind to the suffering of those whose homes and kin the dead had taken. They were all strangers in the land, bereft of shelter and beset on all sides by the stench of death. Knowing that she was herself a stranger in the land, unhomed and unclean, no other woman or man could any longer be strange to her. Hurriya had been right—their dwellings, and those of the Canaanites, were threatened alike. And they'd be strongest facing the dead together.

For seven days she would remain unclean, but it might well take those seven to get to Shiloh on foot. She might find the dead all about her. If God meant her to meet them as she now was, alone, she would do so. Such things had been required before of those God called. Moseh had been sent against the Pharaoh of Kemet and all his chariots and his cities with just a stick in his hand and the promise whispered from a burning bush: *ki ehyeh immakh*, I will be with you.

Devora did not have even that promise, or any stick that would perform wonders. But she understood now the story of the burning bush as she never had before. It was not enough simply to sit beneath her olive tree and decide what to do about the suffering that was brought before her. The *navi* must go out into the land and do what she could for the suffering she found there, whether she witnessed it in the eyes of her own people or in the eyes of a bereaved stranger wrapped in a salmah. She could not sit with the Law at her back, for the Law must look into the eyes of the People. The Law must listen to the heart. Otherwise the Law, which was alive like an olive tree, would blight and decay, until it became unable to yield any life-sustaining fruit.

She would deliver Hurriya's message to the People. And she would blow the shofar, call together the chieftains of the tribes. Tell them what Heber had said. Tell them they were all marching north, and the Ark of God with them. Maybe they would find tens of thousands of hungering dead when they returned to these hills. It didn't matter. She had to trust that they would see the fire of the *shekinah* burn like wildfire on the slopes, hotter than any *navi* had ever been touched by it, hotter than anything made of flesh and bone could endure. That they would see the dead razed from the land, even as they had been razed from Shiloh thirty years ago. But even if the Ark lit no fire, still they must stand together against the dead.

For a moment she looked to the north over the tops of the oaks, where hills mounted higher and higher until she could glimpse the sharp line of the mountains of White Cedars beyond them, where snow fell like white feathers out of the sky. Somewhere north of her was an olive grove where a girl used to watch over her sister from the branches of a high tree.

"I'm sorry, Hurriya," she whispered. "I don't know where Anath is or how to find her. But I know she will be all right. You trusted me to help you, you hoped you could trust me when you came to my seat. I let you down then. Maybe I'm letting you down now. My daughter." Her voice choked. "Please trust me again. She will be all right. Your Anath. I know she will; she survived this camp and she survived the dead and she has a horse that will carry her far. I have to trust her to that horse and to God. I have to. The People need me, Hurriya, both our peoples."

She turned her back on the oaks and the higher ridges and the distant suggestion of peaks that knew the softness of snow and the seductive death of the extreme cold. She could do nothing more here.

Waterskin and goatskin pouch slung over her shoulder, Devora carried Mishpat at her side and began walking south along the high bank. She listened and watched intently, for it was not a question of whether she would encounter more walking corpses today, but when. She thought of Lappidoth waiting for her in the white tents, but this did not lighten her heart.

Whether God stayed silent or roared loud as thunder in the hills, her longing for rest was a seduction and a luring away from her responsibilities. She was the *navi* and the judge, but she understood that she too was judged. As she watched the pain of the People, God watched her. She knew she would not rest nor set Mishpat aside until there were no dead walking anywhere in the land. The burden of facing the dead was finally and entirely hers to bear. She *would* bear it. She had to.

FINIS

ACKNOWLEDGMENTS

I AM SO EXCITED to offer you this new edition of the third volume in *The Zombie Bible*, and I could not have done it without the help of many people. I offer my thanks...

To Andrew Hallam, for his diligent and enthusiastic reading of my work; to Ever Saskya and JR West for their moral support; to all those who generously gave feedback on excerpts; to my pastor, for his excitement about the series; to my editor Jeff Vandermeer; to Johnny Shaw, who gave me some of the best writing advice I have ever received over a few beers in New York, advice I kept firmly in mind as I worked on this volume ("if it takes another six months to make a good novel a great novel," he told me, "you take the six months"); to my wife, Jessica, and to my daughters River and Inara—it can't always be easy living with a husband or father whose mind wanders with such frequency into daydreams of the hungry undead, or who leaps often from his chair to scribble a note; if it were not for their patience, their laughter, and their love, you would not now be holding this work in your hands; and to all of you, my readers—it is you who make these stories breathe.

***

SPECIAL THANKS TO

THEA DEE, RON GIESECKE, ANDREA G MANN, DARREN WAGNER, JEREMY KERR, SCOTT ROCHAT, JUHI MENDIRATTA, KATY FLYNN, TODD BERGMAN, AND ALL MY PATREON MEMBERS WHO HAVE HELPED FUND THIS SILVER EDITION!

A NOTE ON PLACES

I ASK THE FORGIVENESS of any readers who live in Israel for the occasional liberties I have taken with their country's geography, such as nudging Hazor (Walls) a little nearer the shore of Lake Hula (Merom) and, more severely, lifting the elevation of Merom (a choice originally suggested by the name *Merom* itself, "high place").

I have always said that a novel needs to tell the truth and take no prisoners, but in this case I have proven more focused on the truths of the human heart than the truths of topography. I can say only that when I first conceived this story (the first volume of *The Zombie Bible* that I undertook), my entire means of traveling to that beautiful land consisted of a few colorful but barely sufficient maps, a shelf groaning beneath the weight of historical texts, and the seaworthy if makeshift vessel of my imagination. When I travel there at last, I hope to find that land as lovely in fact as it has proven in my heart.

ABOUT THE AUTHOR

STANT LITORE doesn't consider his writing a vocation; he considers it an act of survival. As a youth, he witnessed the 1992 outbreak in the rural Pacific Northwest firsthand, as he glanced up from the feeding bins one dawn to see four dead staggering toward him across the pasture, dark shapes in the morning fog. With little time to think or react, he took a machete from the barn wall and hurried to defend his father's livestock; the experience left him shaken. After that, community was never an easy thing for him. The country people he grew up with looked askance at his later choice of college degree and his eventual graduate research on the history of humanity's encounters with the undead, and the citizens of his college community were sometimes uneasy at the machete and rosary he carried with him at all times, and at his grim look. He did not laugh much, though on those occasions when he did the laughter came from him in wild guffaws that seemed likely to break him apart. As he became book-learned, to his own surprise he found an intense love of ancient languages, a fierce admiration for his ancestors, and a deepening religious bent. On weekends, he went rock-climbing in the cliffs without rope or harness, his fingers clinging to the mountain, in a furious need to accustom himself to the nearness of death and teach his body to meet it. A rainstorm took him once on the cliffs and he slid thirty-five feet and hit a ledge without breaking a single bone, and concluded that he was either blessed or reserved in particular for a fate far worse. He married a girl his parents considered a heathen woman, but whose eyes made him smile. She persuaded him to come down from the cliffs, and he persuaded her to wear a small covenant ring on her hand, spending what coin he had to make it one that would shine in starlight and whisper to her heart how much he prized her. Desiring to live in a place with fewer trees (though he misses the forested slopes of his youth), a place where you can scan the horizon for miles and see what is coming for you while it is still well away, he settled in Colorado with his wife and two daughters, and they live there now. The mountains nearby call to him with promises of refuge. Driven again and again to history with an intensity that burns his mind, he corresponds in his thick script for several hours each evening with scholars and archaeologists and even a few national leaders or thugs wearing national leaders' clothes who hoard bits of forgotten past in far countries. He tells stories of his spiritual ancestors to any who will come by to listen, and he labors to set those stories to paper. Sometimes he lies awake beside his sleeping wife and listens in the night for any moan in the hills, but there is only her breathing, soft and full, and a mystery of beauty beside him. He keeps his machete sharp but hopes not to use it.

zombiebible@gmail.com
@thezombiebible
www.stantlitore.com
www.facebook.com/stant.litore

POSTSCRIPT

THANK YOU FOR READING *Strangers in the Land*, I hope it has touched your mind and your heart. If you have enjoyed this novel and would like more, please consider supporting my writing by becoming a member of my Patreon community: www.patreon.com/stantlitore.

I believe passionately that storytelling is a communal act. Our ancestors sat around a fire sharing tales and giving each other chills. Patreon is a way to use modern-day patronage to achieve that again. It means taking writing fiction from something that just happens on a dining room table to something that happens around a community fire or a community table, with boisterous laughter and shared tears.

If you're the kind of reader who has always wished you could sit down on a porch with one of your favorite writers to just listen to the rain and ask them that question you've always had or even just hear them spin out new ideas, then you belong here. That's the kind of connection I want with my readers; that's the kind of connection I want with you.

I hope you'll consider joining me there. We are a vibrant community of 155 members, and growing. I share all of my work with this community first, and the membership dues (which are set by each reader at whatever amount they think best) go toward funding my creative work and paying my daughter's medical bills. I hope you'll come join us: www.patreon.com/stantlitore.

I can be reached by email at zombiebible@gmail.com.

May your life be one of great courage and great stories.

STANT LITORE
NOVEMBER 2015

CPSIA information can be obtained at www.ICGtesting.com
Printed in the USA
LVOW08s1806110416

483081LV00007B/735/P